A GREEN

A GREEN BAY TREE

Margaret James

PAN BOOKS

This edition published 1999 by Pan Books
an imprint of Macmillan Publishers Ltd
25 Eccleston Place, London SW1W 9NF
Basingstoke and Oxford
Associated companies throughout the world
www.macmillan.co.uk

This first world edition published in Great Britain 1994 by
SEVERN HOUSE PUBLISHERS LTD of
9-15 High Street, Sutton, Surrey SM1 1DF
This published in the USA 1994 by
SEVERN HOUSE PUBLISHERS INC., of
425 Park Avenue, New York, NY 10022.

British Library Cataloguing in Publication Data
James, Margaret
Green Bay Tree
1. Title
823.914 [F]

ISBN 0 330 39668 4

Typeset by Hewer Text Composition Services, Edinburgh.
Printed and bound in Great Britain by
Mackays of Chatham plc, Chatham, Kent.

Note and Acknowledgement

A Green Bay Tree is set in England and Wales during the latter half of the eighteenth century. Whereas I have based my accounts of life in Birmingham and the surrounding district on historical fact, those parts of the story set in Wales owe rather more to my imagination. *My* Gower village of Llangynnydd is a Welsh-speaking community, which bears little resemblance to the real Llangennith – for this, together with most of South Gower, has been Anglicised since the Middle Ages. I have repopulated it with Welshmen.

I wish to thank Mr Robert Evans and his daughter Mrs Awen Brockbank, who kindly translated some phrases from this novel into the appropriate regional Welsh. Any errors in transcription are, of course, my own.

Chapter 1

"Call again, why don't you?" Irritably, the elderly man in the fusty black morning coat adjusted his wig. He frowned at the woman by his side. "Call again. He must be here somewhere."

Obligingly, the woman cupped her hands to her mouth. "Master Alex!" she cried. "Master Alex, where are you?" She turned to the tutor. "Yes, I know they're late for their lessons," she muttered. "But I have work to do. If you want them, you must find them yourself."

"Martha, please – "

"I'm sorry, Mr Sandford. I can't perform miracles."

Alex Lowell's nurse, long redundant but kept on at the house as a general servant, peered up at the roof of the stables. Perhaps she expected her former charge to materialise upon the tiles. He didn't. "It's my belief they've gone off to Martley," she said. "To the fair."

"Maybe." The tutor removed his spectacles. Spitting on the lenses, he began to polish them with his dirty pocket handkerchief. "Oh, I expect you're right," he admitted. He sighed. Unsteadily, he made his way back towards the manor house.

From the safety of the barn, the two little boys watched him. Now they breathed a sigh of relief. They resumed their interrupted conversation.

"Yes, as it happens, I do know how it's done." At ten years old, Ellis Darrow was as worldly-wise and infuriatingly world-weary as he'd be at sixty. He had greeted Alex Lowell's revelations with bored disdain. "I've seen the bull serve the cows. Arrowsmith says it's the same with humans. You needn't think you're telling me anything new."

"Well! You never said anything to me." Annoyed to have had such interesting information deliberately withheld from him, Alex glared. "So when did you find out?"

Ellis yawned. "Years ago," he lied.

The two children were lolling comfortably amidst the hay which filled the upper storey of the biggest barn. From here, they had a clear view across the cobbled courtyard of the home farm. They could look right into the dairy where Lyddy Searle was skimming pans of milk, carefully taking off the cream.

Alex nudged Ellis. "Someone's been serving *her*," he said. "But it wasn't a bull."

"Wasn't it?"

"No."

"Who, then?"

"Wouldn't you like to know?"

Ellis took a bite out of the apple he'd chosen from a heap by his side. "Yes," he admitted. "I would."

"Give me one," said Alex, pointing to the neat pile of fruit. "Then I'll tell you."

"Get your own apples," Ellis replied.

Alex kicked him.

Ellis kicked Alex back. A brief scuffle ensued, resulting in the whole pyramid of apples tumbling down and rolling all over the floor. Each child filled his pockets. Then they lay down on their stomachs and observed Lyddy Searle again.

"She's going to have a child." Alex poked Ellis in the ribs. "Didn't you hear me? I said, she's pregnant!"

"Is she?" Impressed at long last, Ellis stared. "How do you know?"

"I heard my mother talking about it." Alex grimaced. "She's very upset."

"Why is *she* upset? What's it to do with her?"

"Ah." Alex looked very knowing. "She's upset because

Lyddy was served by my father. So, she's going to have his baby."

"So it'll be your half brother! Or sister."

Alex shrugged. "It'll be a peasant," he said, shortly. "Like its mother." Standing up, he brushed the straw from his breeches. "It'll be a bastard. A peasant woman's brat. Nothing to do with me. Look! She's seen us."

Alex sniggered now, making Ellis grin too. Glancing up, Lyddy Searle stared coldly at the two boys. Her lips moved, but of course they were much too far away to hear what she said. They could, however, see her face was red. That she looked absolutely miserable. Meeting that desolate stare, Ellis had the grace to look away. But Alex glared straight back at her, and pulled a face.

Still blushing, Lyddy bent over her work again.

"I'd have thought your father was a bit old to – you know." Ellis frowned. "Well, he's an old man. Isn't he?"

"Oh, men can do it until they're a hundred," Alex replied. "Papa's nowhere near that. He was born in – oh, he must be about fifty now, I suppose. I'm twelve, and I was born in '48, so – "

"About the year ten." Ellis's mental arithmetic was much better than his friend's. "Your father must have been born in 1710."

"Yes. I was just going to say that."

"Liar." Cruelly, Ellis laughed. "As Mr Sandford says, *you* have all the mathematical genius of a backward donkey."

"Pig!" Alex punched him. Still Ellis grinned. So, shoving him on to his back, Alex got astride him. Easily dodging Ellis's flailing fists, he landed blow after blow on the younger child's face. "There, Darrow!" he crowed. "I can thrash you any day. So, do you give in? Do you beg for mercy?"

"No!" Bloody about the nose and cut above the left eye, Ellis squirmed and tried to wriggle away, but was held fast by the bigger child's weight. So he was obliged to stay where he was, and be hit.

Eventually, Alex got tired of thumping him, and rolled away. "Ellis?" he demanded. "What's the matter?" For his friend simply lay supine. "Are you all right?"

"I think so." Ellis staggered to his feet. Now he tried to staunch the torrent of blood which poured from his nose. "Yes. I'm fine."

"Come over to the pump. Get washed." Alex helped the smaller boy down the stairs. He led him across the yard, to the water trough.

"What shall we play?" Now a little cleaner, but still somewhat battered about the face, Ellis kicked a stone across the cobbled yard. "What about a round of quoits?"

"I'd rather fight."

"Only because you always win." Ellis dabbed at his sore face. "Why can't we ever have a game of anything?"

"Such as?"

"Tennis?"

"No. I hate tennis." Alex thought for a moment. "We'll play French and English," he said. "You be the Frog. I'll be the English Milord."

"Oh. Vaire well." A natural clown and mimic, Ellis shrugged in the approved Gallic fashion. "Then, *cochon anglais*, I damn your eyes. Defend yourself!" Twirling an imaginary cloak, he bared his teeth in a snarl. "What, you disgusting villain? Do you laugh at me?"

Alex grinned. Taught from birth to despise everyone and everything French, this sort of foolery delighted him.

Ellis liked a responsive audience. So now he posed and postured all the more.

The boys' mothers were distant cousins. But, whereas pretty Anne Chalmers had married wealthy Henry Lowell and now queened it over the entire parish, Jane Collins had been landed with Peter Darrow, who was a miser. An improvident miser, at that.

The first issue of Jane and Peter Darrow's uneasy union, Ellis often stayed at Alex's house. There, he was company for Alex. He also spared his own parents the expense of bringing him up.

Despite his habitually barbarous treatment of the younger child, Alex loved Ellis dearly. On the day the storm finally broke, when Lyddy Searle dropped her lighted taper into the powder keg of his parents' marriage, he had been particularly glad of Ellis's company.

For, if he'd not had Ellis to thrash, to torment, if Ellis had not been there to provide a diversion, Alex would probably have battered his own head to bloody ruin against a convenient out-house wall. His nonchalant indifference to the fact of Lyddy Searle's pregnancy concealed a terror which was making him sick with fear.

That morning he had, as usual, sneaked into his mother's bedroom. There he meant to enjoy a clandestine embrace and a few minutes' conversation, before the real business of the day began.

Instead of lying back against her embroidered satin pillows, however, instead of placidly drinking her early morning chocolate, today his mother was up. She was dressed in a loose gown. In tears, with her hair unpowdered and disordered about her face – upon which the marks of her own fingernails plainly showed – she was pacing the floor of her room.

Alex's father was also there. Clad in his long padded morning robe, Turkish slippers on his feet and a purple silk turban on his head, he stood by the window, idly taking snuff. He watched his wife with the detached interest of a man observing a wild animal in a zoo.

Hiding in his mother's dressing room – for neither parent had noticed as he slipped in – Alex overheard the whole exchange. He learned how Lyddy Searle had had the effrontery to come to Mrs Lowell herself. To tell her, face to face, that she was expecting Henry Lowell's baby.

"She was here!" Meeting her husband's languid stare, Anne Lowell glared. "The slut sneaked past all the servants, and got in here. She told me you are the father of her child!"

"Indeed?" Henry Lowell took more snuff. Elegantly, he sniffed the powder up each nostril, smiling with gratification as the stimulant had the desired effect. "The assurance of the jade."

Alex's mother stopped pacing. She stood before her husband. "Well?" she demanded. "Will you have her whipped?"

"My dearest Anne, why ever should I have the girl whipped?"

"For her insolence, of course!" Mrs Lowell clenched her fists. "For lying. For slandering. For defaming a gentleman's character!"

"Ah." Henry Lowell smiled. "No, my dear Anne. I can't have her whipped for that."

"Why not? Henry, you're a magistrate. It's your duty to keep these dirty slatterns in their place."

"Anne, my dearest. Listen to me." Expressively, Henry Lowell shrugged. "You must understand that this particular dirty slattern was neither lying, slandering, nor defaming. She was merely – although I must admit it was extremely tactless of her – stating an established fact."

"What?" Anne Lowell's face lost all its colour. "What did you say?"

"I said – or as much as said – that the girl was not lying to you."

"She is pregnant? The child is yours?"

Alex's father bowed an elegant assent.

"It was conceived in this room?" Wildly, Mrs Lowell stared about her. "So that was how she knew the way. You and that creature came up here. You had her in my bed. You defiled my own clean sheets."

"Anne, you forget yourself." Henry Lowell shook his head. "I shall go and dress."

Mrs Lowell gaped at him. Her mouth hung open. Then, to Alex's horror, she threw herself against him. She punched his chest, she kicked his shins, and soon her nails had marked his face with the same sort of long, livid weals which disfigured her own. "Beast!" she screamed. "Dirty libertine! Disgusting, filthy brute!"

For a moment or two, Henry Lowell stood quite still. He let her attack him. But then he raised his right hand. He slapped his wife across her upturned face, with a force that felled her to the ground.

Terrified, Alex ran. Scuttling from the dressing room, he was violently sick on the landing outside.

By late afternoon, Alex was feeling less distraught. He and Ellis had spent an hour or two in the orchard, climbing the apple trees and stealing the fruit. Now, a large heap of it was collected and secreted for their own private use. Then Mr Sandford came to fetch him. It was time to see his parents. He went meekly, leaving Ellis to enjoy a quiet hour alone, before the children had their supper.

Every afternoon, at four o'clock, Alex was washed, brushed and taken to see his mother and father. This was by way of a diversion before they went in to dinner. As the first family in the district, the Lowells dined fashionably late – their neighbours took their main meal of the day at three, or even two o'clock.

"Sir. Madam." Alex bowed to each parent in turn. To his relief, he saw that neither bore any visible marks of their morning's contretemps. But then, his mother and father painted so heavily that all the scratches, bruises and scars were bound to be concealed by thick, white cosmetic, rouge, and the usual profusion of patches.

His mother patted the sofa. "Sit down, child," she invited.

"Thank you, madam." Alex sat. Covertly, he glanced at her. He could have wept at what he saw.

Never robust, she now looked positively ill. On edge, too. Even a child of twelve could see she was barely in control of herself. A vein throbbed in her neck. Her hands were practically knotted together, their restless fingers twisting and fiddling with her rings.

But, as usual, she had dressed with the greatest care.

Her hair was powdered and curled. She was clad in the finest silks and satins, which rustled as she fidgeted in her seat. "Have you completed your lessons for today?" she enquired.

"Of course, madam," Alex lied. "Mr Sandford is very pleased with me. He especially commends my progress in grammar. He says I may go on to Book Six tomorrow."

"Indeed?" Henry Lowell looked first at his watch, then at his son. "Well, sir. You are evidently destined to become a great scholar."

Alex winced. Fond of pointing out that *he* had memorised the whole of Virgil by the time he was ten, it was plain Henry Lowell thought his son a blockhead.

An oppressive silence filled the room.

As Alex walked back to his own part of the house, he thought about Lyddy Searle again. He remembered his father as he'd just seen him. Immaculate in his powder-blue coat and breeches, in his white silk stockings and cream kidskin shoes, his fine cambric shirt had been of such snowy beauty that it dazzled the eyes. He could not imagine his handsome, beautifully dressed Papa so much as touching, let alone doing that filthy thing with a rough peasant girl like Lyddy, who always stank of wood smoke and mutton grease.

Perhaps it was nonsense. An adult's joke he had not understood. Surely a man who washed every day, who scented his face and hands with rose water and had his hair dressed by an Italian barber, could never have done that awful, intimate, sweaty thing with a girl like Searle's daughter?

As the two boys wolfed their supper, as greedily as if neither expected to see food again, Alex brought the subject up for the second time. "Ellis," he began, "do you think my father could have – well – "

"Could have what?" Ellis picked a shred of meat from between his front teeth.

"Could have made Lyddy pregnant."

Ellis shrugged. "You said he did."
"Yes, I know. But do you think he really – "
"I expect so." Ellis grinned. "My father does it with Nell Purvis. He takes her up to the attic in the east wing."
"How do you know?"
"I heard her telling one of the housemaids about it. She said my father gives her a shilling every time."
"Oh." Alex swallowed his bread, then gulped some ale. So it was quite normal, then. All gentlemen did it. There was no need to worry any more.

By the time September turned into October, Lyddy Searle's belly had swollen enormously. She walked awkwardly now. Her legs wide apart, her body was tilted backwards, to balance the ballooning weight of her unborn child.
Village women said the creature should be turned out of her parents' cottage, and sent to the Bridewell. "She ought to be well whipped," said one.
"At the cart's tail," added another. "That would teach the baggage some shame. I remember when Molly Lucas was tied up and flogged all along the Warwick road."
"Miscarried, she did."
"A good thing, too. Seeking to lay her bastard at the expense of the parish."
"Miss Lyddy needn't hold her head so high. This time next week she'll be in the House of Correction, picking rope."
"With her head shaved. Serve her right."
But, in spite of her neighbours' charitable good wishes, Lyddy met no such harsh fate. Instead, she paraded around Squire Lowell's estate sticking out her pregnancy for all to admire. Evidently, she was proud of it, for she stared boldly back at everyone who dared look at her.
Mrs Lowell was much pitied. As for Mr Lowell – well, said the village women, the slut had obviously encouraged him. He was, after all, a man. Mrs Lowell's maid added her mite to the debate by revealing in confidence – to

anyone who would listen – that her mistress had not allowed her husband into her bed since long before Alex was born. "So what else was the poor gentleman to do?"

Denied the society of siblings, Alex thought of Ellis as his little brother. Scared of the dark, he always wanted Ellis's company at night. Then, curled round each other like a pair of kittens, one blond and one dark head resting on the same pillow, the two children kept each other warm.

"Ellis?" murmured Alex, as they lay in bed one evening, on the point of falling asleep. "Ellis!"

"What?"

"I wish you were here all the time." Alex levered himself on to one elbow. "I was thinking. If I asked Papa, perhaps he'd allow it. You could share Mr Sandford with me. Your father could pay off the curate then."

A thin, grey-haired, gentle old man, Mr Sandford was nearing the end of his teaching career. Kindly and over-indulgent, he had so far failed to push anything much into Alex Lowell's thick head. On the other hand, Ellis rather liked Mr Newstead, the local curate who taught him. He thought about Alex's suggestion, and decided it would not be a good idea.

"I don't think I'd want to share Mr Sandford," he said. "He smirks at me." Ellis imitated Mr Sandford's leer. "He makes my skin crawl."

"That's because you have lice," retorted Alex. "Not because Sandford smirks at you."

"I haven't got lice. But you've got fleas." Ellis grinned. "I saw one on your shirt yesterday."

"You didn't."

"Yes, I did."

"Beast!" Picking up a pillow, Alex hit his friend over the head with it. The ticking burst open. The room filled with feathers. "I haven't got fleas!" Alex caught Ellis's arm. He twisted it behind his back. "Say I haven't!"

Ellis shrugged. "Let go," he said, equably. "You're hurting."

It was boring, torturing Ellis. However much Alex hurt him, the younger child would never cry, or beg for mercy. He simply waited for his tormentor to get tired. So now, Alex released him. "Will you stay?" he pleaded. "If my father agrees?"

"No. I've been here long enough. I must go home soon."

"Home!" sneered Alex. "That tumbledown hovel. That great barn, that cowshed. How can you call that place home?" Gazing all around the warm, airy chamber in which the children lay, he sighed. "Ellis, surely you like it here?"

"Yes, I do. But – "

Indeed, Ellis was sorely tempted. The Lowells' home was a new mansion, raised on the ruins of a Jacobean manor house. The huge cellars and vaults of this still survived, and were the most marvellous of playrooms.

The place was so comfortable. So warm. Even in the children's rooms, fires always burned. The windows were a snug fit, so excluded all draughts.

The whole house was light. The gracious oblong casements let in all the sunshine. This lit up the pale Georgian greens and blues in which the interior was decorated. It illuminated the neat candy stripes of the wallpapers in the large drawing room and dining room downstairs.

By contrast, Ellis's own home – a Tudor hall in the last stages of dereliction and decay, riddled throughout with worm and rot – was a hovel indeed.

Seeing Ellis wavering, Alex pursued his advantage. "Stay!" he cried, pathetically. He hugged his friend around the neck. "Stay, stay, stay!"

"I can't, Alex." Ellis pushed him away. "I must go home. To see Lally."

Chapter 2

Lyddy Searle's father was the village blacksmith. A devout, God-fearing man, he was a Dissenter of the most narrow-minded, puritanical kind. He was also a mainstay of the local chapel.

He had no time for women. In his opinion and experience, they were feckless, irresponsible and generally contemptible. All the same, his own daughter's disgrace was a terrible burden for Jeremy Searle's broad shoulders to bear.

Lyddy, however, seemed not to feel her shame. When the alteration in her shape finally brought her condition to her father's attention, he took her into the kitchen to examine her soul. He did not find it clad in the white raiment of repentance. Instead, he discovered it was very black indeed.

"Well? Did you encourage the squire?" he demanded, of a surly, silent Lyddy. "Set out to entice and ensnare him? So that the man, being but flesh, was tempted beyond resistance?"

Despising this Presbyterian cant which she had, in any case, heard a thousand times before, Lyddy was silent. Her father took this to mean she gloried in her disgrace, and was not in the least repentant of her sins.

"Speak to me, child!" Jeremy glared at her. "Tell me now! Have I not brought you up in godliness and righteousness? Have I not taught you to conduct yourself as a Christian maiden should?" He shot a spiteful glance at his wife, who sat weeping quietly in the chimney corner. "Did I not seek to check the sinful indulgence of your mother, and guide your steps in the ways of holiness?"

Lyddy neither spoke nor moved.

So, grind his teeth and glare at her though he might, Jeremy Searle failed to bring his daughter to a proper state of contrition. Worse, Lyddy as good as admitted she had led the man on – so he was in no position now to go up to Mr Lowell's house and cross-examine the other sinner in the case, the father of this little child his daughter was about to bear.

Had Lyddy wailed and wept, had she declared herself a poor innocent seduced by a vile adulterer, Jeremy would have hauled her up to the great house there and then, to confront the squire with the evidence of his crimes. But since she sat and said nothing at all, what could Jeremy do?

Detesting both the idolatrous Church of England and the Tory squirearchy which supported it, for years the blacksmith had been a thorn in the side of the squire. A fierce and outspoken critic of almost everything Henry Lowell did, Jeremy Searle particularly opposed the squire's determination to enclose most of the local common land. For such enclosure robbed the peasants both of grazing rights, opportunities to gather fuel, and any chance to keep livestock of their own.

As far as the squire was concerned, the blacksmith did not know his place. Jeremy Searle never touched his forelock to Mr Lowell. He never shrank into the hedge as the gentleman's coach swept by. He never crept or fawned or asked a single favour of the lord of the manor. He would rather have starved than beg.

Now the squire had taught him a lesson. Had sired a bastard grandchild upon him. Was this simple retribution? If so, for what? For the squire's hunters being kept waiting at the forge, while the tenant farmer's work horses were shod? For the making of Mrs Lowell's fancy wrought-iron plant baskets being held up, while a ploughshare was repaired?

"Why, girl? Why?" Jeremy was determined to have an answer. "Did he force you? If so, I'll have the justices on him, lord of the manor or no! So tell me. Was it rape?"

Still dumb, Lyddy looked at him. Then she shook her head.

"You went to him willingly?"

Lyddy nodded. Folding her arms across her stomach, she braced herself for the blow which must surely fall.

But, with a disgusted snort, Jeremy jumped to his feet. He strode out of the house. He went into the forge, pumped the bellows, then beat the squire – in the form of a new horse shoe – completely senseless.

Lyddy and her mother remained in the kitchen. There, the silence was broken only by the older woman's sniffs, and the squeaking of needles piercing the leather of the gloves they made. For this part-time occupation was common to all village women who had skills in needlework.

Still smarting from her husband's reference to the sinful indulgence with which she'd treated Lyddy, poor Mrs Searle blamed herself for everything. Now, she sighed. Her daughter had been such a beautiful child! She was beautiful still. As fair as an angel, this girl had been given her as consolation for the loss of two sons, both in their early infancy. "Lyddy," she ventured, "when you've finished that pair, shall we have some tea?"

Lyddy rose to her feet. She went into the scullery, where she filled a kettle. On her way to the fire, she touched her mother's shoulder. "Don't cry, Mam," she said, softly. "It doesn't help."

The village continued to seethe with gossip, rumour and speculation. Then, one chilly winter morning, the Searles – Jeremy, his wife Judith, and their now almost spherical daughter Lyddy – piled their luggage on a wagon borrowed from a tenant farmer and left the forge, the village, and possibly even the county itself.

Jeremy had told no one they were leaving, and gave nobody – not even his travelling companions – any information about where they were bound.

The forge was the freehold property of the Searles, and now it was boarded up. Nor was it subsequently let. Soon, the inconvenience of having no local blacksmith, of being obliged to wait for the visits of an itinerant farrier cum tooth-drawer cum smith, was keenly felt by the entire neighbourhood, from the squire downwards.

"Maybe they'll return." A disgruntled farmer, whose cart-horses' shoes were by now in a terrible condition, looked hopefully at his neighbour. "After the girl's had the child, like, maybe they'll come back."

"I doubt that." The neighbour, whose own Cleveland bays were unfit for carriage work on account of having cast most of their shoes, sniffed morosely. "Jem Searle wasn't deaf. He heard what Meg Gowan and Ellen Wheeler were sayin' about him and his family. He's done this to spite us."

"You reckon?" The farmer shook his head. "Women. Eh, Jack? Bloody women."

"Downfall of many a good man."

"It's a fact." The farmer sighed. "A true fact indeed."

The blacksmith's savings were sufficient to convey the family to Warwick, and to lodge them all at a respectable inn. There, the baby was born and Lyddy recovered her strength.

But, as his neighbour had predicted, Jeremy Searle had no intention of returning to the village of his birth. An avid reader of newspapers and broadsheets, he was well aware of the opportunities which awaited the talented and ambitious in the newly burgeoning towns of Birmingham, Bradford, Manchester and Liverpool.

He had often wondered if he too could become a manufacturer. He yearned to belong to that new breed of men, who now dominated the economy of the country. Who were demolishing the old order. Who would smack the squires and fine gentlemen, who infested the land, squarely in the eye.

The time was ripe. He would realise his dreams.

It wouldn't matter if the women assumed it was Lyddy's disgrace alone which had driven him from the village. Indeed, this notion would help keep them properly docile. So he took these two vessels for sin aside, and harangued them thoroughly on the subject of their wickedness. He then informed them they were all going to Birmingham, a place where they were not known, to seek a new living there.

"Now listen, the pair of you," he said. He fixed his blue glare on his cringing wife and tearful daughter. "Pay close attention to what I say. The baby – as far as the world is concerned, anyway – belonged to Lyddy's sister-in-law."

"What sister-in-law?" Astonished, Lyddy broke her vow of silence. Covering the baby's little hand with hers, she gaped. "Father – "

"Your sister-in-law who died in childbirth." Still Jeremy glared. "Her husband – a good-for-nothing scoundrel since disowned by us all – deserted her on her deathbed. He went for a soldier. Abandoned both mother and child."

The blacksmith shook Lyddy's shoulder, wrenching it so viciously that the child she was feeding lost her grip on the breast and cried out in alarm. "You're this baby's aunt," he repeated. "Do you understand me? Her maiden aunt."

Milk streaming down her chest and soaking her clothes, Lyddy nodded helplessly. Now she tried to pacify the squealing baby who, after some choking and squawking, finally consented to get on with her feed.

"So you won't be seen nursing her in public," added Jeremy, giving the child a baleful stare. "You'll feed her in private only. Do you hear me? If she cries when you're out in the street with her, you let her cry."

Lyddy opened her mouth to protest. But, as Jeremy's own lips compressed themselves into a cold, hard line, she closed it again. She held the baby close, to hide it from her father's hostile gaze.

It was a frosty morning in late February when the family climbed into the farmer's creaking cart which Jeremy had hired to make the journey to Birmingham. The blacksmith took up the reins. The horses shook themselves and stamped their great feet. Then, slowly, the rickety contraption moved off along the pot-holed road.

"It's time that infant was given a name," said Jeremy, as they bowled along. "Have you thought of one?"

"I wish to call her Susannah." Lyddy looked down at the baby. "I think it suits her."

"No doubt it does." Jeremy snorted. "Yes, it's a fine name for a bastard child. Susannah! Who enticed the elders. Who exposed her body to men with no more shame than a common harlot might feel. Who – "

"But father, Susannah didn't entice – "

"Rebecca." Sucking in his cheeks, Jeremy nodded, as if agreeing with himself. "Rebecca. That's the babe's name."

So Rebecca, of course, it was.

There was a great deal of traffic on the road that morning. Farm wagons, gentlemen's coaches, private cabs and public diligences all bounced and swayed along the muddy, rutted highway which led to the great manufacturing town in the distance.

In due course, the baby in Lyddy's arms began to cry for her dinner. "Wait until we get to the inn." As Lyddy began to unhook her bodice, Jeremy glowered at her. "You know what I told you."

"But Father, she's hungry. She's crying!"

"Let her cry." Jeremy stared straight ahead. "She'll come to no harm. She'll maybe learn some Christian patience, too."

But now Mrs Searle covertly ripped a shred of cloth

from her cuff. She passed it to her daughter. "Here," she whispered. "Make a comforter for her."

So Lyddy twisted the piece of linen into a spiral. Sliding her hand inside her bodice, she dabbed her nipples until the material was soaked. She pushed the milky fabric into Rebecca's little mouth.

Disgusted, Rebecca spat it out again. But Lyddy persevered. Half an hour later, still puzzled and famished, the baby fell into a fitful, whimpering sleep.

Just as the sun was falling beyond the horizon, the family reached the outskirts of the town. Dying rays of day cast a feeble, ghostly light on grimy buildings, dingy manufactories, and smoke-stained houses. Behind these, the sky was a sickly yellow. Higher up, it became a ghastly red.

Until today, Lyddy had never seen a manufacturing town. Now, cradling Rebecca in her arms, she gazed in dismay at its dismal, blank-walled manufactories, its huge, forbidding warehouses, and its filthy slums where starved, half-naked children wailed or played.

Hearing the unceasing din of industry, she wanted to cover her ears. Feeling soft flakes of soot settling on her head, she wondered if coming to this awful place were a divine judgement. A punishment for her sins.

Taking lodgings in one of the less squalid of the town's two hundred and fifty inns, the elder Searles lay down to sleep. But Lyddy paced the floor, trying to feed a baby so exhausted by crying that she had no energy to suck.

"Here we are then, Master Ellis. Home again." The Lowells' under-coachman, who had just driven the boy the twelve miles to Easton Hall, grinned encouragingly. "Well, down you get then. Aren't you glad to be back?"

"What?" Ellis sniffed. No, he wasn't. Not particularly. In spite of what he'd told Alex about being obliged to return home, he wasn't especially glad to see Easton Hall again.

After the elegance and luxury of the Lowell household, his own home was a wretched place. Cold, uncomfortable and squalid, its fabric was crumbling and its drains had been blocked so long that it stank.

His parents were seldom on speaking terms, so the atmosphere indoors was frosty in every sense. The servants, whose wages were generally in arrears, were obstructive, quarrelsome and sour.

But Lalage was there. Ellis's beloved little sister Lalage, who chattered and babbled enough for three children, made coming home more than worthwhile. Now, having heard the sound of wheels on gravel, she escaped from her nurse and ran out to meet her brother.

"Ellis!" she squealed. Hysterical with delight, she tore across the weed-infested drive. "Ellis! Oh, Ellis! You've come back! What have you brought me?" Launching herself at his stomach, she beamed up at him. She tugged at his coat-tails in anticipatory glee.

Ellis swept her into his arms. He hugged her. In return, she gave him a very sticky kiss, redolent of her breakfast. Monkey-fashion, she wrapped her legs around his waist. Clinging like a vine, she buried her face in his hair.

But now he realised she'd wet herself. So, unfastening her ankles, he put her down again. "Oh, Lally," he scolded, wiping his hands on her already grimy pinafore. "Why can't you go to the close-stool, like everyone else?"

Lalage's nurse came out now. She found her charge fishing in her brother's pockets.

"Marzipan!" Thrilled, Lalage crammed a large yellow lump into her grubby mouth. She thrust her hand in again. "A doll!" she cried. "Oh, Ellis! A real china doll!" Her happiness was complete.

Ellis laughed. "From Mrs Lowell," he explained. Taking it from her he held it, teasingly, just out of her reach. "She says you're to have it only if you've learned your alphabet."

"My alphabet?" Lalage sniffed in derision. "I learnt that weeks ago. Give her to me, Ellis. Please!"

He tossed the doll into the air. "Here, then. Catch."

She caught it just in time. Had it hit the ground, it would certainly have smashed. Now she examined it and was pleased to discover that, if yanked at hard enough, its pink satin gown would come off. So now, stuffing another lump of sweetmeat into her already bulging mouth, she ran off. She must show her treasures to her mother.

Lalage was Mrs Darrow's youngest child. Her baby, her darling, she was a much-wanted daughter, born after two difficult and distressing pregnancies which had both ended in the delivery of a stillborn son. Petted and spoiled by her mother but totally ignored by her father, who despised girls, at five years old she was still a baby. Ellis wondered if she'd ever grow up.

He went upstairs to his room. This, he found, bore all the signs of his sister's recent occupation. She'd scribbled in his books, piddled on his floor, and slept in his bed. He pulled a face. Instead of Alex, he'd now have Lalage as a bedfellow each night.

For, in spite of threats from him, smacks from her nurse and rebukes from her mother, he knew that at dead of night Lalage would sneak out of her nursery and make her way along the pitch dark corridors to her brother's room. In the morning, he'd wake to find his hair being pulled by a smelly little visitor.

Ellis groaned. Alex might squirm and kick and snort throughout the night, but Lally was far more trying. She lay on top of him, practically smothering him in her embrace. She dug her sharp toenails into his shins. Worse than that, the little wretch soaked his bed.

She didn't care. If he pulled up her nightgown and slapped her bottom, she just laughed.

When he was grown up, Ellis decided, he would have a bed all to himself. In his own private room. There would be a padlock on the door.

Both the Lowells and Darrows lived on their estates, amidst ancestral acres deep in the green Warwickshire countryside. The Darrows had held these same acres since Domesday, but the Lowells were relative parvenus, having received their sizeable grants of lands for backing the (eventual) right side in the Civil War.

Captain Alexander Lowell had gone into exile with Prince Charles. When King Charles came back to claim his own, faithful Alex had been suitably rewarded.

Henry Lowell and Peter Darrow were both country squires, both dyed-in-the-wool Tories, but there any resemblance ended. Squire Lowell had vision. Realising industry was the key to the future, he had invested in mines and factories and mills. A keen agricultural improver, he was also busily enclosing his open fields and turning his peasants off their common land.

But Peter Darrow seemed unaware that the eighteenth century had begun, let alone was more than half over. A heavy drinker, a spendthrift when it came to hunting dogs and the new breeds of faster horses, he was a miser in every other respect.

The expense and fatigue of agricultural reform ensured there would be no changes on his property. As far as he was concerned, the peasants were welcome to cut firewood and keep pigs on the common. Provided, of course, they left his game birds alone.

Left very much to their own devices, his tenant farmers called him a fine squire and a good man. Henry Lowell's tenants, respect and fear him though they might, called him a grasping, heartless devil. Since the Searle affair, he was branded a reckless libertine, too. It was his fault the village had lost its forge, after all.

Mrs Lowell did not long survive the misery of her husband's public betrayal. She wasted fast. Refusing to eat, she dosed herself on opiates, and washed these down with brandy. She died in the winter of 1760, soon after Ellis had returned to Easton Hall for the Christmas holidays, and just before the birth of the little child whose conception had hastened her demise.

Alex was with her when she died. That night he'd crept

into her room and smuggled himself under the bedclothes, staying there while she dozed.

Usually, Anne Lowell was a fidgety sleeper. Tonight, however, she lay like a statue. "Mama?" whispered Alex. He was concerned that she lay so still. "Mama, can you speak?"

Mrs Lowell did not reply. Only her hand, which Alex had taken in his, gave his fingers an answering squeeze.

He held her hand throughout that night. It was only in the early hours of the morning that he realised it no longer generated any heat of its own. That the wrist above it was cold.

Sent to stay with the Darrows while the inconsolable widower indulged his private sorrow, Alex was first of all white and silent. He refused to speak to anyone, even Ellis.

But soon he progressed to the second stage of grief. Clinging to Ellis for hours together, he wept his heart out for his poor, gentle, ill-used Mama. Covering his face, he rocked to and fro, keening like a beaten dog.

Like a pair of human bookends, Lalage and Ellis sat one on either side of him, trying to comfort him with simple animal warmth. Every night, the three of them curled up together in Ellis's large, sagging bed.

Snuggled up close one early morning, Ellis took Alex's cold hand in his. He chafed it. "We're to go to school, Alex," he said. "Your father will pay. I saw his letter to mine."

"I want to come." Wedged against Alex's side, Lalage woke with a start. Now, afraid she'd missed the chance of some wonderful treat, she turned her great, dark eyes on the boys. She grabbed her brother's arm. "Ellis, I want to come too."

"You can't. It's only for boys."

"That's not fair!"

"Nothing's fair." Ellis pushed her away. "Don't be such a baby."

"I'm not a baby."

"Yes, you are. You're a smelly, noisy brat." Ellis glared at her. "Just shut up."

"Shut up yourself." Lalage scratched his hand. She scowled.

Alex, meanwhile, was trembling with apprehensive dread. At the very mention of school, visions of floggings, of himself as a tormented fag – of his fingers broken or burned by older boys, of his back raw from the birch – rose like horrid spectres in his mind. "School, Ellis?" he croaked, appalled. "Truly?"

"Truly." Wanly, Ellis grinned. "Don't look so horrified. We'd have had to go sometime."

"Oh. Ellis?"

"What?"

"You won't tell anyone, will you?"

"Tell anyone what?"

"That I cried. For Mama." Blushing, Alex buried his face in Lalage's sticky nightgown. "Ellis, you must promise me that."

"I shan't tell." Ellis sighed in sympathy. "I love my mother. I'd cry if *she* died. Although I know you'd laugh at me if I did."

But now, Lalage decided there'd been enough chat. Reaching across Alex, she nudged her brother's leg with her own left foot. When Alex tried to push her away, she jumped on top of him, and grinned.

"Lally! I wish you'd ask Nell to cut your toenails." Ellis spat on the scratch. "Let's tickle her," he said. "Alex, get her arms. Hold her wrists."

"No!" Squealing like a piglet, Lalage squirmed away. When Ellis tried to grab her, she dug her sharp fingernails into his neck.

The scrum which followed put all thought of school right out of Alex's head. The three children went down to breakfast rosy, cheerful, and in fits of barely supressed giggles.

January saw an intense amount of activity at Easton Hall.

The boys' clothes were prepared, their luggage packed, and sent off by stage coach. It was decided Alex should leave for Harrow from Ellis's home, rather than face the double disruption of a return to the Lowells" estate, followed by the long journey down south.

"Tomorrow we go." Staring gloomily out of the bedroom window, Ellis looked down on the snowy scene below. "It'll be damned cold in that coach," he muttered. "But it'll be even colder when we get to school."

"Will they beat us hard, do you think?" Since his arrival at Easton Hall, Alex had felt no need thrash his friend. Instead, he was tormented by visions of grinning ushers armed with huge canes and other weapons of assault, all bent on beating him senseless.

"Don't know about beating." Ellis turned round. "My father had his leg broken at Winchester. Some monitors crushed it in a doorframe. He still limps."

"Oh, God!" Alex paled. "Ellis, you don't suppose – "

"But no one's going to break *my* legs." Forcing bravado, Ellis laughed. "Don't worry, Alex," he said. "I'll look after you."

"You?" Alex sniffed. "I can give you a hiding with one arm tied behind my back. How can you look after me?"

Ellis grinned. "Well then, we'll look after each other," he replied.

Over the next few years, Ellis grew tall and broad, becoming much bigger than his friend. Remembering Mr Sandford's oft-repeated prophecy that one day Master Ellis would be larger and stronger than him and would hit him back, Alex was inclined to be wary of his tall, broad-shouldered companion.

But he need not have worried. Ellis would have scorned to hit anyone smaller than himself.

Another year went by. Two years. While Alex still looked like a child, Ellis was fast becoming a young man. Ellis was the first to suffer the embarrassment of his voice breaking, the first to wake to find himself soaking wet but not with Lally's piddle, the first to take a razor to his previously smooth cheeks. He was also the first to lose his innocence, to a chambermaid who made a speciality of deflowering virgin gentlemen.

"*Did* you?" Fascinated and horrified by his friend's latest exploit, Alex lugged Ellis off to the privacy of the school chapel. There, they discussed it. "You did the whole thing?" he demanded.

"Yes." Ellis yawned. "Nothing to it, you know."

This was a blatant lie. Far too nervous to concentrate on what he was doing, Ellis's ignorance had astonished even the chambermaid. Now he shrugged, nonchalance incarnate. "She's an obliging girl," he said.

"Will you see her again?"

"May do." Ellis yawned again. "If I have time."

"Oh." Alex frowned. "Ellis, this girl – is she clean?"

"Oh, certainly." Ellis grinned. "She's spotless. Unlike you!"

Chapter 3

Alex had no ambitions. No plans for his future. Lazing his way through life, he did just enough work to safeguard himself from beatings. He was like a frog on a lily pad. Inactive himself, he was washed gently this way and that by the flow of the tide.

But Ellis had designs, ideas and schemes. While Alex took most pleasure in doing nothing at all, Ellis had – as Alex scornfully called them – enthusiasms. He took everything so seriously that he made Alex yawn with fatigue.

Outside lessons, boys were left very much to their own devices. They might play, study, or doze their lives away, just as they pleased. Ellis was constantly occupied.

He loved all kinds of games and sports. Unlike Alex, he did not simply endure the new and, in Alex's opinion anyway, insufferably tedious abomination of cricket. He organised matches, he captained the house team, and he always played to win.

Ellis was also determined to be the best scholar in his form. So, although his education at home had hardly been of the finest, he now worked very hard indeed, catching up with and passing most other boys in his year with ease. Not only that. When there was any scheme of riot or mischief among his peers, Ellis was generally the ringleader, and usually took the soundest thrashing afterwards. Which, of course, made him more popular still.

He made Alex sick.

"You'll burn yourself out by the time you're twenty," he said, as he loafed against a wall watching Ellis fastening the latchets of his shoes, in preparation for yet more cricket.

"I shan't rust away, like you. Idle devil you are." Picking up his bat, Ellis gave him a slap on the back which sent Alex flying. Calling to another white-flannelled idiot, he strolled away.

One Christmas holiday, Ellis was rummaging around in his father's library when he discovered a book of woodcuts. A musty, leather-covered volume, badly bound and worse printed, it was called *The Beauties of England*. Three of the faded illustrations depicted Easton Hall in its Elizabethan heyday.

The printing was appalling, but the intrinsic quality of the woodcuts themselves was excellent. Obviously, they were the work of a master. Ellis stared at them, entranced. In 1580, evidently, the roof of the manor house had not sagged in the middle. Its walls had not bulged outwards. Its lines had been perfectly straight, and its tall, intricately constructed chimneys had been set at ninety degrees to its roof. Its now worm-eaten carvings and sculpted gable ends had once been things of great beauty. The house had been surrounded by ornate, formal gardens, which set it off to perfection.

Looking at the pictures again, Ellis compared the crumbling ruin which was now his home with the pristine charm of the original house. He realised the Hall was, in fact, an architectural gem.

The long, low, deliberately irregular building, rising gracefully from the foundations of the original Norman fortress, was in the form of an ornate capital E – for Elizabeth, of course. This was an elaborate compliment to the Virgin Queen. It was built of mellow, rosy-red bricks, which served to enhance the great, grey beams which formed the framework. The small, leaded windows were set with pleasing symmetry in the red walls. The elaborately pantiled roof perfectly balanced the whole.

When it was new, thought Ellis, the Hall had surely

been splendid. "One day," he decided now, "it will be splendid again."

Having hated his home for a great, cold, echoing barn of a place, Ellis now found he rather liked it. He set out to examine every part and aspect of it, from its beautifully carved staircase to its dozens upon dozens of dark, panelled rooms. All these were admittedly rather small for modern taste, but they were well-proportioned and, for the most part, had the most marvellously elaborate plaster ceilings – many of them in urgent need of restoration.

The long gallery on the first floor, which Ellis and Lalage had always used as an indoor race track and whose scuffed, pitted walls bore witness to many a collision and bump, was certainly deserving of preservation. As Ellis looked up at the yellow, crumbling plaster of the cornices, he decided that when he could afford it, this would be the first room he would tackle.

The day Ellis found the black metal box, which contained the original plans and drawings for the construction of Easton Hall, was the day which crystallised his ambitions. Excitement fizzing and buzzing inside him, he had to share them. The Hall's present owner was the obvious person to see now.

"Sir?" he began, startling his father who was dozing over a late breakfast of strong coffee and slops. "If you please, sir? I've been looking at the designs for the house."

Mr Darrow glanced up. "Designs for which house?" he enquired, blearily. He'd had a heavy night, and the three bottles of port he had consumed were making their presence felt in the area of his gouty foot. "What the devil's the boy talking about?" he asked his wife. Who, as usual, did not deign to answer him.

"I've been studying the original plans and drawings for Easton Hall." Unperturbed, Ellis sat down. "I think we ought to discuss some refurbishment. Some restoration. I've made some rough calculations, and I – "

"What?" His father's sarcastic snort stopped Ellis in

mid-sentence. "Restoration?" he demanded. "Refurbishment? Has the boy run mad?"

He thrust his red, bloated face into his son's. "So who do you think is going to pay for this – this restoration of yours? Who's going to find the ready cash?"

"I just thought – "

"Well, child, you can just stop thinking." Scowling, Mr Darrow slid down into his chair. "If I had my way," he muttered, "I'd sell this mausoleum. Buy myself a decent, modern house. But it's entailed on you. So I damned well can't."

"But, sir – "

"But nothing, boy." Mirthlessly, Peter Darrow grinned. "The entail ends with you," he growled. "So, forget about restoration. Hang refurbishment. *You* can have the pleasure of pulling the place down."

With that, he got up and stumped out of the room.

Ellis was not disheartened. He lugged the black box up to his bedroom, from which Lalage was nowadays firmly excluded, and spread out his treasures.

There they all were. The ground plans and the elevations. The designs for the carvings which embellished the gables, the patterns for the plasterwork ceilings, the sketches for all the various kinds of panelling. Ellis smiled. Now he had some concrete guidance. He could see what he should be attempting, and work out what to do.

As he walked through the long gallery, he passed the portrait of an earlier Ellis Darrow, the courtier who had caused the old castle to be razed and the new Hall to be built. Ellis stopped. He grinned up at this ancestor who, serious and dignified in his embroidered jerkin and starched ruff, gazed solemnly down at him.

"Don't look at me like that," said Ellis. "You just wait until I've finished. I'll give you something to smile about. You'll see."

"But why?" asked Alex, when Ellis confided his plans.

"Why not let it all rot? Then pull it down and start afresh?"

"I couldn't do that." Ellis was appalled. "It's my heritage," he said. "It's going to be mine. Then it will be my son's. Alex, families like ours have duties as well as privileges."

"Do they?" Rubbing his eyes, Alex yawned. "Such as?"

"We are the guardians of our nation's history. Of its traditions, of all that's best about it. Our homes reflect this. We – "

"God, Ellis. What a pompous bore you are." Alex grinned. "You'll be insufferable by the time you're thirty."

But Ellis was not to be silenced. "Alex," he went on urgently, "*you'll* marry. You'll have children. Your sons will expect – "

"Don't." Alex shuddered. "I hate children," he muttered. "Puking brats. Whining babies. Odious! Ellis, when *I* marry – if I marry – it certainly won't be in order to beget heirs."

"But you – "

"It's *not* my duty. Don't be ridiculous." Alex grinned again. "Anyway, I've many things to do before I wed."

"For example?"

"I want to travel." Alex laughed out loud. "I want to see the whole wide world!"

So, while Alex went on the Grand Tour of Europe, ransacking France, Germany and Italy for fine furniture, ancient pictures and marble statuary, and developing his amatory skills in the beds of foreign whores, Ellis Darrow stayed at home in Warwickshire.

Here, he relieved his father of the fatigue of managing a country estate. He saved the wages of a land agent, too. Intent on understanding exactly how an estate like this was run and how profits could best be made, Ellis took over the agent's duties himself.

He made plans, plans, yet more plans. Constantly frustrated by lack of money and his father's pig-headedness, he gradually learned how things might be improved. When he finally inherited, he was confident he could become a rich man.

As Ellis soon realised, the land itself was excellent. Prime agricultural acreage, in fact – but it was under-used, with much of it actually gone to waste as common and furze. Enclosed, it could yield splendid profits. So Ellis bothered and badgered his father into taking steps to implement those changes which recent legislation allowed him to make.

"I'll leave Westcott Common alone," he said, as Squire Darrow muttered about the huge expense of fencing, not to mention tenants being dispossessed. "There'll be no evictions. But we have forty acres of bracken out there, simply going to waste. We could have sheep on that land. Cattle, even. Why not go ahead?"

"Oh, very well. Very well." Sick of being harangued by his son, the squire sighed his agreement. "But I tell you now. Things are perfectly well as they are. All this running after innovation is a waste of time. It makes me tired."

Mr Darrow went back to his bottles. Now, he spent all his time hunting, pickling his liver or sleeping off his hangovers. Ellis became master in all but name.

If Ellis irritated his father, he upset his sister even more. A young lady well into her teens, Lalage was disgusted by her brother's uncouth behaviour. His lack of interest in the world of fashion made her want to hit him.

So, he felt his true calling was that of glorified bailiff. But that was no reason, surely, for him to behave like a provincial rustic all the time?

Maybe not. But he did. Forgetful of all social obligations, he had to be nagged and bullied for days before he would shake the straw out of his hair and take his sister to a dance, a party or a rout.

There, he'd be an embarrassment. At even the most dignified gathering, he would simply buttonhole some other rural bore, then spend the entire evening discussing crop rotation. Or the relative advantages of speading horse shit as opposed to cow muck all over the wretched fields.

Mrs Darrow also preferred to be at home. Cajoled and bamboozled into chaperoning her daughter to those few balls and assemblies to which Lalage managed to arrange invitations, she sat all evening with the rest of the Mamas, grumbling about her servants and her ailments. When she should, of course, have been finding a rich man for her daughter to marry.

"God's teeth, girl! You're only sixteen." As her maid laced her into a horribly constricting pair of stays, in order that she might then squeeze into her one fashionable gown and take her daughter to an evening party in Warwick, Mrs Darrow groaned. "You've plenty of time to become a society beauty," she muttered. "Dawkins, that's enough. If it won't fasten, leave it. I shall wear my brown silk."

"Your brown silk?" Lalage screwed up her face in despair. "Oh, Mama! You can't wear that odious old sack."

"Lally, do you wish me to accompany you to the Harrisons' rout?"

"Yes Mama, I do." Lalage bit her lip. "But couldn't you just *try* to get into the blue satin? Please? Breathe in. I'm sure the hooks will meet."

In view of the dullness of her home circumstances, Lalage was always more than glad to see Alex Lowell. Recently returned from Europe, Alex had acquired delightful French manners and a wardrobe full of beautiful Italian clothes. Blond, slim and so elegant in his embroidered waistcoats and snowy white breeches, the very sight of him made Lalage's heart lighten.

He was so unlike her shabbily-dressed bore of a brother. In everlasting black broadcloth or brown homespun, Ellis looked like a parson down on his luck. His coarse cotton shirts and woollen stockings seemed especially repulsive when compared with Alex's cambric linen and fine silk hose.

"I don't see why Alex bothers with Ellis any more," she muttered, as she and her mother sat in Mrs Darrow's bedroom one dull morning, watching the rain slide down the window panes. "He's such an eternal bore. Bragging about his precious wheat yields. Rhapsodising over his tenant farms."

"Alex is a farmer too, Lally." Mrs Darrow shrugged. "Perhaps he finds Ellis's conversation interesting."

"Interesting?" Lalage tossed her curls in scorn. Yawning, she scratched her left armpit. "Has Nell finished turning my pink silk yet?" she asked.

"I expect so. Don't fret. It will be ready in plenty of time for Lady Ingham's party."

"Good." Lalage inspected her finger nails. She really must stop biting them – she wasn't a child now. "Oh God!" she wailed. "I wish we weren't so poor!"

"My love, we're not poor."

"We *are*! We live in a hovel, and we dress in rags." Lalage rose to her feet. Now, irritably clicking her fingers, she paced the room. "Turnips," she muttered. "Fences. Drains. Manure. Great heavens! How can Alex bear it?"

Alex couldn't bear it, in fact. As it happened, he found Ellis's unremittingly agricultural conversation every bit as tedious as Lalage did. So he never listened.

Instead, he watched. As Ellis's dark eyes flashed with excitement, as his handsome face was animated by his latest enthusiasm, Alex sat and gazed. It was enough to be there. To be with the person he loved best, in all the world.

The sole heir to a large, unencumbered estate, at twenty four Alex Lowell was by far the most eligible bachelor in the district. Fair game for every Mama with a daughter to wed, he was bombarded with invitations to every single music party, assembly, ball or evening gathering for miles around. He was also being nagged by his father, who wanted him to find himself a decent wife. She should be a woman with fortune, further expectations and good wide hips, who could present him with a dozen strong sons.

Mr Lowell even had a list. Inspecting it, Alex found most of the girls upon it were fat, imbecile or ugly. Usually all three.

So, whenever he could, he was glad to make his escape to Easton Hall, to the peace and sanctuary of the Darrows' placid, undemanding society. But, even there, he was not safe. Just turned sixteen, Lalage Darrow was a tall, strong-featured, dark-haired girl of the sort Alex usually found very attractive. She was on the look-out for a husband.

A rich husband, naturally. Old or young, handsome, plain or even downright repulsive, these considerations were irrelevant provided he had cash.

Alex was wealthy. Lalage began to eye him in the greedy, covetous way a tigress might gaze upon a nice, fat deer. She started to court his good opinion.

"Ah, Mr Lowell," she began sweetly, bumping into him as he stood idly in the entrance hall one cloudy morning, looking up at the darkening sky. "Are you going out today?"

"Perhaps." Ellis had gone to visit a tenant farmer, and Alex was bored. Now, he was trying to decide between a short walk round the shrubberies or a nice little nap. He stifled a yawn. Perhaps he'd go for the nap. "What about you?" he enquired.

"I'm going to the village." Lalage smirked. "I have an errand of mercy to perform. One of the cottagers – "

"Is sick?" suggested Alex, smiling.

"Yes." Lalage licked her lips. She grinned back at him. "Well, I told Ellis I would take her some broth. You know how conscientious he is about his tenants."

"Indeed I do. He's an excellent landlord. Or he will be, one day."

"Quite." Lalage did not wish to hear a speech in

praise of her brother. "Do you think it may rain?" she askcd.

Alex looked up at the clouds. "It's quite probable," he replied. "But it may hold off for an hour or two. If you were to go now, you'd probably escape a soaking."

"Do you think so?" Lalage sighed. "But it's so tedious, walking such a distance all alone."

"Would you like me to go with you?"

"Could you?" Lalage grinned. This was easy! "Have you the time to spare?"

"Of course." Alex offered her his arm. So Lalage picked up her basket, and off they went.

They had plenty of subsequent opportunities to be together. Lalage made quite sure of that. Delighted to find Alex seemed to like both her company and conversation, she sized up the state of her other personal assets.

Sighing, she saw that her complexion was too sallow and her chest too flat. Her feet were rather big. Her wrists were inescapably bony. Her knuckles were lumpy, too.

But she had thick, black hair, big, dark eyes and a full, red mouth. She decided these little charms would have to do. She set out to enchant him.

For his part, Alex observed that Lalage Darrow had changed. Once a rather dirty, smelly, scrawny child, she'd become an extremely good-looking young woman. A beautiful one, in fact. As tall as he was, and as straight as an arrow, she had none of those awful bumps and protuberances which distort the average female shape, making it vastly inferior to any handsome boy's.

For Lalage had no hips. Not much in the way of a bosom, either. Mere pincushions, *her* little breasts were far removed from the horrible, pendulous mammaries Alex found absolutely repellent. He imagined Lalage dressed as a boy. Her long hair tucked under a highwayman's three-cornered hat, breeches tight on her long, straight legs, she had a velvet jacket slung over one shoulder. The very idea made his heart thump and his pulse race.

He flirted mildly with her, and she grinned back at him. She came down to meals with her bodice so tightly laced that even her tiny bosom bulged dangerously above it. Ellis appeared not to notice. Or, if he did, not to care. There was nothing to care about. He did not imagine Alex would seriously court a penniless, sixteen-year-old girl. He would never seduce the sister of a friend.

"Are you particularly anxious to learn all about the cultivation of winter wheat?" demanded Lalage. It was early evening. Dinner was long since cleared away, and Lalage and Alex were walking in the knot garden. Lalage stooped to pick a sprig of rosemary. "Are you especially interested in the domestic habits of the turnip?" she enquired.

"Not really." Alex laughed. "Not at all, in fact. But you were sitting next to me, you see. That more than made up for the tedium of your brother's dinner-time conversation."

He took Lalage's hand. Raising it to his lips, he kissed it. "Nothing could be as fascinating as you are," he said.

"Ellis wouldn't agree." Lalage pouted. "He adores a parsnip. But when he looks at *me*, he merely sees his grubby little sister."

"Ellis doesn't look at you with my eyes," Alex said.

It was becoming chilly now. The wind was getting up, and in the east the stars began to glow. Lalage was dressed in the flimsiest of silk gowns, and soon she started to shiver.

"Are you cold?" asked Alex.

"A little." Lalage was in fact half-frozen. That evening, her hair was combed away from her forehead and coiled in braids at the back of her head, so her shoulders, most of her back and a great expanse of her bosom were bare. "It is rather fresh out here," she said.

"Then shall we go indoors?" Alex increased the pressure on her fingers. "We can enjoy each others' company as well indoors as out."

"Yes." Lalage looked at him. "Come to my room," she whispered. "To talk a little."

"Had we not better sit with your brother and Mama?"

"Mama has gone to bed. Ellis has ridden over to Hadley, to see some boring stock-breeder." Lalage sighed. "Oh, Alex! I get so lonely. Every night, it's the same. I sit at my window in the twilight, all by myself."

"Poor Lally. You need someone to cheer you up."

"Yes, I do." Lalage sighed again. "Come up with me. Just for half an hour."

"Won't your maid be there, turning down your bed and so on?"

"The servants are all in the kitchen at this hour, stuffing themselves. Alex, please come. No one will know."

Alex pulled her towards him. He kissed her on the mouth. Together they went into the house.

Then Alex took over completely. Shutting Lalage's bedroom door behind him, he bolted it. Crossing the room, he pulled the curtains closed.

He threw off most of his own clothes, leaving them in tumbled, tangled heaps all over the room. But, after tugging ineffectually at a few of her laces, he abandoned his efforts to undress Lalage herself.

Instead, he pulled her over to her bed, then told her to lie down. Dragging up her voluminous skirts and petticoats, he took her without further ceremony, as greedily as a man dying of thirst gulps water.

She let him get on with it, lying supine and relaxed as the most available of harlots. When he'd finished, she laughed. "So that's what it's about," she said, smirking up at him. "That's all there is to it. So now, negotiations can begin."

"What?" Alex frowned. "What exactly do you mean by that?"

"Well." Lalage giggled. "You *have* been rather presumptuous, haven't you? If I told Ellis about this, he'd break your neck. Then roast your carcase on the village green."

"I doubt that."

"Really? Then you don't know him as well as you think you do." Her bodice hanging open and her skirts up round her waist, Lalage licked her lips. "Rape, Alex," she whispered. She stroked his neck with a ribbon. "That was rape. The wanton violation of a helpless child. A capital offence, yes?"

Alex said nothing.

"Oh, well." Lalage affected a huge yawn. "Don't speak to me. I don't care. I shall get dressed."

Alex eyed her appraisingly. He shook his head. "Lally," he said casually, "give me a kiss."

"No. You've had enough kisses for today." Lalage pulled the lace out of her bodice. Then she began to re-thread it through the eyelets, frowning in concentration as she worked.

"I said, give me a kiss," repeated Alex. But rather more sharply this time.

"I said, no." Not looking at him, Lalage sucked the end of the thread, and went on with the job in hand.

So she was taken completely by surprise when Alex pushed her on to her back, and pinned her down to her bed. When he let his whole weight fall on top of her, and gave her a bruising kiss which cut her lips against her own teeth.

Laying one forearm across her throat, he tugged viciously at her skirts and petticoats, snapping the laces which held them. He took her again, but far more roughly than before. This time, it hurt. Lalage would have screamed if her mouth had not been gagged with his.

For such a small, slim man, Alex was very strong. Much stronger than she was. Although she struggled and fought, Lalage was unable to push him away. For when she tried, the pressure of his arm increased, crushing her windpipe, half choking her.

"Now," he said, ten minutes later, "*that* was rape.

That's what men are hanged for, that's the capital offence. Do you see?"

Lalage glared at him. Her throat in spasm, she was unable to speak.

Alex pushed damp blond hair out of his eyes. "I didn't take you by force that first time," he went on. "If anything, you seduced me. I didn't even take your virginity. But I have now. So go and tell your brother all about it. If you dare."

Her eyes bright with anger, Lalage stared at him. Licking her lips, she found they tasted of her own blood. "Beast!" she croaked. "Filthy pig! I'll see you hanged, I swear I shall!" Then, suddenly pathetic, she sobbed. "How could you do that, to me?"

"Yes, I thought a few tears would come next." Alex laughed. "Lally, my darling, don't cry. I may be a vile seducer, a filthy satyr and all the rest of it, but I'm also a very wealthy man. You like that, don't you? That's why you find me irresistible, after all."

"I hate you! I hate you worse than poison. I don't find you irresistible, not in the least!"

"Yes, you do." Complacently, Alex smiled. "I'm the heir to the biggest estate in the area. I'm richer than your brother will ever be. That's why you set out to captivate me. Why you grin and leer at me. Why you walk round the house with your bosom falling out of your gown."

Lalage sniffed.

Alex rolled on to his stomach. "Lally, may I touch you?" he asked.

She did not reply. So now Alex traced the outline of one little breast. He trailed one finger down her stomach, then let it lie in the pool of her navel. "I can buy anything I want," he said. "I could buy you. You are, after all, for sale."

"I'm not!" Covering her face, Lalage burst into tears of humiliation and distress. "I'm not for sale at all."

"Of course you are. Forgive me for contradicting a lady, but you should understand this. Girls like you are so many heifers. Bred for the marriage market. Think about it, and you'll see it's so."

He looked at her. "Aren't you white?" he whispered. "White, smooth and perfect. Darling Lally! You needn't have gone to all this trouble, you know."

"What?" Lalage sobbed again. "I was a virgin," she wept. "I gave you something I can never give another man."

"I know, darling. I know." Alex moved her hands away from her face. He kissed her lips. "You're so like Ellis, aren't you?" he murmured. "Same fine eyes. Same straight nose, dark hair and pale skin. Except for a few essential differences, you're almost the same person."

"Are we?"

"Yes, indeed." Alex kissed her again. "I was about to fall in love with you," he said. Wistfully, he sighed. "I would have liked just a little more time. To flirt a while. To undress you in my mind. To plan my first meal of you, to linger over the bill of fare."

He shrugged his shoulders. "It doesn't matter. I'll marry you, anyway."

"You'll what?" Incredulous, Lalage stared at him. "What did you say?"

"I'll marry you. That's what you want, isn't it?" Alex laughed. "Well, you want my money. I'm afraid being bedded by me is the price you'll have to pay."

Lalage licked her salty, bloodied lips. Money! Masses of it, coffers of it, full to overflowing. She looked into Alex's eyes. "It's a bargain," she said.

"Of course it is," Alex agreed. "You must cut your hair," he told her. "It's too long for the modern fashion."

"Is it?"

"Indeed it is." Fingering her gown, Alex shook his head. "Good God, look at this rag. Was it your mother's once? We must get you some presentable clothes. I'll see about an allowance for you, straight away."

Lalage cheered up.

As Alex dressed, she watched him. She would take his money. She'd spend it like water. He owed her that, at least.

She wouldn't forget what he'd done to her, or what he'd said. One day, she would make him suffer as she just had. Justice would be at her hands, not at a rope's end. But, like the rope, she would show no mercy.

Alex Lowell married Lalage Darrow, taking her for his wedded wife a mere three months after he'd taken her to bed.

Defying his own father, he'd amazed hers, who had quickly given his consent before the young squire changed his mind.

Now she was his, signed, sealed and delivered. Now, he could have her any time he pleased. He could summon her to his presence. She would have to do just as he said. That was the deal.

On the whole, Alex thought he'd made an excellent choice of bride. Young, ignorant and unschooled, Lalage was biddable, co-operative and obedient. As receptive to new ideas as ever her brother was, she learned the language of love as fast as Alex could teach it, and soon became eager to contribute new words and whole phrases of her own.

"You're exhausting," groaned Alex, after an afternoon spent reworking some especially difficult syntax and going over it yet again. "Lally, you wear me out."

"Do I?" Jumping from the bed, Lalage stretched. Still full of energy, she danced across the room. Stopping in front of a looking-glass she studied herself, turning this way and that. "I'm getting fatter," she said. "Especially around my behind."

"Nonsense." Alex grinned. "You're as thin as a rail. There's no meat on you at all."

"I must eat more. I'll stuff and stuff."

"Don't do anything of the sort. You're perfect as you are." Alex held out his hand to her. "Come here."

Lalage flung herself on the bed. "When do you wish me to have a child?" she asked.

"A baby?" Alex winced. "Surely you don't want to be pregnant? Not yet?"

"Well, you want an heir, don't you?" Lalage frowned. "I assume you married me so I could provide you with one."

"No!" Violently, Alex shook his head. "Absolutely not. What I mean," he added, seeing his vehemence astonished her, "is that I think you're too young."

"I see." Believing she'd been wedded and bedded in order to breed a clutch of little Lowells, and intending to have at least six children, Lalage shrugged. "I just wondered. Alex, I need a couple of new gowns."

"Order them." Relieved to get off the subject of pregnancy, for the idea of Lalage's beautiful skinny body bulging and swollen revolted him, Alex smiled. He kissed her. "Order what you want. Two, twenty-two, a hundred and two. As many as you please."

Lalage narrowed her eyes. She wondered what else she needed. If Alex was feeling generous, now would be a good time to ask.

She kissed him in return. "Do you know, Alex?" she whispered.

"What?"

"I'd so like to travel." She stroked his shoulder. "I'd love to go abroad."

"You shall." Feeling desire rekindling, Alex kissed her again. "Where would you like to go?"

"Italy." Dreamily, Lalage smiled. "I'd like to go to Italy. To Venice. To Rome."

"Then you shall. I'll make the arrangements later today. Darling, lie down again now."

Chapter 4

Lyddy Searle's baby daughter became a lively toddler, then a merry, good-humoured little child. Growing up in a dark, shuttered, poky little house in the shadow of the button works where her grandfather was first the solitary labourer, but soon enough the overseer of a dozen men, and finally – having acquired an adjacent yard and some outbuildings – the owner of a fair-sized button, buckle and trinket manufactory, Rebecca was well content with her lot in life. With good reason. In a hard, unforgiving world governed by a stern, Prebyterian God, she knew her own family had been singularly blessed.

In spite of its thriving industries and bustling commerce, Birmingham was a byword for poverty, dirt and despair. Even for starvation. Ragged, homeless children, their bony little bodies riddled with disease, their eyes huge in their emaciated faces, sat all night against the warm wall of the factory furnace. But Rebecca slept in a soft, feather bed. Thin, pale women, often with babies in their arms, walked the filthy streets where they begged for coppers or scraps of food. But Rebecca's grandmother and Aunt Lyddy had plenty to eat, good warm clothes, and a comfortable home.

As Rebecca knew perfectly well, this was because her family was industrious and God-fearing. Because her grandfather worked hard, went regularly to chapel, and did not swear.

Orphans were not a rarity, so the fact that Rebecca's mother had died when she was born did not particularly distress her. She sometimes wished her father would come home. But her grandfather evidently hadn't got on with his son.

"You must never ask Granda about your father," said Aunt Lyddy, taking the child on her knee and looking earnestly into Rebecca's cornflower-blue eyes. "Becky, you must promise me now. Never ask him about when you were born. Or anything like that."

"Will it make him angry?" asked Rebecca.

"Very angry." Aunt Lyddy sighed. "Also very sad."

"Oh." Rebecca thought for a moment. "Aunt Lyddy, did you like my Papa?"

"Yes, at first." Lyddy shrugged. "But later, after you were born, I didn't like him at all. We'd best forget all about him."

Always obedient to her beloved aunt, Rebecca did as she was told. Besides, she loved Jeremy Searle dearly. She would not have upset him for the world.

Although universal in the more ancient English towns, there were no trade guilds in Birmingham. There were no closed shops, no long years of formal training before a man might be initiated into a trade, or mystery as they were still known in places like Winchester, Coventry or York. Any man with his own small savings, rather more ambition, and a hefty dollop of luck, could push his way into the hierarchy of manufacturers. He might even become rich.

At the age of forty one, Jeremy Searle became one of those men determined to create his own little kingdom, a New Jerusalem of which he would be king. He was already a fine craftsman. Back in that quiet Warwickshire village, he had often undertaken small commissions for fancy wrought-iron work. He'd made ornate metal baskets for planting up with summer flowers, and taken regular orders for hanging brackets, elaborately worked coat-stands, and even garden gates.

For a man as dour and self-righteous as Jeremy, the blacksmith had a surprisingly well developed feeling for proportion and beauty. This was coupled with an artistic talent and natural sense of line which he expressed through even his most ordinary work.

Although running the factory left him no time to make anything himself, he still had the patience to seek out, encourage and expect good craftsmanship. In each of the many workshops, excellence was always demanded, and frequently attained. But, although he inspired and encouraged them, his workers feared his temper. As Jeremy made his daily inspections, both foremen and hindsmen held their collective breath.

"Here, you. James Adderby, isn't it?" Today, Jeremy collared one of his current apprentices. He glared at the lad. "You call this finished?" he demanded. He held up the snuff-box in question. He glowered at it in disgust. He was seriously displeased.

A child of eleven or so, whom Jeremy had literally taken from the street, James Adderby bit his lower lip. "I buffed it well, master," he whispered. He was terrified of all grown men, and Jeremy scared him almost witless. "Truly, sir. I finished it as best I could. W-where do you see the fault?"

"Here, idiot. Here again!" Now, on a minute shaving of rough metal near the hinge, Jeremy deliberately cut the ball of his own thumb. "If a man wants to cut meat, he buys a carving knife. Smooth and polish it again."

"Yes, sir." The boy reached for the steel wool.

"Not now, child." Jeremy's stern features relaxed a little. "The other lads stopped work five minutes ago. Go and get your dinner."

"Thank you, sir." The boy managed a faint smile of gratitude. Then he scuttled off.

Jeremy trained his apprentices personally. He drove them very hard. But he paid them well, and he treated them humanely. In the factories and workshops of his competitors, child operatives slept on rags spread over the hard factory floor, but Jeremy lodged his apprentices in a purpose-built dormitory adjacent to the works. While other men's juniors were thrown scraps fit only for animals, Jeremy Searle's boys ate nourishing meals, with butcher's meat every other day.

In return, their master expected complete loyalty, unquestioning obedience, and very hard work. He was seldom disappointed.

As his undertaking prospered, Jeremy diversified from the main business of button, buckle and trinket manufacture and began a line in fine wrought-iron work. Later, as this began to pay dividends, Searle's took deliveries of tin, brass and copper too, turning out candlesticks, snuffers, needlecases, card-holders and all manner of fancy goods. By the time Rebecca was eight, Searle's factory was a byword for excellence. A bright, shining jewel in the crown of that dirty metropolis, which was also the toyshop of the world.

"Here come the carters. Aunt Lyddy! The delivery men are here." From her bedroom window in the house alongside the factory, Rebecca loved to watch as drays loaded with sheet metal or bar-iron rolled heavily into the cobbled yard. Begging an apple or two for the horses, she would rush down to feed them as they stood calm and patient, waiting for their drivers, jangling their brasses and stamping their enormous, iron-shod feet.

"Becky! Come away!" Passing through the yard, Jeremy often had occasion to scoop the little girl out of harm's way. For, docile and tractable as they were, the carthorses still fidgeted and shifted about, and a careless kick could have crushed her skull like a nut. "What have I told you, my maid? How many times must I say it? Keep out of the horses' way!" With a great, rough forefinger, Jeremy tapped Rebecca's little nose. "Will you never learn obedience? Have you no common sense?"

"I'm sorry, Granda." Rebecca tried to look contrite. "They're gentle beasts," she whispered. "They'd never hurt me."

"Not on purpose, no." Jeremy shook his head. "You

must heed your elders, child. Do as you are told, come when you are bidden. Remember, a lesson not willingly learned must be beaten in."

But, in spite of these warnings and threats, Rebecca still darted among the horses. Offering apples or carrots, stroking their velvety noses, she was sure she'd come to no harm. She loved the warm, bran-and-molasses, ultimately reassuring odours of those great beasts. The crunching, grinding sound of heavy, metal-rimmed wheels rolling across cobblestones was music to her ears. She would always associate these with the more familiar sounds and smells of hot iron being worked by perspiring human beings.

Standing in the factory forecourt, she was happy. This was where she belonged. Where she would always belong.

"Are you there, Lyddy? Where is the woman? Lyddy!" Jeremy Searle's harsh, peremptory shout was the alarm which always roused Rebecca to wakefulness early each morning. "Lyddy, you idle good-for-nothing! Bring me some hot water! Where's my shirt?"

At the sound of these and half a dozen other equally strident demands, Rebecca would sit up, rub the sleep from her eyes, and frown. Her stern but loving grandfather was so hard on her poor aunt. He was just as curt with his wife. Why? It was a mystery indeed.

It was not as if Jeremy were a cruel man. He was kindness itself to children. He plainly adored his grand-daughter who, from earliest infancy, had been actively encouraged to sit on his lap, pull his side whiskers and dribble all over his lapels. She was his precious Becky, his dear little maid, and his sour, hard-featured face creased into lines of pleasure when his grand-daughter was at his side.

From Jeremy, Rebecca heard her first Bible stories. From him, she learned the names of birds and flowers which, as a town-dweller, she seldom saw in real life.

From the age of five or so, she spent most of her waking hours in his poky little hole of an office, learning her alphabet and then, painstakingly, transcribing lofty sentiments and copybook phrases for his ever critical scrutiny. Thus occupied, she desired no other company.

"Here," he would say, as he rewarded her with the sweet or farthing which meant he was satisfied with her efforts that day. "That's good, child. Very good indeed. But don't make those fancy hooks and curls. Plain writing's the thing, you see. They'll expect it when you go to school."

School was a torment which began when Rebecca was seven. Made to sit still, to learn by rote, to repeat the same lessons over and over again, Rebecca was bored and irritated from day one.

By the end of her first week, she had decided enough was enough. "Don't want to go there any more," she declared. As Lyddy brushed the child's straight, fair hair, Rebecca folded her arms. "I'll stay at home and help you today."

"You must go to school." Lyddy fetched Rebecca's clean cap. "Here. Let me tie the strings, then you must be off."

"I'm not going. I told you." Rebecca stamped her foot. "I don't need to go to school. I know everything already. Aunt Lyddy, I do!"

"Hush! Granda will hear." Looking fearfully round for the old man, Lyddy tried to pacify the child. "Granda will be so angry – "

"Don't care if he is." Scowling, Rebecca plucked at the pintucks on her bodice. "Aunt Lyddy, it's horrible there. Mr Harker shouts and yells all the time. He takes so much pipe tobacco that he stinks. Like a dirty old hog."

"Rebecca!"

"Well, he does. He's a disgusting, smelly pig."

Hearing his grand-daughter's voice raised in anger, Jeremy came across the yard. Now he walked into the kitchen. "Pig, is he?" he asked, mildly enough. He swept his grand-daughter into his embrace. He tickled her cheek. "Rebecca, I should whip a little maid who calls her schoolmaster a pig."

"Whip *me*, Granda?" Rebecca grinned. "You wouldn't do that. Anyway, it's true. Mr Harker doesn't smell at all like a Christian."

"Eh? Stinks of fire and brimstone, does he? Of the fumes from the fiery pit?"

"Yes!" Delighted, Rebecca laughed.

In spite of himself, Jeremy chuckled too. "You must go to school," he said. "To learn your numbers and your letters. So you may cipher, read and write. You must study the Scriptures, too."

"I can read and write already. I know the *Twelve Principles for a Godly Childhood* by heart. You could teach me to add and subtract."

But Jeremy was firm. "You shall go to school," he said. "You must learn everything you can. Then, Becky, you will grow up to be a sensible, well-educated, modest woman."

"But – "

"Be silent!" Jeremy's fierce, pale eyes met hers. "A maid's first duty is obedience. So, Rebecca – you will do as I say."

Rebecca was defeated. Sulkily, she allowed Lyddy to fasten her into her pinafore, then to cover her shoulders with a plain, worsted cape. Her hair tucked under a cap of such starched white purity that it gleamed, she set off along the grimy street, towards the school where she would be systematically drilled into a narrow, Nonconformist view of the universe in which she lived.

Along with Rebecca, there was a whole group of children who were habitually bored. They took care not to show it, however, for yawning, fidgeting and scratching were offences of the gravest kind, and punishable by flogging on the hands or the back of the neck. Protestations of innocence merely incurred a double dose of stripes.

So the children took correction meekly, even if it was unjust. Beaten on the hands until her palms were split and disfigured with great purple weals, Rebecca knew better than to argue with Mr Harker about the fate of a piece of chalk, which she'd allegedly stolen. She knew full well that same chalk was in Anthony Rider's breeches pocket. Biting her lip, she took her punishment, hoping she would not cry out – and thus be given additional stripes, for insolence.

Friday afternoons, twice blessed Friday afternoons, were usually made unpleasant by readings from Foxe's *Book of Martyrs*. Rebecca watched in disgust as Mr Harker's yellow jaws dribbled tobacco-stained saliva, as he read out details of the most appalling torments.

"The children too were stripped, and cast naked into a circle of flames," he intoned, his bleary eyes roving over his own class of little sinners. "Searle, I saw you fidgeting. Step up to my desk."

"I must be naturally wicked and ungodly," thought Rebecca as she walked home, her hands stinging and her spirits depressed. "That's why I hate old Harker, and why he hates me."

But then, inspiration dawned. She came to a sudden decision. "I shall mortify my flesh," she resolved. "I shall subdue my passions. From now on, I shall accept chastising in a meek and maidenly fashion. I try to like Mr Harker, then he may like me."

In this unnaturally high-minded mood, Rebecca made her way to a piece of waste ground, where she picked a handful of burrs. Making sure no one was looking, she yanked open the front of her gown, then stuffed the prickly objects deep inside her shift. Lying next to her skin, they scratched and tickled horribly. So now, feeling as complacent as the most self-satisfied of martyrs, she went home.

Smugly, she sat down to her supper. "Whatever's the matter, child?" asked Lyddy, as Rebecca ate her bread and drank her tea. "Why do you fidget so?"

Rebecca smiled beatifically. "I don't mean to fidget," she replied. Longing to have a good scratch, now she forced herself to sit absolutely still. She nibbled her bread and butter.

She retired to bed early. She spent half an hour on her knees, then climbed into a bed from which she'd removed most of the bedclothes. She'd suffer in earnest now, for the autumn night was very cold, and there was no fire in her little room.

Downstairs, Lyddy shook her head over the half-finished meal. She wondered if the child was sickening for chicken-pox.

After a chilly and almost sleepless night, Rebecca rose early, washed, and observed she had an unpleasant rash all over her chest. All that day, she itched horribly. Mortification of the flesh was supposed to be uplifting, but this was nothing of the sort. It just hurt. "Searle!" Glancing up from his own work, Mr Harker finally noticed her furtive scratching. "What are you doing?"

"Nothing, sir."

"Indeed?" The master grimaced. "Come up here."

Meekly, Rebecca bowed her head. Rising to her feet, she approached his desk.

"You have fleas, Searle?" enquired the master.

"No, sir." Rebecca folded her hands. Instead of giving the master her usual bold stare, she looked humbly at the floor. She hoped God was watching her. That He was impressed.

Mr Harker wasn't. He merely picked up his cane. "Searle," he said, "you are a disgrace to this school. You are not only forward and disobedient, but evidently dirty as well. A liar, to boot. What are you, Searle?"

"Forward, disobedient and dirty, Mr Harker."

"Sir."

"Forward, disobedient and dirty, sir."

"Hold out both your hands."

Rebecca did so.

The master found children like Rebecca thoroughly exasperasting. Too clever by half, they finished their own tasks in record time, then fidgeted and distracted the others. This Searle child was the most aggravating of them all. Today, she would be taught a particularly difficult lesson. He raised his cane.

He hit her on the palms of her hands, reopening some already festering welts, and bringing tears to her eyes. Coolly and methodically, he gave her six stinging cuts, then told her go and sit down.

She looked at him. The injustice of his words and actions now burned stripes into her very soul. Her spirit was roused in earnest. "No," she cried, "I won't!"

"What?" Mr Harker stared.

"I'll never sit down in this place again!"

"Searle, go back to your desk!" Nonplussed, the master glared at her. "Sit down!" he repeated. For added emphasis, he rapped the cane across his desk. "Do as I say!"

Rebecca went back to her desk, but not to sit down. With hands which felt as if they were on fire, she picked up her books. She strapped them together. Aware that twenty pairs of childish eyes were goggling at her in awe and disbelief, she kept her own gaze on the master. "Good afternoon, sir," she said. Then, her head held high, she walked out of the classroom and out of the school.

On the way home she took the burrs out of her clothes and threw them into the road, where a passing donkey ate them. Reaching the factory, she went straight to Jeremy's little office. She sat down. But now she felt somewhat apprehensive. That sense of elation created by defying Mr Harker gave way to a nervous fear of Jeremy Searle's wrath.

Her grandfather was doing some paperwork. Glancing up, he blinked at her in surprise. He looked at the ancient pewter fob watch which always lay on his desk. "Well, my maid?" Kindly, he smiled. "Why are you home so early?"

Rebecca opened her mouth to speak. But now, the tears behind her eyelids spilled over. She heard herself sob. She held out her hands, turning them over to expose the palms. Jeremy stared in horror at the damage Mr Harker had done.

He left the office at once, returning a few minutes later with a basin of hot water and a handful of clean cotton waste. He held out one huge, gnarled paw. "Left hand first," he said. He wrung out the wadding. "I'll try not to hurt you."

Later that day, Jeremy jammed on his wig, brushed his best coat, and went out. He returned an hour later red in the face, his mouth set in the most terrific scowl Rebecca had ever seen. Lyddy kept out of his way for the rest of the evening.

Rebecca did not go back to school.

By the time Rebecca was fifteen, Jeremy regularly employed upwards of seventy men. Engaged in a huge variety of operations – for Jeremy would try anything which promised to yield a profit – his workforce was of all ages and abilities. At one end of the scale, he had children turning out nails, bolts, screws and buttons. At the other, he employed a dozen highly-skilled craftsmen, who made the most delicately wrought brass, iron and copperware for a growing and discriminating clientèle.

Rebecca's own training began when she was a very small child. Hand in hand with her grandfather, she went in and out of all the workshops and into all the sheds, courts and yards. Her childish ears accustomed to the most horrendous din, she watched the processes from beginning to completion. Say what he might about the value of studying the Scriptures, Jeremy knew perfectly well that it was in the factory Rebecca's real education took place.

When she was very small, he carried her on his

shoulders. "What's he doing, Granda?" she asked from her lofty eminence, as she watched a man punch holes in metal discs.

"Well child, what do you think?"

"Is he making buttons?"

"Indeed he is, my maid." Jeremy grinned. "Birmingham buttons, the best there are! Now, see these two fellows here? They're making buttons too, but the operation is quite different. Watch closely, and learn how it's done."

Rebecca spent all her free time amidst the rattle and commotion of the factory. She studied brass-founding, general casting and iron-smithing, she watched plating, gilding and embossing. She learned how Jeremy co-ordinated and managed his workforce. She met his suppliers, customers and fellow manufacturers, too.

"You'll be a manufacturer in your own right by the time you're sixteen," said Jeremy, grinning as she pointed out a defect in a new type of door hinge, then went on to suggest how a change in soldering technique could correct the fault. "If I didn't know otherwise, I'd have said you were a master craftsman yourself. That you'd worked your way up from 'prentice boy, and laboured at the furnace with the other little hinds."

"Would you?" Rebecca shrugged. "Don't dismiss Jonas Trotter," she said, referring to the journeyman who'd spent the past week wasting both expensive materials and his own time, together with that of three apprentices. Hundreds of hinges would now have to be scrapped. "He's a good workman. This particular fault is hardly obvious, after all."

"Trotter's task is to make things fit for the purpose. It was his responsibility to see the hinge worked." Jeremy tossed the offending artifact aside. "So, Becky. My little maid. Will you like to be an ironmaster?"

Rebecca frowned. "You're the master," she replied. "The men would never take orders from me."

"Of course they will. They see you understand the processes. They know you're a clever lass. They have as much respect for your opinion as they do for mine." Wryly, Jeremy grimaced. "Perhaps more."

"I doubt that."

"You don't hear what I hear." Jeremy's sour-featured face creased into a smile. "You must learn to trust yourself," he said. "To be ruthless. To believe you know best. Never pity the incompetents, and don't keep the idle in your employ. Womanish compassion has no place in business."

"No, I suppose not."

"So harden your heart. Then you'll be a match for all of them, competitors and employees alike."

Months went by. Year followed year into oblivion. Jeremy made his will, leaving everything he possessed to Rebecca. "Yes, yes, I trust you to provide for your grandmother and aunt," he muttered testily, when Rebecca objected that the older women had rather more right to inherit than she herself did. "You won't prove unworthy of my faith in you. I know that."

Rebecca did not have the chance to provide for her grandmother. On hearing the details of her husband's will, the old woman took to her bed, and five days later she died. Jeremy did not appear to care. He arranged the most perfunctory of funerals. Brushing aside all sympathy, and leaving his daughter and grand-daughter to listen to the condolences of neighbours and friends, he was back in his office before the sexton had finished shovelling soil over his wife's grave.

One fine spring morning he came downstairs to breakfast, glared at his daughter, smiled at Rebecca – then dropped his bombshell. "I intend to take the maid on a jaunt," he announced. He stirred his chocolate, then broke some bread. He dipped the crust in his drink.

Lyddy stared at him. Jeremy never took holidays. His only respite from work was the sabbath day, when he stood before his Lord for eight hours at a stretch. "A jaunt?" she asked. Fearful of annoying him, she hardly raised her voice above a whisper. "What exactly do you mean?"

"What I say." Jeremy drained his cup. "Cuthbertson can oversee the factory for a week. The clerks know their business well enough. Becky and I deserve a holiday."

Although rather sorry to leave her aunt behind in the dirty town while *she* rode through the pleasant spring sunshine in a comfortable hired coach, Rebecca was nevertheless determined to enjoy herself. The sensation of travelling was so new, so delightful and so interesting that it gave a glow to her complexion and kindled such a sparkle in her blue eyes that even her grandfather, who affected to despise personal beauty, grinned complacently whenever he chanced to look at her.

She had no idea where they were going. When she asked Jeremy where he was taking her, the old man merely looked foxy and replied she would see soon enough.

They were now in Shropshire. Two days and two nights of easy travelling brought them, at dusk, to the Severn Gorge and the bleak, industrial landscape of Coalbrookdale. Here, so much iron was smelted that the countryside for miles around was barren, blackened and dead. The noise from the forges and mills, together with the sight of scarlet-orange flames bursting from the hundreds upon hundreds of furnaces all around, made the night hideous. Rebecca wondered why her grandfather had come to such a place. Merely to exchange the sights and sounds of one pandemonium for another?

Jeremy would not say. After taking a leisurely supper at a comfortable inn, he grinned and told her not to ask so many questions, that persistent curiosity did not become a virgin of her tender years. "Wait until morning," he said. "Then you'll see."

"See what?" Engagingly, Rebecca smiled. "What *is* this great wonder, which you've brought me so far to gaze upon? Or is there nothing here at all?"

"Don't be saucy." Jeremy's bushy grey eyebrows came together. "You're not too old to be whipped."

"I'm sorry." Rebecca stroked his hand. "Can't you tell me tonight?" she wheedled.

"No. You must wait and see." Jeremy grimaced. "You've never had any patience," he muttered. "Even from a babe, you've known neither forebearance nor restraint."

Rising to his feet, he called for a candle, then went up to bed.

"The iron was cast here, at Coalbrookdale." His granddaughter by his side, Jeremy gazed. He shook his head. "I can hardly believe my own eyes."

"It's extraordinary." Rebecca gazed too. "I'd never have thought it possible."

"Possible or not, here it is."

"Yes." Now, Rebecca walked closer. "How high is it, would you say? Fifty feet? Fifty five?"

"Nearer sixty, I'd guess. Out of the water, that is." Jeremy eyed the half-completed bridge. "Becky, we'll talk to the fellow in charge. We'll find out."

They picked their way through a mass of building materials, then hailed the foreman.

By now, Mr Brading was used to tourists. This great arch spanning the Severn was the first iron bridge ever to be constructed, anywhere in the world. So, from all over the country, people had come to stare. To mutter privately that the whole thing was impossible. It would all fall into the water one day.

"Well, master," began the foreman, "it's cast iron. Every last bit of it. All the parts have been made here. All levered into position by hand." Impressively, he pointed. "Those pieces over there weigh near on six ton."

"So the whole?" asked Rebecca. "The whole weighs what?"

The foreman scratched his head. "Well, at a rough

computation, about five hundred ton." He grinned. "Yes, at least that."

"How is it all fixed together?" Rebecca peered at the work. "Have new methods of construction had to be found? Here, I see, you have wood-working joints. This is a mortice, is it not? Over there – a dove-tail?"

"Indeed it is." Surprised to find a woman had even heard of such things, Mr Brading nodded. "Come higher up the bank," he invited. "Step over the cordon here, and come with me. I'll show you how the rest of the work goes on."

Rebecca and Jeremy followed him.

From their new vantage point, they could see everything. Awestruck, they gazed. So many ribs of iron! Such a glorious, soaring arch! So much weight, so much metal, all so elegantly poised, so effortlessly suspended over the wide gorge of the river. The daring of it took the breath away.

Rebecca turned to her grandfather. His faded eyes met her much bluer ones. "That, my maid, is worship," he said. He took her hand. "That is the work of a living God, who has taught men to do the impossible."

Understanding perfectly, Rebecca agreed.

Lyddy never understood why her father loved Becky so well. A loud and insistent critic of the whole female sex, he bullied Lyddy herself from morning to evening. There was no doubt at all that he'd worried and driven his own wife to her premature grave.

But Becky was special. For one thing, she stood up to him. Rebecca spoke to him as if to an equal, always had done, ever since she could prattle. Somehow, the child had melted the cast-iron casing of Jeremy Searle's hard, Puritan heart, had discovered something soft and pliable inside. More than that, she commanded the old man's respect.

Chapter 5

When Alex had just turned twenty seven and been married long enough to cause his father some concern that no son – and no daughter either, for that matter – had been born to him, Henry Lowell took to his bed with his last illness. A slight summer cold, taken while out riding, turned to pneumonia. This weakened Mr Lowell so seriously that a physician was summoned, something almost unheard of in the Lowell household, where illness was simply not allowed to occur.

The doctor examined his patient, looked grave, and said he was unable to offer much hope. The lungs were failing. The death rattle could be heard as plain as day. Soon, little groups of tenants and villagers stood at the lodge gates. Silently, they waited for the passing of the squire.

"I wish to speak to you about the child." Summoning Alex to his bedside that fine June morning, Henry Lowell frowned. The effort to retain consciousness was exhausting him, and now he gripped Alex's wrist. "The girl," he croaked. "We must make provision for the girl."

"What girl?" Annoyed to have been called so early in the day, Alex sighed. He raised his eyebrows in bored enquiry. "Come, sir. Which particular girl is this?"

"My child, Alex!" While his son watched impassively, Henry Lowell coughed. Hawking up great gobbets of phlegm, he groaned in disgust and pain. "My daughter, damn you!"

"Ah. Yes." Alex had forgotten all about her, that little by-blow whose conception had undoubtedly hastened – or perhaps even caused – his own mother's demise. "Well sir, what did you wish to say?"

His father grimaced. "God," he muttered. "Great God in heaven. If this isn't the very pattern of a death-bed. Here's old sinner, confessing his crimes. Here's the son in tears at the bed's head. But you're not in tears, are you, boy? Far from it!"

Alex shrugged. He tried to look concerned. "Sir," he began, "before I came in, I spoke to your physician. He is most optimistic today. He is sanguine – "

"Sanguine?" Henry shook his head. "The man's a fool. He cups me, he bleeds me, nods, looks wise – he's an entertainment, I'll admit. But he's no Saint Luke.

"Listen to me, boy. That child of mine, my flesh and blood, I want to provide for her. I've seen my lawyer. He's taken my affidavit on the circumstances of her birth. When I die, I want you to set aside some cash. For her. Use the interest by all means, but keep the capital in trust for her."

"But where is this girl to be found?" Alex grimaced in irritation. "Why leave her money in trust to me? Why not simply make a bequest, in the normal way?"

"There's no point in tying up cash in perpetuity." Henry Lowell coughed again. "All I ask of you, is that you make a few enquiries. Give yourself five years or so. If you find the girl, give her a couple of thousand pounds. Two thousand, three – that's all. It won't make much of a dent in what you'll receive."

"But sir, why – "

"Why indeed." Henry Lowell sighed. "Why should you decrease your inheritance, for the sake of some harlot's bastard?"

"It's not that, sir. I don't begrudge the woman a legacy, not in the least. As you say yourself, it's a trivial sum indeed. But is she still living? If so, how am I to discover her? Where should I look?"

"I don't know. Just before the child was expected, the whole family moved away from here. I last heard of them in Warwick, but God knows where they are now. Their name was Searle." Henry Lowell glared. "Say it!"

"Searle," repeated Alex.

"So try to find her, won't you?" The old man shook his son's arm. "Promise me."

"I promise." Alex prised the yellow fingers from his sleeve. He went downstairs to find the doctor, who was anxious to bleed his patient yet again.

Alex then went to look for his wife. As he'd expected, Lalage laughed immoderately when she heard the details of her father-in-law's last request. "But that's charming," she cried. "Like something out of a romance! So, you will discover this slattern's brat. You will raise her from the gutter, clothe her in silks and satins, and bring her home again. Oh, darling! Imagine the pathos of the scene. We'll invite all the neighbours round, to watch."

"Do be quiet, Lally." Alex grinned. "I knew you'd laugh."

"I'm not laughing, darling."

"You are." Alex sighed and shook his head. "Well, then. I asked where I should look for this woman, girl – whatever she is."

"What did your father say to that?"

"Very little. He knows the family went to Warwick. That the slut he seduced had a baby daughter. After that, he lost sight of them completely."

"What a pity." Lally slipped her hand into her husband's. "There are some strawberries today," she said. "The very first, fresh out of the frames. I've told my maid to dress them with orange juice and sugar. Then take a bowlful up to my room."

"A little private banquet, darling?"

"Yes. For just the two of us."

"Ah. Then dress can be informal."

"Or optional." Lalage bit Alex's ear. "Do you remember when we had all those peaches? You used my lap as your plate. I made you lick up the juice."

"It ran everywhere."

"So it did."

"Come on, darling. Let's go inside."

They ran across the bright summer lawns towards the house. They clattered noisily upstairs and into Lalage's room. They were still gorging on strawberries and each other when Henry Lowell finally breathed his last.

"Do you happen to remember that time my father disgraced himself and his family by siring a child on one of the peasants?" Riding with Ellis along the southern perimeter of the Easton estate, Alex was disposed to chat. "The creature bore him a daughter. Or so he said."

"Did he? These fences are in a terrible state." Preoccupied with the condition of his fields, and thinking what a good year it would be for wheat – provided, of course, the rain kept off – Ellis frowned. But then, valiantly, he tore himself away from thoughts of muck-spreading. He turned to his friend. "A girl, eh?"

"Yes. Well, as I told you before, the old fellow had me hauled to his bedside. Confessed his sins. Then he made me promise to look for the girl. To provide for her."

"I see. What will you do?"

"I don't know yet." Sardonically, Alex laughed. "I don't know why he was so concerned about that particular bastard. There must be a dozen more besides. I was half expecting him to produce a list. To lay half the poor of the parish at my door."

"Oh." Ellis shrugged. "So what have you done about the bequest?" he asked, not that he was interested.

"I've set aside a few thousand. It's in the three per cents. I've laid the relevant information with my own attorney-at-law, so he knows as much as I do now.

"If this person is alive, she has only to present herself at Creech, Willis and Son. Then she can claim her reward. I don't feel I'm obliged to advertise for her, do you? That would be taking altruism a little too far."

Ellis shrugged again. "But if it's what your father wanted, perhaps you should at least – "

"Oh, come now." Alex grinned. "I shall look on that money as something put by. For a rainy day. It's still mine, after all. There's no formal bequest."

"No." Kicking his mare into a canter, Ellis rode off across a stretch of common. Alex was left to catch up as best he could.

The following morning, Ellis was left alone with his parents. His sister and her husband were tired of Warwickshire. They were to drive to Wales, where they would meet some fellow idlers for a short summer holiday.

"Won't you reconsider, Ellis?" Laying her white hand on his sleeve, Lalage made a *moue* of disappointment. "Dear Ellis, couldn't you get away for just a little while? We'd so like you to come. Wouldn't we, Alex?"

"What?" Sleepy and contented after a very busy night, Alex yawned. Dozily, he agreed. "What about meeting us in Llangollen?" he suggested. "On Wednesday night?"

"I can't." Ellis shook his head. "I've a new stockman arriving tomorrow. We're going to look out the best of the bull calves. Then we shall start a stud."

"How charming," murmured Lalage, shuddering.

"Fascinating," Alex agreed.

"Well, I think so." Ellis grinned.

Alex and Lalage exchanged pitying looks. They climbed into their equipage, a vehicle so magnificent it could never have been described as a mere carriage, and drove away.

Ellis watched until the dust from their wheels was out of sight. He sighed. What a pair of butterflies. It was time Alex and Lalage had some children. They should stop gadding about, and settle down.

But they showed no inclination to do anything like that. In fact, they travelled all the time. On the Continent in spring and autumn, they spent the winter in London and the summer wandering all over England in the company of other rich, idle wasters who had nothing better to do.

In spite of a round of almost constant pleasure, Lalage

was often bored. Being rich was no longer a novelty. She wanted power, too. Soon, she hit upon a scheme.

When last in London, she had attended a rather special ladies' tea-party, an afternoon *salon* where politics – rather than fashion – had been the topic of the day. Listening fascinated, she came away thinking hard. She made up her mind. Alex must become an MP.

"Darling," she began, as they dawdled over their breakfast one morning, "how would you like to enter Parliament?"

"What?" Alex stared at her. He looked appalled. "Whatever for?" he asked.

"Well, I was at Mrs Marchant's the other afternoon, and I was listening to Lady Grey. She talked so knowledgeably about the current session. She knows so much about Mr Fox."

"She would. She's his doxy." Alex grinned. "He spends half his time at the House abusing the government, and the other half in her private apartments. Probably with his snout up her skirts."

"Alex!"

"Lally, it's a well-known fact."

"Is it?" Lalage was astonished. Could Lady Grey, so dignified, so clever, so fashionable, really be a harlot? "Alex, is she truly his whore?"

"So the report goes." Alex broke some bread. "She's an atheist, too. Not the sort of woman you should be seen with at all."

"Oh." Lalage sighed. There was another embryo strangled at birth.

"Poor Lally." Alex took her hand. "You don't fancy yourself as a hostess, surely? You don't want the fates of nations settled in your drawing room? Or in your bedchamber?"

"I just wondered if you'd like to enter Parliament, Alex. That's all."

"I wouldn't." Alex shook his head. "Oh darling, imagine it. The tedium, the boredom, the *ennui* of the whole wretched thing! Consider election times. There'd be absolute hordes of dirty fellows around then, all tramping through our house. Drinking our sherry. Rubbing their lousy heads against our wallpapers. Wiping their greasy hands on our upholstery. Soiling our floors."

"You're so lazy!" Her dreams of glory shattered, Lalage glowered. "Idle! That's what you are. Bone idle. Half dead!"

"I'm not!"

"Yes, you are."

"Nonsense, Lally. I was in the estate office only yesterday, going over proposals for the new enclosure. I was there two hours."

"Two whole hours?" Lalage tossed her curls. "My poor darling. How could you bear it?"

"Do be quiet, Lally." Alex picked up his newspaper. "You make my head ache. Look, why don't you go and harrass your maid? We're off to Brighton next week. I expect some of your gowns need trimming. Or replacing. Or something of the kind."

After a month in Brighton, the Lowells yawned their way back to Warwickshire, where they stayed for a week at Easton Hall – which, if they wished to see Ellis at all, they were more or less obliged to do.

"I've never known a fellow for taking life as seriously as old Ellis," muttered Alex, as he watched his brother-in-law ride away into the early misty chill of a summer morning. Snug in his quilted powdering gown, still he shivered. "Where's he off to today?" he enquired.

"What?" Not intending to leave her bed until noon at the earliest, Lalage yawned. She sipped her chocolate. "Oh, Ellis. He's gone to see some beastly farmer, I think. The fellow's whole quarters behind with his rent. So, instead of turning him out and getting a reliable tenant, Ellis has gone to find out if he has a sick wife or anything like that."

She grimaced. "They'll fob him off with some excuse

or other, no doubt. Perhaps the cat died, and they're all broken-hearted. They'll tell Ellis they've been keeping a wake. They were too desolate to work."

"Ah." Alex laughed. Then, getting back into bed, he unfolded the letter which had arrived earlier that morning. "Darling," he murmured, "how would you like to be rich?"

"Rich?" Lalage frowned. "I'm rich already, aren't I?"

"Richer, then. How would you like to be richer?" Alex smiled. "We could double or even treble our present income. If we dare."

"How?"

"Well, this letter is from a fellow in London. A stock-jobber, who has contacts in the East India Company. He needs investors, you see."

"Investors?" Lalage's frown deepened. "Well, I don't know about that. Is it safe?"

"Undoubtedly. The fellow out in Calcutta is an old school friend of mine, a very sound man. I was considering putting in – let me see – twenty thousand, perhaps?"

"That's a great deal of money." Lalage narrowed her eyes. "Maybe you should discuss it with Ellis first."

"Ellis!" At the mere mention of his skinflint brother-in-law, Alex sniffed in derision. "Lally, my darling, you know as well as I do that Ellis wouldn't risk a hundred pounds on a Government loan. Let alone thousands on a long term investment like this. Discuss it with Ellis, indeed!"

"Well, speak to your lawyer, then. Don't rush into it, that's all I'm trying to say."

"Don't worry. I shan't do anything rash." Alex put his letter down. He smiled at his wife. "That's a pretty nightgown," he said.

"Do you like it?" Lalage smoothed the neckline, then shook out the lace at the wrists. "It's from Paris," she said. "It's real Valenciennes."

"Is it?" Alex undid the ribbon at Lalage's throat. "Take it off now, darling," he murmured. "We don't want to tear it, do we?"

By mid-day, Ellis was back at Easton Hall. His coarse fustian breeches muddied and his neck-cloth awry, he explained he'd helped pull a ram out of a ditch. Grinning at his sister and brother-in-law, he asked what time they'd got up.

"We rose early, as it happens." Lalage stroked the ruffles on her new silk gown. "We had business to discuss."

"What?" Ellis grinned all the more. "Lally, what a little goose you are. You don't know a thing about business."

Lalage scowled. "Talk to him, Alex," she said. "Tell him about the East India scheme. Otherwise, he'll start lecturing us on the merits of this pig or that cow, and I shall die of boredom. You'll have to carry me out in a box."

"Well, Alex?" Ellis sat down. He began to tug off his filthy boots. "What have you got to say?"

"So there it is," concluded Alex. "All things considered, I think it would be a very wise investment. You're not convinced?"

"No. But I'm not a gambler."

"It isn't a gamble." Alex shrugged. "I don't see what could possibly go wrong."

"My dear Alex, almost anything could go wrong! Take this fellow Hickson, for a start. What's to stop him swindling you? He could grab your money and run."

"He wouldn't do any such thing. He's a gentleman. I've known him since I was twelve years old. He'd never cheat a friend." Again, Alex shrugged. "Anyway, I won't advance more than I can afford to lose. Are you sure you don't want to come in?"

"Quite sure. I can't afford it. But even if I had cash to spare, I'd never go in for anything like this."

"You're over-cautious. You'll never achieve anything if you're afraid to take risks."

"I'm not a speculator." Ellis was serious now. "Alex, I'm not a feudal throwback, afraid of the modern world. But since I've been running this estate, I've learned some very hard lessons. I've learned them well.

"It's taken me years to consolidate what I have here. It'll take me a whole lifetime to recoup what my father has squandered, to recover what he's let go to waste. You, on the other hand, inherited a fortune. You have a large, steady income. Why do you wish to risk losing it?"

"I won't lose it." Alex slapped the arm of his chair. "I can't lose! It's a watertight scheme. I've looked into everything. Ellis, believe me. I'm not doing this on a mere whim."

"What about Lally?" Still Ellis looked grave. "Very well, I'll accept you've taken all reasonable measures to investigate this plan. But if it should go wrong – if you lose heavily – well, I think you ought to settle something on Lally now. Make some funds over to me. Then, if you're ever distressed for cash, that money will be available. I shan't cheat you," he added, observing Alex's sceptical grin.

"I know that." Alex shook his head. "My dear Ellis, I don't expect you to become my banker. Lally agrees with me, anyway. She thinks I ought to invest heavily in this scheme."

"Lally's ignorant and greedy. She doesn't know what's involved. All she understands is that she'll get more pocket money – for a while." Ellis frowned. "You spoil her. You've taught her to think she can have whatever she wants. Look at the gown she's wearing today. It must have cost at least a hundred pounds."

"So what if it did? It pleases me to indulge her." Alex yawned. "I'll see my lawyer tomorrow," he said.

Searle's manufactory continued to expand its range of production, enlarge its workforce and see its profits increase. By the end of the 1770s, the Searles were tinsmiths, lorimers and coppersmiths, in addition to being ironmasters with a reputation throughout the Midlands second to none. As the years went by, the former village blacksmith became a wealthy man.

Searle's supplied not only wholesalers and shops, but also, if the commission were worthwhile, private individuals too. One March morning, Rebecca and Jeremy were busy sorting the day's correspondence. Segregating invoices, bills and enquiries, they speared each letter on the appropriate iron spike. "What's that?" asked Rebecca, noticing the sheet of expensive white vellum in her grandfather's wrinkled hand.

"From a fellow by the name of Darrow," muttered Jeremy, who was still reading. "Wants a pair of ornamental park gates. Large ones, by the sound of it." Reflectively, he scratched beneath his wig. "We'd have to think hard about that," he went on, frowning. "They'd have to be made out in the yard, which would cause difficulties with the deliveries. The drays, and that."

"Yes." Rebecca took the letter from him. "Easton Hall," she read. "That's about ten miles away, isn't it?"

"Ten, fifteen. No more." Jeremy sucked his gums. "I've passed the lodge a couple of times. In my younger days, that is. There's a fine big house, I believe. Tudor or Jacobean, they say."

"It could be a very good commission, couldn't it?"

"It might. There again, it might not. Gentlemen are a fussy lot. Not so keen to pay their bills either, some of them." Jeremy grimaced. "Darrow. Mr Ellis Darrow. I know the name, but I can't place it."

"Has he done business with us before?"

"No. Says here in the letter he saw some of our work at a friend's house. He was impressed." Jeremy sniffed. "So he should have been. Searle's manufactures the best decorative ironware in the Midlands."

"Will you send Mr Cuthbertson to see him?" asked

Rebecca. Michael Cuthbertson was the firm's finest craftsman.

"No, I won't send him. Don't want to offend a gentleman with plenty of money to spend." Jeremy sucked the insides of his cheeks. "Cuthbertson's manners aren't anywhere near fit for a gentleman's drawing room. His linen is always foul. I'd best go myself."

"You, Granda?"

"Why not?" Jeremy grimaced. "I can see what's wanted then. Agree on a price. Nail this Mr Darrow there and then." Getting up from his chair, Jeremy walked out of his office and into the yard. "Has that good-for-nothing aunt of yours made our breakfast yet, do you suppose?"

"I'm sure she has." Rebecca frowned. "You must not abuse my aunt," she said. "She's a kind daughter to you, and she's been almost a mother to me."

"Yes, maybe." Jeremy scowled. But then he grinned. "Come along in then, my maid. We've a full day's work ahead of us."

Two days after receiving Ellis Darrow's letter, Jeremy Searle complained of a severe pain in his chest. He said it must be indigestion. "I told you those rolls were too fresh," he muttered, scowling balefully at Lyddy. "Fetch me a spoonful of chalk."

Jeremy swallowed his powdered chalk, gulped down some water, and went into the factory. Here, while examining the mechanism for a clockwork music-box, he collapsed.

The men laid him on a workbench. Frantic, Rebecca sent for a doctor. But the old man's own clock had run down for ever. A stroke – apoplexy – whatever the physician chose to call it, Jeremy Searle was dead before the doctor even arrived.

Three days later, he lay beside his wife in the local cemetery. Rebecca realised she now owned a large tract of real estate, a factory, and everything in it.

Chapter 6

Lyddy spent a most frustrating day. Worrying and fretting, she was unable to settle to anything. She wasted the whole time Rebecca was away on a series of unnecessary household tasks.

As if bent on both irritating her housemaid and aggravating her cook, she took all the household brassware into the back kitchen, where she polished it until it gleamed like gold. To the annoyance of her laundry woman, she took down, folded and refolded all the bedlinen, then turned out the whole family's chests of drawers. Exhausted, she was nevertheless waiting up for Rebecca when she finally returned from Easton Hall.

Of course, Lyddy knew perfectly well who Mr Ellis Darrow of Easton Hall in the county of Warwickshire was. The mere sound of his name took her back a full twenty years. To a month of sweet kisses and perfect rapture, which had given way to broken promises and universal disgrace. To abandonment, misery and a bitterness which even a whole lifetime could not allay.

Lyddy remembered the Darrow boy. She could see him now. As children, he and Alex Lowell had often lain together in the barn loft, staring at her as she worked in the dairy across the stable yard. When Lyddy's condition had become public knowledge, they'd not been slow to add their two pennyworth to the general currency of disapprobation. Their childish sniggers resounded in her ears still.

Ellis Darrow had succeeded to his inheritance fairly recently, or so Lyddy thought. Racking her brains, she tried to remember when that paragraph in the local newspaper had appeared, mentioning that Peter Darrow had died. Had it been last year? The year before? She tried to recollect.

Sitting down, Lyddy attempted to be rational. She knew nothing about Easton Hall. Nothing about the Darrows, except that the boy – now the man, and owner of the property – had been friendly with the Lowell brat. But such a friendship was more than enough to condemn Ellis Darrow. Try as she might, Lyddy could not help but fear for Rebecca's honour, her virtue – her very life itself.

She wished Rebecca would come home! It was dark now, and very cold. "Why couldn't she have sent Michael Cuthbertson?" Lyddy asked herself for the twentieth, for the hundredth time. "It's not proper, a girl of her age careering all about the country by herself."

Having borrowed an old-fashioned, lumbering carriage and its equally stolid coachman from one of Jeremy's business associates, who had been most anxious to help the young heiress in any way he could, Rebecca ate her breakfast, put on her best black bonnet, and said goodbye to her aunt.

Climbing into her conveyance, she spread her black silk skirts, then settled back to enjoy the long drive through the Warwickshire countryside, which was just now quite lovely in its livery of fresh, April green.

Neither the terrible state of the roads nor the bone-shaking jolting of the vehicle did anything to spoil her pleasure, and she was almost sorry when the coachman passed a lodge cottage, turned into a gravelled sweep, and hailed a man on horseback who had followed the coach for a mile or so and now caught up with it.

"That's Easton Hall, is it?" demanded the coachman, pointing his whip in the vague direction of a large house whose tall chimneys were just discernible through some trees.

"That's right." The man on horseback who was, Rebecca

guessed, a land agent, apothecary or well-to-do yeoman farmer, nodded. "Take the fork to your left. It's a quarter of a mile or so. No more."

"Thank you." The coachman touched his hat. He drove on and, five minutes later, drew up before a perfectly beautiful house. The most beautiful house Rebecca had ever seen, or expected to see.

Rust-red brick combined with pale grey timber to produce an architectural perfection which, although its irregularity was hardly in keeping with the modern concept of beauty, delighted her. Dozens of small, leaded window panes winked and sparkled in the sunlight. The uneven, red tiled roof, surmounted by tall, Tudor chimneys, completed the picture charmingly.

There were birds everywhere. Black rooks cawed and squabbled among the tall oaks which sheltered the house from the cold east winds. White doves strutted along the apex of the roof. Starlings and song-thrushes gathered on the lawns, while peacocks stared haughtily from across a beautifully-kept gravel courtyard. Enchanted, Rebecca gazed. Forgetting why she'd come, she began to walk towards the exotic blue birds.

But then, with a start, she recollected herself. She remembered why she was here. After conferring with the coachman, who assured her his own employer always used the front door when calling on business, and Rebecca should certainly do likewise, she walked up the main steps and rang the bell.

Admitted by a very smartly-dressed butler, she was asked for her card. Having none of her own yet printed, she handed the servant one of Jeremy's, and explained she was Miss Searle, Jeremy Searle's grand-daughter. A few minutes later, she was led into a large, panelled drawing room where a man – another indoor servant, or perhaps a tutor – stood looking out of a window, apparently in a daydream.

Now, Rebecca wondered what Mr Darrow would be like. Most probably, he'd be a fop. A dandy in a brocade coat, who would look at her as if she were the source of a bad smell. Who would –

"Sir? Here is Miss Searle. From Birmingham." Raising his voice in order to gain his master's attention, Simmons sounded extremely put out. As if Miss Searle from Birmingham had no business whatever to call at Easton Hall.

To Rebecca's astonishment, the man standing by the window turned to greet her. He was tall, dark-haired and dark-eyed. He was, in fact, the man she had first seen a quarter of an hour ago, who had directed the coachman to the house.

Looking at his face, Rebecca guessed he must be about ten years older than she was. At any rate, he was no more than thirty. Was this some sort of joke? For, thought Rebecca, as her nervous hands smoothed the black silk of her mourning gown, the man could not possibly own a house like this. To begin with, his clothes were all wrong. They were of the kind seen on the back of a respectable tradesman. A shopkeeper's Sunday best. Indeed, the butler wore finer broadcloth than this man did. Of the two, the servant looked far more the gentleman.

As was increasingly the fashion, the tall man wore his own hair. But this, innocent of powder or any other sort of dressing, was cut so short that its curls stopped well short of his collar and left his ears bare. Anyone even aspiring to gentility would surely have grown his hair just a little longer. Used just a little powder. Even Jeremy Searle had worn a wig, although this had admittedly been a penitentially uncomfortable thing of coarse, brownish tow, and sat most uneasily upon his large, craggy head.

Rebecca's heart sank into her shoes. This Mr Darrow was an eccentric. Eccentrics were notoriously lax about paying bills. Eccentric misers were more lax still. Was Mr Darrow a miser? Well, even if he was merely careful, someone whose coat was made of stuff costing sixpence a yard could hardly be expected to commission anything very lavish in the way of wrought-iron gates.

As she looked at this freak of a man, Rebecca made up her mind. She would make her excuses, and leave.

But then Mr Ellis Darrow smiled at her. "You have come on behalf of Mr Searle?" he asked. He glanced at the letter in his hand. "I was expecting a Mr Jeremy Searle," he explained. "Mr Searle, the ironmaster. You are?"

"I am Rebecca Searle. I too am an ironmaster."

"Indeed?" Mr Darrow's fine black eyebrows rose.

"My grandfather died two weeks ago. I am the manager of the manufactory now." Rebecca met Ellis Darrow's eyes. "It was always intended I should take over the business. I'm perfectly competent, let me assure you of that."

"My dear young lady, I'm sure you know your business through and through." Mr Darrow smiled again. "Well now, Miss Searle – may I offer you some tea? We'll take it in my study. Then I can show you some drawings of what I had in mind."

Opening the door, Mr Darrow held it while Rebecca walked into the passage. "Simmons," he said, "be so good as to arrange tea. Ask Mrs Dale to send up some cake or shortbread. Miss Searle, it's this way. Down the corridor here."

He led her into a small, square room, oak panelled like the drawing room, but furnished with a desk, cabinets for papers, and a tall thin cupboard, presumably for maps or plans. Laden bookshelves lined the walls, and two new, upholstered armchairs were placed either side of the fireplace. A new Turkey carpet covered most of the floor. It was a pleasant, comfortable room, and Rebecca felt far more at ease here than in the larger, more splendid salon.

Delving into a drawer, Ellis produced a sheaf of papers. "These are my provisional plans," he said. He spread the sheets on the desk. "Look, consider. Then tell me what you think."

Rebecca looked. "This is perhaps possible," she said,

pointing to the drawing on the top of the pile. She leafed through the other sketches. "This, however, isn't feasible at all. The weight of metal at the top of the gate would eventually distort the whole thing. That is, unless it were braced here, and here. Which would spoil the symmetry of the design entirely."

"Yes. I see." Ellis nodded. "Then perhaps something like this?"

"Yes. That's better. Perhaps, though, we could have a little extra detail there. Then here, we might add some arabesques." Rebecca pencilled in an alteration.

"That's splendid." Ellis Darrow nodded. "Well now, what about this? "

Both client and expert were soon thoroughly engrossed. Delighted to find that far from simply demanding his whims must be satisfied, Mr Darrow was interested in technical difficulties and constraints, Rebecca now began to rough out a proposal of her own. One which included most of the features Mr Darrow seemed to like best.

As for Ellis, he was pleased to discuss his enthusiasms with someone who treated them as seriously as he did himself. An hour, then another, quickly went by.

Finally, Rebecca sketched a design for a pair of gates representing a near perfect compromise between what Ellis wanted and what her craftsmen could produce. "What do you think of this?" she asked.

"That looks splendid." Ellis took the drawing. He studied it. "Could we perhaps have a *fleur de lys* here?"

"Certainly." Rebecca drew it in.

"Perfect." Ellis nodded. "Miss Searle, that's exactly it. What is it, Simmons?" he added, absently. For now the butler came silently into the room.

"You have a visitor, sir."

"I'm very busy just now." Ellis picked up a pencil. "Tell him to wait."

"Ah." Simmon sniffed. "Well, sir – "

"I'm engaged for the next ten minutes. If the fellow can't wait, tell him to go away."

Simmons sniffed again. "Mr Lowell, sir," he said.

Pushing past the servant, Alex Lowell flicked fastidiously at the point where the fine twill of his own coat had made contact with the coarser broadcloth of the servant's attire. "So what keeps you so occupied?" he enquired, smoothly. "What can possibly prevent you from talking to *me*?"

"Alex!" As if waking from a dream, Ellis shook his head. "I thought you were in London."

"We came home yesterday." Alex looked quizzically at his friend. Then, glancing at Rebecca, he smirked. "I understand now," he said, somewhat waspishly. "All becomes plain."

"Indeed?" Standing up, Ellis brushed pencil shavings from his breeches. "This is Miss Searle," he said absently, still examining the drawing which Rebecca had completed just a few minutes ago. "She came over from Birmingham earlier today. Miss Searle, my close friend Mr Lowell."

"A most exquisite pleasure." Alex held out his hand. "How do you do?"

Rebecca took his hand. His fingers were as cold as glass. She let them go almost at once.

"Do go on with whatever you were discussing," Alex murmured now. "I'll sit here by the fire, and read. Do you know, it's devilish cold outside. Damned chilly for April!"

While Rebecca and Ellis talked, Alex Lowell took books from the shelves, flicked through them, then tossed them aside. Every so often, he yawned. It was clear to Rebecca that he wanted her gone. So very soon, her business concluded, she stood up to take her leave.

She gathered up the drawings and walked towards the door. As she reached for the latch, Alex Lowell coughed. "Miss Searle?"

"Yes, Mr Lowell?"

"A family by the name of Searle once lived very near this place. Would you happen to have relations in the area, by any chance?"

Rebecca shook her head. "I've no connections in this district," she replied. "My parents were born in Birmingham. My mother lived and died there, and I myself have never lived anywhere else."

"Indeed?"

"Certainly." Rebecca smiled. "Mine is not an unusual name," she said. "There are at least a dozen Searles in the town gazetteer. As far as I know, none of them are related to me."

"I see." Alex looked at Rebecca again. He wondered if there were a likeness. She was the right age, after all. She was the right sex. Her light build, fair features and blue eyes were characteristic of the Lowells. But then, he reflected, such colouring and stature was common enough everywhere. There were girls like this throughout the whole of the British Isles.

Initially puzzled by Alex's apparently pointless questions, now Ellis realised why his visitor was being interrogated. Lyddy Searle. That was her name. He remembered now.

He looked at Alex Lowell's face. There, he saw relief. The ironmaster's grand-daughter was not, after all, the abandoned by-blow for whom he'd promised his father he would provide.

Alex settled into his comfortable armchair. Ignoring Ellis and Rebecca completely now, he picked up his book and began to read.

Instead of ringing for the butler to see her out, the master of the house took his visitor to the front door himself.

"The gentleman whom you met in my study is anxious to trace a connection of his," he explained, as he led her across the hall. "A young woman who happens to share your surname. I have an interest in the matter too. You see, Mr Lowell is my brother-in-law. As well as my particular friend."

"I see." Rebecca nodded. None of this was of interest to her. "I shall write to you within the next couple of days," she said. "I shall let you have an approximate price. Then, if you wish to take the matter further, I shall send a man over to take the exact measurements."

"Excellent." Ellis met Rebecca's eyes. He held out his hand. "I'll look forward to hearing from you."

Ten minutes later, Rebecca was in her carriage, bouncing along the ill-made country roads on her way back to the dirty town.

She was pleased with her day's work. Although she had not received a firm commission, she felt it was more than likely Searle's would be asked to make Mr Darrow's gates. Then all Mr Darrow's friends would see them. They too would admire . . .

Rebecca stretched. Contentedly, she yawned. After years of being Jeremy Searle's mere grand-daughter, the irrelevant female relation of a difficult old man, it had been delightful to be treated as a businesswoman. To have been taken seriously, to have had her opinions asked for and, finally, accepted.

Of course, the men in the factory obeyed her. They had no choice. But Mr Darrow was under no obligation at all to listen to her.

Yet he had done so. He had listened to what Rebecca Searle had to say, and spoken to her as his equal.

Rebecca's intensely Puritanical upbringing had not given her any great idea of her own consequence, however, and it had certainly not prepared her to meet such fine gentlemen as Alex Lowell on equal terms. His languid tones and faintly insolent demeanour had embarrassed her. The way he looked at her had made her flinch. She did not feel at all easy in the company of persons of quality. She now decided that she much preferred the style of the plain-speaking merchants in the manufacturing town where she had always lived.

So she returned to Birmingham as disquieted by the stares of Mr Lowell as she had been charmed by the courtesy of Mr Darrow.

* * *

"You shouldn't have waited up," she said, looking with concern at her aunt's tired face.

"I wanted to see you safe home, that's all." Wearily, Lyddy smiled. "Well, how did you get on?"

"Splendidly!" Rebecca replaced her empty chocolate cup on the tray. "He was such a charming man. So easy, so pleasant. Not a trace of stiffness or reserve!"

"He was familiar, you mean? He spoke to you as if you were a woman of the streets?"

"Oh, no!" Vehemently, Rebecca shook her head. "I don't mean that at all. He listened to my advice. He didn't insist on having everything his own way, as gentry often do. I have the commission. I'm almost sure of that. He was very pleased with the final designs."

"Good." Lyddy rose to her feet. "I'll fetch your candle."

"Thank you." Rebecca yawned. "I met a friend of his, too. A Mr Lowell. He looked pretty rich to me. So, if I please Mr Darrow, perhaps Mr Lowell will take an interest in our work."

"You think so?"

"Yes." Rebecca took the candlestick. "But he was not as pleasant as Mr Darrow. Nothing like it. He looked as if he might have whims. Order a thing, then not like it when it's made."

As one whose entire life had been blighted by the whims of men, whose very soul had been warped and twisted – first by Henry Lowell, then by her own unforgiving father – Lyddy drew breath sharply when Rebecca mentioned Alex Lowell. But of course she could say nothing about him. Could admit to no previous knowledge of this man.

It was hardly likely, she told herself, that Alex Lowell would take any interest in a manufacturer's grand-daughter. Either professionally, socially or otherwise.

Chapter 7

Peter Darrow had died in the cold winter of 1777, expiring at last of what his physician said were natural causes. As he'd followed his father's coffin to the church, watched while the vault was opened and the most lately dead of a long line of Darrows interred amid the dust and bones of his ancestors, Ellis was inclined to wonder how his father had lasted so long.

Always a heavy drinker, Peter Darrow had punished his constitution for fifty years or more, but thought nothing of it. After all, his friends had been tipplers too. Then, one evening, he had gone rather too far. At the conclusion of a particularly successful day's hunting, he had stopped to eat his supper at an inn. There, he drank his usual three bottles of port, chased these down with a pint of spirits, then fell dying into the arms of his companion, a fellow Nimrod who later came to comfort the family. Who called the gods to witness that Peter Darrow was a moderate man.

"He was a sot." Disinclined to weep for a father who had certainly done her no favours, who had sired her then ignored her existence, Lalage pursed her lips. "We're well rid of him," she muttered. "Ellis is worth twenty such wastrels. Come, Mama. Dry your eyes. You can't deny it's so."

"All the same, Lally – "

"You hated him! You know you did." Lalage took her mother's hand. "Don't cry," she whispered. "Look forward now. Not backwards, into the past."

But still Mrs Darrow wept. Within a fortnight of her

husband's death, she had retreated into a self-imposed purdah, and seldom left her room. She was to survive the man she had always insisted she loathed, but evidently could not live without, for a mere eighteen months.

The new squire had no time to grieve. Indeed, he was happier than he'd ever been, for he could now do just as he pleased. No entail frustrated his schemes, no disappointed relations disputed his inheritance. Lack of cash was indeed a problem, but he solved this by selling off some of his best agricultural land, and re-mortgaging large parcels of the rest.

He thus incurred the reproaches of his mother, who wept that he had diminished an estate held intact since Domesday. But he brushed these complaints aside. "He *couldn't* sell," said Ellis tartly, as Mrs Darrow sobbed that not even her drunkard of a husband had sold land. "I did what was necessary, that's all. From now on, this estate will pay its way."

Two years later, Ellis began to see financial daylight. At long last his childish dream of restoring his family's home to its former glory was about to come true. He would live to see Easton Hall free from rot and decay. Once again it would be beautiful, as it had been two hundred years ago.

The restoration of Easton Hall was Ellis's folly. It would be his downfall, negating at a stroke all his hard work on the rest of the estate. So said his neighbours, his relations and most of his friends.

But Ellis ignored them. He called in the very best architects, he consulted the finest craftsmen, he summoned specialists from as far away as London to assess, estimate and advise.

All these experts said the same thing. The old Hall would cost twice as much to repair as to tear down and replace.

"Build a new house," said the most famous architect in England, who had been called in at enormous expense and now gave his august verdict. "One of brick and stone, not timber, lath and plaster. Sir, I could build you such a house – "

"I don't want a new house," said Ellis firmly. "I want this one. Will you restore it for me?"

Alex Lowell had long thought his friend a little eccentric. Now he realised Ellis was completely mad. Shaking his powdered head over the latest stack of bills, he laughed in disbelief. "Good God," he muttered. "You're insane."

Lalage agreed. She hated the Hall. Its poky little rooms, full of nooks and angles and awkward corners, were ugly, smelly and dark. They could never be otherwise, for their tiny leaded windows admitted the minimal amount of light and fresh air. The place was equally hideous outside. Those outlandish half-timberings were so out of fashion! As for the roof – it was so full of wells and gullies that it was bound to leak. Rain and melt-water simply collected in pools, to stagnate and seep into the fabric, eroding and rotting it away.

That roof, indeed, was a landscape complete in itself. As children, Lalage and Ellis had often clambered out of their bedroom windows, to play among its many hospitable gullies. To lie on mossy tiles warmed by the summer sunshine, to read or, more adventurously, to play hide and seek between the numerous tall chimney stacks.

As a child, Lalage had loved her home. As an adult, she loathed the place. The house had no elegance. No style. Just like its owner, in fact.

Seeing her brother had money to throw away and determined to drag him into the eighteenth century somehow, Lalage now suggested the landscaping and enclosing of the small park which surrounded the house. She'd watched with bored indifference as Ellis refurbished the Hall. But she became enthusiasm personified when he allowed her to lay out some plans for the park.

For a fortnight, she and Alex walked about the grounds. Tape and stick in hand, she measured, calculated, considered her options. She consulted the best pattern books of the day, and in due course she presented Ellis with a detailed design.

"I didn't know you could draw." Looking at his sister's plans, Ellis smiled his approval. He was impressed. "What's it all going to cost?" he asked.

"Nothing, really. Well – say three thousand pounds." Lalage took him outside. They stood on the gravel sweep. "From here," she told him, "you must have a prospect. Rolling lawns, leading the eye to the beauties beyond."

"Which are?"

"Verdant groves, of ash and beech. A temple to Flora. Clumps of silver birch."

"Which don't exist."

"Which you will plant and build." Lalage touched his sleeve. "Over to the east, where it's hilly anyway, we'll have some rocks and conifers. To make it truly picturesque. Nearer the house, we'll plant ornamental trees. You'll need some statuary, too. Just a little, to set everything off. Along the drive, we must have an avenue. Of limes. Or maybe sycamores. We'll – "

"I don't care for sycamores."

"Oh, Ellis!" Interrupted in full flood, Lalage stamped on his foot. "Oaks, then. Elms. Chestnuts. Whatever you want! Come up to the roof now."

From the roof, they could see for miles. "Over there," continued Lalage, "in the valley, we might have a small lake. We could dam the stream, and maybe build a waterfall. If we cut down those nasty little coppices, we could – "

"Wait, Lally. Please wait!" Ellis laughed. "I'm not prepared to flood, or to fell. We can't dam the stream, it supplies the village. We must definitely keep the timber. Those nasty little coppices, as you call them, must stay."

Lalage frowned. "You must clear some of the woodland on the west side," she said. "It obscures the house. Not that the place is worth looking at – but we won't go into that. You must have some deer."

"Is that the fashion?"

"Yes, it is. So have the walls repaired, and order some new park gates."

"To keep the deer in?"

"To keep the poachers out!"

"Very well." Ellis smiled. "We'll do as you suggest. We'll have a small artificial lake, fed from springs rather than the stream. We'll have an avenue and a prospect. We'll have deer, and some splendid new gates."

"Excellent." Lalage smiled too. Next month, she would get to work on her brother's personal appearance. That would be a challenge, even for her.

Ellis's indifference to the way he looked was a constant source of irritation to Lalage. But she could always comfort herself by gazing at her husband. Today, he looked perfectly beautiful, for he was wearing his favourite yellows and blues. His hair was newly curled, and his hands – whitened daily with paste of almonds – were smooth and clean. Alex Lowell was indeed a gentleman. Her husband always looked like a civilised man.

At dinner, Lalage ate little. For dessert, she merely toyed with a piece of dried fruit. Husband! Yes, that was the next thing. It was high time Ellis got married. But, on the other hand . . .

Conflicting emotions warring inside her, Lalage frowned. Of course Ellis must marry, but who would be a suitable bride? Someone young, strong and stupid, she supposed. Someone docile and obedient, who would warm her brother's bed and bear his children, but otherwise keep out of the way.

But then Lalage had an idea. She smiled to herself. That might be it. The perfect solution. But would Alex and Ellis co-operate? Perhaps. She must think it all through. Then decide what steps to take.

As it happened, Ellis was thinking about marriage too. He was nearly thirty. At long last he had a home of his own, a beautiful house fit to offer any wife, and he also enjoyed an income sufficent to maintain one. He had to have children. Legitimate male heirs were an absolute necessity. Who else should inherit the estate?

There were a dozen young women in the near neighbourhood alone who would have been delighted to become Mrs Squire Darrow. But, turning them over in his mind, Ellis could not imagine himself married to any single one. Thinking of Magdalen Lewin, of Sophie Carlisle, of Harriet Jarrold, he winced. Could he bear the constant company of a woman of quality? Of a creature who thought of nothing but her ailments and her gowns? Who'd been been educated to consider nothing else?

When he felt the need, Ellis visited a friend. A lady's dressmaker living in Warwick, she'd been widowed early in life and had a small daughter to support. He found her physically desirable, admired her independence – but found her conversation tedious in the extreme. For her part, she accepted his money and no doubt laughed at him behind his back.

Alex and Lalage were his real friends. With them, Ellis was perfectly relaxed. Perfectly at ease. Where could he possibly find a woman who would make him as happy as they did?

"Ellis, my dear," began Lalage one evening, after all three of them had enjoyed a good dinner and drunk rather too much red wine, "poor darling Ellis, you look so miserable. So very sad."

"Do I?" Ellis yawned. "I'm not sad. I'm thinking."

"Are you?" Lalage looked soulful. "What about?"

"Don't ask." Alex grinned. "All *he* ever thinks about is the estate. Or this old barn. His mind runs on woodworm, winter wheat or dry rot. Ellis Darrow never wastes his time on daydreams. Or hankers after a whore."

"Don't be so coarse," said Lalage. But then she sniggered, and covered her face.

Lolling next to Alex on the wide drawing room sofa, Ellis grinned too. Now he looked at his little sister, who was sitting on his lap, her skirts spread out across her husband's knees. "That's a pretty gown," he observed. "A pity your dressmaker made it rather too small."

"What do you mean?"

"The neckline is too low. The bodice is far too tight. In fact, it's obscene."

"It's the fashion." Lalage pouted. "Not that you'd know anything about that."

"I suppose not." Ellis rubbed his eyes. "I'm tired. I think I'll go to bed."

"Don't go yet." Lalage pushed his hands away from his face. She hugged him round the neck. "Don't go up there in the dark, to be all by yourself."

"What makes you think I'll be alone?" Ellis stroked his sister's hair which, unpowdered today, lay in thick, black coils on her shoulders. "I might ask Simmons to find me a companion. To send up a kitchen maid to warm my bed."

"You wouldn't do that." Lalage grimaced. "The tenants wonder at you. They say that in addition to looking like a parson, you actually behave like one."

"At least they don't fear for their daughters. They know there'll be no bastards of mine starving in the workhouse, or littering the estate."

"Yet you should have a son." Lalage held him close. Now, she remembered how it had been when they were children. How she'd loved Ellis more than anyone in the world. How he had loved her.

Now, she'd make him love her again. Love her more. She glanced at her husband, and saw he was asleep. "I'm going to take Alex to bed now," she murmured. "Why don't you come with us?"

"Come with you?" Ellis stared. "Lally, what exactly do you mean?"

"What I said." Tipsily, Lalage grinned. "When we were children, I often slept with you. When Alex came to stay, the three of us lay down together."

"We're not children now," Ellis said.

"No, we're not." Creamily, Lalage smiled. "So much the better."

"What?"

"Oh, Ellis!" Lalage kissed his ear. "They do it in France," she whispered. "Brothers and sisters together. Very wicked, I know – but it must be such fun!"

"Alex?" Ellis nudged his friend in the ribs. "Can't you control this creature?"

"Eh?" Alex woke with a start. "What's she doing?"

"She's just invited me to sleep with her."

"Really?" Alex grinned. "Can I come, too?"

"There." Lalage beamed. "It's all settled. Shall we go?"

"Good God." Ellis pushed Lalage away. "Alex, take her. You can entertain one another."

"Just a minute." Devilment flashing from his pale blue eyes, Alex grabbed Lalage's wrists. "If she's been naughty, we should teach her a lesson."

"Shall we?" Ellis's eyes sparkled. "Very well," he agreed. "Get her slippers off first. Pinch her toes."

"No!" Squirming out of her husband's grasp, Lalage held down her skirts. "Ellis, don't you dare. Alex, stop him! Oh, it's not fair, two against one!"

"You started it." Ellis caught her round the waist, and held her. "Now we'll show you the error of your ways."

But Lalage was no passive victim. She fought, she clawed, she scratched. Kicking and biting, she punched her husband and her nails tore long, red pathways down the backs of Ellis's hands.

Soon, the three of them were rolling on the floor, a tangled, writhing mass on the Turkey carpet. Ellis's shirt was ripped from neckband to waist. Alex's beautiful waistcoat was smeared with soot from the fireplace, into which his wife had kicked him. It would probably never come clean.

Alex and Ellis were finally disabled by laughter. But now, half in and half out of her gown, her hair a mess of elf-locks and her slippers, which she had used as weapons, on opposite sides of the room, Lalage was half mad with fury. Sitting astride Ellis, she thumped him hard. She slapped his face and boxed his ears. Too convulsed to defend himself, he writhed and groaned but could not push her away.

Lalage glared down at him. "Well?" she demanded. "Do you give in? Will you do as I said?"

"Oh, take her away!" Choking and gasping, Ellis finally managed to shove his sister aside. "Alex, for God's sake! Take the little baggage upstairs. She's desperate!"

Now pretty desperate himself, Alex did so. Jerking his wife to her feet, he dragged her out of the room. He did not notice the glitter in her dark eyes as she was hauled, ignominiously defeated, up to her marital bed. As she scratched down another black mark against him.

Somewhat breathless but otherwise unmoved, Ellis got up. He brushed himself down and flopped into a chair. Overhead, he could hear his sister's shrill squawks. These were answered by Alex's soothing murmurs. Ellis shook his head. What Lalage needed was a good hiding. Alex ought to give her one, some day.

Ellis found himself thinking about women. But it was a soft, sweet, blue-eyed beauty which he saw in his mind's eye now. He thought of light eyes. Pink-and-white skin. Flaxen hair. A nicely-rounded figure, curvaceous but not at all fat.

Rebecca Searle. His hand had somehow found a pencil. He had scribbled the name on the newspaper by his side.

Five minutes later, he went to bed. He was not lonely for a woman, not at all. But he had a sense, never experienced before, of being incomplete.

Alex made his investments in the East India Company. Soon, he was able to boast that he'd already received several handsome dividends, and expected to receive many more.

"Good for you." Ellis shrugged, then smiled. "Look, Alex, I have work to do. So if you – "

"You don't wish to reconsider your refusal to invest?

After all, the estate is yours now. You have plenty of collateral security. So don't you think you might strike out?"

"No, I don't." Ellis shook his head. "I have all this year's income accounted for. I haven't a penny to spare. But even if I had – "

"You wouldn't invest in the stock market. Ellis, you're a timid fellow."

"Am I?" Ellis pulled a loose thread from his cuff, grimacing as a hole appeared in the cheap worsted cloth. "Yes, I suppose I am."

"To whom do you write?" Bored as usual, Lalage was leaning over her brother's shoulder, reading as he scribbled.

"I write to Miss Searle. As you can see." Looking up at her, Ellis pinched his sister's cheek. "Lally, what an inquisitive little creature you are."

"I take an interest in you, that's all." Crossly, Lalage chewed her lower lip. "So what are you ordering this time?" she demanded. "Gridirons? Ornamental balustrades? A new kitchen range?"

"Do we need one?" Suddenly interested in what Lalage had to say, Ellis looked up again. "Well? Do we?"

"*I* don't know!" Lalage glared at him. "As if I ever go anywhere near the kitchens! Why don't you ask the cook?"

"I shall." To Lalage's amazement, Ellis got up, strode out of the room, and soon she heard the heels of his shoes ringing on the stone slabs of the passage which led to the servants' wing.

Yawning, she turned back towards her husband. "Alex," she said, "do you know what?"

Alex laid his book aside. "What?"

"I should so like a pet." Going over to Alex's chair, Lalage dropped to her knees beside him. Sweetly, she smiled. "I long and long for a pet!"

"Do you?" Indulgently, Alex stroked her hair. "What

sort of pet?" he asked. "A monkey? A kitten? A parakeet?"

"A monkey." Lalage grinned. "A dear little coal-black, curly-headed monkey! Oh darling, Lady Dashforth has a beauty. He's so pretty. So sweet. He brings her chocolate, he waits at table, he warms her bed – "

"Oh. That sort of monkey." Remembering Lady Dashforth had recently acquired her own negro servant, a child of ten or eleven who had evidently been purchased from a Bristol merchant, Alex grimaced. "They're very expensive, you know," he said. "Also, they grow up. A pretty boy of ten soon becomes a great, lubberly black devil. Capable of all kinds of mischief and deceit."

"Darling, I'd sell him long before he became a nuisance." Lalage giggled. "They say Lady Dashforth's boy is rather more than a bedwarmer. Her maid told my Betty – "

"I don't wish to know anything about that." Alex shuddered. "Lally, are you set on this?"

"Yes. As it happens, I am." Now, Lalage pouted. "So I suppose you'll forbid it. Just to upset me, of course. As you did when you refused to go into the House of Commons."

"Lally, my darling, I merely asked – "

"Oh Alex, say you'll buy me a monkey!" Still on her knees, her hands clasped before her, Lalage opened her beautiful eyes wide. "I should so love my own little slave."

"Would you?"

"More than anything else in the world." Taking Alex's hand, Lalage kissed it. "Look," she wheedled, "a child of seven, ready trained and broken, taught to fear the lash, may be had for a mere fifty guineas. Darling, I have the name of the trader – "

"Mr Harbord, isn't it?"

"Yes, that's right." Lalage stroked Alex's fingers. "I am positively assured that, should the child supplied not suit, he may easily be exchanged. If he is recalcitrant, he may be returned to the merchant, who will soon whip him into a better frame of mind. Alex, this gentleman would be so pleased – no, he would be honoured to serve you."

"Oh, very well. Very well." Alex ruffled Lalage's hair. "But darling, please be circumspect. Choose a prettier one than Lady Dashforth's, do."

"Prettier?"

"Copper, rather than jet."

"Oh. I see. Very well." Kneeling up, Lalage kissed Alex on the mouth. "I'll buy the prettiest little boy you ever saw. Then, when he's twelve or so, I'll sell him again. This particular merchant is always ready to buy back. He sends the creatures on to the West Indies, you see."

Over the next few months, Easton Hall provided Searle's manufactory with enough orders to keep at least a third of the workforce permanently occupied. Searle's men re-leaded scores of windows, replaced hundreds of yards of guttering and drainpipes, and made dozens of ornamental planters, together with the cast-iron basin of a garden fountain to stand in front of the house.

Indeed, Ellis seized on any excuse to see Miss Searle. She was often to be found in Ellis's study, discussing projects or estimates. Then she would walk out with him, to examine work done, or in progress.

He could not help but notice she had the most enchanting smile. Her small mouth curved in the most engaging fashion, and her little teeth were so white and well-polished they shone. Her perfect, always spotless neatness delighted him. He was amazed that someone so clean, and who smelled so sweet, could bear to live – could flourish even – in the polluted air of that dirty, smut-laden town. It was as if the filth of Birmingham did not dare settle upon her.

In addition to finding Rebecca personally attractive, Ellis admired her. She was so brisk, so efficient, so competent. A perfect businesswoman, her craftsmen came when she said they would, did what she'd said they would do, and finished their tasks well inside the time allotted.

Although he would never have admitted it to anyone, even to himself, Ellis found he lived for her visits. One bright, sunny morning found him waiting on the front steps, irritably checking his pocket watch, anxious for her to arrive. Which of course she did, right on time, bringing with her the three workmen who would fit the new ornamental leaden gargoyles. These, copied from their Tudor originals, had been meticulously cast in Searle's workshops. Then the men would lay the pipes for the elegant marble fountain which Lalage had had sent from Italy, and which was now going to enhance the knot-garden.

"A lovely day for a ride," said Ellis. He handed his visitor from her hired coach.

"Yes, indeed." Rebecca smiled. "The first wild roses are in bloom. In fact, the hedgerows are full of flowers. After the dirt of the town, it's so pleasant to come out here."

Rebecca's workmen exchanged knowing looks. Then, collecting their tools, they sloped off to begin their tasks. They would pass the kitchens on the way. By now, they had reached an excellent understanding with Ellis's cook.

"Will you come inside? To have some refreshment?" By some oversight, Ellis had retained Rebecca's hand in his, and now he led her into the house. "The day is so warm. You must be longing for a dish of tea."

"Tea?" Freeing her hand, Rebecca looked her client straight in the eyes. "Yes. I should like a dish of tea more than anything in the world."

"Then, Miss Searle, you shall have one."

Taking Rebecca into the drawing room, Ellis sent for tea. Then he spent an hour or more asking about lead casting, in which he had suddenly become very interested. This interest had nothing to do with the fact that the ironmaster's grand-daughter had wide blue eyes, that her hair, under its light dusting of white powder, was of a flaxen gold, that her skin was like cream. That her figure was perfection itself.

Chapter 8

Spring had long turned into summer. The weather was perfect for riding about the estate, for visiting outlying farms and villages, for spying out the land and maybe planning some future enclosure. But Ellis Darrow could settle to nothing. He rose each morning determined to get on with his work, but then found he was dawdling over his chocolate or daydreaming over the previous week's newspaper. Behaving, in fact, more like Alex Lowell than his usual industrious self.

When he set out for Birmingham that hot August morning, he told himself it was quite reasonable to check up on the progress of some work Searle's was currently doing on his behalf. Of course, for a journey into town he was certainly obliged to wear his smart navy-blue coat. It was only natural he should have shaved carefully, tidied his hair and pared his fingernails neatly before finally setting out.

He had other business in town. He needed to see his lawyer and talk to his banker. Since he'd be in the vicinity anyway, it was only polite to call on Miss Searle.

"Searle's manufactory? Yes sir, I know it. Carry on down the High Street, cross the packhorse bridge. Go past the warehouses, through Spencer's Court, and you'll find it." The man of whom Ellis had asked directions grinned. "You'll hear it long before you see it!"

So, leaving behind the prosperous commercial heart of this great industrial town, Ellis set out to find Searle's factory. It was in a suburb he'd never set foot in before.

He had never imagined squalor like it. He'd never even heard of places where grass simply could not grow, where the most obstinate and persistent of weeds were unable to push their way through the blackened earth. Even central London wasn't as barren as this Gehenna of brick and iron. This wilderness of dirt and grime.

All around him was the din and racket of industry, the noise of a hundred small forges and factories turning out thousands upon thousands of nails, hinges, buttons, pots, snuffboxes, tools, locks, bridles, candlesticks, gridirons, grates, firebacks, brooches, pins, buckles, cut and faceted steel jewellery – almost anything, in fact, which could be made of metal, and for which there was a market either in England or abroad.

The air was foul with smuts and thick with smoke. The clear blue sky, which must have been above, was totally blotted out by poisonous man-made clouds. The sweet summer air was displaced by noxious vapours emitted from the factory furnaces, scattered all around. Ellis felt dirt settling on his face. He saw flakes of greasy soot falling all about him. He grimaced in disgust.

But then he shook his head. He even smiled. For he understood that amidst this most unnatural of scenes, there was something wonderfully dynamic, something quite gloriously alive. Although Vulcan had displaced Ceres, creating a little hell in a place where flowers had once bloomed and birds must have sung, this man-made Pandemonium was marvellously vital. It had something about it which, far from depressing Ellis's spirits, made his pulse race.

He reached Searle's. Walking past two great heaps of coal, he stood in the centre of a cobbled yard.

"Can I direct you, sir?" asked a man, who had come out of a workshop by the gate.

"What?" Rubbing his sore eyes, Ellis blinked. "What did you say?"

"Did you want summat?" The man was civil, but brisk. "Come to collect, have you? To deliver, maybe?"

“Ah. No. I wish to see the master here.” Ellis spoke without thinking. Of course, there was no master at Searle’s.

“You want to see Miss Searle, you mean? She’s in charge.” The workman grinned. “Come along with me. I’ll find her for you now.”

They walked towards a large, brick-built shed. Passing through a narrow doorway, Ellis was led into a scene from hell, complete with acoustics to match. For, if the noise outside the factory had been loud, inside it was deafening. Literally so, in fact. A few minutes after entering this demons’ hall, Ellis found he could hear nothing but a confused murmuring and growling, as if he were under water.

He looked about him. In a stifling hot, white-washed chamber, a dozen or more manufacturing operations were simultaneously taking place. By the glowing red of the furnace, men in leather aprons sweated and grunted over their work. As they fashioned the hot metal, white sparks showered into the air, making arcs of vivid light against the dingy walls. The scorching smell of red-hot metal hurt Ellis’s nostrils. The soot-laden air made his eyes run with tears. How anyone could exist, let alone stay sane in such a place, was beyond his understanding. How Rebecca Searle could be the presiding genius was the most profound mystery of all.

“Miss Searle?” Ellis’s personal guide to the modern Underworld tapped someone on the shoulder. “Miss Searle!” he bawled, into the general din, “there’s a gentleman here. Wants to see you!”

For a moment or two, Ellis failed to recognise her. Clad in a coarse black cotton gown, she had a large white handkerchief tied around her neck, while a sacking apron enveloped her from ankle to chest. Her golden hair was invisible, for it was bundled inside a linen cloth. This, like the rest of her clothes, was liberally bespeckled with smuts.

Rebecca Searle was engrossed. With a stern proprietor’s

eye, she watched as a workman burnished a trinket box, bringing it to shining perfection. He handed it to her. She studied it closely. "That's very good," she said – or rather mouthed, for of course she could not be heard. She ran her fingers over mouldings. She checked the hinges and clasp. "It's excellent, in fact. Could we turn out sixty a day?"

She clearly expected an affirmative. Now the workman, who was evidently a fluent lip-reader, grinned. He nodded vigorously. Then, finally heeding the tap on her shoulder, Rebecca turned to see who had touched her. She saw Bill Walters, one of her foremen. Standing diffidently at his side was Ellis Darrow.

She was astonished. "Mr Darrow?" she articulated, her blue eyes round with surprise. "What ever do you want here?"

But, even as she spoke, she smiled. That smile, together with her own fair beauty, emphasised rather than diminished by the white turban round her blonde hair, made Ellis's heart turn over. She was pleased – was rather more than pleased – to see him.

He did not speak. He couldn't. But Rebecca wouldn't have heard him anyway. She put one small, square hand on his sleeve. "Come into the yard," she mouthed. She led Ellis out of hell into the comparatively clear air of the factory forecourt.

Once outside the factory, Rebecca took off the white turban. She shook her head, to clear the ringing in her ears.

Ellis looked at her. Today, her hair was neither dressed nor powdered. Neatly parted down the centre, it was braided close to her head and secured with pins. This gave her the air of a prim little Quaker. She looked about fourteen years old. Ellis cleared his throat. "I was in the vicinity," he began. "What I mean is, I had to come to town. So I've called to enquire after the progress of the gates."

To Ellis's surprise, Rebecca seemed to find this perfectly reasonable. Without further ado, she led him across the yard, through an archway and into a covered court. There, two men were working on the objects in question.

"There, Mr Darrow." Proudly, she smiled. "They will soon be completed. Another week or two will see the work all done."

"I see." Ellis coughed. "Miss Searle, I – "

"A project such as this, you see, is so complicated and involved that it must necessarily take time." Rebecca bent to touch the hard iron, stroking it with an almost maternal tenderness. "The scroll work at the sides is extremely delicate. It could not be rushed. These blackbirds, fashioned by Michael here, took six or seven days to make. Each, that is."

Complacently, Rebecca met Ellis's gaze. "Will you look at them, Mr Darrow? Then tell me if you think it was time well spent?"

Ellis looked. He saw six blackbirds, wings outstretched, fluttering amidst metal foliage which twined through the bars at the tops of the gates. "They're perfect," he said, impressed. "They look quite real."

"Thank you, sir." Gratified, Michael Cuthbertson nodded.

Rebecca stood up. "Do you see this pattern of oak-leaves, with branches interlaced?" She smiled again. "The branches support some weight here, and here. So in addition to looking delicate, they must be strong."

"Yes. I see." Forcing himself to be interested, Ellis touched the metal. "How was this work done?"

"Mostly in the forge, while the metal was red-hot. Later, some cold shaping was required." Rebecca folded her arms. "All that remains now is the finishing. Then you may have your gates. They will be the envy of the county." She looked directly at him, her smile now almost arch. "I hope you do not think we neglect our commission?"

Ellis blushed red. "I – I had no idea of catching you out," he muttered. "I was in town anyway. I had business with my lawyer. I have long been curious to see the manufactory, so I didn't think you would mind – what I mean is, I had no intention of checking up on you."

"Visitors are always welcome." Rebecca herself blushed now. "Provided they are not spies for our competitors, of course."

She pushed a stray lock of hair behind her ear. Then she examined her hands. Seeing how dirty they were, she pulled a face. "I must go and wash," she said. "While I do that, please feel free to walk about. Speak to the workmen, look at anything which takes your fancy. Then, before you leave, will you come to the house for some tea? My aunt Lyddy will be perfectly happy to entertain a third at her table."

"Your aunt who?" Ears still ringing, Ellis shook his head.

"Aunt Lyddy." Rebecca laughed. "It's a strange name, I know. I suppose her baptismal name is Lydia. But oddly enough, I've never thought to ask."

"Ah. I see."

"Is anything wrong?" Seeing Ellis look thoughtful, Rebecca frowned. "Mr Darrow, you've gone very pale."

Ellis looked at her. "There's nothing wrong," he said. "But the factory was so hot. The air so close – "

"Then, a dish of tea – "

"I can't come in." Ellis couldn't face Lyddy Searle. Not just yet. "I have more business in town, you see. I must be back at Easton Hall by six."

"Then, perhaps, another day. When you have more time."

"I should be delighted." Ellis forced a smile. "Miss Searle, I must take my leave."

As he made his way along dirty streets and through noisy, malodorous courts, Ellis realised she'd been disappointed. He told himself he was imagining things. But he knew he wasn't. As he'd said he must go, her face had clouded, the sun had gone in.

He arrived at the stables. Mounting his horse, he

grinned at the boy. He gave the stable lad the biggest tip he'd ever received.

As Rebecca turned to go back to the factory, her step was leaden. Her shoulders drooped and her heart was heavy. Her Puritan upbringing had taught her that only the lowest of women lusted after men. So she was dismayed to find that the merest sight, or even the idea of Ellis Darrow was enough to set her pulse racing, her temples throbbing and to set her face on fire. She daydreamed constantly. In her mind's eye, she saw herself mistress of Easton Hall. The mother of a whole brood of little Darrows, each child the image of Ellis himself.

"Why isn't he married?" she asked herself, as she stood watching a man stamp patterns on bright steel buttons, as the boy assisting him placed blank after blank in the press, as the press came down, thud, thud, thud, as regularly and quickly as the beating of her own heart.

Perhaps, she conjectured, his wife had died. Perhaps he had been betrothed, but the lady had changed her mind. No. That, surely, was impossible.

Conclusive proof that Rebecca Searle was nothing but a fanciful, feeble-minded woman merely masquerading as an ironmaster was provided towards the end of that day. A second visitor arrived, demanding to see the proprietor of the manufactory without delay.

Rebecca went out to meet him. Cordially, she shook his hand. A mild-mannered, well-dressed, soft-spoken gentleman, the visitor carried with him a close-wrapped object which, seated in the comfort of Rebecca's little office, he handed over for her inspection.

"You know what it is?" he demanded affably, languidly tapping his front teeth.

"No." Examining the object, Rebecca frowned. "I've never seen anything quite like it before."

"You cannot guess its use?"

"Is it for an animal?" At a loss, Rebecca shrugged. "Maybe for a dancing bear?"

"Not exactly." Retrieving the heavy iron collar, the man grinned. "It's for a negro," he said.

"Indeed." Rebecca winced. She narrowed her eyes in disgust.

Her visitor appeared not to notice. "Miss Searle," he began, "I have lately seen many fine examples of this factory's work. Your craftsmen can execute the most intricate of designs. Now – I require at least a hundred of these decorative collars. Maybe more. Ladies and gentlemen who have purchased negro servants for use in this country like to adorn their slaves thus. For quality workmanship, they are prepared to pay high prices."

"Are they?"

"Certainly." The man grinned again. "It's the fashion, you see," he drawled. "So. Will you name a price?"

Rebecca considered. Never turn away trade. Never be short with any man who might put business one's way. Never let private sentiments override good commercial sense. Her grandfather's maxims came crowding into her head.

She looked at the thing on her visitor's lap. It was indeed a work of art. As a connoisseur, she could admire the workmanship and respect the skill of the man who'd wrought it. Decorated with a pattern of scrolls, arabesques and acanthus leaves, it was delicately fashioned and beautifully finished. It locked with a pretty gilt key, which at present hung from a pale blue ribbon attached to the man's fob.

It weighed about five pounds. Innocent of padding or anything else which could protect the skin, it must necessarily chafe. Rebecca imagined having this thing around her own small, white neck. She winced again.

A minute or so ticked by. The man's grin had not faltered. "Miss Searle," he began softly, "do you not approve of the trade in slaves?"

Rebecca met his eyes. "The fact that my fellow creatures can be bought and sold like cattle disgusts me," she replied.

"I see." The gentleman sighed. "Mr Hall in Dowley's Court has expressed great interest in this commission."

"Has he, indeed?"

"Oh, yes." The man toyed with the gilt key. "Miss Searle. I can see you are a lady of fine susceptibilities. You are concerned lest these collars be misused.

"But these objects are for show. For display. In short, they are badges of office. I doubt if any lady or gentleman in our most Christian kingdom would even dream of shackling a negro. By day or by night."

Rebecca stood up. "At present," she said coldly, "my order book is full. I suggest you go back to Mr Hall. Since I myself have no men available to work on this commission, I heartily recommend him."

"I quite understand." The gentleman's smile was positively wolfish now. "I apologise for taking up your time. For obtruding upon your sensibilities. I bid you good day."

After seeing her visitor off the premises, Rebecca went back to her office and sat down again. She felt quite faint. Sternly, she told herself that Richard Hall, a manufacturer of locks, bolts and fetters who already supplied a Liverpool merchant with a range of manacles, padlocks and chains, would be thankful for the work. She further reflected that she really was busy. That the factory was working to full capacity already, and it was simply impossible to take on any extra work just then.

But she knew this was so much nonsense. She could always find men to work for her, could always put up a temporary wooden shed, clear a space in one of the courts, or squeeze a few more benches into the finishing shop.

She stood up. Five minutes later, she was back in the main part of the factory. There, amid the racket and clatter, her mind began to wander again. She was so weak. So womanish! Trade was trade, business was business, and there was no room in business for squeamishness, for mawkish sentimentality, no room at all. Rebecca's common sense told her she was a fool. Only a simpleton turned custom away.

Now, she was thinking of Ellis again. Despairing, she let her inward eye gaze on his kind face. She was comforted.

"You saw him from the window, you say?"

"I did." Calmly, Lyddy ladled out soup. Breaking into a new loaf, she offered Rebecca bread. "Yes, I saw him."

"Do you not think him a fine looking man?"

"Oh, very fine." Lyddy grimaced. "Hardly a man of fashion, though. Not what I'd call a beau."

"No, indeed." Rebecca started on her soup. "He's certainly no dandy."

"He's providing us with a great deal of work at the moment," said Lyddy now. "I hope he's paying something on account?"

"He does better than that. As each individual order is completed, he pays." Rebecca smiled. "The clerks in the counting house have never seen anything like it. It's almost unheard of for a fine gentleman like that to keep his account so up to date."

"Oh." Lyddy frowned. "Well, he's taken one thing he hasn't paid for."

"Has he?" Rebecca stared. "What?"

"Your heart, child! Your own dear heart." Agitated beyond discretion, Lyddy threw down her spoon. "Oh, Becky!" she wailed.

"Aunt, really!" Blushing crimson, Rebecca blinked. "I only said he was a fine looking man."

"Becky, Becky!" Lyddy sighed. "Don't let him see you think so. That's all. Whatever you do, don't let him see he bewitches you. Never put yourself in his power!"

The following morning, Ellis rose early and, his day's paperwork completed in good time, rode over to see Alex and Lalage. Hauling a befuddled and still dressing-gowned Alex into his study, Ellis pushed him into a chair and shut the door behind him. "I've found her," he announced. "I've found her at last."

"You've what?" Blearily Alex looked at his watch. He yawned. "God, Ellis. Do you know what time it is?"

"Long past eight. Alex, did you hear what I said?"

"I heard." Still yawning, Alex closed his eyes. He lay back in his chair. "Ring for some tea, could you? Tell them to bring a bottle of brandy, too."

"You don't need brandy. Not first thing in the morning."

"I know what I need. At least, I know far better than you do." Alex opened his eyes a little. Setting his turban straight, he selected a pipe from the rack. He pulled a jar of tobacco across his desk. "Now," he continued. "You were saying something about finding women."

Readily, Ellis explained. "When I looked at her yesterday," he concluded, "I saw it. The resemblance is marked. She has the same eyes, the same hair, the same shape of face as your own. Lyddy Searle had a birthmark – a little sickle-shaped mole. It was just above her left eyebrow. Rebecca has it too."

"Fascinating." Alex yawned. "Where the hell's that brandy?"

"Damn the brandy!" Ellis shook his friend's shoulder. "You owe her something!" he cried.

"Do I?"

"Yes!" Ellis glared. "You told me all about it. When your father died, you set aside so many thousand pounds. In Consols. Or at any rate, that's what you said."

Alex frowned. "We don't even know if it's the right girl," he muttered. "How can we tell – "

"Of course it's the right girl." Ellis grew angry now. "Very well then, break your promise. Betray your trust. That's nothing to me. But don't give me so much cant about it not being the right girl. There's no doubt of it. No doubt at all."

Just then a manservant came in. He set down a loaded tray. Dismissing him, Alex poured himself a cup of tea, to which he added a large measure of brandy. In a couple of greedy gulps, he drank it down.

"Look here, Ellis," he began. "If you seriously imagine I will impoverish myself – and beggar your sister, remember Lally will suffer too – in order to force money on a girl who is wealthy enough already and who may not even be the proper person to receive it, you must be mad. Think of Lally! Be concerned for her, even if you care nothing for me."

"What nonsense you talk." Ellis laughed. "You're worth millions. You can't pretend it will hurt you to part with a couple of thousand pounds."

"Worth millions, eh?" Alex looked up at his friend. "Oh yes. How pleasant it was to be rich. But alas, I'm not rich any more. In fact, I'm a veritable pauper now."

"Alex, what are you saying?"

"I wasn't going to tell you. Not just yet." Alex looked down at his fingernails. "But you'd have found out soon enough. You read the newspapers, after all."

He glanced up. "Ellis, if you say, 'I told you so,' I shall hit you."

"Good God!" Ellis stared. "Is it bad?"

"Bad enough."

"You can bear a loss of twenty thousand, surely?" Ellis looked stunned "To someone like you, it's a trifle."

"Ah, but it was rather more than twenty thousand." Alex sniffed. Pouring more brandy, he drank it down. "I shan't tell you exactly how much. Well, I'm hopeful some of it will be salvaged. But I'm afraid my sister – if she is my sister – will have to wait. The cash I set aside for her is all I have left."

"Oh." Shocked, Ellis poured a large brandy for himself. "Does Lally know?" he asked.

"Yes." Alex sighed. "So far, she's been very good. She has every right to blame me. But it seems she doesn't. Yet."

"Ah." Ellis rolled his brandy round his glass. "Well, what are your plans for the future?"

"I think it's my turn to ask some questions now." Tipsily, Alex grinned. "Well, Ellis? Explain yourself. Why are you so interested in Rebecca Searle?"

"I – "

"Why's it important to you that my father's bastard gets her inheritance?" Pale blue eyes fixed on his friend's face, Alex grinned even more. "Do you know what?" he demanded.

"What?"

"I think you're in love. You're besotted. Bewitched. Ellis Darrow, the direct descendant of Rafe D'Arreau, whose Norman blood is some of the purest in the kingdom, is in love. With a lady of equal rank? No. With my father's bastard. God, that's so funny!" Alex laughed out loud. "Just wait until I tell Lally!" he cried.

Eliis did not even smile. "There's nothing to tell her," he said, stiffly. "But if it makes you happy to speculate, do please continue."

"Speculate?" Alex winced. "Oh Ellis, that's cruel."

"I'm sorry." Still Ellis looked grim. "But I won't be teased. Even by you."

"You're not about to do anything foolish. Are you?" Alarmed, Alex grabbed Ellis's sleeve. "You've taken a fancy to her, yes. But you're not considering marriage? Not with that baggage?"

"You're going to be needing friends." Ellis pulled away. "You'll want all the support you can get. So don't upset me!"

"Ellis, I only meant – "

"I don't care what you meant." Ellis scowled. "I'll come back later today," he said. "We'll discuss your finances then." Still very angry, he stalked out of the study. He slammed the door behind him.

Chapter 9

Alex sat alone in his study, staring at the latest letter, the written confirmation that he was indeed ruined. Things were as bad as could be. Dropping the flimsy piece of paper on his desk, he passed his hand across his eyes. He sighed.

Corruption in the East India Company was legendary. Any fool, any idiot knew that. But, with the assurance of one who has never been knowingly cheated, and the confidence of someone who has never known want, Alex Lowell had assumed *his* investments would be safe.

He had known George Hickson from a schoolboy. After Ellis, George had been his best friend. It was with George that Alex had sneaked out of school, made his way to the city taverns and got drunk. It was with George he had heaved his heart out into a gutter on rainy London nights. Scared half to death that the Watch would come upon two fourteen year old schoolboys throwing up in the drizzle, and cart them off to some insalubrious lock-up, Alex and George had encouraged one another. Told each other to bear up and be a man.

It was with George and their respective valets that he had gone off on the Grand Tour. With George Alex had spent month after fascinating month in France or Italy, drinking more wisely now, and improving his knowledge of the languages of love.

So where was George Hickson now? If there was any justice, in the pit of hell itself. Damning George for all eternity, Alex opened his desk drawer and found a key. Taking the big black cashbox from its shelf, he unlocked it.

He looked at the certificates and papers inside. He was worth about four thousand pounds. Could one live in any style at all on the interest from four thousand pounds? Alex doubted it. The money itself was bespoke. Dared he hope Ellis would not tell that wretched woman all about it?

Cursing himself for ever having told Ellis anything, Alex closed the cashbox. He stood up. "There's no need to worry," he muttered. "No court in England could enforce payment of that particular bequest."

With terrifying speed, Alex's many creditors closed in upon him. In the space of a few weeks, huge tracts of the Lowells' land were seized and auctioned off. The house which Henry Lowell had built, on which he had lavished more love and affection than he'd ever shown his own flesh and blood, was sold to a speculator. He immediately let it to a young man of substantial fortune, but no social worth, since his income derived from the mills of Lancashire.

"I suppose it will do." Looking round the small sitting room of the house, or rather cottage, which Alex had decided to rent for the time being, Lalage sniffed. "It could be made tolerable. But Alex, why – "

"You know why!" Alex threw himself down on the sofa. "I won't live at Easton Hall. That's final. If you think I'm prepared to let the neighbourhood say my brother-in-law has to keep me, you can just think again."

"I see. You must have a home of your own. A little space, of which you can be master." Scornfully, Lalage glared all around the little space in question. "Well Alex, you have it here. I wish you joy of it. A more wretched, miserable little rat-hole I never yet saw."

Sitting down beside him, Lalage looked into her husband's eyes. "What are we going to do about Ellis?" she asked. "He's positively maudlin these days. What's that woman done to him?"

"I don't know." Wearily, Alex rubbed his eyes. "I don't understand it at all."

"It's got to stop." Lalage scowled. "It's ridiculous, running after a woman like that. He forgets who he is."

Lalage Lowell, née Darrow, was in no danger at all of forgetting who *she* was. Ever mindful of her aristocratic Norman origins, she knew her place. It was at the top of the tree.

But Ellis was different. He was enthusiastic, in the very worst sense of the word. The result of this was an unfortunate tendency to latch on to unsuitable people or things. To squander his time, money and emotions on creatures or objects of very little worth.

"First, it was Alex." Lalage grimaced. Once, for Ellis, the sun itself had shone out of Alex Lowell's pale blue eyes. "Then he fell in love with his wretched house. What's the current fancy? That woman."

Lalage ground her teeth. A manufacturer's granddaughter. A bastard, to boot. God in heaven! Why couldn't Ellis see sense? If he wanted somebody to love, Lalage was always there for him. *Her* arms were open wide.

If he wanted a child, she'd give him one. A child of her body, legitimately her husband's but bound to Ellis by ties of affection and blood – what heritage could be better? What more could Ellis ask?

"He needs a wife," she told Alex. "But he must choose wisely."

"Yes, of course." Alex looked at her. "Did you have anyone in mind?"

"I'll find someone." Lalage narrowed her eyes. "She must come from good stock. She must be young, foolish and obedient. She must be someone I – or rather, someone *we* can control."

* * *

Ellis practically fell over himself to be tactful. He never so much as mentioned his brother-in-law's failed speculations, so their easy friendship was unaffected by Alex's financial disasters and consequent social disgrace. The Lowells often visited Easton Hall, where they kept Ellis company and saved on housekeeping, too.

One fine autumn morning they arrived for what they intended to be a whole day's visit, but found Ellis away from home. He had left the house early that morning, and was not expected back until nightfall.

"Where's he gone?" Slapping her gloves into the butler's hand, Lalage glared at him. "Speak up, man. Where is he?"

"Mr Darrow has gone to Birmingham." Simmons avoided Lalage's gaze. "More than that, I cannot say." Without waiting to be dismissed, he walked out of the room. Alex and Lalage looked at each other.

"That fellow gets above himself." Crossly, Lalage picked at a loose thread in the upholstery of her chair. "I suppose he's gone to see his precious gates," she muttered, as she flicked a speck of dust off her skirt. "Alex, they've been almost six months in the making. I sometimes wonder if they'll ever be finished at all."

"So do I." Rubbing his eyes, Alex yawned. "But they're so very special, you see. They can't be rushed."

"Evidently not." Lalage grimaced. "I expect Miss Searle is making them herself."

Ellis sat in Rebecca's dusty little office. He was happier here than he would have been in paradise. Reluctant to leave, he took a full ten minutes to examine his bill, and another five to sign the banker's drafts. Finally, he could spin things out no longer. He passed the papers across the desk.

"Thank you." Rebecca hardly glanced at them. "Well, Mr Darrow, it's been a pleasure to do business with you. I'm glad you're so pleased with the gates. When would you like them fitted?"

"Fitted?"

"Yes." Opening a ledger, she consulted it. "If I send two workmen down on Thursday, would that be convenient for you?"

"I'm sorry." Ellis shook his head. "I didn't quite catch what you said."

"Could two men come on Thursday? To fit the gates."

"Oh. Yes. Yes, of course." Ellis knew he had to think of something. Quickly. He stared all round the little office, as if searching for inspiration. He found none.

"The men could be there at ten. Is that too early?" Rebecca looked him. "Mr Darrow? Is ten o'clock – "

"That would be splendid." Ellis took a deep breath. "Miss Searle," he began, "I wonder – what I mean is, I was thinking you might like to see the gates in position yourself. You have lavished so much time and thought on them. It might be gratifying – "

"For me to see them in place?" Rebecca had instantly caught his meaning. But now, too late, she realised she'd been too forward. Her face grew hot. "What I meant was – what I thought you meant – "

"I would like you to come over to Easton Hall once again." Ellis smiled at her. "You would enjoy an outing, I'm sure."

"Yes, indeed." Blushing furiously now, Rebecca nodded vigorously. "I should like that very much."

"Come to dinner, then." Ellis positively beamed. "On Friday, yes? I shall send the carriage. We can dine early, at two. Or three. Whenever suits you."

But now Rebecca was embarrassed. "Well," she began, "I should like to see the gates. But as for dinner, I don't really – "

"Miss Searle, you must come to dinner." Ellis was insistent now. "At this time of year, the country air is so clean. So fresh. It will be beneficial to your health. The drive will delight you. The leaves are turning. The woods are at their loveliest just now.

"You could bring your aunt. Yes, bring Miss Searle as well. That is, if she would like to come."

"That would not be possible. My aunt never goes visiting. She does not like it." Rebecca made up her mind. "But I shall come. I accept your invitation with pleasure. Thank you very much."

"Excellent." Ellis took her hand. "Friday, then? I shall send the carriage over for about ten o'clock. Would that suit?"

"That would be perfect." Rebecca smiled. "I shall look forward to it," she added, astonished at her own daring, and confidently expecting the hand of God to strike her dead at once.

Ellis drove Rebecca through the park. After pointing out the various features of this pretty but wholly artificial landscape, he drew her attention to the new quincunxes of rare flowering cherries. These, he predicted, would be a glory the following spring. He showed her the freshly-planted avenue of elms, which would not reach maturity in his lifetime, but which he was confident his grandchildren would enjoy. He hoped she was not bored.

But, as time went on, he became afraid she was longing to make her escape. She would not talk. In response to any comment from him, she merely nodded, blushed or smiled. Ellis had intended this to be a day of pleasure. Instead, it was becoming an ordeal.

They reached the boundary of the park. Jumping down from the small phaeton which Lalage always used when at Easton Hall, Ellis handed Rebecca down. They looked at the gates.

"You're pleased with them?" Studying them critically now, for when Ellis's carriage had swept into the park earlier that day she'd had barely a chance to glance at them, she frowned. To her enormous relief, they looked right. More than right. They looked splendid. "Mr Darrow? You like what you see?"

"Certainly. They're beautiful." Ellis wasn't even looking at the gates. "Miss Searle, will you step into the wood? It's beech, so the ground is quite open. There's no undergrowth, nothing to snag your gown."

"In that case, I should like it." For the first time that day, Rebecca looked straight at him. Her face glowed, her eyes sparkled. "I should enjoy it very much."

The gates had been expertly fitted, but the carriage wheels had scuffed the gravel from the road into little ruts and heaps. As Ellis pushed, one gate stuck fast.

He shrugged. There was room enough. He stood aside to let his guest pass.

Women's clothes, however, take up far more space than men's. Gathering her skirts close about her, Rebecca tried to manoeuvre her way through. The hem of her gown caught on a wrought-iron spike. She stopped to free it – and Ellis, who'd followed rather too quickly, stumbled against her.

Her shoulder bumped against his chest. Fearing she might fall, he caught her elbow.

Both coloured. "I'm sorry." Still holding her, Ellis looked into her eyes. "I didn't mean to jostle you."

"You didn't." Rebecca was crimson now. Her hem was still impaled on the spike, so now she tugged again. "Mr Darrow, if you could step back a little – "

"Don't pull, you'll tear the material." Ellis let her go. Stooping down, he lifted the hem off the spike. "There," he said. "No damage at all."

"Thank you." Still blushing scarlet, Rebecca walked on. They went into the wood.

For a while, neither spoke. The wood was silent. Their light footsteps, crunching across a carpet of fallen leaves, were the only sounds to be heard.

Ellis felt light-headed. The desire to embrace her was overpowering. In the end, it was too much to bear. He took out his watch. "We should go back to the house now," he observed, wondering if his voice sounded as odd to her as it did to him. "I ordered dinner for half past two."

Dinner could have been dry bread and water for all the notice the diners took. Both Ellis and Rebecca made a creditable pretence of eating, but neither actually consumed very much. Taking turns to start a sentence, they looked at each other, blushed, then dried up. They glanced out of the window. They sipped water. They looked at the food which was congealing on their plates. Their eyes would keep meeting. They would keep smiling at one another. Finally, Ellis stood up.

"I'll show you the house," he said. "If you'd like to see it, that is."

"I would, very much." Rebecca smiled. The fact that she'd seen most of it already was of no consequence at all.

Simmons and the footman cleared away. Significantly, they grinned. But the cook, who had made a special effort, was disgusted.

At four, Rebecca went home. As he handed her into his carriage, Ellis wondered if he should offer to go with her. But he decided against it. Alone with her in the cosy intimacy of the carriage, he would have had to take her in his arms. To kiss her until she begged for mercy.

That Sunday morning, he rode over to Birmingham. Picking his way along mean, Sabbath-quiet streets, he made for Searle's factory.

Finding the gate open, he went into the yard. He knocked on the door of the house, and was admitted by a shy, neatly-dressed maid. Shown into the front parlour, a little square room smelling sweetly of scented beeswax and new furnishing fabrics, he was asked to wait.

He looked around. From outside, the house looked just as disagreeable, as grimed, blackened and down-at-heel, as every other in this ugly neighbourhood. But it was very pleasant within. A lady's home, this room in particular was done up in very feminine taste. Papered in pink and cream, it was furnished with easy chairs and a fat, buttoned sofa, all comfortably upholstered in patterned chintz.

The overall effect was one of quiet, neat elegance. Of basically good, if uneducated, taste. Ellis smiled. But then, having glanced round once more, he let his mind wander.

He was not to know the house had not always been like this. Had he called there a year ago, he'd have found dark colours, heavy, functional furniture – a complete dearth of comfort, or decoration for decoration's sake. But since Jeremy Searle's death, Lyddy had refurbished her home. Now, it was almost light and airy.

The ill-used daughter had laid her father's ghost. She had literally swept it away. So here, no trace of the dour, Presbyterian blacksmith remained.

A rustle of silk, and the sound of the door being closed behind her, brought Ellis to his senses. "Mr Darrow?" began Rebecca, sounding puzzled.

"My dear Miss Searle." Ellis took her hands in his. "Forgive me for disturbing your Sunday. I need to talk to you, however. Most urgently."

"I see." Soberly dressed for a dull Nonconformist Sabbath, Rebecca's blush was more suited to a bright May morning. She pulled her hands free. "Well, Mr Darrow. If you would like to step into the office?"

"No. I don't want to go to the office." Ellis thought for a moment. "Could we go for a walk, instead?"

"A *walk*?" The idea of wandering around Birmingham for pleasure was such a novelty that Rebecca stared. "Well," she said at last, "I suppose we might go along the canal bank. Not that it's particularly pleasant, you understand. This part of town is not the place for sightseeing."

She gave him a faint smile. "For exercise, you see, we would normally drive out to the countryside. I don't think you'll find anything hereabouts to admire."

"That doesn't matter at all." Ellis returned her smile

with interest. "Do you wish to bring your maid?" he asked.

"No. That won't be necessary." Rebecca looked down at her feet. "I must change my shoes," she said. "Then we can go."

Walking along the dirty, dusty streets, watching where she put her feet for fear of treading in something unpleasant – for the pavements in that district were all strewn with rubbish, with great heaps of refuse simply left to rot or await whatever scavengers chance might prompt to pass that way – Rebecca kept her eyes fixed firmly on the ground. When Ellis offered her his arm, she took it. More, he suspected, for support than anything else.

Five minutes after setting out, they reached a branch of the canal. A dirty, polluted stretch of urban waterway, this particular little inlet was used to bring coke from the stockyards to the factories all about.

There was no bridge. "We'll have to turn back soon." Glancing up at her companion, Rebecca narrowed her eyes against the weak autumn sunshine. "There are only factories or furnaces along here. It's very dirty."

"Come just a little further." Since leaving Searle's yard, Ellis had not spoken. Now he covered Rebecca's hand with his. Leading her past another factory, they approached a large, gloomy, blind-walled warehouse. Coming to a high brick wall, they stopped.

The wall was that of a foundry. Still warm, for even on a Sunday the fires were never allowed to go out completely, it was comfortable to lean against. Here, surrounded by high, windowless buildings and screened from public view, Ellis finally took Rebecca in his arms.

To his surprise and delight, she did not resist him. After a minute or two, she even found her voice. "You wish to talk to me?" she demanded. "You have something urgent to say?"

"Yes, indeed." Ellis kissed her forehead. "But perhaps I don't need to use actual words. At any rate, not as such."

"I think you do." Looking up, Rebecca met his eyes. "You must say exactly what you mean. Then we'll understand each other, you see."

"Marry me." Ellis kissed her again. "I want you to marry me. Well, Rebecca? What do you say to that?"

"I – I don't know what to say." Rebecca blushed. She had – and yet she hadn't – expected anything like this. For, although the idea that Ellis might suggest she became his mistress had never even crossed her mind, she had not seriously expected him to propose marriage.

Now he was speaking again. "I shan't let you refuse me," he said. "I don't expect an answer straight away. But when you do decide, it must be in my favour."

"Must it?" Still looking into his eyes, she shrugged. "I don't mean to tease you," she cried. "I would not torment you for the world! But I hardly know you. I – "

"You know me well enough. At any rate, you know what matters most. I love you." He touched her face. "I think that maybe – well, when I took your hand just now, you did not draw away. When I embraced you, you did not flinch. I think I know you well enough to be sure you would not let yourself be kissed by a man you did not like."

"Go on," she said.

He laughed. "You smile when you see me arrive. You frown when I depart. I don't think you are such a fine lady that your smiles are false, or your frowns mere pique. As for me – in your company, I am happier than I have ever been in my life. I consider us well suited. Don't you?"

Rebecca blushed redder. "I – I hope you don't think I've been forward," she stammered. "I never intended to flirt. Or to tease."

"I don't think you know how to flirt, let alone tease." Serious now, Ellis looked into Rebecca's eyes. He saw irises as blue as the cornflowers which could never grow in that dirty town. So it was that, surrounded by high brick walls, hemmed in by heaps of rubbish and industrial spoil, he took her face between his hands. He kissed her on the lips.

At first, she stiffened. Then, however, the first shock over, she relaxed. She let herself be kissed. She closed her eyes. Contentedly, she sighed.

But then, suddenly, she pulled away. "Oh, Ellis," she cried, in real distress. "This is terrible!"

"Is it?"

"Yes!" She looked as if she might cry. "I'm a manufacturer!" she wailed. "A respected member of the community! But I'm kissing a man in a public alley. Behaving like a woman of the streets!"

"It's the Sabbath day, too. So the sin is magnified a hundred-fold." Ellis grinned. "Now, Rebecca. Say you'll be my wife."

"I'll say – "

"What?"

"I may be your wife."

"I see." Ellis took her hands in his. "I shall give you – let me think – a week. But because you keep me in suspense, I shall impose a penalty. I shall kiss you again."

Chapter 10

"You've actually asked her to marry you?" Well aware that her own future prosperity depended on her brother either marrying a rich idiot or dying a bachelor, Lalage stared in horrified disbelief. Her *own* children – for surely there'd be some, one day – must inherit the Easton estate! "You've proposed marriage?" she repeated, aghast. "You can't have done."

"Well, I have." Ellis shrugged. "But I'll admit this here and now. I didn't expect either of you to be overjoyed."

"What did Miss Searle say?" asked Alex.

"That she would consider it."

"Consider it?" Lalage snorted. "The assurance of the woman!"

"What did you say?"

"Nothing, Ellis. Nothing at all." Recovering her composure, Lalage walked over to the sofa on which her brother sat. She flopped down beside him. "She's a Dissenter, isn't she?" she asked.

"I believe so." Ellis shrugged again. "What of it?"

"Well, there you have it. That explains everything." Turning to Alex, Lalage grinned. "Poor Ellis," she murmured. "He had to propose. There was no other way to get her into bed."

Alex swallowed hard. Glancing towards Ellis, he saw an earlier flush had now been replaced by a livid pallor. "Lally, darling," he began, "I really think it's time – "

But Lalage ignored him. Reaching for her brother's hand, she took it in her own. "Won't she let you touch her, then?" she cooed. "Do you have to pay even to look? What's the rate of exchange?"

"What do you mean by that?"

"You order a new fender. She allows you to glimpse her ankle. You buy a kitchen range. She leaves off her neckerchief for the day. But she won't actually lift her skirts until you promise – "

"It's time we went." Alex stood up. "It's late, and I'm sure Ellis is tired."

"How should he be? He's done nothing tiring. Yet." Lalage laughed. "My dear Ellis, I'll confess it now – I know very little of trade. But I imagine women of that kind can readily be bought. What's the going rate? A hundred? A thousand? How much have you offered her so far?"

"Be quiet." Ellis's eyes flashed dangerously. He snatched his hand away. Folding his arms, he glared at the wall.

"Oh, Ellis!" Lalage pouted. "Can't you take a joke? I was only teasing."

Ellis said nothing.

Suddenly, Lalage was afraid. A horrible suspicion crossed her mind. She had to know now. "Ellis?"

"What?"

"You haven't done anything rash, I hope? You haven't got her with child?"

"What did you say?" Whipping round, Ellis grabbed his sister by the shoulders. He shook her like a doll, his fingers digging into her flesh. "Listen to me, Lalage!" he cried. "Listen well! If you make any more insinuations like that, I shall hit you! Do you understand me? I shall take my whip to you, and thrash you so hard you'll faint!"

"You wouldn't dare!" Lalage glared back at him. "Alex wouldn't let you."

"Alex couldn't stop me." Ellis jumped to his feet. He strode out of the room. The door slammed behind him.

"Well!" Shrugging, Lalage rubbed her hot face. "Whatever did I say, to deserve all that?"

"Nothing, dear." Taking his wife's hand. Alex chafed

it. "Nothing at all. Don't fret about Ellis. He's so wound up today, he takes everything amiss."

"All the same, I only – "

"I expect you hit home rather, that's all." Alex rubbed his eyes. "Perhaps Miss Searle's hanging on to her virtue. If Ellis wants her, he'll be taking that hard. He's not the kind of man to endure being denied."

"That's hardly any fault of mine."

"No. But don't annoy him." Alex stared out of the window. "Don't tease him. It'll only make him angry. More determined. If the creature holds out on him much longer, he'll tire of her. Or, he might do as he threatened."

"Marry her?" Lalage gaped. "He wouldn't. Would he?"

"He might, Lally. He just might. So be careful."

For the rest of that evening, Ellis made himself scarce. His sister exercised her wit at will, guessing he was probably wandering through the moonlit woods, sighing to himself and carving Rebecca's name on every tree.

Alex told her not to be ridiculous. "He's gone to his study," he said. "He's working on the design of some cottages. Homes for those peasants, who'll be seen off the next bit of common he means to enclose."

Derisively, Alex sniffed. "He's ever the model landlord. Even when he's in love."

"So it would appear." Lalage shrugged. "Shall we ring for supper?""

"I'm not hungry. I think I'll go to bed."

"Shall I come with you?"

"If you're tired." Alex yawned. "I don't mind either way."

Lalage had nothing else to do. So she followed him upstairs to her own old room, which she and Alex always used when staying at Easton Hall.

Closing the door behind her, she sat Alex down on the bed. Unfastening his cuffs, undoing his buttons, she undressed him. It was as if he were a child and she his nurse.

It had been like this for weeks now. Each evening, Alex let Lalage undress him, then slip his nightshirt over his head. Getting into bed, he curled himself up like a hedgehog. He then went straight to sleep.

That night, Lalage did not ring for her maid. Throwing off her own clothes, she got into bed. "Alex?" she whispered. "Alex! Wake up."

"What?" Alex stirred. Reluctantly, he opened his eyes. "I wasn't asleep," he muttered.

"You were."

"No." Alex shook his head. He yawned. Then, seeing his wife was naked, he frowned. "Hadn't you better find your nightgown?" he asked. "Or did Betty forget to pack it?"

Lalage scowled at him. "Listen to me," she said. "Alex, listen!"

"What?"

"We must have a child. A son. You mustn't hold back on me any more." For emphasis, she shook his shoulder, pinching through to the bone. "Don't deny it," she muttered, fiercely. "I know you don't want me pregnant. You'd hate me to be fat and bloated, like a sow. But if we had a son, Alex – think! He'd be Ellis's heir."

Alex looked at her. Over the past few weeks, he'd taken her for granted, forgotten completely how lovely she was. "Oh, darling," he cried, "you don't want a baby!"

"But I do." Lalage glared. "Alex, I *do*!"

"You might die!" Alex winced, as if in pain himself. "Oh, Lally! If you died, I'd die too."

"Of course I shan't die. Why should I?"

"You're so small."

"Nonsense. There are a million women smaller than me. Some of them give birth every single year, and thrive on it." Taking his hand, Lalage stroked it. "Give me a child," she whispered. "Let's make a baby, tonight."

"We'll see." Alex kissed her. "We'll see."

An hour later, Alex sat up. Lalage lay exhausted, satisfied at last.

He congratulated himself. It had been a near thing, but he had managed to come away just in time. Before a single seed was spilled.

"Do you suppose he's told her?" Wide awake now, Alex lit a candle. He looked at Lalage. "Has he said anything, do you think?"

"About the money, you mean?" Lalage tied the ribbons on her nightgown. She frowned. "No," she said. "I'm sure he hasn't. He's not even sure she's the right person. Not absolutely certain, that is."

"Oh." Alex was unconvinced. "All the same – "

"You're his best friend. I'm his sister." Lalage's huge, dark eyes flashed. "He wouldn't impoverish us!"

"But he loves her. Or thinks he does." Alex sighed. "He might think her welfare is far more important than ours."

Lalage's eyes narrowed. "He won't tell her," she said. "He won't ruin you and me. He loves us, too."

Inexplicably, Lyddy Searle seemed dismayed rather than delighted by Rebecca's news. Calmly, she poured out tea. Carefully, she cut the cake. "So," she said, handing her niece a plate. "Mr Darrow has asked you to marry him."

"Yes, he has!" Rebecca was cross now. "Aunt Lyddy, aren't you pleased? I thought you'd be thrilled."

"Did you?" Lyddy's pallid face became even more pale. "Well, I'll admit I'm surprised. Weren't you?"

Rebecca shrugged. "In a way," she said. "But in another way, I expected it. Or something like it."

"Like it?" Lyddy's eyes grew wide. Her face was ashen now. "Rebecca, it *was* marriage he offered. Wasn't it?"

"Yes, of course." Rebecca frowned. "Aunt, I'm not sure I understand you. Or if I want to."

"My dear child, you say he asked you to marry him. Was he quite explicit? Or did he wrap a sordid suggestion in fine words?"

"No, Aunt! Nothing like that." Rebecca smiled. "Marry me. That's what he said. Could anything be plainer?"

"I suppose not."

"He gave me time to consider, too."

"I see."

"Do you?" Rebecca took Lyddy's hand. "My dear, dear aunt," she cried, "I know how much you care about me. All my life you've watched over me. Nursed me. Taught me. My own mother could not have loved me more. Nor been as gentle and wise a friend, as you have been to me.

"So I hope that now, grown to womanhood, I can judge a character? That I can tell a charlatan from an honourable man? That I know the difference between right and wrong?"

"I hope you do." Lyddy sniffed. "Does Mr Darrow?"

"Yes!" Rebecca searched Lyddy's face. "He's a good man," she said. "He's kind. He's honest. He's plain-spoken. He's never suggested anything improper. He's never, by word, look or deed, offended me. Oh, Aunt! Dear Aunt! Won't you wish me happiness?"

"Well." Pursing her lips, Lyddy did not know what to say.

"I know *you've* never wanted to marry," went on Rebecca, now in full flow. "But I do! I want children of my own. I want to be a wife. I want a man's – a man's company."

"Then can't you find a man of your own class?" Lyddy met Rebecca's eyes. "Let it be known you wish to marry. I'll put it about you've a mind to wed. There'll be men queueing from here to Snow Hill!

"Becky, there's Matthew Harris, the widower. He's a rich man. Henry Prescott. David Kay. If you don't want anyone in the toy trade, there's John Graham – "

"The typefounder?"

"Yes. He'd take you tomorrow! Then again, there's James Ryeland. He always looks at you in chapel. I tell you now – *his* mind cannot be on the word of God for more than five minutes together while you are by! Michael Allen, George Curtis, Francis Holland – "

"I want Mr Darrow." Rebecca bit her lower lip. "No one but him."

"He wants to marry you, too. Or so he says." Lyddy sniffed again. "Or does he merely want you in his bed?"

"What do you mean?"

"In spite of his fine words and splendid offers, does he simply want your virginity? Forgive me for speaking so bluntly, but I feel I must. Does he want to use you? Then, when he's tired of you, will he throw you away?"

"Aunt, it's not like that! Mr Darrow has never even hinted – "

"Ah, but perhaps he has. Perhaps, Becky, he has made himself perfectly plain. You, unfortunately, have not had the wit to take the hint."

Seeing Rebecca's colour rise, Lyddy spoke more gently now. "Becky," she whispered, "they're not like us. Their ways are not our ways. A gentleman's sweet words are like the perfume of roses. Pleasant to the senses, beguiling to the heart, but worth nothing. Nothing at all."

"Oh. I see." Rebecca plucked at the skirt of her gown. "You have a very low opinion of my good sense," she murmured. "You think me a fool, and Mr Darrow a brute." But then her eyes flashed. "You're so wrong!" she cried. "He's not a seducer. He's not a wretch. He's not that kind of man!"

"*All* men are that kind of man!" Lyddy was almost in tears. "Becky, it's so. They take what they can get. They don't care if they break a woman's heart!

"That's not the end of it, either. If a man errs, it's nothing. But if a woman strays, she can be sure other men will punish her. Will make quite certain she suffers, to the very end of her days."

"How do you know?" Rebecca glared. "You've never married. You've – now *I* shall speak bluntly – you've never even had knowledge of a man! What do you know of the breaking of hearts, or inequality of punishment?

"My dear aunt, I know my grandfather was a harsh man, was harder on you than you deserved – but all men are not like that. Consider, too, that despite his stern nature, my grandfather always looked after his kith and kin. As for my own father – he might have abandoned my mother, but he did marry her. Didn't he?"

Lyddy sighed. "Did you give Mr Darrow an answer?" she enquired.

"No. I explained. He gave me time to consider."

"Then consider, child. Consider well. Remember, either way he wins. If he seduces you, he has his pleasure and may walk away. If he marries you, everything you own becomes his." Lyddy rose to her feet. She lit a candle, taking the flame from one fluttering on the table at her side. "I'm going to my bed."

Groping for her clock, Lyddy turned the dial towards her. The rays of a full moon lit up the hands. Three o'clock in the morning. She'd lain awake five whole hours.

She got out of bed and went into Rebecca's room. Gently, she shook her awake.

"Aunt? What is it?" Rebecca started out of her dream. "What's the matter? Is the factory afire?"

"I want to talk to you." Pulling her shawl close, Lyddy sat down on the bed. "Sit up now, and listen."

"Can't we talk in the morning?" Rebecca frowned. "Aunt, it's so late! Can't it – "

"No. It won't wait. It must be now, while I have the courage to speak." Lyddy took Rebecca's hands in hers. "You see, child, there are things you ought to know."

"What things?" Still half asleep, Rebecca pulled one hand free. She rubbed her eyes. "Oh, Aunt! What – "

"About you. About Mr Darrow. Mr Lowell, too."

"Mr *Lowell*?" Rebecca stared. "My dear aunt, Mr Lowell is nothing to do with me."

"Listen to me, dear," said Lyddy, gently. "Listen well."

Chapter 11

Monday morning was a cold, sullen dawn. The sun had risen with as much reluctance as the hundreds of factory workers now scurrying about the great industrial town, hastening to their various employments.

Rising early, Rebecca looked out of her window and saw the day was wet and overcast. A dirty rain fell steadily against the panes, each droplet containing its own speck of soot which would eventually dry, suspended in the shape of a tear, upon the glass.

"Are you awake, Miss Searle? Oh! You're up already." Rebecca's little maid, bustling in with a jug of hot water and a dish of early morning tea, looked curiously at Rebecca's ashen face. She saw her mistress's eyes were heavy, and smudged with purple shadows. "Not a very nice day, ma'am," she ventured, staring still.

"No indeed, Esther." Taking the dish of tea, Rebecca sipped gratefully. "You may go now," she said. "Help my aunt make the breakfast. I shall dress myself today."

Rebecca washed, then put on her clothes. Awkwardly, for without Esther's help she could not manage the back very well, she braided and pinned her hair. Then she went down to have breakfast with her aunt.

Her aunt? Yes, Lyddy was still her aunt. Rebecca could not start calling her by another name now. After all, Lyddy was still the same shy, retiring, unobtrusive soul. Still the very model of a spinster, of a poor relation. Of course, as far as anyone else was concerned, Rebecca and Lyddy would always be niece and aunt.

Taking her seat, Rebecca smiled encouragingly. Her

cordiality would, she hoped, show Lyddy that the revelations of the early morning had not altered her feelings of gratitude, of respect, of love. "Did you sleep?" she asked, carefully, kindly.

"A little." Steadily, Lyddy poured tea. "Did you?"

"I dozed." Rebecca broke some bread. "Not a very nice day," she added, reiterating the observations of her maid. "Cold, and damp."

"Yes." Evidently relieved that Rebecca was not disposed to be sharp, Lyddy nibbled some toast.

After Lyddy had finished her story and gone back to her room, Rebecca lay awake, thinking. By morning, she had made up her mind.

She could never marry Ellis Darrow. She hated the very idea of being married to the man who, as a child, had jeered at and mocked poor Lyddy.

Her other self told her Ellis had been a mere boy. That he had grown up to become a kind, sensible and considerate man. "All children are cruel and thoughtless," this other self said. But then a picture of two sniggering, spiteful brats, gawping and sneering from the safety of the hayloft, forced its way into her mind yet again. The scene had etched itself into her brain. Burned into her soul.

People do not change, she thought. The child must always become the man. Ellis was still cold-hearted, mean-spirited. But, as an adult, he'd learned to hide his true nature. Beneath a thin veneer of good manners and fine phrasing, he was a brute after all.

As for Alex Lowell – one had only to glance at him to see the sort of brat he must have been. Sneering, prurient, censorious, mean. The pale, blond gentleman she had met in Ellis Darrow's study was everything Rebecca despised in men. To think that idle fop was her brother!

One might know a man by his friends. Alex Lowell was Ellis Darrow's dearest friend. The case was proven.

But then Rebecca thought of Ellis himself. Who had

told her only yesterday that he loved her. He had meant it, too. She'd have staked her life on that.

Rebecca finished her breakfast. Stepping into the scullery, she put on her thick, frieze cloak. She slid her feet into wooden pattens. Quickly, she made her way across the cobblestones, clacking across the wide expanse of courtyard where black, sooty rainwater splashed and ran into puddles.

Pushing open the door of the big workshop, she entered the familiar, vaulted cavern. She made her way along the benches. This was going to be a normal day, she decided. Smiling and nodding, she exchanged morning greetings with the men. Since the hammers and anvils were not yet busy, the noise was moderate, so she could stop and chat to her employees.

"A rather nasty morning, Miss Searle." One of her best foremen, a master craftsman who had taken over the guidance and training of Jeremy Searle's three most promising apprentices, grinned at her. Then, directing one of the boys to get on with what his master had started, Peter Crewe followed Rebecca up the gangway. "Could I have a word or two?" he asked, wiping his grimy hands on his leather apron. "If you could spare a minute, I'd be glad of your advice."

"Well, Peter?" Rebecca was now in one of the workshops, where a couple of the newest apprentices were hard at work burnishing a boxful of the cut steel buttons for which Birmingham was famous. Remembering now that the foreman had an ailing wife, and observing his face was drawn and pinched with anxiety, she smiled kindly. "How is Mrs Crewe today?" she asked. "Any better?"

"She's mending, I think." Peter Crewe chewed his lower lip. "You and your aunt have been very thoughtful, sending over those jellies and jars of soup. The apothecary's medicine seems to do her good. As for cash – the friendly society's advanced us a dividend now, so we're not short."

"That's good." At the mention of the friendly society, Rebecca frowned. Theoretically a savings club which helped its members out in times of financial hardship, the society to which Peter Crewe and some of her other workmen belonged was a buzzing hive of radicals. A breeding ground for sedition. At meetings, the members read tracts and pamphlets to their fellow workers, then incited them to strike. To agitate for higher wages, to harrass and scheme against their employers. Peter Crewe would never have dared mention the friendly society to Jeremy Searle.

Rebecca folded her hands. "Well then," she said, but rather less cordially now, "if there's anything I can do for you? Or your family?"

"There is." Embarrassed now, for he was aware he'd made a blunder, Peter Crewe looked down at the floor. "Miss Searle, you've been kind already. You've done more for us and the children than we've any right to expect. But – they're building houses along Marlin's Walk. Where the spoil heaps used to be. Decent houses. Brick-built. Two rooms below, and two up one pair of stairs."

Glancing up, Peter Crewe met Rebecca's eyes. "Miss Searle, I've been in the housing club for three years now. I've saved fourteen pounds, so I can well afford repayments on a mortgage of a hundred."

"Which is what the Marlin's Walk houses will cost?"

"Yes." Peter Crewe shuffled awkwardly. "I need another six pounds, for the deposit. I haven't got the money. But if my Jane had a decent house to live in, if we were out of that court where the water's always brackish and the damp makes her chest so bad – "

"I'll lend you six pounds. Of course I will." Rebecca smiled. "Tell the builder you'll take a house. You're right about that tenement – it *is* damp, and I don't doubt that contributes vastly to Mrs Crewe's indisposition. Come to the counting house at noon, and Henry shall give you the money."

"What about the repayments?" Relieved and delighted, the foreman beamed. "I could afford thirty shillin' a month, easy."

"I'll tell the clerk to take it out of your wages. But thirty shillings is too much. A florin a week will do. You expect to live long enough to clear the debt?"

"I hope so, Miss Searle." Peter Crewe clasped Rebecca's hands. "Thank you, Miss. Thank you from the bottom of my heart.

"My pleasure." Rebecca shook her head. If only her own problems could be so easily solved.

Leaving the workshops, Rebecca walked into the yard again. That exchange with her foreman had soothed her. Being able to offer assistance had given her back her own self–esteem. Now, having made Peter Crewe happy, she felt a warm glow deep inside.

She would, she thought, go and look over those new houses herself. If any of her other workmen asked for her help in buying one, she would certainly consider giving it. Close to the factory, convenient for the nearest school, a colony of Searle's workmen in Marlin's Walk would not be a bad thing at all. Perhaps she should buy a couple of houses herself, and rent them out? Her grandfather would have approved, she knew that.

For, distrustful of workers' clubs though he'd always been, Jeremy Searle had always been concerned for the welfare of his factory hands. He had impressed on his grand-daughter the fact that, as their employer, her interest in Searle's workforce should extend well beyond working hours and reach far outside the manufactory gates.

As Rebecca stood on the cobbles, she gazed up at the sky. A sooty wind blew, and the sun was beginning to break through increasingly ragged clouds. It was a weary, feeble Birmingham sun, true enough. But its faint rays now illuminated a corner of the dirty courtyard, and made the windows in the house at the far end of the square sparkle. Rebecca went into her office, shut the door, and sat down. She would apply herself to the demands of what she was determined would be a normal day.

Soon, as she'd anticipated, there was a tap on the door. Her first visitor was a wholesaler, wanting to re-negotiate the terms of an order for buckles. Together, he and Rebecca went through an established routine. The wholesaler asked the impossible, and Rebecca suggested he took his business elsewhere. Finally, they came to an agreement and shook hands over the deal.

Then she was called over to a workshop to arbitrate on a dispute between two journeymen. As she made her way back to her office, one of the clerks from the counting house handed her some letters. "How many are absent today?" she asked, as she glanced at her post.

"Not many, Miss Searle. Only thirteen."

"That's quite enough." Rebecca pursed her lips. "The usual defaulters?"

"More or less, Miss."

"Make me a list of their names. I'll see them all tomorrow, at eight o'clock sharp."

Monday morning. Saint Monday – upon which, since long before the time artisans had worked in urban factories, the more feckless labourers had traditionally kept holiday.

That Monday, as on any other, dozens of workmen would have taken the day off, and in Rebecca's factory several labourers and at least two skilled craftsmen were absent from their benches.

Tom Farrow, she supposed, would be down at the dog fight. Even now, he'd be pitting his own bloodthirsty cur against opposition from all over the county. George Holland was probably in bed with some drab, confident he could make up all the time lost on Monday, on Tuesday, Wednesday, Thursday, Friday and Saturday, and still earn enough to pay for his beer and his whores. Perhaps, thought Rebecca, she should let these two go. Reliable and conscientious when they actually came to work, their cavalier attitude towards their employer was bound to infect the other men.

Rebecca sorted through her paperwork, then went back into the factory. As she was berating an apprentice, telling him that if he spoilt his materials just once more he would most definitely leave her employ, she was called to her office again. A drayman, who had brought his load of bar iron into the factory yard, wanted her signature on the receipt.

Rebecca sat down at her desk. She found a quill. With a pang, she realised Ellis had signed his last banker's draft with this very pen. She mended the point. She dipped it in the inkwell. She was about to sign her name and tell the man to take himself off – when she saw the price she was expected to pay.

She shook herself. Told herself to concentrate on the business in hand. "No!" she said, sharply. "I shan't sign this. It's far too much."

"Is it, Miss?" The drayman could not read. Perplexed, he scratched his head. "Well, Miss Searle, I dunno anything about that. All they says to me is, Mr Hollis was most particular – "

"I spoke to Mr Hollis last Wednesday. I agreed a price then. That's the amount I expect to pay." Rebecca met the drayman's eyes. "You may take your load back again. Tell your master that from now on I shall deal Adlam's, instead."

"Take the stuff back, you say? But, Miss Searle!" The drayman stared. "Look, Miss, I thought – "

"I would sign anything?" Rebecca had heard what Mr Hollis thought about a woman running a factory. He gave old Searle's chit of a girl another six months at the outside. "Well, I certainly shan't sign this. Good day to you. Mind your horses don't foul my yard."

"Listen here, Miss Searle." The drayman folded his arms. "I only delivers the stuff. I don't know anythin' about prices. But if you want, I'll go back and enquire, like. There might have been a mistake."

"Mr Hollis knows full well what he's about." Rebecca laid down her pen. "Take your load away. If your master can get this sort of price from other manufacturers, then he's welcome to sell his goods to *them*."

"I could take a message, perhaps." It had taken almost twenty minutes to manoeuvre a heavily-laden cart up the steep incline which led to Searle's factory gate, and the drayman was most unwilling to take it back down again. "Miss Searle, I'm sure there's been a mistake."

"Maybe." Clicking her tongue in annoyance, Rebecca seized a sheet of paper. Scrawling rapidly, she told Mr Hollis she didn't want his goods. Since the price of pig iron had not increased for at least three months, she saw no reason to double his profit at her manufactory's expense. "Take this to your master," she said, handing the man the note. "If you're not back within the hour, I shall have your load removed. I can't have your cart blocking the entrance to my factory yard all day."

Twenty minutes later, the drayman was back. There had been a most unfortunate error. Mr Hollis sent his most sincere apologies. He hoped the happy association with Searle's manufactory would not be dissolved because of a trifling mistake.

Giving the drayman a shilling, Rebecca sent him on his way. Was this the beginning of the end? If the foundry owners all banded together to conspire against her, to force an upstart female out of business, there would be little she could do about it.

There'd been remarks and muttering, she knew that. A factory managed by a woman – by a young, unmarried woman at that – was an abomination. Not to be tolerated. Jeremy Searle had not come to dominate the toy trade without making enemies or arousing jealousy. It seemed Rebecca would have to take these enemies on.

After her mid-day meal and a short rest, Rebecca was back in the factory again. As the afternoon wore on, fatigue and lack of concentration claimed their usual handful of victims. A child cut himself on some swarf.

Another, getting some grit in his eye, rubbed until it bled. He had to be taken to the barber-surgeon three streets away. There was a violent argument between two master coppersmiths, and both appealed to Miss Searle for a decision in his favour.

"Please, Miss Searle, might I have an extra boy to work the bellows?" A harrassed furnaceman appeared between the coppersmiths, pushing them firmly aside. "Miss Searle, the big fire's almost out!"

By evening, Rebecca was exhausted. She was too tired even to think. The problems of factory management had driven all idea of Ellis from her mind. As she sipped her evening chocolate, she felt her eyelids droop. Tonight, she would sleep.

Yawning, she snuffed her candle. Rubbing her eyes, she climbed into bed. But sleep eluded her. Until the early hours, she merely dozed. Then dreams, as vivid as reality, rendered her hour or so of actual slumber even more disturbing than wakefulness. At five o'clock, heavy eyed and suffering from the most appalling headache, Rebecca finally got up. She sat on the edge of her bed, and sighed.

She had dreamed of Ellis. Of nothing but him. She had seen his face, heard his voice, and felt his arms around her waist. He had kissed her again and again, his mouth warm on hers.

Tormented by desire and hating herself because of it, Rebecca washed and dressed. Fastening her laces and tying her apron strings, she was almost in tears of frustration, anger and distress. She was ashamed of herself, disgusted she should be so womanish, foolish and fond.

Chapter 12

Some weeks before Ellis made his momentous announcement, Alex had decided he had to get away. Lalage's restless liveliness, which had once seemed so charming, no longer entertained him. Instead, she was wearing him out.

Lalage had changed. Once so carefree, such a butterfly, she'd been enchanting. Delightfully trivial. Her name meant babbler, or chatterbox, and she had lived up to it. She'd prattled endlessly of new gowns, of holidays abroad, of what she would buy next and what she would do with this latest toy once she got it. Alex had found all this most amusing. Her pleasure in each new possession had also gratified him.

But nowadays, she did nothing but grumble. She went on and on about money, or rather the lack of it, and she moaned constantly about the shortcomings of her new, somewhat less than efficient servants.

"He is ignorant, coarse and dirty," she complained, glaring after the departing footman whose wages she could not afford to pay. "As for Sukey – she has no idea of waiting on a lady at all. I'd give her notice tomorrow if Betty could manage by herself."

Recalling Madam's airs and graces, her former acquaintance tended to be cool towards her now. When, one afternoon, a formerly cordial neighbour cut her dead, it plunged her into an evil humour which lasted a whole week. Even her much-petted and over-indulged little negro servant suffered now, for she threw her slippers at his head and gave him such a tongue-lashing that poor Caspar was in tears.

The slights – real or imagined – to which Lalage was subjected in church, at home, while staying with Ellis, began to obsess her. Then again, she wanted a baby. Insisted they must have a child. For Alex, that was the last straw.

He told her he was going to take a short holiday. He would go up to Derbyshire, which he and Lalage had visited a year or two since. Its wild landscapes, full of rushing torrents, steep precipices and cavernous gorges, had delighted him. Lalage, on the other hand, had hated it. So he felt confident she would want nothing to do with the scheme.

"I thought I'd go to Matlock," he told her. "I'll hire a guide there and spend a week or so hill-walking. Maybe fit in a little rock-climbing, too. Darling, I know you hate the rain and damp. I don't expect you to come with me. Stay with Ellis, instead."

"But I'd love to come!" At the prospect of travel, Lalage brightened visibly. "The change will do me good."

"But darling, it's so late in the year. It will be very cold, and it's bound to be wet. You hate walking. You know you do."

"I don't mind a gentle stroll." Warming even more to the idea of a jaunt, Lalage grinned. "Anyway, I can't see *you* doing much rock-climbing. You might scramble up a few cliffs, I suppose. But I could manage that, too."

"I intend to stay in lodging houses, you know." Dissuasion having failed miserably, Alex now tried lies. "I shall be living as cheaply as can be. Taking supper at the coarser type of inn. Eating dinners of bread and cheese."

"There's no need to stint yourself like that." Gaily, Lalage tossed her black ringlets. "I'll ask Ellis for a loan," she said. "No, I'll do better! He asked what I wanted for my birthday. Well, he can pay for this trip."

She shook her head. "Oh, Alex! Coarse inns, cheap lodging houses, indeed. They'd be full of fleas and cockroaches. You'd come back absolutely infested. We'll go in style, and comfort."

Alex knew when he was beaten. He capitulated with good grace. "I didn't think it would appeal to you, darling," he said. "But if you want to come, of course I'd love to have your company."

On the Wednesday following Ellis's declaration of intent, Alex and Lalage set off. Travelling in Ellis's new carriage, they bowled along merrily. The coach was comfortable, the coachman efficient, and they were gratified to find other vehicles always gave way.

The weather was unseasonably fine. Although it was cold and sharp, the sun shone. Lalage loved travelling, and was in an excellent humour.

Arriving in the pretty little town of Ashbourne, Lalage stepped from her equipage and strolled into the best hotel with the air of one conferring inestimable largesse upon this humble place. Taking her for a lady of great wealth and consequence, the owner offered her the best rooms, and told her she must demand anything she wanted. "My daughter will be honoured to wait on your ladyship," he said. "My own private dining room is entirely at your disposal."

Soothed, cossetted and made much of, Lalage relaxed. Looking at her, Alex wondered how he could have even considered leaving her behind.

The following day, the weather was still fine. They set off for Buxton. But soon the road became so rutted and potholed that Lalage was jolted and bumped into a temper as foul as her previous day's mood had been sunny. Thrown against the side of the coach, she fell awkwardly, wrenching her wrist. She began to cry.

Higher and higher they climbed. Instead of sunshine, here there was low cloud, which obscured all the views and masked the landscape in a damp, chilling mist. On reaching the highest market town in England, Alex and Lalage found a dreary little place indeed, the ambience of which the now persistent drizzle did nothing to improve.

"What a dismal hole," observed Lalage. Nursing her

sore wrist, she let Alex help her out of the carriage and take her into an hotel.

Their rooms were cheerless. Damp spotted the walls and mirrors, while mouse droppings speckled the floors and stank out the closets. Lalage shuddered, both from cold and disgust. "Do tell them to light a fire!" she wailed. "Can't they hurry with the supper?"

"Will you not walk out for half an hour?" Anxious to stretch his legs and ease the cramps which sitting in a coach for hours always caused, Alex wanted to investigate the charms of the town. As the newest of English spas, Buxton would surely have something interesting to offer, so he was eager to look around. "Lally, please come out for a while. Some fresh air will do you good."

"Getting soaked to the skin is more likely to finish me off." Lalage scowled. "I want supper, served in my room, before a decent fire. Then I'm going to bed."

Alex went out by himself

"What a wretched place." Eyeing the almost completed Crescent with the severity of one who has seen both the glories of modern Bath and the wonders of ancient Italy, Lalage pursed her lips. "Oh, Alex! Does his lordship really expect the fashionable world to flock here?"

Alex gazed at the elegant stone terrace before him. He shook his head. "It's a fine piece of architecture," he hazarded, examining the Duke of Devonshire's expensive folly with his own hyper-critical eye. "But it hardly rivals Bath."

"Precisely." Lalage turned away. "Well now, shall we sample the famous waters? Drink some of the nasty stuff which doubtless comes straight from the gutter in the High Street, but which these charlatans pass off as some magical potion capable of curing all ills?"

"If you wish." As anxious as his wife to get out of the persistent rain, Alex let Lalage lead him into the pump room.

The attendant filled their glasses. Finding the water

was warm, Lalage grimaced. She drank a little, made a face, and put down her glass.

"It's excellent for rheumatism." The attendant, a neat, respectable-looking woman with a round, honest face innocent of all guile, smiled encouragingly. "It's a specific against the gout, too."

"Is it, indeed?" Lalage blotted her mouth. "Well, my good woman, I suffer from neither. Alex, if you've finished, might we go back outside?" She glared at three rather damp tourists who had just that moment come in. Shaking their umbrellas, they gave off pungent scents of wet wool, soggy shoe leather and perspiring human being. Lalage drew her skirts close about her. "I find it close in here," she said.

They stayed in Buxton for three days. The town, which was admittedly rather dismal in the late autumn downpours, depressed Lalage's spirits extremely. She became thoroughly disagreeable.

Left to himself, Alex would have made the best of things. The hotel was good enough. There was company available. Had he been alone, he'd have played cards with the other gentlemen and flirted mildly with their wives. He'd have ordered delicate little suppers and eaten them in bed, while he skimmed a new novel or book of verse.

But, followed everywhere by Lalage's gimlet glare, there could be no flirting. Not understanding even whist, Lalage complained bitterly if he played cards. So, after breakfast on the third day, the Lowells set off again. They travelled first to Bakewell, then went on to Matlock. The truly dreadful road put Lalage into her vilest temper yet. She ignored the wonderful scenery, refusing even to look at the stupendous views over which, the mist having obligingly lifted, Alex exclaimed alone.

Matlock itself turned out to be a horrible place. Here there were factories, quarries and mills, and a vast industrial wasteland sprawled like a stain across countryside which had once been of great natural beauty. In the streets, Alex and Lalage met cripples and beggars by the score. For, here in Matlock, there was simply no avoiding the sight of people whose twisted or truncated limbs bore witness to the cruelties of the new machine age.

Each morning, from her hotel window, Lalage watched bedraggled women and children make their weary way along the road, en route to Mr Arkwright's Cromford mill. Taken to visit it, the Lowells found a great, forbidding place reminiscent of an ogre's castle, in which men and women laboured like slaves, in thrall to pitiless machines which never tired, and therefore never stopped. Children as young as seven were employed here – though, it was alleged, on light, easy, pleasant tasks.

"Poor little things." Not even remotely interested in the welfare of the lower orders, Lalage was nevertheless very tender towards children. She treated her own little negro servant with a kindness Alex found quite touching, and had been almost tearful when she'd bidden Caspar goodbye, commending him to Sukey's special care.

Now, she watched Mr Arkwright's infant labourers with concern. She turned to the overseer. "Mr Gregory," she began, "are these children properly fed? Do they have the chance to get a little education? Do these little workers have time to play, and enjoy the games of which all boys and girls are fond?"

"Yes indeed." Whenever he showed ladies or gentlemen over the new factory, the overseer took care to leave his whip and his frown behind. Now, he smiled broadly. "Regular meal-breaks are always allowed. On Saturdays, each child receives at least four hours' schooling, all at Mr Arkwright's own expense. On Sundays, the children are at liberty the whole day. Then they are as sportive and playful as any in the kingdom."

Looking at these children toiling in the cotton mill, Lalage doubted if Sunday was anything but a welcome day of rest for them. These wan, pale, scrawny creatures, one with unmistakeable signs of consumption, another coughing like an old man, looked incapable of the frolicking which the overseer assured her was the rule.

Suddenly tired, for the atmosphere inside the mill was extremely oppressive and had made her cough, she took Alex's arm and made her way out into the fresh air.

"So that was a manufactory." Still coughing, for the tickle in her throat refused to go away – indeed, her lungs felt as if they were stuffed with cotton waste – Lalage inhaled the purer air of the river valley. "In other words, a place where little children choke and drudge their wretched lives away. All for the enrichment of a greedy, unscrupulous upstart, who capitalises on their parents' need."

Alex merely shrugged. Lalage glared at him. "But I don't doubt the wonderful Miss Searle manages things *far* more efficiently than Mr Arkwright?"

"I don't believe she employs any children as young as his." Alex flicked some cotton fibres from the sleeve of his coat. "Ellis says Miss Searle's workmen look very hale. He saw apprentices, but they were great strong lads of twelve or more. They looked far more robust than the average country boy."

"Did they?" Again, Lalage coughed. "They are no doubt fed upon chicken wings and cream."

"I don't know about that. But one thing is quite certain. Miss Searle's employees aren't slaves. She doesn't have a real manufactory, either. She merely manages a cluster of workshops, all gathered together for convenience and ease. Miss Searle's men follow the same trades as their fathers and grandfathers, and work in much the same way."

He glanced back at Arkwright's new mill. "But as for that abomination – now that *is* something new. In there, men serve machines, not the other way about. Iron and steel are the masters in that place."

"Whereas Miss Searle's operatives may labour or be

idle, just as they choose. Oh Alex, you do talk some stuff!"

"While you deliberately misunderstand me." Alex put on his hat. "I ordered dinner for two o'clock. So come along. I'm hungry."

After they'd dined and rested, their guide took Alex and Lalage high into the hills and showed them yet more peaks, picturesque rocky outcrops and deep, dripping caverns. Alex loved everything. He even admired the vermin, exclaiming delightedly over the squirrels and pine-martens scampering all around. "Darling, look!" he cried, squinting into the distance. "Is that a red deer?"

"Where?" Lalage looked. She saw a huge stag, even bigger and more aggressive-looking than Ellis's prize-winning Hereford bull, staring morosely back at her. She shuddered in distaste. "Alex," she grumbled, "my feet are wet through."

"Why didn't you wear your boots?" Properly shod and gaitered for scrambling over rocks and rough ground, Alex shook his head. "Those shoes aren't suitable for outdoors, surely?"

"I didn't expect to be dragged through a marsh." Lalage scowled at the guide. "Well, Mr Freeman, it's getting dark. Time we went back, I think."

"What we must do," said Lalage, as she and Alex ate supper before a blazing fire, "is ruin her. Before she ruins us. Think, Alex! What can we tell Ellis? What would he believe?"

Alex frowned. "We'll tell Ellis nothing which is untrue," he replied. "Oh, Lally! Don't be so dramatic. As if she wants to ruin *us*. As if she thinks of us at all."

"I expect she thinks of us day and night." Lalage pushed her plate aside. Having sent the maidservant away, she began to undress herself. Unfastening her gown, she let it slide to the floor.

"She plots," she muttered, tugging at her laces. "She schemes. She makes plans. She'll get her way, you mark my words." Now, Lalage began to sob. "If she takes Ellis, I don't know what I'll do!"

"Well, he's not married to her yet." Shrugging off his own clothes, Alex yawned. "There's no wedding arranged."

"There will be!" Still in her shift, Lalage walked across the room. Pulling off her rings, she tossed them into their boxes, one by one by one. She stared into the red glow of the fire. "Ellis is determined," she whispered. "Once he gets an idea in his head, that's it. There's no stopping him. He – "

"Lally, that's enough." Alex went to her. Taking her in his arms, he kissed her neck. "I don't want to hear any more about this so-called engagement," he murmured, into her hair. "I'm sick and tired of the whole subject. Do you understand?"

"But, Alex – "

"You're getting yourself all worked up about nothing." Alex shrugged. "Oh, I admit he's besotted," he agreed. "I accept that he's behaving as if Miss Searle is the only woman in creation. He's haring off to Birmingham at all hours of the day and night. But what do you think happens when they meet?"

"I – "

"You don't know, so I'll tell you. They go to some dirty little flea-run of a private brothel. He rogers her till he's exhausted. He comes home and stays there contented until he wants her again."

Alex kissed Lalage's cheek. "Darling, Miss Searle is a whim. A passion which will wear itself out. He's had mistresses before. This particular trollop is merely the latest to take his fancy. She won't be the last."

"No, Alex. You're wrong. I – "

"Lally, he's notorious! At fifteen, he'd already had half a dozen chambermaids. God only knows how many bastards of his are gambolling about the estate. Ellis likes women, certainly. But he'll never restrict himself to one alone."

Again, Alex shrugged. "Oh, he might marry some day," he conceded. "But then, he'll take a wife of his own class. He'll sire a dozen children, and leave her to raise his brood while he goes his own way. You'll see."

But Lalage was not to be comforted. "He's doing it to spite me," she said. "That night when I suggested the three of us went to bed together, he was disgusted. He's paying me back."

"Don't be ridiculous." Alex laughed. "Ellis thought it was a stupid idea, that's all. He simply doesn't want you, or not in that way."

"But he loved me once! He – "

"He loves you still." Alex kissed her again. "So do I. Come to bed."

"I don't want to."

"You do."

"I said, I don't!" But, all the same, Lalage's eyes glittered. Her cheeks grew red.

Alex grinned. "Shall we do it in comfort?" he asked. "Shall we be gentle and loving, shall we kiss and hug and be kind? Or shall we play a different game?"

"Let's hurt each other." Now, Lalage's eyes grew huge. "Let's bite and scratch. Make each other cry."

"Very well." Alex grasped her shoulders. "Lie on the floor, then," he whispered. "No, not on the hearth rug. Lie down over there, on the cold, hard floor."

Lalage lay on her back, naked and bleeding. Scraped and grazed by rough wooden floorboards, she had long, jagged splinters in her shoulders, dirt and blood under her finger nails, and dust in her hair. Cold now, she wanted to cover herself. To sit wrapped in a blanket by the fire.

She lifted her hips. "Alex," she whispered. "Let me get up."

Alex groaned. But then, obligingly, he rolled away.

Lalage sat up. Gingerly, she touched herself.

She was very sore, but she was also dry. Bone dry.

Once again, Alex had done it his way, had withdrawn before any seed was spilled, had cheated her of what she wanted most.

Sitting by the fire, Lalage began to cry.

Chapter 13

By the time she and Ellis met again, Rebecca had passed a week of absolute misery. Even the factory hands, who were not on the whole a sensitive or imaginative set of men, observed Miss Searle was out of sorts. Unusually sharp, maddeningly hyper-critical, she countermanded her own orders, argued with people who agreed with her already, and found faults where none existed.

"It's the woman in 'er," averred Michael Cuthbertson profoundly, as he and Peter Crewe sat together in an outhouse which they regarded as their own private dining room, eating their mid-day meal. "Old Mr Searle, he should've wed a girl like her long before now. Put her in harness, like. Not left her to gallop about the meadow all by herself, without bit or bridle, lacking a man's control."

"I reckon she does very well." Unwilling to run his employer down – or at any rate, not while he owed her money – Peter Crewe ate the last fragment of his pasty. He wiped his face on the back of his hand. "Considerin'? she's just a lass, I think she manages the place handily. She's – "

"She's in need of a husband." Michael Cuthbertson grinned. "She's in heat! That's why she's so fidgety. Why nothin's right for her these days."

"Oh." Peter Crewe shrugged.

"If she had a man to advise 'er, look – to guide 'er by day and see she's properly served at night – well, she'd get on much better than she does now.

"A woman needs a firm hand. Don't care who she is,

she can't get on without a man to lead 'er. To show 'er the way. Law o' nature, that is."

"Is it, now?" Peter Crewe shrugged again. He got up. "Best get back," he muttered. "Don't want her goin' for me again. Had a bellyful this morning."

The two craftsmen walked into the polishing shop where, as if to underline the justice of Michael Cuthbertson's remarks, they found Rebecca snapping and snarling at one of the apprentices. "I'm telling you, George Warner," she cried, her voice shrill with irritation, "I'm telling you now, and the rest of you may listen! This is not a charity school for idle cripples, where the halt and the lame may while away their days. This is not an asylum, where the simple-minded may beguile their empty hours with a little light handicraft!

"This is a manufactory. I will have those who work here earn their money. Any who feel disposed to shirk may go and find other masters, for I will not pay good wages for slovenly work!"

Slamming the offending candlestick down on the bench, Rebecca turned to leave. Nervously, Michael Cuthbertson and Peter Crewe looked at her.

"Ah. Michael." Rebecca fixed him with an ice-blue glare. "George here is one of your little flock, is he not? Have you anything to say in his defence?"

Michael blinked. "Well, Miss Searle," he began, "I admit the boy's backward. He's maybe a little clumsy, too. But he's still learning. If he's allowed to go a bit slower, like, he'll make fewer mistakes. As Mr Searle always used to say, the boys – "

"Mr Searle?" Rebecca's blue eyes flashed. Losing her temper completely, she grabbed Michael by the collar. She shook him. "Don't you ever mention Mr Searle to me!" she cried.

Storming out of the workshop, she swept across the yard. The men heard her office door slam.

"It's as I said." Michael Cuthbertson went to his own bench. He picked up his hammer. "Needs a husband," he muttered. "Needs a man, to show her what's what. If she were my lass, I'd tan her backside good and proper. So help me I would!"

Rebecca sat her her office, grinding her teeth. Mr Searle, indeed! How dare that man invoke Jeremy Searle!

For a day or two after Lyddy had made her astonishing confession, Rebecca hardly gave her grandfather any thought at all. She'd been trying to digest the fact that she was Lyddy's daughter. Lyddy's illegitimate daughter, to boot.

But, by the Thursday of that traumatic week, Rebecca had begun to look back over her childhood. Then she thought of Jeremy Searle a great deal.

How could he have been so cruel? So deceitful? So mean? It wasn't just that *he* had lied and deceived. He had forced his wife and daughter to lie, too.

Although Rebecca could understand why Jeremy had not wanted the world to know his private family business, she could not forgive him for deceiving her. She hated him now. If she could have dug him up and spat at him, she'd have done it. Then smashed his headstone and desecrated his grave.

She decided to tell Ellis everything. Then, after he'd turned away in disgust, she would immerse herself in her work. She would never think of marriage again.

For now, the very idea of being a wife, of giving up her own identity to become some man's chattel, was abhorrent. Rebecca Searle would be a great manufacturer. The most ambitious, the most ingenious the town had ever seen. She would show Hollis and his friends what she was made of. If anyone tried to cross her, she would destroy him. She would leave him bruised and bleeding in the dirt.

When Ellis called again, that Sunday afternoon, Rebecca was waiting for him. Clad in her drabbest clothes, her hair was plainly dressed and her demeanour subdued. Her face wore an expression of solemnity better suited to a funeral, or a wake.

Returning her lover's greeting with the coolest of nods, she let herself out of the house. She took Ellis through the yard, out of the side gate, then led him down a lane full of high, blank-walled warehouses. Such dreary surroundings were the perfect setting for what she had to say.

Ellis did not care where he walked. Rebecca's coolness, however, did upset him. When he spoke, when he asked how she did, if she'd been well since he saw her last, she replied in sniffs, grimaces or monosyllabic murmurs. If she replied at all.

As they came to the end of the lane and began to cross a piece of waste ground on which spoil heaps festered and general household rubbish lay rotting all around, Rebecca found her voice at last. "Mr Darrow," she began, "I must – "

"Ellis, if you please." Encouragingly, Ellis smiled. "You've said my Christian name at least once. You could say it again, if you try. My dear Rebecca, since we last met, I have been so – "

"Mr Darrow!" Rebecca would not, could not look at him. "Please, don't talk like this! Will you hear what I have to say?"

"Well?" Ellis was disposed to indulge her. "What is it?"

"Since we met last," replied Rebecca carefully, "I have been told something which amazed me. It concerns the circumstances of my birth. Because of these, it is impossible for me to accept your offer of marriage."

"I see." Ellis did not seem the least bit perturbed. "So – what are these particular circumstances? More to the point, why do they so disastrously affect you and me?"

Rebecca grimaced. She cleared her throat. She might as well spell it out, she thought. Wrapping the sordid truth in fancy phrases would serve no purpose at all. "Since speaking to you last," she began, "I have learned who my parents were."

"Your parents?" Ellis shrugged. "Well, I – "

"Please, Mr Darrow! Don't interrupt me." Now, Rebecca was as pale as her snow-white neckerchief. "I had always assumed – been told, in fact – I was an orphan. That my mother had died in childbirth. That my father had deserted us, never to be heard of again.

"But, last week, I learned my mother is in fact the woman I've always called Aunt. Her name is Lyddy Searle. My father was Henry Lowell." Rebecca stared straight ahead. "The world," she continued doggedly, "has a host of names for the children of unions such as theirs. Names I do not care to repeat, and with which I hope you are too generous to insult me.

"All the same, you will wish to withdraw your offer of marriage forthwith. But, to spare you that embarrassment, I shall assume you never made it. I release you from any obligation. Consider your words unsaid."

Ellis was silent. To fill this yawning void, Rebecca felt obliged to talk on. "Mr Darrow," she cried, "I know all this must both shock and disgust you. That now you must hate the idea of even speaking to someone like me. I – "

"Don't be absurd!" Ellis glared at her. "Nothing has changed."

"What?" Astonished, Rebecca stared up at him. "Mr Darrow, did you understand me? I told you – "

"That your parents were Lydia Searle and Henry Lowell." Ellis looked grave. "I'm surprised you think I must be shocked by something which is common enough. I'm sorry you expect me to despise you for it. That you think I shall hold you responsible for the failings of others."

"Oh." Incredulous, Rebecca gaped. "All this week," she murmured, "all this awful, miserable week, every hour of every day, I've been worrying and fretting about this. I've wondered what I should tell you. How I should tell it. Yet you take it all so calmly, you – "

"That's probably because I know most of the facts already."

"You do?" Rebecca's head spun. She thought she might faint. To stop her falling, Ellis took her arm. Gratefully, she leaned against him. "How do you know?" she demanded, weakly. "Who told *you*?"

"No one told me. I worked it out for myself." Ellis covered Rebecca's hand with his. "When I was speaking to you once, you happened to mention that your aunt's name is Lyddy. I wondered then. Lyddy Searle is not a very ordinary name.

"My family has close connections with the Lowells. In fact, I spent much of my childhood on Henry Lowell's estate. I was staying at the house when he – well, when you were first known to have been conceived."

Ellis began to walk on. Rebecca walked too. Traversing the waste ground, they came to a block of warehouses with factories adjacent. They went up a narrow alley.

Now, Ellis slipped his arm around Rebecca's waist. "I forgot all about the Searles," he continued. "After all, they meant nothing to me. But then, years later, I learned Miss Searle's child had been a daughter."

"How did you discover that?"

"I simply heard of it." Lightly, Ellis touched Rebecca's face. Turning it towards him, he looked into her eyes. "My dear Rebecca," he cried, "I did not investigate you! I have never enquired into your affairs. Mere accidents made these things known to me."

"All the same, you knew." Stricken, Rebecca looked back at him. "So you thought me a liar. That I deliberately passed my mother off as my aunt. Now you assume I am dishonest and scheming. That when you first asked me to be your wife, I was too cowardly to confess. That only an unquiet conscience made me tell the truth today."

"No!" Ellis shook his head. "I assumed no such thing. I didn't consider it at all."

"Didn't you?"

"Well – I suppose I thought it strange to tell the story which you did. But I hoped – no, I was sure – you would eventually confide in me."

"I see." Rebecca wanted to weep. "I understand you perfectly now."

"Do you?" Ellis took her by the shoulders. "Rebecca," he said gravely, "please don't think I had doubts about your personal worth. I asked you to marry me because I love you. For all I care, your parents could be a pair of colliers. Or the King and Queen of England. It doesn't matter to me.

"But now, I don't merely love you. I admire and honour you, too. You are brave and you are honest – you have courage and compassion, as well. My darling Rebecca, say you'll be my wife!"

Rebecca said nothing. So Ellis took her in his arms, and held her.

They stood in silence for a minute. Two minutes. Then Ellis spoke again. "There's something you ought to know," he said. He stroked a stray lock of hair back under her bonnet. "You see, you're not the only one who needs to confess."

"Oh?" Rebecca looked up at him. What could Ellis have to tell? Did he have a mistress, perhaps? One whom he would not, or could not give up? Might he have a bastard child of his own? That would account for his indulgent attitude towards her own illegitimate state. "Well?" she demanded, bracing herself for the worst.

"Henry Lowell left you some money," was the reply.

"Indeed?" Rebecca kept her voice neutral. "I see."

"It is a substantial sum." Watching Rebecca carefully, Ellis was relieved beyond expression to see she was not impressed. No spasm of greed, nor even a glimmer of interest, flickered across her pretty face. "I assume it would be worth having," he said.

"Do you?" Rebecca shook her head. "Is this bequest in your brother-in-law's trust?"

"Yes, it is."

"Does he mean to make it over to me?"

"Well, he did." Ellis shrugged. "Just recently, however, he and my sister suffered a financial disaster. They lost most of their property. So now they are very poor. At present, they could not afford to pay you even a little of what you are owed. Perhaps they never will be able to." Ellis took a deep breath. "I don't think you'll press the point, will you?"

Rebecca bit her lip. "You say they are poor," she murmured. "How poor?"

Ellis shrugged again. "Poverty is always relative," he replied. "Alex Lowell grew up in luxury, you see. To be living in straitened circumstances is new to him. He doesn't know – "

"I doubt if he knows what poverty is!" Rebecca's blue eyes flashed. "You say he's poor. By that, I suppose you mean he cannot keep himself in fancy clothes. Or indulge himself at the table. Or play for high stakes at cards, or dice."

"Well – "

"Is he in rags?" Rebecca's eyes were like flints. "Is he starving?"

"No. But – "

"No doubt he feels he's stricken." Rebecca grimaced. "But then, he hasn't seen the poverty here. He does not know the orphans of this town. *He* hasn't stumbled over bundles of rags, which are actually human beings. Or seen the miserable creatures who huddle against my furnace wall on cold winter nights. Who creep into my factory yard to beg stale scraps, or a bucketful of cinders, or a few bits of coal."

Rebecca sniffed. "Never fear," she said. "I don't want his money. I don't want anything from the Lowells."

"No?" Relieved and delighted, Ellis hugged Rebecca close. "I hoped you'd say that."

"Did you? Why?"

"Because I think I understand you. That when I decided you were generous and good-hearted, I did not deceive myself. I – "

"I shall never sell my factory, you know." Rebecca met his eyes. "If I become your wife – if I become anyone's wife – my husband must not imagine I shall meekly hand all my property to him. To do with as he thinks fit."

"My dear Rebecca!" Ellis shook his head. "What sort of tyrant do you think I am? I offer you everything. My home, my land, my heart. Will you take it all? Give nothing in exchange?"

"If we marry, I shall be obliged to give you all that I have. The law will allow you to call everything of mine your own."

"Not necessarily. In our case, definitely not." Reassuringly, Ellis smiled. "We will see a lawyer. There will be a settlement. It will bind us both. Rebecca, I – "

"You mustn't think I'm mean. That I'm greedy." Rebecca felt guilty now. "You see, my grandfather left everything to me. I owe it to myself, to my children even, to see it prosper. If I marry, I must be the wife of a man who understands this. Who will not destroy everything for which my grandfather and I have worked."

"I understand." Ellis hugged her. "It sounds as if you might have changed your mind," he added. "Have you?"

"I – "

"Will you marry me?" Taking Rebecca's face between his hands, Ellis made her look at him. "Ladies love to torment," he whispered. "To tease. To keep men in suspense, to exercise their power. But all the same – "

"Ellis, that's not fair! Rebecca pushed his hands away. "Whatever I am, I'm no tormentor. I do not tease. I say what I mean. I always have."

"Then say you'll be my wife."

"I – "

"Say it!"

"I'll be your wife." Rebecca looked at him. "With all my heart I will. Ellis?"

"Yes?"

"Our wedding. How soon can it be?"

Ellis kissed her. "As soon as the banns are read," he replied.

Chapter 14

Lalage was furious. She cursed Ellis and his prospective bride roundly, wishing them nothing but misfortune and sorrow for the rest of their days. She found little comfort in the fact that the wedding was to be a hole and corner affair. She couldn't imagine Ellis wanting anything else.

Obliged by law to marry in an Anglican church, as opposed to a Presbyterian chapel, Rebecca insisted on a plain and simple ceremony devoid of idolatry or fuss. Ellis hadn't argued the point. Informed by Lalage that, if no persons of quality or fashion were invited, she wasn't coming either, he simply shrugged. He told her to do as she thought fit.

Married early one Tuesday morning in the plainest, lowest church in the whole of the West Midlands, Ellis and Rebecca had their marriage vows witnessed by Lyddy Searle and her good friend Matthew Harris. Feeling it incumbent upon him to attend, Alex was an uncomfortable and self-conscious groom's man.

After a simple wedding breakfast at Rebecca's old home, the new husband took his bride straight back to Easton Hall. Disgruntled tenants, who had stuffed and tippled for days when Lalage and Alex were married, lined the drive to see the new mistress go by. They waved and grinned, but there were no cheers or whoops of glee.

"They were hoping for a rather more lavish affair. They'd expected there to be feasting and carousing. Dancing on the village green." Taking Rebecca's hands in his, Ellis shook his head. "We'll have to give them all a good dinner, instead."

"Of course! We must see to it at once." Rebecca smiled. "Could we use one of the bigger barns? Would they all fit in? Dear Ellis! I want to know everyone on the estate. Every single person. I must meet them all."

A day or two before the wedding, Rebecca's boxes had been taken to her new home. Now, as the wedding coach bowled merrily along the avenue towards the Hall, her new maid was busily unpacking them, and exclaiming as she did so that the new Mrs Darrow's taste in underclothes was singular. She'd never known a lady who favoured things so plain.

"Oh, she don't need finery. She don't want frills." Detailed to assist the lady's maid, the under-housemaid began to fold bedgowns and shifts. These she would stow in the new cedarwood press. "She's like an angel," she declared. "Fair-haired. Blue-eyed. Her skin's like ivory. She's really beautiful."

The girl grinned. "I expect the master's longing to get her to bed. I'll bet he can't wait for dark."

"Don't be so vulgar, Molly." Finishing her unpacking, the lady's maid looked all round the bedchamber. "Well," she said complacently, "they can come up any time they please. It's all ready now."

"I'm sure we shall be the very best of friends. The closest of sisters, too." Welcoming this new sister into the family, Lalage treated her with a gracious condescension which, at first, Rebecca found extremely unsettling. But she was determined to love her sister-in-law, so she tried very hard to adapt.

She succeeded. A fortnight into her honeymoon, the new Mrs Darrow was receiving small gifts and extravagant compliments every bit as graciously as her sister-in-law could offer them. She decided that although her husband's sister was undeniably affected, very silly and most unattractively overdressed, Lalage was probably good at heart.

So, like a grub burrowing into a wholesome apple, Lalage wormed her way into Rebecca's affections. When she was comfortably established, she would sit down to plot.

"Rebecca! How charming!" Charming herself in blond lace and pale blue satin, the following Sunday morning Lalage cornered Rebecca in the drawing room. She exclaimed and complimented until Rebecca blushed scarlet. Then she turned to her husband. "Alex!" She dragged him across the floor. "Darling, do look at Rebecca! Did you ever see anything so lovely?"

"What?" Alex seldom saw anyone even half as lovely as his wife. He was never attracted to pasty-faced blondes. But, obligingly, he glanced in Rebecca's general direction. Seeing she was simply dressed, in a pink striped gown which suited her very well, he smiled. "She looks very pretty," he said. He took out his watch. "Lally, what's become of Ellis? He's very late."

"No, he isn't. It's only a quarter to. Don't fuss." Lalage took Rebecca's hand. "Shall we go outside?" she suggested. "I told them to bring the coach round here. If we stand on the sweep, we can take the air while we wait."

"Ellis said something about walking to church." Rebecca looked towards the door. "My dear Lalage, a five minutes' walk – "

"A walk?" Scornfully, Lalage laughed. "Oh, my dearest sister! The Darrows never walk to church. Whatever would the parish think of us?"

"All the same, Ellis did say – "

"What did Ellis say?" Coming into the room, Ellis looked from his wife to his sister. "Well, Lally? It's a fine morning, so I suggest we walk to church. If we go across the meadow and up the lane – "

"We will arrive muddied to the knees and frozen to the marrow." Lalage frowned in distaste. "Oh, Ellis!" she wailed now, her voice high in mock despair. "Your breeches! Your hat!"

"What's wrong with them?"

"They make you look like a farmer. A tenant farmer, at that." Eyeing her brother's plain black coat and drab fustian breeches, the elegant Mrs Lowell shook her head. "I had hoped your wife might civilise you," she said. "But I see now that it is not to be. Whatever Rebecca may say, you will have your own way still."

Now Simmons came in, to announce the carriage was at the door. Ellis frowned. But then he shrugged. "Oh, very well," he said. "Ride if you wish." He offered Rebecca his arm. "Will you walk with me?" he asked.

Rebecca put her hand on his sleeve. "Of course, my dear Ellis," she replied.

They watched the carriage bowl away. "Would you have preferred to ride?" asked Ellis.

"No, not at all," Rebecca replied.

"Good." Ruefully, Ellis grimaced. He sighed. "I know things are sometimes difficult," he said. "I'm aware that it's awkward for you, living here. Adapting to a completely different way of life."

"I don't find it *all* difficult." Rebecca smiled up at him. "There are certain things about Easton Hall which I love."

"All the same." Ellis smiled in return. "You don't have to come to church, you know. If you wish, we could drive over to Hensham. To attend the Presbyterian chapel there."

"That won't be necessary. Not at all." Rebecca shrugged. "I belong here now. So I shall attend the church on this estate."

"As you wish "

"I do wish it." Rebecca shook her head. "I have searched my conscience. I've prayed for guidance, and received it. I'm doing the right thing, I'm sure."

Mrs Ellis Darrow kept her controlling interest in the factory, visiting at least twice a week. Usually, Ellis went with her. Soon, he began to understand the toy trade.

But with understanding came the desire to be involved. To interfere.

"You know, Becky," he began, as he and she drove home through the darkness of a winter afternoon, "you *must* get a manager. I need you at Easton now. I can't have you spending whole days in Birmingham, when you might be at home with me."

"Ellis, when I agreed to marry you, I told you quite plainly – "

"That you wouldn't give up the factory. I'm not asking you to. I'm merely suggesting you should appoint a manager, who will make decisions and protect your interests when you can't be there."

"Good managers are as rare as unicorns." Frowning, Rebecca bit her lower lip. "I am the manager," she added, crossly. "*I* make the decisions. I – "

"Why don't you put Miss Searle in charge?"

"Aunt Lyddy?" Rebecca stared. Then she laughed out loud. "Oh, Ellis! That's absurd. Why, she's ignorant. She's old."

"Nonsense. She's not yet forty." Ellis shook his head. "She may not be well-educated, but she's very sensible. Clever, even. She has your best interests at heart. I think she'd be ideal."

"Do you?" Rebecca grimaced. "Ellis, forgive me, but I must speak plainly now. You're meddling in matters you don't understand. Allow me to manage my manufactory as I think fit – and, in return, I shall not criticise the way in which you run your estate."

"Speak to your aunt about taking over."

"No!" Rebecca folded her arms. "Ellis, it's a ridiculous scheme. One which will end in disaster for all concerned."

"Very well." Ellis sighed. "I'll speak to her myself."

"Ellis, you mustn't. You can't!"

"My dear Rebecca, I shall make no proposals which I have not previously discussed with you. But you must at least consider what I say." Complacently, Ellis smiled.

"I'm sure we shall eventually reach an amicable agreement here."

"Are you, indeed?" Turning away from him, Rebecca stared out of the window. But, able to see nothing but the black silhouettes of winter trees made eerie by the flickering light from the coachlamps, she lapsed into contemplative silence.

Long before Ellis had brought the subject up, Rebecca had indeed been wondering how she was to combine the role of factory manager with that of squire's lady. She'd soon realised it was an impossible task. There was simply too much to do. A series of sleepless nights, turning various expedients over in her mind, brought her no nearer a solution to the problem. Tonight was no different in that respect.

The following morning, Ellis told her he and his land agent would be riding over to a tenant farm some seven miles distant, so would be away from home until supper time. "Have a rest today, my dear," he advised, as he kissed her goodbye. "You look tired."

Rebecca ordered the carriage and drove into Birmingham, instead.

Hearing wheels on the cobblestones, Lyddy came out to greet the visitor. Out of the office, not out of the house. "Rebecca!" Delighted, she beamed. "Did you leave something behind yesterday?"

"No." Rebecca kissed Lyddy's cheek. "I merely wished to talk to you again. That's all."

"Well, then. Talk away." Gaily, Lyddy laughed. "My time is yours, after all."

Now, for the first time in months, Rebecca looked closely at Lyddy Searle. She was struck by the changes these few months had made. For a start, Lyddy was smiling – she smiled a good deal these days. Also, there were touches of colour about her attire.

Formerly clad only in penitential browns, greys and drabs, now Lyddy sported blues, pinks and reds. Today, a bright blue neckerchief adorned her shoulders. A pink ribbon was threaded through the bodice of her gown.

Lyddy took Rebecca into the house. On the table were flowers. Fresh, hot-house flowers. "Where did you get those?" asked Rebecca.

"Oh, a friend sent them over. Yesterday evening." Lyddy blushed. "Tea, Becky? You look as if you could do with a cup."

Lyddy always had the tea things ready. Now she picked up the kettle and poured hot water on to the leaves. "You're looking very pretty today," she observed. "Very sweet indeed. Is Mr Darrow well?"

"Ellis is in excellent health." Rebecca sipped her tea. She remembered now. Yesterday, while she went round the workshops, Lyddy and Ellis had been alone together for a full half hour. Maybe more. "Have you and Ellis been discussing me?" she asked. "Talking about me, behind my back?"

"Of course not!" Colouring, Lyddy shook her head. "But yesterday, he did say – "

"The factory needs a manager."

"Well, yes."

"He thinks it should be you."

"Oh, no!" Looking Rebecca full in the face, Lyddy's countenance was open. Her blue eyes were perfectly candid – there was no guile in them at all. "But he did say he was concerned about you. That your duties at Easton were numerous, and he felt you needed – "

"A manager. Quite."

For a moment or two, both women were silent. Each sipped her tea, and considered. Then Lyddy reached across to touch Rebecca's sleeve. "I could do it, you know," she said, mildly. "I could take charge."

"*You*, Aunt?" Rebecca put down her cup. "You, manage a great manufactory?"

"Why not?" Lyddy shook Rebecca's arm. "Over the years, I've seen all that goes on here. I understand the processes. I know how things are done. When you were first married, who managed the place then? Who oversaw the manufactory for at least a fortnight, who – "

"I don't deny you could cope for a mere two weeks. Anyone could. But – "

"Ask me anything." Lyddy was on her feet now. "Test my fitness for the task. We'll go round the workshops, shall we? You can examine me in detail then. I may surprise you!"

So, Rebecca and Lyddy made a tour of the factory. Here, Lyddy displayed such perfect grasp of the processes and profound understanding of the work in hand that Rebecca was astonished.

"Miss Searle?" Michael Cuthbertson spoke now – not to Rebecca, but to Lyddy herself. "I've three boys idle this morning. Shall they go and help the furnacemen, or shall I give them instruction in soldering? I've finished the task I was working on myself."

Accustomed to giving orders, Rebecca was about to reply. But then she realised Michael was not even looking at her. She glanced at Lyddy.

"Take two of them into the workshop, and let one go and help work the bellows. Turn and turn about." Lyddy looked at the boys in question. "Henry here has some experience of soldering, has he not?"

"Yes indeed, Miss Searle. But David and Jacob – "

"Have not. In that case, take them for the morning, then call Henry to join you at noon."

Seated in Rebecca's office, Lyddy started to open the day's post. "Well, Becky?" she asked, as she smoothed letters, sorting them into separate heaps of bills, orders and general enquiries which required more detailed attention. "Did I disappoint you?"

"You amazed me." Always candid, Rebecca smiled. "You have the respect of the men. You know more about the apprentices than I do myself."

Gratified, Lyddy blushed. "So?"

"I think you'd be an excellent overseer. For the time being, anyway."

"Temporarily, you mean. Until you find someone more suitable." Lyddy bit her lip. "You'd really prefer a man to be in charge."

"Oh, no. But I must consider – "

"What about Michael Cuthbertson?" Lyddy spiked the last letter on to its pile. "He and I could do the job between us."

"Could you?"

"Certainly." Lyddy shrugged. "I know he's a rough sort of man, but he does know his trade. He's honest, and the other men like him. Becky, it would be as well to have a man like Michael firmly bound to *us*."

"Bound to us?"

"Yes." Lyddy was solemn now. "They're always murmuring, you know. Among themselves, that is. Even here, they read pamphlets, they discuss policy, they plot and they scheme. After work, they attend meetings. Those clubs and friendly societies – they're just a cover for sedition! Mark my words, Becky. One day, there'll be trouble."

"But what have they to complain of?" Rebecca frowned. "Their work is hard, I grant you. But I pay them well. I'm no slave driver, they could never accuse me of that."

"No, indeed. They think well of the Searles. They've no quarrel with you or me." Lyddy sighed. "It's the system they hate. They want no more divisions, no more distance between master and man. So, trust me. Speak to Michael. Offer him the chance to be a manager, answerable only to you and to me."

"I'll consider it." Rebecca stood up. "I'll think about it, and let you know in a day or two."

"Good." Opening a ledger, Lyddy made an entry. "Shall you stay to dinner?" she enquired.

"I don't think so." Rebecca pulled on her gloves.

"I must get back to Easton. A builder is coming this afternoon, to look at some damage to the roof. I promised Ellis I'd be there. To speak to him."

She glanced round the office. "It's not as if I'm needed here," she said.

So, Ellis had his way. Lyddy Searle took over the management of the factory. She did very well. So much so that Rebecca gave up all talk of temporary measures and stop-gaps. Lyddy was up to the job. Ellis had been right.

But husband and wife did not always see eye to eye. Where his personal health and safety were concerned, Ellis was so careless that Rebecca wondered how he'd managed to live so long.

One rainy morning, in the very depths of the coldest, most sodden February imaginable, he went out riding. He came home soaked through. His coat was a saturated dishrag and his boots were waterlogged entirely. He refused to go and change. He wanted his dinner *now*.

"Ellis, you're drenched." Meeting him at the table, Rebecca stared. He was literally steaming. "Go and get changed," she said. "I'll tell Simmons to put the meal back, until three or four."

"You'll do no such thing." Ellis sat down. Pushing wet hair out of his eyes, he broke bread. "Simmons!" he cried. "Where the devil is the fellow?"

"But Ellis, you'll take cold." Unable to believe her husband could deliberately court chills, fevers or worse, Rebecca frowned. "My dear, you must get out of those wet things."

"Oh?" Ellis met her eyes. "I am not your child," he said, coldly. "Nor am I one of your factory hands. I am your husband – your master, if you like. Do not presume to tell *me* what to do."

"You will take a fever!" Rebecca wanted to hit him. "Dear Ellis! Please be sensible."

"Ah, Simmons. At last." Ellis scowled at his butler. "Well, come along. Don't be all day."

Ellis ate his dinner. Then he fell asleep before the fire. By evening, he was sneezing violently. The resulting chill kept him indoors for the rest of the week.

"I can't think how I picked this up," he grumbled, sniffing miserably and rubbing his aching head. "I hope I'm not taking the smallpox."

"You have a slight fever. That's all." Rebecca could not help but smile. "You'll probably survive."

The factory made Ellis richer. Involvement in trade and industry opened his eyes to commercial possibilities he'd never previously considered. Rebecca's business acumen sharpened her husband's wits.

A year or so after their wedding, Ellis had what he thought was a very good idea. Discussing it with Rebecca, he received her permission to go ahead. Then, acting in what he thought were Alex's and Lalage's best interests, he opened negotiations for the purchase of the Lowells' former home.

In a matter of weeks, it was his. Alex's old home was expensive to maintain – and the speculator who'd bought it, finding his present tenant had an intention to purchase property in the north of England, decided to cut his losses and sell up.

The mortgage, which Ellis raised now, was so large that he was obliged to find another tenant. It would be at least ten years before he could afford to let Alex and Lalage repossess the place. But he felt it was far better to have the house in the family than let it be sold again, to another stranger.

He'd signed the purchase order quite happily, and took on the commitment with a light heart. Alex and Lalage had suffered greatly when their house was sold. "But one day," Ellis told Rebecca, "God willing, I shall give it back to them."

"Have you told them so?"

"No. Not yet." Ellis shrugged. "I *hope* my income will remain sufficient to pay off the mortgage. But I'd be a fool to bank on it. I told Alex I regarded it as an investment. He accepted that."

Indeed, Alex heard of Ellis's latest venture with absolute indifference. "If he wants to saddle himself with that old barn, it's his affair," he said.

But Lalage was furious. Suspecting deep plots and subtle manoeuvrings, especially on Rebecca's part, she ground her teeth and stamped her feet in rage. "She wants it for herself!" she howled. "She already has my brother. Now, she means to infest my home!"

"Don't be silly. She's perfectly happy at Easton." Alex shrugged. "As Ellis says, it's an investment. Merely that. Letting the old place will provide him with some extra income. But if in due course he wants to live there, why shouldn't he?"

"Because it's not his house!" Recalling the splendour amidst which she had once dwelt, Lalage began to cry. "Alex, your father built that place for the Lowells. Not the Darrows. *You* belong there!"

"It's only bricks and mortar. Not a holy shrine." Yawning, Alex picked up a newspaper. "Lally, don't upset yourself. Not over a house."

"Your house. Not that interloping bastard's."

Alex sighed. "It's not mine now," he said. "Nor ever will be again."

Alex's house might be lost to her forever, but Lalage was determined to realise one ambition. She would certainly have a child.

But it appeared the Lowells were destined never to become parents. No child was even conceived, let alone brought to term. Obsessed by her desire to have a baby, Lalage often woke Alex in the middle of the night, or roused him in the small hours of the morning, to do his duty by her.

But nothing happened. Hope was born and flourished

– but then it died. Each twenty eight day cycle ended in the same bloody epilogue. Lalage looked for someone to blame.

"I don't hold back on you. I haven't done so for months now. It's not my fault you don't conceive." As sullen as the dismal winter's morning, Alex scowled. "You blame me for everything these days."

"Not absolutely everything." Having just got out of bed, Lalage was wandering naked around the bedroom. "But there's no one else to blame for this."

"I suppose not." Alex sniffed. "Put on your dressing gown," he said. "You'll take cold, walking about like that."

Lalage sat down on a hard chair. She picked at her finger nails. "Give me a child," she muttered.

"What?" Mirthlessly, Alex laughed. "Now?"

"Yes, if you like!" Lalage slid from her chair. Lying spreadeagled on the cold wooden floorboards, she narrowed her eyes at him. "Well, Alex?" she demanded. "Surely you don't need a map?"

Alex looked at her. He grimaced in disgust. "Get up at once," he said.

"Can't you do it any more?" Lalage licked one finger. Suggestively, she stroked herself. "You know you want me," she whispered. "Darling, look! I'm doing most of the work. You play just a little part. Towards the end."

Alex yawned and turned away. "It's nearly time for breakfast," he said.

He rang the bell.

They went downstairs together. While Alex mended the fire, Lalage made tea. Then they sat down, as companionably as any husband and wife in the universe.

Opening an envelope by his plate, Alex took out a letter. It was accompanied by a banker's draft. "Money," he observed. He handed it to his wife. "Use it wisely, Lalage," he advised. "Use it well."

"*Her* money." Lalage looked at the bank draft in her

hand. "How long before he tells her, I wonder? Alex, how long?"

But, very gradually, the terror that Ellis might tell his wife all about Henry Lowell's bequest receded. Now, the far more dreadful fear that Rebecca would produce children and shut the Lowells out of Alex's family home forever, condemning Alex and Lalage to poverty for the rest of their lives, began to gnaw at Lalage's very vitals.

She'd disliked Rebecca on sight. Being perfectly well-bred, however, she hid her loathing absolutely, being always civil and on occasions positively charming towards Ellis's wife. She instructed Rebecca in the polite arts both of making tea and presiding over a genteel afternoon party. In her more generous moments, she was relieved to observe the bastard was not entirely beyond hope of refinement. In time, she might even be knocked into some semblance of a lady.

"Rebecca," said Lalage, as they took tea together one afternoon, "now you are married, I feel you should cease to visit that factory. You have a manager. You have a husband to advise the fellow. It's hardly necessary for *you* to be concerned with affairs of trade."

Rebecca shook her head. "On the contrary, dear sister. I intend to concern myself with them for many years yet. My aunt and foreman do indeed oversee the daily running of the place. But you must understand that any business of that size needs a firm, guiding hand."

"But now you are a wife, that hand should be your husband's." Graciously, Lalage smiled. "Dear Rebecca! You are a lady now. Ladies do not soil their hands with commerce."

Rebecca laughed out loud. Lalage winced. A lady never laughed, not in company. She merely nodded. Or, if her teeth were good, she smiled. But worse was to come. "Would you like to see over the factory?" asked Rebecca now. "I could take you there myself. You could see the workshops. Meet the men. You might find the processes very interesting. Such an outing would be an education for you."

Lalage's face froze. "I don't think so," she managed to croak, at last. "I have no desire to observe the ways of the manufacturing classes." Rising to her feet, she left the room.

The day Ellis remarked, quite casually and as if it were the most natural thing in the world, that Rebecca was to have a baby, Lalage fainted. Her face grew ashen, she gripped the arms of her chair, and her breathing almost stopped. For a few seconds, she lost consciousness completely.

When she opened her eyes again, the first thing she saw was the mother-to-be. Leaning over her, loosening her gown, the creature was actually touching her. She nearly fainted a second time.

"Simmons? Fetch a cordial." Rebecca rubbed Lalage's cold hands. "Stand back, Ellis. She needs air."

Pleading indisposition, Lalage went home. She left Alex at Easton Hall. "I don't want you to come," she hissed, as he handed her into Ellis's coach. "Betty will look after me far better than you can."

Taking her mistress upstairs, Lalage's maid undressed her, put her to bed and waited for the storm to break. She then sat impassive by the bedside while Lalage screamed and cursed, while she bit her lips, tore her hair and ripped her tear-stained handkerchief to shreds.

"I'll kill her!" wept Lalage. "I'll kill her. I will! I'll cut her throat. I'll drink her blood!"

"Hush, madam. Don't say things like that." In Lalage's service for at least the past three years, Betty was used to her rages and well aware that she often said things she could not possibly mean. She stroked her mistress's hair. "You'll have a child of your own one day," she soothed. "God willing, you'll have several."

"I'll never have any. Ever!" Covering her face, Lalage burst into tears again. But gradually the sobs abated. She groped for her maid's hand. "Betty?"

"Yes, madam?"

"Look at me." Pushing damp, bedraggled hair from her shoulders, Lalage glared with fevered eyes. "Look closely, look well. Am I hideous, do you think?"

"No, madam. Of course you're not."

"Answer me honestly, girl." Lalage tugged at the tapes of her nightgown. Pulling the garment over her head, she threw it off. "Look again," she snapped. "Look here, and here. Am I foul? Repulsive? So ugly that I am not fit to breed?"

"No, madam. You're not foul." Betty sighed. "But you're far too thin."

"What of that?"

"Well, if you were to eat more – if you made a good meal now and then instead of always picking at your food – you would grow robust. Then, you would be even comelier than you are now."

"You think I should grow fat. Like the bastard."

"I think that while you are so frail, it would be hard indeed to conceive."

"Ah." Stretching out her arms, Lalage saw for herself how slender they were. Looking down the length of her body, she realised her ribs could be counted. Her hip-bones jutted sharply. Her belly was concave. Indeed, she was much too thin. "Mr Lowell likes me," she whispered. "Alex thinks I'm beautiful."

"Madam, you are." Betty stood up. "I'll fetch you some chocolate," she said. Picking up the discarded nightgown, she held it out. "Let me put this on back on," she urged. "It's cold in here. You're bound to take a chill."

"Give me my glass." Lalage held out her hand. "My looking glass, I want it. Give it to me!"

Betty handed it to her.

"Now go away." Lalage began to study herself. "I'll ring when I want you again."

By the time Alex came home, Lalage had been asleep for hours. Well versed in the lore of sedative draughts, Betty had doctored her mistress's chocolate. When she was sure Lalage was sleeping soundly, she covered her with a great heap of bedclothes, drew the curtains against the winter chill, and had Caspar make a great fire in the grate.

"You had a pleasant evening?" Roused by her husband, Lalage rubbed her eyes. She glared at him. "You spent a convivial few hours with your sister and your friend?"

"I came away early. I was concerned about you." Alex took his wife's hand. "Betty told me you were feverish," he added. "But you seem cool now."

"She put something in my chocolate." Lalage sniffed. "She's a witch, Alex. Did you realise that? She knows all about me. Do you know what she said?"

"No. What?"

"She thinks I'm too thin to conceive. That's the problem. If I ate better – "

"Perhaps she's right." Alex nodded agreement. "Yes, maybe some pies and pasties would do you good."

"Alex?"

"Yes, darling?"

"Do you love me?"

"Of course I do." Alex sighed. "Why do you doubt it?"

"If I were fat and hearty-looking, would you love me more?"

"Oh, God!" Wretchedly, Alex shook his head. "I don't want you to be *fat*!" he cried. "You're lovely as you are. But it wouldn't hurt you to be just a little heavier."

"You never kiss me now." Picking at a loose thread in her cuff, Lalage let a tear roll down her nose and splash on to the crumpled linen sheet. "You'll come to bed tonight, read for ten minutes, then fall asleep over your book. You don't care if I lie awake, lonely and unhappy."

"Sweetheart, I didn't know you lay awake, unhappy." Taking her face between his hands, Alex kissed her. "Lally, shall I come to bed now?"

"If you wish. Don't do so just to oblige me."

"I'd like to come."

Alex undressed. Taking Lalage in his arms, he kissed and lulled her into contentment. Tonight, he did not hold back at all. "There, darling," he said afterwards. "Do you doubt I love you now?"

Lalage began to cry again. "No," she wept. "But – oh, Alex! Everything's so horrible these days! Why can't we be happy again?"

"I don't see why we should be sad." Alex kissed her soft, red lips. "We've had a rather difficult time, I agree. But I'm sure everything will be better now. No, don't put your nightgown on. I'll keep you warm."

"Will you?"

"Yes." Alex hugged her. "It's nice, to feel you next to me."

So, curled round one another, Alex and Lalage closed their eyes and drifted off to sleep.

Lalage made the best of things. She smiled charmingly, asked after Rebecca's health, and cautioned her against over-exertion. Watching anxiously for changes in Rebecca's figure, she saw that her sister-in-law's well-rounded bosom was becoming even larger. Her generous hips grew broader still.

As Rebecca's girth increased, Lalage's hatred of her blossomed. The poisonous flowers of jealousy opened, and scented all the air.

Chapter 15

"Mrs Darrow, would you kindly look over last year's accounts some time soon?" Bobbing a curtsey, the housekeeper offered the leather-bound ledgers for Rebecca's inspection. "His honour told me to bring all the household books to you," she explained. "He was sure you'd wish to see them."

"Ah. Yes. Thank you." Seated at Ellis's desk, Rebecca was busy with some paperwork concerning the Birmingham factory. Now, she looked up. "Leave the books here," she said. "I'll glance at them when I have time. But I'm sure everything is in order?"

"I hope so, madam." The most meticulous of managers, Mrs Redman folded her mittened hands. "Your ladyship won't find anything amiss. I'll stake my life on that."

"Good." Rebecca picked up her pen. "I'll let you have the books back by supper time," she promised.

As the door closed behind the housekeeper, Rebecca shook her head. When she had first been addressed as your ladyship, or your honour, she had suspected sarcasm. But, very soon, she realised Ellis was his honour, too. The indoor servants, the tenants, the peasantry, even the farmers who rented his land, all referred to him thus.

Rebecca finished her letter to a toy merchant. Then, since the cramping backache from which she now suffered all the time tended to become even worse if she sat down for an hour or more, she stood up. She walked towards the window.

This window looked out over the gardens to the front of

the house. Now, Rebecca saw Lalage. Loitering by some ornamental planters, she was smirking at Alex Lowell, who sauntered across the gravel sweep. Observing the whip in his right hand, Rebecca deduced he'd been out riding.

As he glanced towards his wife, he noticed Rebecca at the window. Solemnly, he raised a hand in greeting.

Politely, Rebecca nodded. Then, frowning, she looked away. For Alex Lowell upset her.

Why did he spend so much time at Easton Hall? Just recently, it seemed he was there every day. Almost every single meal was eaten under his scrutiny. Watching Rebecca – judging her, perhaps – his pale blue eyes roamed freely over her face and body. But, if she ever met that baleful gaze, he looked sharply away. Sometimes, he even shuddered.

He hardly ever spoke to her. If directly addressed, he replied as briefly as possible, then turned away. For Ellis's sake, Rebecca would have been happy to conciliate Alex Lowell. But it appeared Alex had no desire to be friends with her.

"Becky, my dear? You're very thoughtful today." Shaking out his table napkin, Ellis nodded to Simmons and the footman to serve dinner. "What's bothering you?"

"What? Oh – nothing." Jolted out of her anxious contemplation of Alex Lowell's bland, blond features, Rebecca shook her head. "My mind was quite empty."

"That, I can't believe." Ellis broke bread. "Well, now we have your attention, tell us what you think of our plan. Since the weather is so fine, we wondered if a couple of days' rambling might not be the very thing?"

"Rambling?" repeated Rebecca, blankly.

"Yes." Ellis smiled. "We shan't go very far afield," he went on, for now Rebecca looked doubtful. "We thought we might take you to Warwick. We'll show you the castle, which is very splendid – you'll admire it, I'm sure. Then we could go on to Stratford. Put up at an inn, maybe. Spend two or three days there."

"Do say you'll come." Lalage's sharp, clear voice chimed in on Rebecca's left. Grabbing at her sister-in-law's hand, she held it. "It's taken Alex weeks to talk Ellis into this."

"I see." Rebecca shrugged. "Ellis, can you spare the time?"

"Of course he can." Lalage tossed her black curls. "You and I will ride in the new carriage," she said. "The men will go on horseback, I expect. But we two shall travel in style."

"Ah." Rebecca met her husband's gaze. "When did you mean to set out?" she asked.

"On Tuesday." Reassuringly, Ellis smiled again. "You won't find it arduous, I promise you. Such easy travelling as this will not harm the child."

They drove to Warwick and took rooms in a pleasant, half-timbered coaching inn. Taken to see the castle, Rebecca wondered aloud what such a magnificent place could be like inside. So, always anxious to please her, Ellis asked if the family were in residence. Told the earl and countess were abroad, he enquired if the housekeeper could show their party round. The housekeeper proved delighted to oblige.

Rebecca stared, amazed. Such wall-hangings! Such massive, splendid plate! Such enormous, lofty apartments, so thickly carpeted and draped – so much luxury, in fact, that it made the blacksmith's grand-daughter feel quite faint. She concluded her tour looking solemn, and thoughtful indeed.

"I hated it all," she murmured, when Ellis asked what she had liked best. "Here, in this very town, people go hungry. Some even die for lack of shelter and food. While there is so much want and starvation at their very gates, it's wicked to live in the style which the earl and countess do."

"Well – where would your factory be, if the aristocracy had no money to spend?" Ellis took his wife's hand. "Your own workmen are engaged in the manufacture of toys and trinkets for the rich. Searle's finely-wrought snuff-boxes and pretty candlesticks all help contribute towards the sinful luxury of the age."

"Ellis, that's not so!" Rebecca stared at him. "My factory makes plain buttons. Steel buckles. We strike tradesmen's tokens. We may help to make life easier for ordinary people – but we do not pander to the whims of earls or dukes. We've never sought the patronage of the great!"

"No." Ellis had been teasing, but now he saw Rebecca was really upset. So he changed the subject.

The sun came out. Rebecca's mood lightened. Unable to hear Alex Lowell and Lalage muttering about radicals, levellers and revolutionaries in general, and low-born bastards in particular, she looked and listened with great interest as Ellis pointed out the landmarks of the pretty mediaeval town.

Reaching the market, she bargained for some ribbons, inspected fat, yellow cheeses and chatted to a farmer's wife, who sold her a bunch of sweet herbs. As the sun shone down, Rebecca's pretty face glowed too.

But then, walking past Lord Leycester's Hospital, she had to negotiate some narrow steps. There, she tripped.

She was sure she'd been pushed. Even as Ellis caught her arm, even as she heard him exclaim and ask if she were hurt, she knew Alex Lowell had nudged her. For all his politely concerned smile, for all his offer of his arm to lean on, it was as much as she could do to bite her lip. To stop herself crying out, "you pushed me! I know you did. Don't grin like that, you hypocrite. You meant to hurt me just then!"

She stared at him. But Alex's blue eyes were opaque. His smile did not waver. Turning away, she leaned on Ellis's arm, flushed and upset.

Later, back at the inn, when Alex and Lalage had gone

to their own room and Ellis and Rebecca were alone in theirs, Ellis took his wife's hands in his. "What's the matter?" he asked, his voice low with concern. "Were you hurt this afternoon?"

"Hurt?" Rebecca shrugged. "What do you mean?"

"When you tripped. Did you twist your ankle, maybe?"

"No." Rebecca forced a smile. "I'm a little tired, that's all. I think I'll go to bed."

"I'll have the girl make you some chocolate." Ellis let her go. "I shall take a turn about the streets, breathe in a little night air. Then I'll join you."

When Ellis finally came to bed, Rebecca was still awake. Sitting up against her pillows, she was obviously brooding, and frowned as he walked in. "There *is* something wrong," said Ellis. "Is it what I said about the factory? I was teasing, you know."

"It's not that."

"Then won't you tell me what is bothering you?"

"It's your brother-in-law." Rebecca looked down at her hands. "He frightens me."

"Old Alex?" Ellis shook his head. "Why's that?"

"He stares at me."

"Is that all?"

"It's enough." Miserably, Rebecca sniffed. "I don't know what he means by it."

"He thinks you're pretty. Worth staring at." Reassuringly, Ellis smiled. "He means no harm."

"He doesn't like me."

"Why do you think that?" Taking her in his arms, Ellis hugged her. "What's he done? What has he said to you?"

"Nothing. But he hates me, all the same. So, if Alex dislikes me, I expect Lalage – "

"You're being ridiculous now." Ellis kissed her cheek. "You're with child," he murmured. "Women in your condition often have strange fancies. Absurd ideas. Lalage loves you dearly – she's told me so time and again. Alex has no reason to dislike you."

"All the same, he – "

"You cannot pretend he avoids your company. Or criticises, or slights you. If he stares, he means no harm. He's rather near-sighted, as it happens. I doubt if he realises how disconcerting his gaze can be."

"Maybe not." Drawing away, Rebecca looked into his eyes. "I'm safe with you, aren't I? *You* love me?"

"Of course I do. I've loved you from the moment we met."

Far from hating her, Alex found his half-sister quite likeable. Of course she was vulgar, of course she was ill-bred, of course her horrible Birmingham accent and coarse expressions grated unmercifully on his refined sensibilities. But Rebecca had a sparkle and vitality which he found rather charming, and he thought she was, on the whole, quite a dear little thing.

She was pretty, too. Not beautiful, of course. She was too well-rounded and healthy-looking to be a beauty. But she was a sweet little armful. Dark, slender women were Alex's fancy, and Rebecca's blonde, milkmaid looks did not attract him at all – but he could see why Ellis was besotted. Rebecca looked edible. Making love to a woman like that, thought Alex, must be like eating a perfect, ripe peach.

But as for Lalage, she abused the peach all the time, moaning about her morning, noon and night. "I do wish she'd make more effort with her hair," she muttered, as she and Alex stepped from Ellis's carriage one Sunday morning. Collected early so that the four of them could go to church together, the Lowells had been obliged to rise betimes. Alex was still yawning and rather dozy. He would have preferred to stay in bed.

Now, Lalage watched Rebecca and her brother crossing the wide lawns which lay to the west of the Hall. She wondered where they'd been. Rebecca wore a cloak and stout shoes. Ellis was clad in his usual outdoor rig of boots and a heavy frieze great-coat, so he looked more like a parson than ever. She pinched Alex's arm. "Just look at her," she hissed. "What an absolute fright!"

Alex rubbed his arm. He grimaced. "I wish you wouldn't nip me like that," he complained. "You make quite a bruise. *I* think Rebecca looks charming. That simple style of dress becomes her very well."

"It suits her simple heart and simple mind." Lalage glared at him. "So I suppose you think *I* am too fine? Far too elaborate for your exquisite taste?"

"You're perfectly lovely. You always are." Looking at his wife, Alex saw that today she was dressed from head to foot in violets, mauves and purples. Her black hair was elaborately coiled and plaited. Her milky complexion was flawless, and as pale as the ivory combs at her temples – or perhaps even paler still. Huge, dark eyes burned like glowing coals in her beautiful face. Her neck was an alabaster pillar. Her shoulders were white as swan's wings.

Her full skirts billowed and rustled in satin cascades. Her sleeves, by contrast, were cut very narrow, to show off the elegant slenderness of her arms. As was the fashion, her bodice was laced tight.

Since Lalage was extremely proud of her snow-white bosom, she always had her stomachers cut so low that her little round breasts were almost bare. But today, Alex observed, even her nipples were on view. Intentionally so, it seemed. Painted a soft, raspberry red, they glowed invitingly through a cloudy trimming of fine Brussells lace.

Alex decided he would like to bite them. Damn the woman, he thought. Damn the church and vicar, too. Couldn't Ellis and Rebecca go to divine service alone? Then, he and Lalage would go back to bed.

But now, to his annoyance, Ellis and Rebecca stood before them. "Good God, Lalage!" Staring at his sister in amused derision, Ellis laughed like a jackass. "Where do you think *you're* going today?"

"Good morning, Ellis." Coldly, Lalage met his startled gaze. "What do you mean? I'm going to church, of course. With you."

"I see." Still Ellis grinned. "Well – you'll give the vicar apoplexy. You'll frighten the choirboys. You'll strike the curate dead." He turned to his wife. "Becky, my dear?"

"Yes, Ellis?"

"Could you lend this wanton a scarf? Poor silly creature – she's always forgetting hers."

"I don't need to borrow anything from Rebecca." Lalage squared her shoulders. She turned her glorious profile towards her husband.

Alex groaned.

"Tell me, Ellis dear," said Lalage, as she got back into the coach, "where have you been, so early in the morning? Picking mushrooms? Gathering herbs? Or showing Rebecca some of your old trysting places, where you used to take trollops from the village? I'm agog to know."

"We've been over to Hensham. One of the cottagers is sick, so we went to enquire after his progress." Meeting Lalage's eyes, Rebecca smiled. "He's very much better today."

"I'm so glad." Lalage's own smile would have frozen oil. "Do hurry up, Rebecca dear. We're late as it is."

"We could call in again on our way home," suggested Ellis, as he handed his wife into the coach. "I reckon a sight of Lalage here could bring a corpse back to life. She'll have poor Harry Brewer back on his feet and scampering around, in no time at all."

After morning service, Lalage lagged behind. There'd been whispering and pointing all through the psalms and responses, so she knew her beautiful new ensemble had struck just the right note.

What a bore Ellis was these days! Droning on about scarves and looking at her as if she were some kind of freak. One would have thought he was about to take holy orders himself.

It was all that woman's fault. Before he was married, Ellis had loved to see a pretty bosom on elegant display. He'd gawped at hers almost as much as Alex did.

But now he was bewitched. He must be. How else could his behaviour be explained? How could a man like him even have fancied, let alone fallen in love with, a vulgar little woman whose coarse Midlands accent and unpolished manners must disgust any gentleman of education or taste?

Then there was his house. That horrible heap of bricks, timber and plaster on which he had lavished so much time, energy and money, it was a wonder he hadn't bankrupted himself.

She saw Ellis take Rebecca's hand. Her breakfast rose in her throat.

"Lally!" Standing on the steps of the Hall, Ellis called to her. "Oh, Lally! Do come along. Don't dawdle so."

"I'm coming." Lalage quickened her pace. Suddenly, she felt such hatred for Rebecca that it almost choked her. Looking at Ellis, she hated him, too.

He was a traitor. He had betrayed his class, his name, his inheritance. By marrying that upstart, he had disgraced his entire family.

Traitors should be arraigned and sentenced, if only to discourage further betrayals. How could Ellis best be punished? Wondering, Lalage licked her lips.

Chapter 16

Standing on the steps of her little house, Lalage watched Ellis hand Rebecca out of the gig. The fat blonde baggage was almost spherical these days. The slightest nudge would send her sprawling and rolling in the dirt. The idea of Rebecca helpless on her back, kicking and wriggling like some giant ladybird, amused Lalage so much that she was able to greet her sister-in-law with a perfectly brilliant smile. She bade her enter the little sitting room with such an excess of cordiality that Rebecca was bemused.

"Alex will not be long," she told her guests, as Betty brought in the tea things and arranged the china just so. "Dear Ellis! Darling Rebecca. It's so good of you to come. I know how busy you are."

"We'll always make time for you, Lally." Ellis took a dish of tea. "What did Alex wish to discuss?"

"He's got some scheme or other." Lalage poured her own tea. "I don't know exactly what it is, he won't tell me. But I believe it affects the East India business."

"Oh. That." Ellis shrugged. "Well, if there's any chance of recouping some of your capital, I'll be glad to give him all the assistance I can."

"So kind." Lalage turned to her sister-in-law. "You're looking very pretty today," she observed. "I trust you're well?"

"Quite well, I thank you." Rebecca smiled.

"I'm so glad." Lalage bared her teeth.

Had she lived in a more superstitious age, Lalage might have brewed up magical potions, danced naked in the moonlight, or sacrificed to some ancient deity who'd lived in the greenwood since before time began. Anything, to make Rebecca miscarry.

Indeed, as a child she'd had a nurse who was a witch. Hannah Jewell had the witch-mark on her neck, the witch-spot deep inside her private parts, and devil's kisses all over her left breast.

But Lalage's mother was a modern woman who didn't believe in witches. Hannah was a good nurse, and Mrs Darrow wasn't at all perturbed when a frightened chambermaid told her the witch was corrupting her daughter. For Hannah nursed her own fat, healthy son at her right breast, while she offered poor weazen Lalage devil's milk only, from her left.

Whispering spells over her little charge, she'd charmed away all Lalage's infant maladies. Years later, she put the evil eye on a housemaid. The girl was pregnant, so Hannah bewitched her womb. The child was born a monster, with long, yellow teeth and nails like claws. Yes, Hannah Jewell would have known a charm powerful enough to abort any child. But alas, poor Hannah was dead these five years.

Left to herself, Rebecca seemed most unlikely to lose her baby. Her cheeks glowed pink with health. Perfect happiness gave her a radiance which even the most cunning painting could not have supplied. As for Alex, who had recently referred to a heavily pregnant neighbour as Madam Cow and refused to sit next to her in church because she sweated so much – he thought Rebecca looked quite lovely. He even told Lalage so.

In her less rational moments, Lalage seriously considered murder. She would stick a knife between her sister-in-law's shoulder blades, perhaps, or spike a dagger through her heart. A sharp stab, followed by a downward thrust into the belly, would kill both mother and child at once.

For days on end, Lalage had brooded. But then one evening, as Betty prepared her for bed, inspiration dawned. She had her marvellous, her brilliant idea.

As she watched her flickering bedside candle, she realised she need hardly go as far as murder. All it needed was a sudden shock. A bad fright would certainly bring on a disastrously premature birth.

Lalage smiled to herself. The creature was about six months gone. Perfect. She'd miscarry of a dead child, and maybe even bleed to death herself. How could a fright be arranged? Lalage ranged the options and tried to decide.

"Another thing, too. She's turned him into a peasant. He looks like one, talks like one, eats like one. It's odious, Alex. Quite vile." Picking crossly at a piece of chicken wing, Lalage lost patience with the bones, and tossed the whole thing into the fire.

"I wish you wouldn't waste so much food." Partial to chicken wings himself, Alex frowned. "Lally, we can't afford to throw good meat away."

"Oh, I quite forgot. I am to eat, and grow fat. Like Rebecca." Grabbing a piece of bread, Lalage stuffed it into her mouth. She chewed vigorously. "He's clean and decent, I suppose," she continued, speaking with her mouth full and spewing crumbs everywhere. "But he looks like a dispossessed labourer these days. He's always without a hat. In fact, he's so sunburnt I'm ashamed to be seen with him. I've half a mind to tell him so."

"Don't upset him, Lally." Alex looked grave. "He's doing his best to help us just now."

For, in addition to acquiring a sun tan, Ellis had been studying the newspapers. Prompted by Alex's chance remark that he had recently read something encouraging about the East India Company's current financial situation, Ellis sent for a packet of the latest London journals. A fortnight or so after the subject had first come up, he called on his brother-in-law, hauled him into his cubby-hole of a study and closed the door. Lalage was left to entertain Rebecca for an hour. This first hour lengthened into two.

"Why is he so excited?" demanded Lalage. Burning with

curiosity, she forgot to be cool and aloof. "Dear Rebecca, do tell me!"

But Rebecca merely smiled all over her smooth, pale face and told Lalage she would know everything soon.

Lalage sighed, and wondered if it were worth trying to choke it out of the smug little sow.

Eventually, Ellis came out of Alex's study. He was grinning broadly. Soon, he was followed by his friend, who looked just as pleased. "We're going to London," announced Alex. "To mend my fortunes."

"Indeed?" Lalage raised her eyebrows. "Ellis? Is this so?"

"In a manner of speaking." Ellis took his sister's hand. "I have business there myself. Alex is to be my travelling companion."

"But the East India scheme! What – "

"Ah. Now we come to it." Sitting down, Ellis rubbed his face. "Well, Lally. I've recently been in touch with a gentleman who has contacts in the company. He thinks there's a chance we could salvage some of the money Alex invested there. I must write a few letters, get more information.

"In the meantime, my dear sister, keep your fingers crossed. Be sure to say your prayers."

It was as if a sudden burst of sunlight illuminated a pathless, rainswept moorland. Lalage beamed in delight. Her prospects, once forever blighted, looked brilliant now. "Do you think he can do it?" she demanded, as she and Alex watched Ellis and Rebecca drive away. "Is there any chance of recovering the cash?"

"Perhaps." Alex shrugged. "If Ellis thinks it at all possible, we might as well try. But if it turns out unlikely we'll recoup anything, I shall still go to London. For the ride."

"Oh, of course." Lalage eyed him narrowly. "The chance of a merry jaunt is not to be foregone."

"No." Mildly, Alex met her eyes. "I'm looking forward to it. I admit that."

* * *

Ellis and Alex expected to be gone a month or more. Rebecca, it appeared, did not consider herself fit enough to travel. As for Lalage – she was informed her presence was not required.

"You'd have taken Rebecca!" she cried. Having instructed Betty to look over and remodel all her hats and gowns, Lalage was very upset. "If that creature had expressed even the slightest interest in the scheme, you'd happily have taken her!"

"Yes, indeed." Salting the wound, Ellis nodded vigorous agreement. "But Rebecca understands business. You do not."

"You'd be so bored, my darling." Having had his trip to Derbyshire thoroughly spoiled, Alex was determined to enjoy his month in Town. "Even if you understood what we were talking about – which you wouldn't – you'd find it insufferably tiresome to sit in a fusty little office all day, discussing stocks and shares."

"I see." Lalage grimaced. "Then, during the evenings, while the two of you were sitting in some stinking tavern with a whore on each knee, I'd be just as bored alone in my lodgings."

"Exactly." Alex blinked. "I mean – "

"When it was time to bring the drabs back for a good rogering, I'd get in the way."

"Oh, darling! We'll be doing nothing like that!" Alex wrung his hands. "Lally, please don't be difficult. Look – I'll bring you a present. Anything you want. Something pretty, yes?"

So Lalage was left behind. Stuck in the muddy solitude of a Warwickshire village while her husband enjoyed the pleasures of the Town, she brooded and schemed. A invitation from Rebecca to spend a few days at Easton Hall was torn up and thrown down the servants' privy. "How dare she!" Grinding her teeth, Lalage glared out across the fields. "As if I'd wish to seek *her* out!"

She went over her plan once again. Yes, it would do. Before Alex and Ellis returned from London, Lalage would have taught the trollop a valuable lesson.

Needing a fellow conspirator, Lalage decided to enlist the support of Betty. Dear, loyal Betty, she had served her mistress well, accepting Lalage's fall in fortune as philosophically as she'd accepted her munificence in her heyday of prosperity.

As well she might. Even when Lalage had – in her own opinion, anyway – been near destitute, Betty's wages had been paid. Betty had a warm room, good food and a new gown twice a year, woollen in winter, fine cotton in summer. So, whereas Sukey the housemaid wore Betty's cast-offs, Betty always went to church in smart new clothes. The lady's maid was as beautifully dressed as the lady herself.

"Betty," began Lalage one morning, as the maid brushed her mistress's long, black tresses and began to coil them into an elaborate pleat, "do you know of any rascally fellows who might like to earn an honest shilling or two?"

"Rascally fellows, madam?" Tugging out a knot, Betty smoothed a lock of hair into place. "Felons, you mean?"

"Maybe." Twisting round, Lalage looked up. She met her servant's gaze. "Betty?"

"Yes, madam?"

"I've always been a kind mistress, I hope?"

"You have indeed, madam. No one could be kinder."

"You have nothing to complain of in my treatment of you?"

"Nothing, madam. On the contrary."

"Then, Betty – "

"Madam, wouldn't Mr Darrow be the best person to ask about this?" Betty resumed her brushing. "If you wish to give employment to some poor creature, I'm sure he could recommend – "

"You misunderstand me." Lalage frowned. "Well, leave

it for the present. What do you think of yellow satin? Lemon yellow, with a broad black stripe? I need a new morning gown, you see."

Over the next few days, her mistress gave Betty no peace. Every conversation eventually worked its way round to rascally fellows and honest shillings. "You must know *someone*, Betty," insisted Lalage, as Betty laced her into a cherry-red gown which the maid had always coveted. "That brother of yours, the one who was taken before the justices on suspicion of trapping deer. The one whom I persuaded Mr Darrow to let off with a warning, even though I had to tell my own brother a pack of lies in the process – surely he knows somebody?"

Reminded of the favour Lalage had done her family, Betty blushed. "We were grateful indeed for your kindness," she muttered. "Poor William would have kissed your hands, had he – "

"Your father, Betty?" Sweetly, Lalage smiled. "He goes into the squire's woods. Your mother is not averse to a hare, or a pheasant. All those little brothers and sisters of yours, the ones still at home – I'm sure they know where to look for game-birds' eggs?"

Poor Betty grew scarlet. "We're not a family of thieves," she wailed. "I can't deny that sometimes in the winter, when there's snow on the ground and my father can't get work, he'll maybe take a few rabbits. But he – "

"Rabbits!" Lalage grinned. "Pheasants, more like. Partridges and hares, as well. Oh, Betty! Do you think I'm stupid?"

"I think you're a dear, sweet lady, and a good friend to me." Betty smoothed the folds of the red gown. "But I don't know why you're examining me like this! My family is poor. If my brothers take a little game now and then, they *do* break the law. I admit it. But is it right that they should starve?"

"Hush, girl. Hush." Seeing tears in Betty's navy-blue eyes, Lalage laid a kind hand on her shoulder. "I'm no sport-loving squire. I wouldn't care if all the pheasants in Warwickshire found their way into your brothers' nets."

"Then why – "

"Listen to me." Releasing the maid, Lalage walked over to the window. "My dear Betty," she began, "you know how severely poachers are dealt with by the justices round here. You also know how easily a man may be taken up. Sent to the county assize. Sentenced to a public whipping, to gaol – or even the fatal tree!"

"Oh, madam!"

"Betty, I need you to help me."

"How, madam? What – "

"Find me someone!" Lalage glared. "Find me a man. Two men. Criminals if you please, but two strong, hardy fellows, who will – who will – "

"What, madam?"

"Serve me." Lalage bit her lip. "Who will do as I tell them, and not ask the reason why."

That evening, Betty visited her cousin. He called on a friend, who said he knew a likely pair of men. A chain of enquiry which, had Lalage given the matter a moment's thought she would have seen must lead directly back to her, ended a fortnight later when two scruffy men presented themselves at the kitchen door, demanding to see a Mrs Curtis and refusing to be denied.

Not in her mistress's confidence, Sukey insisted they'd come to the wrong house. But Lalage spotted them from her window, and ran after them as they loped off down the lane. Cloaked and veiled, she caught up with them by the village pond. "I am Mrs Curtis," she gasped, breathless. "You wished to speak with me?"

"Aye." The taller of the men, a thick-set fellow with the marks of irons still fresh on his wrists, eyed her suspiciously. "Was told you 'ad a job for us," he said.

"You've been in prison." Observing the bracelets of scars, Lalage glanced at the man's ankles. On his shins, she saw evidence of recent shackling. His friend had been shackled, too. "Were you committed by the local justice?" she asked. "Or by the Assize?"

"By Squire Darrow." Wiping his hands on his dirty breeches, the man spat. "Six months at stone-breaking, we was. Never even saw the bloody deer!"

Sympathetically, Lalage shook her head. "It's that wife of his," she said. "Upstart that she is. She was born a labouring woman's daughter. She gets above herself now. Teaches her husband to despise her own people."

"She does?" The smaller man, a weasel-faced individual without a single tooth in his head, shrugged. "I've heard she's a good lady. She sends food and blankets to the poor, and makes sure the children go to school."

"She sends weak broth and mouldy cheese, to the wives of men her husband has sent to prison! She makes their children go to school, but she knows full well those same children are needed in the fields. To earn the pittance her husband pays them."

Lalage grimaced. "Squire Darrow and his wife are hypocrites. They're cruel, they're unjust. They've certainly injured *you.*"

"Aye." The taller man nodded. "You're right, they have."

"So now, if you will perform a small service for me, you could pay them back a little."

"How's that?" The weasel-faced man scowled. "The likes of us can't strike at people like them."

"Ah, but you could." Lalage folded her hands. "I have a quarrel with Mrs Darrow," she began. "She has injured me, and I wish to repay her in kind. I don't want her killed, or hurt," she added, seeing the men become alarmed. "Just badly frightened."

"What do you want done?" The smaller man shuffled a little. "Frightening ladies," he muttered. "I dunno if we're the fellows for that sort of work."

"You won't have to touch her." Lalage spread her hands. "I only want her house set alight."

"You want Easton Hall burned?" The tall man stared. "No," he said. "We're not the men for a job like that."

"I'll pay you well." Engagingly, Lalage smiled. "Look, all you'll have to do is go up there late one night. Sneak into the kitchens. Pile up rags or other rubbish, make a spark. Simple! I'll pay you twenty pounds."

"For firing the Hall?"

"For starting a little, harmless blaze." Lalage's eyes flashed. "The squire sent you to prison," she cried. "He punished you for something you hadn't even done. Was that justice? Was that fair?"

"It wasn't." The weasel-faced man shook his head. "George, the lady says true."

"A few sticks and tinder," murmured Lalage. "Light a fire, just a little one, then leave the county. Ten pounds apiece richer, to boot."

But the larger man hesitated. "It could turn out to be murder," he muttered. "It could become a hanging matter for us. Look here – I reckon we'd be taking a big risk. One worth a lot more than twenty pounds."

Lalage sighed. "There'll be no deaths," she assured him. "The place is full of servants. The alarm will be raised, and everyone will escape."

"No." The weasel-faced man shook his head. "It can't be done."

"Fifty pounds," said Lalage. "A year's wages for you two."

"That's true." Greed kindled the tall man's dull, grey eyes. "Aye, that's true enough."

"So?"

"Twenty pounds down."

"Ten." Lalage was firm. "The balance to be paid when the thing is done."

"How do we know you won't cheat us?"

"How do I know you won't cheat me?" Lalage glared at them. "Ten pounds, and forty to follow. Do it any night this week, and when I hear of your success I'll arrange for forty pounds to be sent to the White Feather on the Addingley road."

"Ten pounds isn't much." The smaller man was still doubtful. "If we're caught – "

"Don't be caught!" Lalage grimaced. "They keep no dogs. The service doors are never locked. Most of the upper servants live in the Dower House. Only a few kitchen maids and the butler sleep at the Hall."

"I thought you said the place was full?"

"It is! Well, it sometimes is. Depending on the time of day or night." Now in a state of near frenzy, Lalage took out her purse. She clinked the coins. "Here," she said, counting out money. "Gold. More than you've ever had in your lives. Still more to follow. All for striking a flint."

The men gazed at the cash. Then, grabbing at it, the larger man scooped up his share. "It'll be done," he said.

"This week?"

"Yes. Day after tomorrow. Mrs Curtis?"

"Yes?"

"The rest of the money. If it's not a-waitin' for us, we'll be back to see you. We'll alter the look of your pretty face."

Lalage shuddered. "The money will be there," she promised. "Ask the ostler, and you'll receive it."

Lalage watched the men go. Perspiration beading her brow, her heart hammered. She was gasping for breath.

Flopping down on a grassy bank, she waited until she could trust her legs to carry her back up the lane. She would, she decided, give Betty the cherry-red gown tonight.

Chapter 17

Ellis took himself off to London most reluctantly. For, although he knew such a long journey would be bad for her, he was extremely unwilling to leave Rebecca behind.

"Stay well, Becky," he said, as he took his leave. "Take care of yourself and the child."

"Don't worry, Ellis." Feeling more tearful than she cared to admit, Rebecca forced a smile. "What harm can come to me here?"

Rebecca missed Ellis badly. In the course of that first week of separation, she was several times on the point of packing her boxes and taking the public stagecoach to London. Only the certainty that Ellis would be extremely angry with her for risking both the child's safety and her own stopped her. So, to assuage her restlessness, she went twice or three times a week to Birmingham, where she walked about the factory and workshops feeling completely redundant.

For Lyddy had taken over. The wretched, dejected, downtrodden Aunt Lyddy of Rebecca's childhood no longer existed – instead, the self-willed, high-spirited Lyddy Searle, whose strong passions had once betrayed her into a reckless love affair which was bound to end in disaster for all concerned, was a force to be reckoned with.

"Orders for buckles," she was saying, as she led Rebecca out of the casting-shop and back into the yard. "Well, Becky – they're down again. Of course, the shoe buckle is no longer in demand. The fashion for laces has seen to that. But now, every other kind of buckle seems démodé, too. I think we should finish our last order and wind up the process. Concentrate on polished steel buttons and brooches, instead."

"Maybe." Somewhat breathless now, but inclined to blame the heat and noise of the factory for her nagging headache and general fatigue, Rebecca nodded. "Yes, do that. Now – you said you were having problems with one or two of the hands."

"Ah. So I did." Seeing Rebecca was flushed and looked extremely tired, Lyddy led her towards the office, where she could sit down. "John Dixon and Timothy Hartley must go. They steal scrap, they drink to excess, and they swear like Irishmen. Michael tells me their work is poor. They're no use to us."

"No, indeed." Wearily, Rebecca sighed. "Well then, shall we call them in? I'll tell them today. They'll have no more employment here."

"I can tell them. When you've gone." Lyddy grimaced. "But if they then come whining and moaning to Mrs Darrow, she must support me."

"Of course she will." Rebecca toyed with a teaspoon. "Whom had you in mind to replace them? Idle and inefficient they may be, but we'll surely need to find others to do their jobs?"

"Not necessarily." Opening a drawer, Lyddy took out some papers. "I wish to speak to you about the furnace," she said.

"What about it?" Rebecca frowned. "It's efficient, isn't it?"

"Efficient enough. But it could be more so." Lyddy passed the papers across. "Becky, we need an engine."

"Ah." Rebecca smiled. "I see."

Of course, as Rebecca knew perfectly well, the big factories in the centre of town all used steam power these days. Engines were the latest thing, and everyone who aspired to any sort of credibility as a manufacturer wanted one. But Rebecca had decided that, in Searle's case, taking into account its diversified, generally small scale of manufacture, mechanisation would probably be more trouble than it was worth.

She picked up the first sheet. It was a scale representation of a basic steam-engine. Very detailed, it was meticulously drawn. "You had this done on your own initiative?" she enquired.

"Not exactly." Lyddy blushed. "You remember Mr Harris? The toymaker? Well, he sometimes calls here of an evening. Just to chat, sort of thing. Well, *he's* had one of Mr Boulton's engines installed. He says he wouldn't be without it now."

"So?"

"So, look at this." Lyddy handed Rebecca another drawing. "A small engine," she urged now. "A neat, unobtrusive work-horse, that's all we need. Twelve or fifteen horsepower – no more."

"You're sure of that?"

"Oh, certainly!" Complacently, Lyddy smiled. "Such a one could easily power a forge the size of ours, and provide us with the means to work other machinery, too. Think of it, Becky! Think how wasteful it is to have apprentices working bellows, or men blowing air through coals. An engine could do all that for us, leaving human hands to do what machines cannot."

"How much would it cost?"

"Eight hundred. Maybe a thousand. No more." Lyddy found a letter, which she passed over. "I wrote to Mr Boulton myself. It was merely an enquiry, you understand. He estimates a round thousand, all in. Becky, I agree the Soho engines are expensive. But everyone says they're by far the best."

"They still break down." Rebecca shook her head. "Parts wear out, or are found to have been ill-made. Then they need to be replaced."

"True. But here in Birmingham, it would be easy to find engineers who could do the necessary work." Clasping her hands together, Lyddy looked earnestly at her child. "Mr Boulton's own engineers are close by, after all."

"I suppose you're right." Rebecca did some rapid mental arithmetic. "Where would we find the money?"

"We can raise credit. Mr Harris says – "

"Ah, yes. Mr Harris." Rebecca grimaced. "Well, Aunt. If you are determined, I suppose I could – "

"Becky, the factory is yours. I'd do nothing, take no action whatsoever, without first consulting you."

"Or Mr Harris." Rebecca put the papers down. "A thousand pounds," she said. "Well, the factory's insured for four and a half thousand. It's worth at least four. Could we borrow against that?"

"Of course." Lyddy clapped her hands. "So you agree!"

"I'll speak to Ellis. But I'll let you know one way or another long before the month is out."

"Excellent." Lyddy had become quite pink. Rebecca smiled. It was delightful to see her so happy. Whether it was worth a thousand pounds of steam engine, however, was a different matter entirely.

By the end of their third week in London, Ellis and Alex had finished all their business. Late one Friday evening, a full seven days before he was expected, Ellis walked into Rebecca's bedroom. She had just begun to brush her hair. In the candelight it shone like a saint's diadem, cascading over her shoulders and framing her pretty face with tendrils of pure gold.

"Becky?" he whispered, unwilling to startle her.

"Ellis!" Dropping the hairbrush, Rebecca spun round on her stool. Jumping up, she fell into his embrace, kissing him, hugging him, laughing and crying, all at once. "I thought you were Molly, come to plait my hair."

"Ah. Molly is dismissed for tonight. I told her to have her supper, then go to bed." Ellis kissed his wife. "Well, darling?" he demanded. "How are you?"

"I'm in excellent health. Never, ever, better!"

"What about the baby?"

"He's well, too. Feel!" Taking Ellis's hand, Rebecca placed it on her stomach. "He kicks and kicks. He gives me no peace at all. I'm sure I shall be brought to bed of a goat."

"I see." Ellis laughed. Then he yawned, hugely. "Oh God," he groaned, "I'm so tired. I couldn't sleep at all in that wretched inn."

"Because it was so noisy?"

"Because I was away from you."

"Come to bed." Rebecca hugged him again. "Sleep the whole night through. You can tell me what happened in London tomorrow morning."

Unlike Ellis, Alex had slept perfectly well while he was in London. So now, he ate a good supper, finished a second bottle of wine, then told Simmons he could go to bed. Leaving the dining room, he walked about the salon for a while, observing how much this had changed for the better.

Since Rebecca had been mistress of Easton Hall, her presence had filled the old house. Now, in addition to modern conveniences like efficient flues and effective draught-proofing, there was close carpeting and new furniture, too. Comfortable sofas had joined awful old settles, and some other modern pieces, carefully chosen or specially made to compliment their setting, gave the rooms a more up-to-date air.

Rebecca's own little parlour had been papered in a pale Chinese print, and completely new-furnished. But that remained the only room in the house which was entirely modern. The rest of the old barn stayed more or less as Ellis wanted it. Old-fashioned and grotesque.

Alex shook his head. The trip to London had been exhausting, the business meetings interminable. There'd been no opportunity whatsoever for the licentious pleasures in which Lalage supposed her husband would indulge. Meek as a lamb, Alex had trotted behind as Ellis strode from bankers to brokers, from attorneys to stock-holders, more or less bludgeoning them into taking an active interest in Alex's affairs. Eventually, he'd worn them down. So, the business had been concluded in three weeks instead of the originally anticipated month.

As a result of Ellis's efforts, it now seemed likely that a little of the Lowells' money – three or four thousand pounds, certainly no more – might be recovered.

Alex had expressed his thanks. Then, taking a last, longing look at the Town and miserably recalling all the pleasure gardens and theatres still unvisited, he packed his boxes and waited for the coach to take him back to the green solitude of Warwickshire.

On reaching Easton Hall, Ellis went haring off to Rebecca's bedroom, leaving Alex to his solitary supper and his reflections. What a fool Ellis was now! What an uxorious, drooling zany. That girl had bewitched him. She'd cast an absolutely unbreakable spell.

Alex rang for more candles. His supply of new novels – for he had managed to snatch one visit to a bookseller, and made the most of it – would beguile the next few hours.

At about three o'clock in the morning, when Alex was nodding over Miss Burney's latest effort and deciding it was much inferior to *Evelina*, he smelled smoke. He wrinkled his nose in disgust. Simmons the butler liked his pipe of tobacco, the more evil-smelling the better. Now, presumably, he was coming up the passage, no doubt returning from a visit to whichever of the more comely kitchen maids was his current fancy. Alex rose from the sofa and opened the door of the salon. He would tell the wretched butler to get to bed at once.

The passage was full of smoke. Puffs of it invaded the room, while belching black fumes rose up the stairs, swirling in menacing spirals all around the banisters above.

"Good God!" At a loss, Alex blinked. Then, coming to his senses, he shut the door again. But the room was already polluted. The whole atmosphere was thickly fogged with acrid, stinging smoke. Taking out his pocket-handkerchief, he stuffed it into a flower vase, then clamped the wet pad of cambric to his mouth.

He went back into the passage. "Fire!" he shouted, coughing and choking as he inhaled a foetid mouthful of smoke. "Fire! Oh Christ Almighty, where's Simmons? FIRE!"

No one seemed to hear him. So, half-blinded and gagging horribly, he made his way to the front door.

Dead asleep for the first time in weeks, Ellis was roused by Rebecca pushing his shoulder and repeating his name. When she smelled burning she'd pulled back the bed-curtains at once, thinking the candle had caught. But now, by the light of that same candle, she could see wisps of smoke snaking into the room. They were coming from around the door.

Ellis opened his eyes and sat up just in time to see his wife get out of bed. "No!" Suddenly wide awake, he caught her hand. "No, Becky! If the corridor's full of smoke, you mustn't open the door."

"Ellis, there's a fire!" Her eyes wide with alarm, Rebecca stared at him. She tried to free her hand. "What else can we do?" she demanded. "Burn alive?"

He shook his head. His hand still held hers, and now it increased its vice-like grip. He thought for a moment. He glanced towards the window. "The roof," he said, at last. "We must get out on to the roof. It's the only way."

"What?" Already very frightened and now panicking, Rebecca struggled to get free. "But it's pitch dark!" she wailed. "We'll never – "

Her hand was within inches of the latch.

"Rebecca, you will *not* open the door." Now, counting on her obedience, Ellis released her. "Put on your wrap," he said. "Then get over by the window."

Reaching for his shirt and breeches, he pulled them on. Opening the casement, he peered out. "There's a full moon," he observed. "It's quite light enough to see."

"But Ellis, I'm pregnant! I've no head for heights. I'm bound to fall." In tears now, Rebecca gaped at him. "You're mad," she sobbed. "Stark, raving mad!"

"I'm not." Ellis forced himself to be calm. "Darling, I've climbed out of this window many a time. I've spent whole days scrambling over the tiles, going where I pleased. I – "

"Yes, you told me." Still Rebecca wept. "It's so steep!" she cried, staring in horror at the dizzying drop below. "I can't go out there. I'm sorry, Ellis. I just can't."

"You can. You must." Ellis grabbed her wrist. "No shoes," he said. "Bare feet grip better, you see. Now. Swing your legs over the sill. Hold tight to the water-spout here. Trust me."

Running through the cold night air, Alex made his way to the kitchen wing, where he located the source of the blaze. Now, he and the butler, together with three kitchen maids and the cook, were trying to put it out. Other tenants and servants, who had seen the flames and smelled smoke on the night breeze, came to join them.

"The master, sir! The master and mistress!" Beating ineffectually at the inferno which now completely engulfed the stairs, Simmons stared tearfully through the flames. "What will become of Mr Darrow, sir?"

Alex told him to shut up and keep beating. There was a chance, a slim chance, that they'd get the fire out before it reached Ellis and Rebecca.

But the single staircase was now well ablaze. *Why*, Alex wanted to cry, had Ellis never thought to put in a second, servants' stairs? For there was now no other way to reach the upper floor.

Half an hour went by. Sweating, dirty and exhausted, the labouring firefighters realised they would never get the blaze under control. If they valued their own lives, they should leave the house very soon.

Alex was sure Ellis must be dead. Standing on the gravel

sweep, watching the house burn, he gazed blearily into the fire.

Now, he reproached himself bitterly. Why hadn't he roused Ellis? Why had he not even thought of his friend? What would Lalage say? She would revile him absolutely. Hate and despise him forever. He buried his face in his hands, and sobbed.

"Alex!" An angry shout from above made him start. "Simmons! Alex! Get ladders, damn you!"

Alex looked up. He stared in disbelief. For there, on the roof of the long gallery, stood Ellis. Rebecca crouched beside him like a suppliant, clinging to his knees.

"Ladders!" cried Ellis again, his eyes blazing as brightly as the fire. "For God's sake, fetch ladders. This roof's red hot!"

But nobody moved. The firefighters merely stared, hardly believing what they saw. The man in the torn white shirt, whose black hair streamed in the burning wind, was surely a vision. A ghost.

Alex recovered first. He let out a whoop of joy. "Jump!" he shouted. "Jump, Ellis! We'll catch you."

"Don't be ridiculous." Ellis glared down at Simmons. "Ladders, man!" he howled, desperate now. "Hurry!"

At last, a dozen or so tenants raced off to one of the barns, to do Ellis's bidding. They found ladders. They lashed them together. They propped them against the walls, and held them.

Then, very carefully and slowly, Ellis and Rebecca were brought down from the roof. Rebecca went first, assisted by three or four labourers who steadied and encouraged her. Then, Ellis followed.

As his foot cleared the bottom rung, the roof of the long gallery collapsed. With a great roar, the timbers fell. Scarlet flames shot a triumphant sixty feet into the sky.

It was pointless to go on fighting a fire like this. Helplessly, tenants, villagers, master, mistress and servants stood together. They watched the house burn. It was a terrible sight, which held them all entranced.

By the time streaks of dawn appeared in the sky, however, Easton Hall was no longer a spectacle. It was a blackened, empty ruin.

Chapter 18

Instead of taking to their heels and putting as much distance as they could between themselves and Easton Hall, the two arsonists stayed to watch the results of their evening's handiwork. Enthralled by the awesome sight of a great house ablaze from end to end, they gawped like idiots, hardly able to believe they'd been so successful.

Then, coming to their senses, they joined the fire-fighters. They took their positions in the chain and passed leathern buckets full of water, to be hurled into the flames.

His arm around his wife's shoulders, Ellis stood for an hour or more, watching his house burn. "Your honour?" Now, a villager touched his arm. "Mr Darrow, sir?"

"Yes?" Ellis peered into the gloom. "Oh. James Tarrant, isn't it?"

"That's right, master. I lives down yonder. In the house on the green. This here fire, sir – "

"What about it it?"

"I reckon those two over there might know summat the rest of us don't." Tarrant jerked his thumb towards a couple of men standing just a few feet away. "I think they ought to be asked to explain theirselves, like."

"I see." Ellis glanced towards the two strangers. He frowned. "Do they come from the village?" he asked.

"No, sir. They do not." Rubbing his tired eyes, Tarrant grimaced. "But they've been round and about the place for the past few days at least. Harry Green's seen 'em in your park. Fred Brewer noticed 'em too. Thought they was after the deer."

"Oh." Still too shocked and upset to think at all clearly, Ellis shrugged. Helplessly, he sighed. "Well – "

"I think you ought to question them, sir." Boldly, Tarrant shook Ellis's arm. "Beat it out of 'em even, if your honour has to! But you should definitely make them buggers talk."

"Oh, very well." Ellis sighed again. "Bring them over here."

Farming his own little bit of freehold in addition to those acres he rented from the squire, James Tarrant was well respected by his peers. He nodded to a friend. Now, the two strangers were surround by a mob of villagers, all hostile and all excited. Their arms were pinioned, then they were dragged unceremoniously to where Ellis and Rebecca stood.

Looking at them, Ellis realised they were vaguely familiar. "Well?" he asked. "Did you two burn my house?"

Normally a rather more subtle inquisitor, Ellis's extreme fatigue and personal distress were responsible for the bluntness of this demand. But now, questioned so abruptly, the two men reddened. Usually bold and fearless, tonight they shuffled like a pair of embarrassed virgins. They grimaced. They would not meet the squire's eye.

A silence or two or three minutes ensued. But then, prods from behind and audible muttering that there was an oak tree handy and plenty of rope readily available, helped one of the men to find his tongue. "We were just passing," he mumbled. "We saw the flames, like. So we – "

"We were on the road, see. Tramping." The other man shrugged. "We're tinkers, sir. Poor travelling men."

"Poor travellin' poachers, I'd say." Tarrant poked one of the men in the chest. "I seen you before," he said. "You was at the Sessions. His honour sent you down for six months."

He turned to Ellis. "Mr Darrow, sir!" he cried. "This fellow was tried at the last Session but one. You give 'im 'ard labour. Now he's come back, to take his revenge!"

"Hang 'em both, that's what I say." This shout from the back of the crowd made Ellis look up. Now, as the tenants gazed at their landlord's blanched, stricken countenance, the cry was taken up with a vengeance.

"Hang them both!"

"String them up, like dogs!"

"Hang them, your honour. Do it now!"

"But the lady made us!" Now, the smaller of the two men sank to his knees. He grovelled at Ellis's feet. "*She* put us up to it," he wailed. "It was the lady as wanted it done!"

"What?" Ellis stared at the man. "What on earth are you talking about?"

"The lady, sir! She gave us gold."

"A lady gave you gold?" Now, Ellis took hold of the man's upper arm. Jerking him to his feet, he glared. "What lady is this?" he asked.

"Sir, I – "

"The lady! Tell me her name!" Shaking him as violently as a terrier shakes a captive, doomed rat, Ellis's hard fingers bit almost to the man's bones. "Speak!"

"Your honour, I – "

"Answer me!" Ellis's eyes glittered. "If you won't talk to me," he hissed, through clenched teeth, "I'll hand you over to the local militia. They'll not be half as tender of your limbs as I am."

At the mention of the militia, various tenants who served in the ranks of those trained bands rattled farm tools. They made martial noises. The two men made up their minds. They made a full confession there and then.

"We heard there was a lady wanted a job done," began the first. "Betty Hardwick's cousin put us on to her."

"She met us in the lane leading to Fairfield Common. She came from the house with the white gable ends."

"Mrs Curtis, that was her name."

"Fifty pounds she offered us!" One of the men was sobbing now. "She said there'd be no one hurt. The fire would be spotted, and put out straight away. Sh-she said – "

"Her name again." Ellis wrenched his captive's shoulder. "Her name, damn you!"

"Mrs Curtis." The man winced. "Mrs Curtis, your honour. That's God's own truth."

"Is it?" His face ashen, Ellis looked ready to pass out. "The house with white gables," he muttered. "You're sure she came from there?"

"Yes, your honour. Certain."

"What did she look like?"

"She had d-dark hair." Terror made the man choke on his words. "B-big eyes. She was a handsome lady."

"She was veiled," put in his friend.

"But we could see she was very pretty."

"Young, too."

"She wore a blue velvet cloak."

"A smart blue cloak, with black braid. A black straw bonnet."

Standing near at hand, Alex heard all this. As Ellis turned to him, he flinched. "I know nothing," he whispered. "As God's my witness, I know nothing at all."

"Don't you?" Ellis's eyes blazed. "You're quite sure of that?"

"Ellis, I swear before God – "

"I'm going to see Lalage." Accepting the cloak now offered by a tenant, Ellis reluctantly let Rebecca go. He glared at the two strangers. "If you have lied to me," he muttered, "I shall have you beaten. You'll be flogged until your backs are broken."

He turned to Alex. "As for you – look after Rebecca. Guard her with your life, until I get back."

"Ellis, please!" Distraught, Alex caught at his friend's sleeve. "Don't go while you're so angry. Just – "

"I shan't be long." Ellis fastened the cloak. "Simmons, find me some boots."

"But, Ellis!"

"Take Rebecca to the Dower House." His voice clipped but calm, Ellis met Alex's anxious eyes. "But first, listen to me. If Becky comes to harm – if her labour begins, if her child comes too soon – I'll make you sorry."

Seeing his brother-in-law was far too enraged to be rational, Alex shrugged. Taking Rebecca's arm, he led her away. Chattering and jostling, a group of tenants and servants accompanied them to the Dower House, a hundred yards down the drive.

Left unprotected, the two criminals provided the rowdier elements of the mob with some excellent sport. But then, seeing the men grow increasingly bloody, James Tarrant intervened. "I don't suppose his honour wants them killed," he said. Wading through the press, he hoiked the smaller man to his feet. "Put 'em in the lock-up. That's what I say."

"I reckon we should deal with 'em now." A rather less pacific villager, whose cudgel had done good service and was now liberally splattered with blood and stuck about with human hair, shook his fist. "I'm telling you, James Tarrant. I reckon – "

"Listen, George Siddons. All of you, listen to me. They've yet to be tried. They're entitled to the process of law, same as every man here." James Tarrant turned to a couple of labourers, who frequently worked for him. "What do you think, Peter Dummett? Timothy Fowler, what say you?"

"Put 'em in the lock-up." Sagely, Peter nodded. "Aye, that'd be best."

"So it would." Another villager agreed. "His honour might want to question 'em again, like."

"They oughter 'ave a trial," added a different voice.

"It's every man's right."

"That's so."

"Put 'em in Nick Drayton's cellar."

"Aye, that'd be the best thing."

So in the end, justice and reason prevailed. Now so bloodied and beaten that they could barely move or stand, the strangers were hustled to the village. There they were thrown into a cellar, to await the pleasure of the squire.

Clad like a highway ruffian in his grimy shirt and blackened breeches, a pair of ancient hessian boots on his feet and a tenant's greasy cloak thrown about his shoulders, Ellis walked into his sister's elegant dining room just as she was starting her breakfast.

He sat down – or rather collapsed – on a little gilded chair. "Why?" he demanded. "Lalage, first you must tell me why."

"Why what?" Lalage had heard all about the fire. She had spent the past half hour both comforting and threatening a terrified Betty. Now, blandly, she smiled. "Well, Ellis? I thought you were still in London," she said.

"I came home yesterday." Ellis felt sick. "Lalage, they say you – "

"Coffee?" Lalage's smile was charming. "You look as if you need some. Dear Ellis, your boots! What on earth have you been doing?"

"Stop it!" Staring at Lalage, Ellis saw the triumph in her eyes. Her delight was obvious. Her guilt was plain. "You know perfectly well what's happened!" he cried. "You know why I'm here!"

"Do I?" Shrugging, Lalage sipped coffee. "You know, I'm not absolutely sure I follow – "

"Damn you!" Jumping to his feet, Ellis dashed the cup from her hand. Scalding coffee soaked the tablecloth, and dripped on to the rug beneath. He pulled Lalage from her seat. Grasping her by the shoulders, he made her look at him. "I got back yesterday night," he muttered. "Alex and I had – "

"Alex was with you?" For the first time, Lalage's face registered concern. "Ellis, is he – "

"He's unhurt. He roused the household, in fact."

"I see." Forgetting she wasn't supposed to know what had happened, Lalage stared into her brother's eyes. "He saved you?" she whispered. "You, and everyone else?"

"Yes. But if he hadn't been awake, I doubt if anyone would have escaped. Woodsmoke kills in minutes. Well, of course you know that."

"Do I?"

"Yes!" Ellis shook her. "Why?" he repeated. "God in heaven – you'll tell me if I have to thrash it out of you!"

"How did you get out?"

"Over the roof." Ellis grimaced. "Did you think of that? When you decided to burn me alive, had you forgotten that as children we often climbed out of our bedroom windows? We spent hours playing in the gullies. Hiding amid the chimney stacks."

"I remember. Of course I do." Lalage squirmed. "But Rebecca didn't know anything of that."

"No, indeed." Ellis's grip tightened. "Rebecca would have roasted, unaware of the means of escape so readily to hand. Was that what you intended? Oh, Lalage! How could you sink so low?"

"You dare to ask *me* that?" Now Ellis's grip relaxed, just a little. So, Lalage escaped from his grasp. "Fool," she muttered, rubbing her upper arms and grimacing in pain. "Stupid, ridiculous fool. He asks me how, and why. The blockhead. The mooncalf. The clod!"

"What?"

"You disgraced us all!" Her dark eyes blazing, Lalage glared. "You ask how I could sink so low! Well, you sank lower than I did! Far lower. Yes, indeed!"

"What on earth – "

"You married a peasant's bastard!" Lalage's eyes flashed fire. "You courted and married a dirty little drab!"

"Lally!"

"Now she's with child," spat Lalage. "Whose, I wonder? The land agent's? The cowman's? No matter. You're her husband, so she'll drop her brat at your expense regardless. In the meantime, she parades around your estate like a washerwoman who's won the national lottery. Sticking out her belly like a trophy, for all to gaze upon!"

Lalage drew breath. "I hate you!" she cried. "I've hated you from the day you took up with her. I despise you more than I despise the common, stinking, low-bred slut herself!"

Ellis gaped at her. Bone-white beneath the dirt, his face was a picture of such incredulity, such horror, that for a few moments Lalage was afraid for his sanity. For her own safety, too. She thought he might attack her. Even kill her. But then, rallying, she tossed her curls. "Is she injured?" she asked, hopefully. "Is the creature hurt?"

"No. Not as far as I can tell." Still ashen, Ellis stared like a hypnotic. "She's with your husband just now," he went on, tonelessly. "At the Dower House."

"Oh. I see."

Ellis shook himself. "But if she dies," he went on, "if she suffers, if she loses the baby, Alex will pay."

"Why should Alex pay?"

"For his part in this, of course."

"He had no part!"

"You expect me to believe that?" Ellis shook his head. "Well – it doesn't matter what I believe. If things turn out badly for Rebecca, Alex will suffer too."

"How?"

"I shall make the matter public." Ellis narrowed his eyes. "I shall have the pair of you arraigned, and brought to trial. I'll see you hanged for what you've done!"

Lalage blanched. She hadn't bargained for this. As her schemes and plans had led her down the primrose path to insanity, she had convinced herself that it was Ellis who must see the error of his ways. It was Ellis who would confess his sins, and repent.

As for Lalage herself – she was the one Ellis loved best. Of course she was! That fat blonde doxy was his harlot, the object of his lust, it was true. But she was nothing more. Surely?

Lalage looked into her brother's eyes. "What do you want me to do?" she asked.

"What?" Ellis stared at her. "I don't know," he muttered. "But I don't want to see you any more."

"Never again?"

"Never."

Lalage shuddered. Reaching out to him, she touched his hand. "I'm sorry," she said, meekly. "Ellis, I'm so sorry. I must have been mad. I – "

"Don't touch me!" As if she were a scorpion about to sting his flesh, Ellis dashed her away. "You're not sorry," he said. "You're annoyed, of course. You failed to kill the woman I love. Who loves me – "

"Ellis, *I* love you!" Clutching at her heart, Lalage collapsed on the carpet. Sprawled in a heap, she caught at her brother's ankle. "I love you!" she wailed. "Ellis, you're my life! My soul! No one could love you as I do!"

"Shut up." Ellis tried to shake her off. "Let me go."

"I can't."

"Release me, Lalage. If you don't, I'll kick you."

"Do that. Kick me all you please, beat me black and blue." Lalage began to sob. "Beat me to death, if you wish."

"I just might." Ellis lost all sense of reality now. "For God's sake," he cried. "Let me go! Lalage, are you mad?"

"Yes." Lalage stared up at him. Her bosom heaved, and tears sparkled like jewels in her beautiful eyes. "It's all your fault," she wept. "You made me like this. When you married that fat slut, you – "

She got no further. Ellis's precarious self-control snapped. He pulled Lalage to her feet. He shook her like a doll, jarring every bone in her body. His hands found their way around her neck. He was choking her. The pressure on her windpipe grew.

Her head spun. Blackness was before her eyes. Soon, she thought, soon it will all be over, and I shall be at peace. Now, she felt his grasp relax a little. "Go on," she urged, gasping. "Don't stop now!"

Her eyes were glazed. She was fainting. Losing consciousness. But then Ellis chanced to look into those blank, black eyes, and the red anger which had fired his attack lifted like a sea mist. He slackened his grip still further.

"Go on, Ellis." Crazily, Lalage grinned at him. "Kill me. If I have to die – I'm happy – to be strangled – by you."

At last, Ellis understood. If he killed her, she would win. Dying, she would break Rebecca's heart, because she would kill him too. As he climbed the scaffold, her ghost would mock him. Her soul would be waiting, to drag his down to hell.

She had destroyed his home. She had probably killed his child. If she took his life too, her victory would be complete. So he pushed her away from him, letting her fall heavily on the coffee-stained carpet. He strode out of the house.

Chapter 19

Accustomed to being in charge and expecting to be obeyed, Rebecca took command. Summoning Ellis's farm bailiff, she told him to get a group of labourers together, then set them to drag what they could out of the smoking ruins of the house. When he'd done that, he should report to her at the Dower House.

In the servants' dining room there, Alex and his sister began a late breakfast. Warmly wrapped in dressing gowns, with caps on their heads and slippers on their feet, they nibbled toast and drank comforting hot chocolate.

"I always knew you hated me." Too wound up to rest and far too upset to eat the substantial meal the cook had now provided, Rebecca warmed her hands around her cup of chocolate. Then, toying with a piece of bread, she tried to read her brother's expression. "All the same," she went on, "I'd never have thought Ellis's own sister could have done – what she did."

"Neither would I." Alex looked on the verge of tears. His hands trembled and his cup shook, making the chocolate slop over. "Rebecca, please believe me. I had no idea. Not the slightest inkling! I knew she was upset, but I never imagined she could be as – as downright wicked as this."

Two fat tears welled up in his light blue eyes. First one, then the other, trickled lazily down his pale cheeks. He dashed them away. "Rebecca? Do you believe me?"

"I don't know." Rebecca shrugged. "Should I?"

"Yes, I think so." Alex met her eyes. "May we talk?"

So, over a somewhat dishevelled breakfast, Rebecca Darrow and Alex Lowell began their first and last private conversation.

Alex explained himself, or tried to. Disclaiming all knowledge whatsoever of his wife's schemes, he insisted he was in no way involved in anything Lalage had planned. He loved Ellis dearly. He would never have hurt his best friend. As he spoke, he wept.

Watching him, Rebecca was inclined to believe everything he said. Weak and pathetic as he was, she didn't think Alex Lowell even capable of planning, let alone committing such a crime. Fop he might be. Criminal he almost certainly was not.

"I believe you," she said. She covered his soft, white hand with her own. "Please, Alex. Don't cry."

He sniffed. Eventually, he managed to control his tears. But then he began to babble again, explaining about Lalage. He spoke of her disappointments, her trials, her worries. Of her distress, that she should be childless. Of her lack of cash, which made her miserable. "Lally always wanted money," he explained. "Money. Power. That's why she married me, you understand – she thought that as my wife she'd have both. But now, of course, she has neither.

"When Ellis took out that mortgage on my family's old home, it upset her dreadfully. She thought he meant to live there, you see. I didn't care what became of the wretched place. But Lally did."

"He meant to give it back to you!" Covering her face, Rebecca felt tears behind her own eyes. "You pair of fools, how could you think Ellis would want to live there? Or anywhere, but at the Hall?"

"He meant to give it back?" Sceptically, Alex frowned. "Oh, Rebecca. I don't think – "

"He did!" Rebecca glared. "Ellis loved you both," she muttered, so bitterly that Alex winced. "He meant to see you back in your former home. Living in the style you used to do. He meant to mend your fortunes, to see you both happy. His generosity almost cost him his life." She sighed. "Mine, too."

"Yes." Embarassed, Alex stared at the floor. "Fortunately, however, things didn't turn out that way."

"Has she always disliked me?" Genuinely curious, Rebecca frowned in puzzled enquiry. "I don't understand. What have I done? How have I hurt *her*?"

"She was prejudiced before she even met you." Alex sniffed. "For one thing, there was the matter of the legacy. You don't know about that, do you? The thing is, just before my father died, he asked me – "

"To provide for his daughter." Rebecca grimaced. "I've known about that all along."

"You have?" Amazed, Alex stared at her. "Rebecca, tell me. How – "

"Ellis told me all about it. Before we were married. He asked me to forgo any claim on you, never to mention it in fact. He thought it would embarrass you to feel I was an unpaid creditor. So to speak." Mirthlessly, Rebecca laughed. "Poor Ellis. He needn't have been so scrupulous, after all."

"What else did he say?" asked Alex. "Did he tell you what sort of sum was involved?"

"No." Rebecca sighed. "He said it was several thousand pounds, but he'd never known exactly how much. There's no written legacy, is there? No formal bequest?"

"No."

"Then, had I been disposed to defy my husband, and determined to secure my inheritance, do you think it would have been worth my while to try? To fatten a lawyer, in an attempt to prove title on such a vague intention?"

"I suppose not."

"Anyway, Alex, I don't want anything from a Lowell."

"No." Alex bit his lip. "I don't suppose you do."

Getting up, he walked over to the window. He stared at the wisps of smoke, which still spiralled above even the tallest trees. "Ellis will always suspect I had a hand in it," he muttered. "He'll never believe I – "

"Well, you did save yourself. You left the house and never thought of us." Rebecca joined him at the window. She watched with him as the evidence of the fire blew away on the breeze. "You could have made your way upstairs, and woken us."

"The place was full of smoke. I couldn't breathe. I did shout." Alex shrugged. "I accept you probably didn't hear me."

"No, but – "

"Don't let's quarrel." Alex took her hand. "I panicked. I admit it. I left it to Ellis to save you. But we mustn't fall out now. We're relations. Henry Lowell was your father, as well as mine."

"You think I therefore owe you something?" Rebecca's eyes narrowed. "Your father hurt my mother very cruelly. You yourself haven't behaved honourably by me."

"No." Alex hung his head. "I haven't, I agree."

"It's such a shame." Rebecca sighed. "Such a pity that neither you nor Lalage could forgive me for a mere accident of birth."

"I don't care about that!" Alex crushed Rebecca's fingers. "Rebecca, don't think I'm so small-minded that I hold your illegitimacy against you."

"Don't you?"

"No! Of course not."

"Oh." Rebecca sniffed. "When Ellis announced he was going to marry me, how did you feel about it?"

"*I* didn't object." Alex looked at her, blue eyes wide. "When I saw you together, I could see he loved you. Since I love him, I could hardly begrudge him a wife so likely to make him happy. Who would love him in return." Alex looked into Rebecca's eyes. "Because you do love him, don't you? As much as I love Lally."

"You still love her? After all she's done?"

"I can't help loving her." Alex sighed. "She's not Ellis," he conceded. "She's not the person I love more than my life. But she's almost as dear. She's his living image, you see."

"But she's nothing like him!" Rebecca was angry now. "How dare you even begin to compare those two? Oh, they may have the same features. The same mannerisms, the same accents – physically, I'll admit, they're complementary faces of the same coin. But inside, they're completely different. No two people could be less alike."

"Couldn't they?" Alex sighed. "Rebecca, they're both ambitious. Both determined. Both headstrong, both passionate. Both repay being loved."

"But only one is worth loving!"

"No." Alex shook his head. "Lally's worth loving, too. As for Ellis – well, he'll be back soon. He won't want to find me here. Rebecca? "

"Yes?"

"Don't hate me. Don't remember me with disgust. After all, you can afford to be generous. You have everything now."

"Have I?"

"Of course. You have Ellis. One day, your child will be in possession of my old home. The Searles will have their revenge on the Lowells." Alex smothered a yawn. "I'll have Simmons find me some of Ellis's clothes. Then I'll be off."

After a rest which took up the remainder of the morning, Rebecca rang for her maid, put on a servant's red woollen cloak, and went to look at the damage to Easton Hall.

Coming out from among the trees, she gazed at her home. It didn't look so bad by daylight. The shell was still whole, for the basic structure of the place had proved solid enough to withstand even the fiercest flames.

It might, she thought, be rebuilt. The inside was badly damaged, certainly – ceilings had caved in, all the elaborate and painstaking plaster-work had crumbled to black dust, and most of the panelling was destroyed – but the interior walls still stood. Solid brick, in places these were two feet thick. As for the stout oak beams, these were merely charred on the outside.

But, she thought now, Ellis might want the whole thing levelled. Totally obliterated, so a new house might rise phoenix-like, from the ashes of the old.

Rebecca did not care either way. Her husband was unhurt. That was worth a hundred houses. A thousand. Everything in the world.

Amidst the general salvage, her maid discovered some trunks full of her mistress's clothes. These had been hauled out practically undamaged. Rebecca had them conveyed to her new lodging. There, she put on a clean cambric shift and a loose calico gown. She had a servant dress and powder her hair. She washed her face and hands. Properly dressed, she felt better. Much more in control.

By mid-day, the main rooms of the Dower House had been scoured and polished and were ready for the squire's and his lady's occupation. The servants who had previously used these quarters were found lodgings in the village.

Miraculously, no one had been injured in the blaze. Now, on a bright, sunny afternoon, there was almost an air of holiday about the place. The scavengers picking over the ruins of the Hall went about their work with good-humoured interest and enthusiasm. The combination of novelty without danger lifted everyone's spirits. Some parts of the Hall had escaped damage completely, and into these unaffected rooms whatever could be salvaged was piled high.

It was mid-afternoon when Ellis finally walked into the Dower House. Dismissing his valet, who had been anxiously awaiting his master's return and had clean clothes all ready, the squire went to find his wife.

Rebecca had heard him walk in, and now she came running, to lead him to the improvised drawing room.

Ellis let her take him where she pleased. Sitting down heavily, he buried his face in his hands.

Rebecca went to sit on the sofa beside him. "Did you see your sister?" she asked.

"Yes."

"Was she responsible?"

"She planned it all." Ellis rubbed his dirty face. "Lalage meant to kill you."

"I see."

"I think she's mad." Taking his wife's hand, Ellis held it. "She's demented. Insane. From now on, I shall oblige Alex to keep her closely confined. If he refuses, I shall have her placed in a private asylum."

"I talked to Alex." Gently, Rebecca stroked Ellis's untidy hair, pushing it back from his forehead. "He'll look after her. He said so. He also said I'd have my revenge on the Lowells." Rebecca sighed. "I don't want revenge!" she cried. "Why should I want revenge?"

"You don't need to take it." Turning to his wife, Ellis took her face between his hands. "Becky, are you hurt? You and the child – "

"We're both perfectly well."

"Thank God." Ellis shook his head. "I shouldn't have rushed off so hastily," he muttered. "I know that. But I had to see her! I had to ask – "

"I understand."

"She thinks she's won." Bitterly, Ellis sighed. "As far as she's concerned, this is a victory. She's destroyed my home. She's hurt *me* past understanding. She's spoiled everything for you."

"Nonsense!" Taking Ellis by the shoulders, Rebecca shook him. "Ellis, that's not true. She's won only if we let her win. My dear love, a house can easily be rebuilt. I shall have my baby, and others to keep him company. We can't let this – this setback ruin our own lives."

"She meant to hurt me. To cut me to the heart. She has."

"My dear, you're very upset. The shock's made you ill.

You can't see things in proportion yet." Letting him go, Rebecca took one of Ellis's hands. She held it between her own. But, as she stroked his fingers, she noticed her own were wet. She realised she had opened a cut. "That's nasty," she observed.

"Is it?"

"Yes." Rebecca examined the wound. Used to dealing with cuts, gashes and lacerations, for at the factory hardly a day went by without at least one of the workmen hurting himself, she understood that this gaping slash across Ellis's palm needed prompt attention. "Let me wash this," she said. "Then I'll bind it up."

"Don't fuss, Becky." With dirty fingers, Ellis dabbed at the wound. He grimaced. "It'll heal," he muttered. "Leave it for now."

"Ellis, left to itself it will fester. Look, it's dirty. It's full of grit and mess. You must let me wash it."

"Later." Ellis pushed the offending hand deep into his breeches pocket. "Why?" he asked, his eyes dark with distress. "Why should she want to hurt you?"

"I don't know." Helplessly, Rebecca shook her head. "But if you grieve for her, if you torment yourself about her, then she will have won. Ellis, dear – do you love me?"

"Of course I love you! If you'd been hurt last night, if you'd been killed, I would have died, too."

"So there it is. We're both safe. Surely that's enough?" Rebecca rose to her feet. "Aren't you hungry?" she asked. "It must be twenty four hours since you ate."

Ellis had forgotten all about food. But now he realised he was ravenous. Starving, in fact. "I could eat something," he replied. "What is there?"

"Roast mutton. A couple of fowls. A pudding." Rebecca smiled. "Simmons has worked wonders. Shall we go and eat?"

"Yes." Ellis managed a faint smile. "Let's."

As he broke bread, Ellis glanced at his wife. "I've thought what to do," he said. "I shall instruct my banker to release a quarterly allowance. It will be payable to Alex. With the few thousand he'll get back from the East India Company, they'll be able to live. Becky?"

"Yes?"

"Don't speak of them to me. I never want to see or hear of them, ever again."

Chapter 20

"Where?" Lalage stared. "Where did you say we're going?"

"To South Wales." Alex shrugged. "It's as good a place as any," he went on. "Rather cheaper than most. I shall tell Ellis we're going to London. But you and I will go down to Swansea. I shall rent a house there, and – "

"Keep me locked up for the rest of my life." Lalage flashed him a look of utter scorn. "Alex, I'd rather die now. Tell Ellis to have a gallows set up in the garden. He can hang me himself."

"Don't talk like that!" Alex wanted to weep. "Lally, you did a terrible thing. But I still love you. I couldn't live without you. I'll always look after you, I – "

"Ha!" Lalage's harsh, barking laugh brought him up short. "You'll forgive me too, I expect. I've spoiled everything for you. Yet still you love me. You insist you'll look after me."

"I'm your husband," said Alex, simply. "For better or worse – and so on."

"Alex, you're a saint. Now you're going to be a madwoman's gaoler, too." Crazily, Lalage grinned. "I *am* mad, you know. No doubt about it."

"Oh, darling – "

"Darling!" Lalage laughed again. But then she began to cry. "Oh, Alex!" she sobbed. "Poor Alex! Don't you deserve a better fate?"

Alex went to her. Taking her in his arms, he kissed her wet cheeks. "You're not mad, darling," he whispered. "You're troubled in spirit, certainly. You're very upset.

But you're not raving. You're still my sweet wife. My Lalage, whom I love best in all the world."

"After Ellis, of course."

"Ellis never wants to see either of us again. From now on, you'll be all in all to me."

"Ah." Resigned, Lalage relaxed in his embrace. She said nothing more, but let her mind wander. Softly, Alex talked on, soothing her as if she were a child cheated of a promised treat.

Swansea, a mean little manufacturing town with nothing whatsoever to offer a woman of Lalage's cultured tastes and high sophistication, appalled even Alex. Generally willing to take an enlightened interest in whatever he found, wherever he found it, he had the insatiable curiosity of the born traveller.

But even Alex Lowell found nothing to admire amid the acres of squalid tenements. The local metal industries did not interest him. The men who worked in them babbled a language he did not understand.

Unlike most of the foreign visitors to the town, the Lowells had not come as investors or speculators. Consequently, they were bored. A few days in a disagreeable hotel made Alex determined to find a house of his own, and find it very soon. He must make a pleasant home for himself and Lalage. She must be settled, she must be comfortable, she must be content. Then her recuperation could begin.

He could not bear Swansea itself, so he resolved to explore the countryside round about.

The Gower peninsula, a parcel of land to the west of the town, proved to be a pretty place. Driving through green valleys, bowling across broad stretches of common land and skirting wooded hillsides, the Lowells deplored the bad roads but admired the undeniable beauty of the landscape. Arriving at the village of Llangynnydd, they found lodgings for the night. Over supper, Alex asked their landlady if she knew of any houses available for long lets.

"John Rhys Morgan is looking for a tenant. Or so I hear." The landlady had set a plain but well-cooked and substantial meal before her guests, and been pleased to see them enjoy it. Now, she smiled. "I don't know if his house would suit."

"It might." Alex returned the woman's smile. "What kind of house does Mr Morgan have to offer?"

"Oh, a very good one. Excuse me just one moment." The landlady went to the door. In rapid Welsh, she rattled off instructions to an unseen servant. Then she returned to her guests. "Margiad is making your tea now," she said. "So. About the house. Well, as I said, it's a good one. A farmhouse. Not a cottage, no indeed! It's a fine, stone-built Gower farmhouse. You'd find nothing better if you walked for a week."

"Then why does Mr Morgan not live in it himself?" Breaking a silence which had lasted all through supper, Lalage fixed the Welshwoman with a sharp, suspicious stare. "Well, Mrs Gethyn? If it's such a splendid place?"

"It's far too big for him, that's why." The landlady was finding this conversation rather a strain. English was such a strange, such a difficult language. Although she had learned it during her days in service and spoken it with some fluency then, she'd never felt really at ease with the Saxon tongue.

But now she made a big effort. She sat down between her guests. "He's a single man, see," she said. "As a boy, he was a bit wild. Never settled to anything. But then, a year or two ago, his father passed away. He inherited some land. His mother? Oh, she died when he was a child."

Mrs Gethyn sighed, as if pitying John Rhys Morgan's orphaned state. "Old Huw Morgan lived in style," she continued. "Kept servants. Entertained, he did. But John Rhys – well, he doesn't go in for any of that. Doesn't want the expense of keeping up a large house.

"He's quite happy in a little cottage. Out in the fields

all day, so he is. Why'd he want to come home to a great empty place like that farmhouse there?"

"Might he not marry?" asked Alex. "If he had a wife and children, he'd need a substantial home."

"I really don't know about that." Rising to her feet, Mrs Gethyn began to clear away the dishes. "It's a fine house," she repeated, with emphasis. "You'd be wise to look it over."

Lalage thumped her feather pillows, then buried her face in the hollow she'd made there. "So you're going to shut me up in a filthy little slum of a farmhouse," she muttered. "I'm to be locked away in a fine, stone-built prison."

She lifted her head and glared. "It sounds just the place to keep a lunatic confined."

"I'm merely going to see what Mr Morgan has to offer." Climbing into the high, elaborately carved tester bed, Alex lay down beside her. "I'm becoming rather tired of all this talk about locking you up," he added, mildly. "We'll go and see Mr Morgan. We'll look at his house. If it pleases us, we'll come to some arrangement."

"If it pleases *us*?"

"Of course, Lally." Alex sighed. "I wouldn't want you to live in a place you disliked."

"No?" Lalage scowled at him. "As if I have any choice in the matter."

As Mrs Gethyn had promised, the house was indeed fine. A perfect example of the best sort of Gower farmhouse, it was solidly built of dark grey stone. With walls which were, in places, three feet thick, it looked capable of withstanding all the punishment Atlantic gales could ever throw at it. Small windows, the biggest no more than three feet by three, together with a substantial thatched roof, increased the aura of general impregnability.

"Well, Mr Lowell?" A dark-haired, well-built young Welshman of twenty five or so, John Rhys Morgan had the direct, searching gaze of the experienced stockman.

He met Alex's eyes. "What do you think?" he asked now. "Will you wish to see inside?"

"I'm not sure." Largely unimpressed, but not keen to stand around for much longer in the penetrating Welsh rain, Alex thought about it. Then he nodded. "Yes, Mr Morgan," he replied firmly. "I think we would."

Shut up for the past twelve months at least, the house smelled airless and musty. Unused. But there was also a faint fragrance of herbs and lavender and, more to the point, no suspicion whatever of damp or rot.

Downstairs, there was an abundance of dark-stained, solid furniture. In the great, square kitchen, a table, chairs and settles were placed confidently on thick, rush matting. Cupboard beds lined the walls, and upon these little cots lay intricately-worked quilts – the handiwork, Alex guessed, of whole generations of Morgan women, whose nimble fingers had beguiled the tedious winter evenings by stitching these domestic works of art.

"Furnished, you see." Opening a shutter, the farmer let clear daylight flood the room. It illuminated a wide hearth, stone-flagged floor, and plenty of old-fashioned kitchen-ware. It lit up the great carved blanket-press which lurked in the chimney corner, and revealed the huge dresser in an alcove probably built specially to accomodate it.

Tapping the oak table in the centre of the room, the Welshman nodded complacently. "Old stuff," he admitted. "But good." This was the extent of his recommendation. Here was another native Welsh speaker obviously ill at ease with the language of the Saxon overlords.

Politely agreeing that the furniture was splendid – for although he deplored its old-fashioned lines, he could appreciate its quality – Alex glanced round once more. Then, satisfied, he smiled. "May we see upstairs?" he asked.

"Of course." The farmer opened the door to the staircase. "You go on up. Have a good look round. Take your time."

Upstairs, the rooms were large and high-ceilinged – or rather, they were without ceilings as such, for the great wooden beams supporting the roof were exposed, and there was no loft. But the underthatch was completely weatherproof, security against the worst of storms. On this rainy day, the decoratively-woven rope mats which lay behind the rafters were as dry as dust.

Accustomed to rooms which had elaborate plastered ceilings, Lalage looked up at the thatching. She scowled in disgust. Turning on her heel, she made her way down the stairs. Observing her grimace, the farmer opened another door. "Will you look at the parlour?" he asked.

Surprised to be addressed so confidently and directly an ignorant Welsh lout, Lalage stared. But then, very coolly, she nodded. "Very well," she replied. She swept past him.

The parlour was a pretty room. The walls had been smoothly plastered, then painted – or stencilled – with a repeating pattern of blue *fleurs de lys*. The effect was of papering. Comfortable, upholstered chairs were arranged round an open fireplace. The brasswork on the mantelshelf winked at the pewter mugs adorning the small dresser in the corner. On the painted mortar floor was a large Indian carpet, of excellent quality.

"Do you like this room?" asked the farmer, who was standing behind Lalage.

"Yes." Dark and shuttered though it was, the little parlour had a positively seductive air of comfort and warmth. In spite of herself, Lalage smiled. "I like it very much," she replied.

"It was my mother's room." The farmer smiled too. "When there's a good fire, when the kettle's singing on the hob and the toast is fresh made, there's no better place to be."

"I don't suppose there is." Lalage shook her head. "Mr Morgan, I'll confess it now. I like your house. Or at any rate, I like this particular room. It more than makes up for the rusticity of the rest."

Alex came back down the stairs. He glanced into the parlour, shrugged, then walked out into the yard. Motioning the farmer to follow, he strolled round the garden. As he walked, he spoke. When Lalage came out of the front door, she heard Alex laugh. "So," he said now, "provided Mrs Lowell agrees, we'll come to an arrangement."

Then he saw his wife. "Shall we take the place, my dear?" he asked.

"Yes." Decidedly, Lalage nodded. "It's a charming house. I should like to live here."

John Rhys Morgan smiled.

He treated her so carefully. As if she were an invalid convalescent from a serious illness. One for whom a sudden shock or nervous upset might prove her undoing.

"I'm not mad, Alex," she said one morning, as they sat at breakfast. "You said so yourself. There's no need to behave as if I were a lunatic, or a freak."

Alex merely smiled. "Sukey?" he called. "May we have more coffee? Some fresh toast?"

The Lowells' own servants, lodged together in a Swansea boarding house until their employers found a new home, had arrived the previous week. So now, this household consisting of a small, pale, fair-haired master, his beautiful dark-eyed wife, their two rather comely female servants and a footman as black as the devil himself, was a source of fascinated curiosity to everyone in the district.

As far as most of the shepherds and farmers of North Gower were concerned, John Rhys Morgan's new tenants were a rum lot, not to be trusted an inch. Caspar in particular was an object of fear. The *cythraul du* – black devil – of enchantments and nightmares, he was now a tall, well-grown adolescent. His coal-black face, tightly-curling dark hair, huge brown eyes and white, white teeth combined to mark him out. He was a fiend, a creature from the burning lake. Meeting him out on errands for his mistress, older women crossed themselves and muttered protective charms.

But their daughters found him attractive. They eyed him flirtatiously, and dared one another to cross his path. One or two, bolder than the rest, actually grinned at him.

Sukey was alarmed. While in Swansea, she had initiated the boy into certain grown-up rites and rituals. She had even taken him into her bed, and let him discover some of the secrets of her body. Caspar was hers, not some Welsh trollop's.

"But they're so dirty, child!" she wailed, when Caspar told her Bronwen Powell and Angharad Evans had invited him to go walking after church on Sunday. "You don't want to bother with them! They're like the beasts. Backward, and stupid."

"Stupid, eh?" Thoughtfully, Caspar picked his teeth. Bronwen Powell might be backward. Indeed, she did seem a bit of a goose. But she certainly wasn't dirty. Her complexion was cream and pink, smooth and delicate as the inside of a seashell. Angharad Evans's wild, red hair, emerald-green eyes and clear, transparent white skin made his pulse race.

But Sukey had a pretty face. Her figure was trim and neat. She need not be jealous of Bronwen Powell. The footman grinned. "Why don't you like the Welsh?" he asked.

"I told you. They're dirty. They smell."

"They look as clean as the English to me. You white people all smell the same."

"Nonsense." Sukey flounced off, to turn out the bedrooms, or so she said.

Caspar grinned. He loved Sukey dearly. When he was a terrified, bewildered child, whose only memories were confused nightmares of beatings, cold, hunger and loneliness, she had been kind. She had warmed and comforted him.

All the same, he liked to see her jealous. He knew he

was a handsome man. Sukey was a pretty woman. He'd marry her some day. But not just yet.

The Lowells settled down. Deprived of any social life, for he did not want the company of shepherds or farmers, and his limited income did not permit him to meet the few English families in the area on anything like equal terms, Alex began to make a collection of flowers and butterflies. Gradually, he became something of an expert on the flora and lepidoptera of Gower. He even began to enjoy living here.

But Lalage did nothing but fret. She thought of Ellis a hundred times a day. Often and often, she picked up a pen, determined to write, to beseech his forgiveness, to be recalled from exile. If she closed her eyes, she could see his face. Feel his presence. If she shut her ears to the world, she could hear his voice. Was it possible to die of sorrow? Lalage thought it might be.

She longed for news of home. But there was none. Betty could tell her nothing. Her mother had died, and she was not on good terms with her brothers or sisters. In any case, none of them could read or write.

Searching for specimens, Alex strode across desolate moorlands. He scrambled up and down the stark sea cliffs. Sometimes, Lalage went with him. She trailed after him as he stalked butterflies. She lay with him on wet grass while he exclaimed over a new species of orchid or speedwell. Soon, she thought, *he'll* be mad. The very picture of a mumbling, wild-haired recluse. Living with him will deprive me of my reason, too.

Their hurts untended, the two fire-raisers were locked in a filthy cellar. Fed only when someone remembered to push a bit of bread through the trapdoor communicating with the outside world, they had plenty of time to repent of their sins. It was a full week before the squire thought of them again, and decided to question them. After he'd heard anything they might wish to say, they could go to the municipal gaol. To await trial at the next Assize.

The cellar where the two men were confined was a malodorous underground pit. Dripping with damp, it was infested with vermin, and was not a good place in which to recuperate from the savage beating they had received. By day, a little light crept into the place. At night it was pitch dark. Then, rats came out and licked their blood.

Sometimes, curious villagers came, to stare through a narrow grating at the caged creatures within. But such was the esteem in which the squire was held that no one felt the least pity for their plight.

Having ridden over to the village and ordered their temporary release, Ellis had the men taken to the justice room. This was a chamber kept for the purpose of examining local petty criminals, and was on the ground floor of the local inn.

"God in heaven!" The justice stared at the men in disgust. Brought before the magistrate who'd sent them down once already, they cowered. But Ellis did not thunder curses, nor order further tortures. He merely covered his face with a handkerchief. "Tarrant?" he barked, breathing through his mouth. "Tarrant! Get yourself in here! Are you responsible for this?"

"Yes, sir." Tarrant had indeed arranged for the men to be confined. Now he was expecting praise for his initiative. Swaggering slightly, he strolled into the room. Seeing the look on the squire's face, he stopped dead. He shuffled. He coughed. "Well, sir," he began, "I thought – "

"Get them into the fresh air." Ellis scowled. "Good God, man. Look at them. Why weren't they sent to the local prison? Who gave you authority to keep them here?"

"Well, your honour didn't tell anyone what to do. You hadn't signed your mittimus. So I thought – "

"Did you?" Ellis glared. "Well, Tarrant – the next time you feel like thinking, apply your mind to some agricultural matter. Leave judicial affairs to me."

But now, despite being removed to a slightly more

salubrious place, the men were past help. Alive with vermin, their wounds were badly infected. Soon, a fatally high fever racked their bodies. Their fellow prisoners, usually more than anxious to relieve new arrivals of their valuables, refused to go near them. Left food and water but otherwise neglected, allowed neither wholesome air nor medical attention, both were dead long before they could be brought to trial.

"It's better this way." Having searched his heart and conscience, James Tarrant found he'd acted in the best interests of all concerned. Now, complacently, he watched the sexton shovel earth over the two narrow paupers' graves. "Dunno as I'd care to be strung up by a mob. That was what lay in store for this pair. No doubt about it."

Badly cut in the course of that dreadful night, Ellis's hand had eventually been cleaned and bound up. But, as Rebecca had predicted, the wound festered. It began to smell so horrible that even Ellis was concerned. Nevertheless, he refused to see a doctor. He insisted it would heal.

It did not. Eventually a foul, greenish matter filled the whole lesion. Then, one evening, as Rebecca changed the dressing, she was alarmed to see the palm was swollen like a puffball. Blackened, soft and rotting. She pressed the swelling, and found it gave beneath her touch. "This should be lanced," she said. "Tomorrow, you must send for Mr Steele."

"There's no need for that." Snatching his hand away, Ellis scowled. "I've had cuts before. They've always mended. It doesn't hurt," he lied. "This time next week, it will be better."

"All the same, Mr Steele comes tomorrow. You'll see him then."

"I shan't."

"You shall!"

"Rebecca, you forget yourself." Coldly, Ellis met her eyes. "As your husband, it is *my* place to command. Yours is to obey."

"Yes. I agree." Rebecca forced herself to be calm. "But I have a duty towards you, too. You seem set on a course which may end in your own destruction. I seek to divert you. To – "

"To know better than me. Is that what you mean?" Ellis was angry now. He was shouting. "Well, Rebecca? Is it?"

"No!" Rebecca glared at him. "All I meant was – "

"That you will have your pleasure. That you will defy me. Decide what is best for me, deny me the – "

"Ellis, you're a fool." Rebecca turned away. "Do as you wish. Suffer if you must. I'm going to bed."

She walked out of the parlour and into the hallway. But then, seeing the butler emerge from the dining room, she collared him. "Simmons!" she hissed. "Come here."

"Yes, madam?" Simmons had heard his master shouting, and now he looked at his mistress askance. "What is it?"

"I want you to go over to Feldon. Call at Mr Steele's house, and ask him to wait on Mr Darrow first thing tomorrow morning."

"Ah." Simmons had heard what Ellis thought of seeing Mr Steele. Now, sensibly, he demurred. "Well, madam – "

"Now, Simmons. Go now!"

"I – "

"No matter." Rebecca sighed. "Simmons," she whispered, "did you overhear Mr Darrow talking just now?"

"Well actually, madam – "

"Of course you did. The whole house must have heard him." Rebecca grimaced. "Simmons, you know how passionate your master can be. How angry in his own defence. Especially when no one has attacked him!

"Think, man. Just think. How many times has Mr Darrow gone out riding in the rain, and returned home with his clothes soaked through? Then refused to change them? How often has he taken cold, in consequence?"

"But – "

"Listen to me." Rebecca's voice was still low, but it was also urgent now. "Listen well. Mr Darrow's hurt is grievous. I have seen such wounds before. I know how dangerous neglect of them can be.

"My husband needs to see a surgeon! If he does not have the necessary care, I am afraid he will take a fever. Simmons, I am about to become a mother. I do not wish to become a widow first."

"No." Meeting Rebecca's eyes, Simmons nodded. "I'll go now," he said. "But if Mr Darrow asks for me – "

"I'll tell him where you are. That I sent you there." Weakly, Rebecca smiled. "Go quickly," she added. "Before my husband overhears us, and countermands what I've said."

Mr Steele examined the hand. Gravely, he shook his head.

"There, Becky." Imagining he was about to be reprimanded for wasting the surgeon's time, Ellis grinned. "I knew quite well this gentleman would have a wasted morning. Mr Steele – I'm sorry to have called you here unnecessarily. Will you have a glass of wine before you go?"

"Thank you, sir. I will." Mr Steele sat down. "You should have one yourself, perhaps," he added. "As for Mrs Darrow here – will she join us, too?"

Told to fetch refreshment, Simmons closed the door behind him.

Mr Steele had attended the Darrow family for twenty years or more. He had bound up the results of scores of riding accidents, then treated the fevers which frequently ensued. Having tried in vain to persuade Ellis's father to moderate his drinking, he was well aware that the son, though on the whole a far more reasonable man, was in some ways just as stubborn as the old squire.

Taking the tray from the butler, he poured three glasses of port wine. "I'm sorry, sir," he said, as he handed Ellis a glass. "If I'd been called in a week ago, I could have lanced the palm. Let out the humours, and cauterised the wound. But now, sir – well, I'm afraid I can do nothing. The hand must come off."

"Come off?" Almost choking on his wine, Ellis stared. "It's just a cut!" he cried. "For God's sake, man! If all doctors went around hacking off the limbs of every man who scratched himself, this country would contain nothing but cripples."

"You haven't merely scratched yourself." Irritated into plain speaking, the surgeon met his patient's eyes. "Mr Darrow, that cut goes through to the bone. The wound is putrid. If nothing is done, the whole hand will mortify. The taint will spread throughout the body. Fever will result."

"I've had fevers before. You know that." With a dismissive sniff, Ellis poured himself more wine. "What's a fever? Nothing. The physician is called in. He bleeds the patient, he prescibes medicines, looks grave – but soon all is well again."

"In this case, all the cupping, dropping and bleeding in the world will not avail." The doctor took Ellis's glass. "Believe me, sir. You'll die raving. You'll run mad with pain, and you'll expire cursing the God who made you. Who gave you the life it seems you are too stubborn to wish to preserve."

"Ah. I see." Glancing towards his wife, Ellis sighed. Shrugging his shoulders, he accepted defeat. "Well, then," he muttered, "you may as well set about your task. Have you instruments with you here?"

"Sir, I'm an old man." The doctor shook his head. "I'd take half an hour. Perhaps more. Mr Darrow, you must permit me to call in a colleague."

"To give a second opinion?"

"No, sir! In your case, the opinion of every doctor in the land would be exactly the same." Mr Steele shrugged in enquiry. "Well, Mr Darrow? Have I your permission to send for a younger man?"

"I'll see him tomorrow." Pale now, and unwilling to

meet Rebecca's eyes, Ellis looked down at the floor. "How long, do you suppose – "

"He'll take twenty minutes. No more." Mr Steele himself sighed now. "Mr Darrow, I think you ought to see him today. Further delay might well prove dangerous. Fatal, even. I'll send my boy over to Birmingham at once."

"Would you like me to stay?" Wishing with all her heart that she had flouted Ellis's wishes and sent for the doctor a week ago, Rebecca touched her husband's shoulder. "Dear Ellis, shall I stay?"

"Could you bear it?" His face a dull, lifeless grey, Ellis's dark eyes were blank with dread. "Becky, you're pregnant. You might faint. After all, you've no experience – "

"But I have. Once, at the factory, a boy caught his arm in a piece of machinery. It mangled his hand. I had to do something for him. Then, when the surgeon came, I – I helped."

"Oh. I see."

"Ellis, this will be very hard for you." Wrapping her arms around his shoulders, Rebecca kissed her husband's brow. "You'll suffer, and I shall hate it. But I shan't scream. Nor pass out at the sight of blood. So, if it will comfort you to have me here, of course I'll stay."

"Thank you, Becky." Wretchedly, Ellis shrugged. "You were right. I am a fool."

"I'm the stupid one." Rebecca began to cry. "I'll never forgive myself!" she sobbed. "I knew quite well what needed to be done, and I ought to have done it."

Mr Steele's friend came over from Birmingham that same afternoon. A surgeon at the new General Hospital there, he was a stout, brisk, lively young fellow who liked an outing, and today he thoroughly enjoyed his pleasant ride through the green Warwickshire countryside. He brought with him his new assistant, a lumbering great brute of a lad with shoulders like a pugilist. Gerard's job was to hold the patient down.

Arriving at the Dower House, the surgeon entrusted Gerard with his gelding and his bag, and dispatched him to the kitchens, with instructions to get himself something to drink. The surgeon himself would go in by the front door.

Invited into the sitting room of the Dower House, he beamed at his patient. The niceties of introduction were soon over. Mr Steele's diagnosis was confirmed.

"Well, sir?" Taking off his coat, the lapels and cuffs of which were stiff with dried blood, the surgeon dropped it on a chair. "All prepared?"

"As prepared as I shall ever be." As melancholy as the surgeon was jaunty, Ellis was nevertheless relieved to see such a strongly-made, self-confident young man. One whose manner, even though it did not soothe, at least inspired some faith in his abilities.

"Will you have a draught of something?" Rolling up his sleeves to display tough, brawny forearms, the surgeon shrugged a general enquiry. "Half a pint of rum, sir? Whisky? Believe me, a glass or two of spirits – "

"No." Ellis took his wife's hand. "I don't want anything."

"I see. Well, as you wish." The surgeon glanced around the room. "Now," he muttered. "A table. Or a suitable chair. Ah – this chair here, with wide elbow rests. It looks ideal. May we use it?"

Ellis shrugged agreement.

"Good. What's become of my assistant? I told him to take some porter, then ask to be shown up here directly."

But now Simmons and Gerard were heard coming down the passage. The operation could begin

"Is the lady staying?" Unwrapping his instruments, the surgeon eyed Rebecca's swollen belly. "You know, sir – I don't honestly recommend – "

"I wish to remain." Rebecca met the surgeon's eyes. "My husband would like me to stay."

"Are you prone to fainting?" The doctor whetted his knife. "Because if you are, I must warn you – "

"I've never fainted in my life. I don't propose to begin now."

"Good." The surgeon spread his hands "Well then, Mrs Darrow. You stand behind the chair here. Gerard, you know *your* duty. Yes, I think one strap will certainly be required. Maybe even two. Mr Simmons, have you a bowl ready? Some cloth?"

"Sir." Co-opted to assist and already a faint shade of green, Simmons nodded. "Here they are."

"Splendid." The surgeon flexed his fingers. "So, Mr Simmons. You must hold the hand quite steady. Gerard will show you how. Well, ladies and gentlemen? Shall we begin?"

Taking his newly sharpened knife, the doctor repeated his instruction to hold the patient's hand steady. He also told Simmons to keep his own fingers well out of the way. "I wouldn't want to slice off more than is necessary," he remarked, in a facetious manner which Rebecca found offensive indeed. He checked that the tourniquet was tight. Then, he cut deep into the flesh some four inches above the wrist.

Set on the edge of the bone, the knife was drawn round in a matter of seconds. Now, with the muscle cut and bleeding freely, the surgeon forced up the flesh to expose the bones. Picking up his saw, he started to use it.

Teeth gritted, sweat beading his brow, Ellis fixed his eyes on a point in the corner of the room. His face ashen, his breathing became harsh. Harsher still. Soon, he was literally gasping for air.

Simmons kept his eyes tightly closed. Eventually, even Rebecca found she could look no more. She shut her eyes. But nothing could cut out the sound of the saw. Of the awful grating, rubbing and grinding, as the metal blade parted living tissue.

"Excellent!" The surgeon pushed the discarded hand to

one side. He was perspiring freely now. Taking ligatures of catgut, he began to tie off the artcrics. Finishing this most delicate of tasks, he grinned. "Worst part over, sir," he muttered. "Not long now. Gerard, support Mr Darrow's shoulder. Mr Simmons, do open your eyes. To your mopping directly, if you please."

Simmons mopped with a will. Then, as he was dropping a third or fourth blood-soaked cloth into the bucket provided, the doctor began to draw the flesh down again. Carefully, he eased the skin over the ends of the bones.

He smiled to himself. He'd done a very good job. The flaps of skin met just so. There was no need even for trimming. Nor – as sometimes happened with beginners at this game – was there any need to cut off more bone. That was a great relief. On those occasions, patients sometimes went mad with pain, never to recover their reason.

Applying sticking plaster then neatly bandaging the limb, the surgeon was almost singing to himself. Ellis, however, was deathly silent. His eyes were closed. Rebecca prayed he'd fainted at last.

"There, sir. It's done." The surgeon patted his patient's shoulder. "All finished. In good time, too."

Good time? Through unshed tears, Rebecca looked at the clock. Eighteen minutes. Eighteen minutes of torture. Eighteen whole lifetimes of pain.

Now Ellis groaned. He slumped forward. As Simmons caught his master, Rebecca began to sob.

From earliest childhood, she had been conditioned to forgive all injuries. To turn the other cheek, to love her enemy as herself. So well had she learned her lessons that she had even forgiven the man who'd taught them to her. She'd long since made her peace with the memory of Jeremy Searle.

But now, hatred for Lalage rose up and overwhelmed her. In this instance, there would be no forgiveness. Ever. Rebecca was Lalage's enemy now, and a fearsome one she would prove to be.

Chapter 21

Three weeks after Ellis's operation, Rebecca was delivered of her first child, a blonde, blue-eyed daughter. Recovering her strength with remarkable rapidity, she was out of bed and walking around her room a mere two hours after her confinement.

She had no time to spare for lying in. The following day, she was up, dressed and taking charge again. Behaving in fact as if she were fully recovered and in perfect health – which, indeed, she was.

"A name, Ellis?" Taking the child from her nurse, Rebecca carried the infant into the sitting room of the Dower House, where Ellis stood gazing out of the window. "Well, my dear? What shall we call this pretty daughter of ours?"

"Whatever you please," Ellis replied.

Following his ordeal, Ellis had taken a fever. After lying delirious for five anxious days, he had at last begun to mend. But slowly. He was still very weak. Sitting down beside his wife, he looked at his child. Blank indifference glazed his eyes, and wretchedness furrowed his brow. "Anything," he muttered. "Call her anything. You decide."

"I thought perhaps Eleanor. Eleanor Jane." Rebecca looked at him. "Ellis?"

"That's rather stiff. Too formal. It sounds – "

"What?"

"Oh. Nothing. It's fine. It sounds very well."

"You like the names, then?"

"I don't dislike them." Ellis glanced at the baby once

again. "She's very like you," he observed. "Not a Darrow at all."

"No," agreed Rebecca. She thought, thank God for that. A child who'd looked at me with Lalage's eyes would have made me sick. "Ellis, will you hold her?"

"I may let her fall." Glancing down at dressings which still bound his right wrist, and would do so for some weeks yet, Ellis groaned in anguish. "I can still feel my hand," he cried. "I can clench my fist. Pick up a pencil, hold a pen. I think I'm going out of my mind. Soon, I'll be mad indeed. Like her!"

"You're not mad." Aching with pity for him, Rebecca laid her baby in her cradle. She took her husband in her arms. "It's quite normal to feel as you do," she said. "To imagine the limb, the hand – or whatever – is still there. Mr Steele told me so. Truly, Ellis, he did. My dear, you're not going out of your mind. Not at all."

"Aren't I?" Ellis sighed. "When I was ill, I kept seeing her. She stood at my bedside, laughing. She called me a fool. She promised to come back. To complete what she'd begun."

"She can't hurt us." Rebecca stroked his hair. "She's miles away. She won't come back."

"How do you know?"

"She can't. She dare not." Rebecca shrugged. "Anyway, we are two. Three, now. She's only one."

"I'm not able to protect you." Wretchedly, Ellis rubbed his eyes. "I can't even look after myself. When the surgeon came, I almost cried. Like a child. I wanted to weep and wail, like this poor infant here. I'm not even half a man."

"Anyone would have wept." Remembering, Rebecca's own eyes filled with tears. "Please, Ellis," she whispered. "Don't fret. Especially about her. She's not worth it. I doubt if she ever thinks of us."

Rebecca was wrong. Lalage thought of Ellis all the time. The days lengthened into weeks, into months, into a whole year – and still she longed for him. Yearned for him.

Why hadn't he killed her? He had wanted to. She'd have died happy then. But now, she would die wretched. For she would never look upon his dear face again.

Why had Alex brought her here, to this horrible, dreary, desolate place? Why couldn't they have settled nearer home? Would she ever see Warwickshire again?

"Oh, madam! You're so melancholy today." Lacing her mistress's gown that chilly autumn morning, Betty gazed with concern at Lalage's ash-white complexion, gaunt cheeks and heavily shadowed eyes. "Is it Mr Lowell?" she asked.

"Mr Lowell?"

"Yes, madam. Is he making you unhappy?"

"That's no concern of yours." Sourly, her mistress grimaced. "No concern at all."

"I just wondered, madam." Calmly, Betty went on with her work. "I meant no offence."

"I hope not." Lalage picked at her finger nails. "I hate this gown," she muttered. "It hangs like a sack."

"Will you change it for your blue stripe, then? Or your green silk?"

"No." Shrugging her thin shoulders, Lalage sighed. "As if it matters what I wear."

Betty sighed too. Lalage was right. This particular garment did hang badly, for it was much too big. But then, all her mistress's clothes were too big for her these days.

Always very slim, Lalage had declined dramatically, and now she was nothing but bones. Thin, bird bones. Betty had to force herself to touch her. She hated seeing her naked, and felt sick when she undressed her at night.

The maid reached for more pins. By making big pleats at the back of the gown, she contrived to make Lalage look presentable. Just about. But the garment had been cut to fit a woman with curves. With a neat little bottom and small but firm breasts. It hung like a limp, silken rag on this walking corpse.

Perhaps Lalage would give it to her soon. She hoped so. It was beautiful material, and the style would certainly suit Betty. She fingered the cloth. Covetously, she smoothed the pleats she'd made.

"What were you saying about my husband?" Lalage's sharp voice broke into Betty's daydreams. "Were you being impertinent? I don't seem to remember – "

"I asked if Mr Lowell was making you sad. That's all." Betty picked up Lalage's cap. "He spends so much time out of the house, leaving you all alone. I know how fond you are of company."

"I'm not pining for his!" Derisively, Lalage sniffed. But then her features relaxed, crumpling into misery. "Oh, Betty!" she cried. "He doesn't love me! He thinks more of his moths and butterflies than he ever did of me!

"He hardly speaks to me now. All through dinner, he has his nose in some book. I might as well be a ghost, for all the heed he takes of my presence. At night, it's worse. He never – well, we're not man and wife any more!"

Lalage began to sob. "Betty," she wailed. "Speak to me! Advise me. What shall I do?"

"Dear madam! Don't cry." Betty took her lady in her arms. "Don't upset yourself," she crooned. "He's not worth it. No man deserves all these tears."

"I hate him." Lalage sobbed harder. "I hate him like poison. I do!"

"You don't, madam. You know you don't." Betty smoothed her mistress's long, black hair. "Soon," she said, "it will be winter. He won't be out chasing butterflies or picking posies then. He'll be here, by his own fireside, with you."

"You think that prospect cheers me?" Lalage ground her teeth. "I don't want him here at all," she muttered. "I wish him gone."

"No, madam, you don't." Betty shook her head.

"You're not at all well today," she said. "Come downstairs. Sit in the parlour, by the fire. I'll bring you a dish of tea, with something in it that will soothe you."

But Betty's soothing draughts could have no effect at all on a woman in Lalage's state of mind. The desire to rid herself of Alex haunted her.

She went over and over the things he'd said, the things he'd done. Always, always, she arrived at the same conclusions. He'd bought her, he'd used her, and now he was discarding her. She was of no more account than a walking stick, a snuff box, or a cheap tin tray. She was an object of desire. Or not, as it would seem nowadays.

He had never considered her needs. When she had wanted a child, had begged for one – had lain on the cold floor, beseeching him to give her a baby – he had denied her. Even her abject submission had not melted Alex Lowell's stony heart. Her vulnerable, naked body had disgusted him.

But he had not always despised her. At the beginning, he'd been mad for her. So mad, he had raped her. He had candidly admitted it. "That was rape," he had said. As if rape were a minor matter, of no real consequence at all.

Lalage made up her mind. Taking Sukey aside one evening, she told her that Mr Lowell had recently developed a liking for cinnamon in his hot chocolate. Since Lalage kept the keys to the spice cupboard, she would in future make his evening cordial herself.

This suited Sukey. Relieved of her last task of the day, she could now keep an eye on Caspar. More to the point, she could see Bronwen Powell kept away. Overheated Welsh bitch, she was still poaching after the boy's virginity. Virginity which Sukey meant to have for herself.

On her next visit to Swansea, Lalage visited a druggist. There, she bought everything she needed. As he wrapped bottles, phials and packets of powder, the druggist grinned. Madam would have no problems with rats or mice this winter.

Madam did not use her purchases straight away. But, a few weeks later, as the really cold weather set in, Alex began to complain of stomach cramps.

It was easy to begin, and easy to go on. Too easy. But yet, in a way, it was very difficult as well. As Alex wasted and sickened, Lalage suffered too. As she measured powder into his cup and stirred it round, she even felt pity. Why was he taking so long to die?

She wished she had the courage to administer a fatal dose. Then, instead of suffering this long agony of slow murder, he could die at once. But if his pains worsened, he might overcome his long-standing distrust of physicians and call in a doctor. That would never do.

Finally, Lalage lost her nerve. As the year turned, she stopped adulterating his chocolate. She gave him a reprieve. Alex must recover, and live.

"Do you feel any better today?" she asked one winter morning. Watching him sip tea, she winced as a spasm of pain shook him and made him catch his breath in distress. "Alex?"

"A little, I think. I'm maybe a little better today." White-faced, Alex replaced the teacup on its saucer. "Lally, my dear? I wish to speak to you. It's important. May we talk now?"

"Certainly." A tingle of apprehension rippled down Lalage's spine. Putting down her own cup, she willed herself to remain calm. "What did you wish to discuss?" she enquired.

"It's about the Hall."

"Oh. That." Relief flared like a secret beacon deep inside her heart. Lalage's colour returned. "What about it?"

"Lally, tell me honestly. When you paid those men to fire the Hall, did you mean us all to die?"

"No!" Wide-eyed, Lalage met his gaze. "Of course not. I didn't know *you* would be there."

"Did you intend to kill Rebecca, then?"

"Don't be so silly." Lalage shrugged. "I wanted to frighten her. That's all."

"Thank God." Reassured, Alex leaned back in his chair. "We may do something," he muttered, as if to himself. He looked at his wife. "Are you happy here?" he asked.

"Happy enough." Lalage sighed. "Why?"

"Because, if you're not – and there's anything I can do to make you so – you have only to say."

"There's nothing." Pushing back her chair, she stood up. "Come along," she said. "I'll help you dress."

"Caspar can do that."

"He's gone into Swansea with Sukey. They won't be back until nightfall." Lalage held out her hand. "Come upstairs, Alex. I'll look after you today."

For a few days more, Alex remained reasonably well. But then, a week or so after asking Lalage if she was happy, he sickened again. Lalage had resumed dosing him. "He used me," she told herself, as she measured the powder into the cup. "He let me plead and grovel and abase myself, but still he denied me a child. He cares about that bastard, too. What's it to him, if Rebecca lives or dies?"

A few days more, she thought. A week. Surely he couldn't last far beyond that? Taking the supper tray into the parlour, she put it on the table. "Chocolate?" she enquired brightly, smiling.

"Thank you, darling." Eyes glazed, his face haggard, Alex took the cup. With a teaspoon, he stirred the liquid round and round. He tasted it. Looking at Lalage, he made a face. "You should have added more sugar," he told her. "If you don't put in plenty of sweetening, the stuff leaves such a bitter aftertaste."

For a moment or two she stared at him. All the colour left her face. "W-why do you drink it?" she managed to stammer, at last. Her throat dry, she could hardly articulate. "Alex, if you know, why – "

"Why, darling?" Alex sighed. "I really don't know why," he replied.

"When did you first realise?"

"Almost at once." Alex met her eyes. "The first time must have been – let me see – about the middle of November, was it?"

"Good God!" Lalage stared. "Then – "

"Why didn't I say anything?" Alex shrugged. "Perhaps I thought it was my fate."

"But how did you know what it was?"

"I was sick. Very sick. I realised then." Languidly, Alex yawned. "When I was a child, I ate some poisoned bait. My nurse made me vomit. The taste in my mouth was the same." He smiled. "It's odd, isn't it, how memories of smells and tastes linger? When visual images have long since faded away?"

Thoughtfully, he took another sip of chocolate. "I know you want revenge," he said, calmly. "I denied you a child. You hate me for that. So you turned Ellis against *me*. For a while, I thought that might satisfy you. But it didn't, did it?"

"I – "

"So you decided to kill me. Well, my darling, why should I live? I'm all but ruined. My wife – whom I adore – detests me. Ellis despises me, which is worse." Alex sighed. "Lally, I should thank you. You've made things easy for me now."

"Have I?" Lalage chewed her lower lip. "Throw that stuff on the back of the fire," she said. "I'll fetch you some fresh."

"Laced with double the strength?"

"Laced with nothing at all." Now Lalage's face was white as chalk. "Alex," she whispered, "you won't inform on me, will you?"

"Would it matter?"

"Yes!" Lalage shuddered. "Women can still be burned,

you know. For the murder of her husband, a woman can be strangled on a gibbet. Then burned alive."

"Oh, darling! Surely not?"

"It's true! When I was a child, a woman in the village stabbed her husband. During a quarrel. They took her to Warwick. Oh, Alex! When the flames reached her, she was still alive. The hangman hadn't even pulled the cord tight."

"I shan't inform on you. I shall die. It's the least I can do." Alex grimaced. "*Why* do you hate me?" he asked. "Is it simply because of the child?"

Lalage sniffed. "That, and a few other things."

"What else have I done? Or not done?"

"Alex, you raped me! Raped me, then bought me. Like a little black slave."

"Did I?" Alex shook his head. "You can't forgive me for it?"

"No woman can forgive violation! I cannot forgive, nor forget."

"Indeed? I'm surprised to hear that." Alex shrugged. "*I* thought we were happy together. Oh, I don't deny it. On that first occasion, I was certainly a brute. But I thought I'd more than made amends."

"Did you?" Lalage stood up. "You're tired," she said, tonelessly. "Come to bed. Lie down beside me. I'll warm your cold bones tonight."

As they lay together, Alex looked into Lalage's eyes. "A knife in the ribs," he murmured. "A dagger. A bludgeon. A couple of felons, paid to do your bidding. Couldn't you have arranged it? Why did you decide to torture me?"

"Oh, Alex!" Lalage began to sob. "Alex, I'm sorry. Don't die. Please don't die!"

But, by the end of the week, Alex Lowell had death in his eyes. Lalage knew she would have to think of her future.

Her relations hated her. She had no friends. Her companions in prosperity had deserted her long ago.

The allowance from Ellis, drawn on a London bank – that would still be paid. Lalage could forge Alex's signature. She could, if necessary, write a whole letter in his hand. Ellis would never visit his sister and brother-in-law. He did not even know where they were.

Whatever happened, she would not starve to death.

Chapter 22

The following morning, Lalage threw the remainder of the poison away. Then she went out for a walk. All through the rest of that week and well into the next, she was out of the house as much as possible.

She left Alex sleeping the sound slumber of one drugged into complete insensibility. If he slept – if no additional strain were placed on his weakened constitution – Betty's draughts would, Lalage hoped, help him recover his broken health.

She skirted green fields, she walked along wide, sandy beaches. She scaled high, dangerous cliffs and clambered over wet, slippery rocks. For the first time, she studied the lie of the land. The contrast between North and South Gower, between the rich, arable landscape of the south and the marshy grasslands of the more desolate north, could not fail to impress.

South Gower was a Saxon shore. In its churchyards, she found English names, memorials and gravestones confidently inscribed with the language of the invaders. North Gower, however, was steadfastly Welsh. It seemed an older, more barbarous land. Lalage now decided that, English though she was, she much preferred the north.

She frequently saw her landlord. Talking to a shepherd, striding down a lane ahead of her, sometimes he spoke to her, sometimes he appeared not to notice she was there. He never engaged her in conversation. Merely bidding her good day, he would touch his hat to her, then walk on.

One morning, as she skirted a ploughed field, she saw him coming towards her. Was she on his land just now?

She didn't actually know. As she watched him draw nearer, she looked at him.

How old was he, exactly? Rather younger than herself, for sure. Twenty two, perhaps? Twenty three? Critically, Lalage studied him. Today, he was wearing ancient fustian breeches, a black coat and a battered felt hat. His dirty boots had seen much better days. But then, she reflected, no farmer went out to the fields in his Sunday best.

"Good morning, Mr Morgan." Politely, Lalage smiled.

"Mrs Lowell." John Rhys Morgan nodded.

Lalage was blocking his path. If he wanted to pass her, he would have to side-step through the mud, or wait until she moved aside.

She stood where she was. "I find it a little warmer today," she hazarded. After all, she reasoned, it wouldn't hurt him to make a little ordinary, workaday conversation. "The air is softer, and the wind seems far less bitter than it did."

"It's a westerly. They're always mild." The farmer glanced up at the sky. "We'll have rain by evening, though. You can depend on that."

"Ah."

"If I were you, I'd stay inland today." Gravely, the farmer looked at her. "Take your walk on the common, or along the lanes."

"Thank you for your advice." Lalage stepped aside. "Well, I expect you're very busy today."

"I am. So I'll bid you good morning." Touching his hat to her, the farmer walked on.

Looking after him, Lalage frowned. It was a pity he couldn't spare even ten minutes to chat. She wondered about him now. In a rough, loutish sort of way, he was quite a good-looking young man. Why was he not married? She'd heard he lived with a housekeeper. Did he take her to his bed?

She'd have to ask Sukey. For, having ingratiated herself with some of the village trollops and even learned a little Welsh, the housemaid apparently knew all about him.

She'd informed Betty he was a holy terror for girls. He was said to have a kept woman in Swansea, an occasional mistress in Oxwich, and an understanding with a shepherd's daughter, whose father was his tenant, so couldn't object.

"Sukey's just a tattler," said Betty sourly, as she dressed Lalage's hair the next morning. "She believes anything she hears. How is Mr Lowell today? Any better, do you think?"

"No." Lalage had repented of her cruelty. Now, she would have given the earth, the moon and all the stars above to have her husband restored to health. Miserably, she sniffed. "I'll stay with him today," she said. "We'll get him up. It's sunny in the parlour. If we wrap him up well, he'll not take cold, sitting by the fire."

Roused at last, but only with difficulty, Alex was dressed, then helped down the stairs. "It's not worth it, you know," he whispered. He stumbled against the skirting board, barking his shin. "I'd much rather sleep."

"Oh, Alex!" Lalage felt her heart contract. "You can't give up now. You've been very ill – but I'm sure you'll get better. Betty's medicine – "

"Is extremely wholesome. Yes, indeed." Alex pressed Betty's hand. "Your sleeping draughts are excellent," he murmured. "Not bitter, either. Not at all."

Lalage had the grace to blush.

The following afternoon, Alex was fretful. Coughing and sniffing, he sat close to the fire, fidgeting and muttering to himself.

He did not want company. When Lalage offered to read to him, he told her to go for a walk. When she demurred, he grew petulant. Why could she never oblige him? So, to please him, she agreed to take just an hour's stroll.

She arrived back at the farmhouse to find Sukey hopping about on the doorstep, looking out for her. The maid was in tears. As Lalage asked what was the matter, Caspar appeared behind her. Taking his mistress inside, he bade her sit down by the fire.

"What's the matter?" repeated Lalage. Anxiously, she looked from the footman to the maid. "Where is Mr Lowell?"

"Upstairs." Caspar bit his lip. "He was tired. So Betty and I took him back to bed."

Now, Betty appeared in the doorway. "Oh, madam!" she cried. Her face drawn and white, she was sobbing. "Oh, my dear madam! Whatever will you do now?"

"Is he dead?" Lalage's own face grew pale. "Betty, dear?"

"We took him to bed." Still Betty wept. "We left him sleeping, as we thought, but a few minutes later he called out. I went up to see what he wanted.

"I found him in his chair, gazing out of the window. He looked at me. He smiled. He asked me to stay awhile. He didn't want to be alone, he said."

Now Betty's sobs were choking her. "He was such a kind person," she wailed. "Oh, madam! Such a sweet-natured, considerate gentleman!"

"Betty, what happened?"

"I sat on the window seat. I had my needlework in my pocket, so I took it out and began to sew. Mr Lowell closed his eyes.

"I stitched a whole border. I thought, soon it will be time to fetch the lamps. Sukey is supposed to bring them, but she often forgets. So I got up, to call.

"As I passed Mr Lowell's chair, he groaned. He shook a little, but then he was still. I touched his hand – and there was no pulse! No life at all! Nothing!"

"I see." Lalage blinked. But then she looked at Betty. She met her eyes. There, along with the grief, she saw – what?

Disgust?

Suspicion?

Anger?

All three?

She knows, thought Lalage. Wincing, she looked away. Betty knows what I've done. Will she betray me? Will she ever use it against me?

Lalage grieved. For a month, six weeks, two months and more, guilt and sorrow deprived her of sleep and took away what little appetite she had. Had she been confronted with evidence of her crime, she would have confessed everything. Then gone quietly to her execution.

To avoid Betty, she went out. The weather was fine, so she walked for miles, wearing herself out.

The widow often came across John Rhys Morgan. Whatever he was doing – talking to a herdsman, inspecting a drainage ditch, checking on the progress of a new crop – he would break off, and touch his hat to her. He would then ask, very softly and kindly, if there was anything he might do, either to help, or on her behalf.

"Nothing. There's nothing," she would reply. Then walk on.

When Alex had been buried for nearly three months, the landlord called at the farmhouse. Lalage was surprised. The village people had been to make their condolences long ago. Why John Rhys Morgan chose to come now, she couldn't imagine.

She received him in the parlour. Her pale face and thin figure accentuated by her mourning black, Lalage looked as if she would shortly be worm's meat herself. Black ribbons fluttered against her gaunt cheeks. Black crape clung to her bony chest. All in all, she was the very picture of a grieving relict.

"Mr Morgan?" She offered him a near-transparent, skeletal hand. "How kind of you to call. Will you sit down?"

John Rhys Morgan smiled. "Thank you, Mrs Lowell," he replied. "I will."

Both seated now, they looked at one another. "Tea?" offered Lalage.

"Please. No cream, thank you."

Betty brought in the tray. Lalage poured out two cups of tea, one of which she handed to her guest.

He drank a little, then put the cup down. "You're still grieving, I see." His voice was soft and caressing, warm like new milk. "You're very sad."

"That's only natural, isn't it?" Chancing to meet his gaze, Lalage blushed. She looked away. "When a husband dies, of course his widow mourns."

"Yes, indeed." John Rhys Morgan toyed with his teaspoon. "Especially if she has no one to console her in her sorrow. You never had a child?"

"No. Never."

"You wished for children?"

"Yes." Tears coming into her eyes, Lalage hung her head. "Indeed I did."

"I'm sorry for you." The farmer sighed. "So very sorry."

"Thank you." Lalage sighed too. But then, glancing up again, she rallied. She looked the farmer full in the face. "Mr Morgan," she began, "you have no children. You're not even married. Why is that?"

"Why?" The farmer shrugged. "I'm waiting for the right woman to come along," he replied. "That's all."

"Waiting, you say?" Lalage shook her head. "So she'll simply appear, will she? As if sent from heaven? If I were you, I'd go and look for her myself."

"Go a-hunting, you mean. Perhaps I should." The farmer smiled. "Don't you worry about me," he said. "When the time comes, I'll marry. My wife will be special, you see. She'll be a witch."

"Really?" Nervously, Lalage laughed. "Well, Mr Morgan. How very singular."

"Singular?" John Rhys Morgan frowned. "That's a word I don't know."

"Odd, is what I meant." Again, Lalage shook her head. "Strange."

"Oh, I see." The farmer nodded. "Yes," he agreed, "it's very strange. I don't understand it myself. But it's so."

Lalage narrowed her eyes. The man was mad. A pity, for he was a fine-looking fellow. Very dark, tall for a Welshman, he was heavy in build, but carried no fat at all. On his strong features, a weatherbeaten complexion was attractive. Sunburn was acceptable on someone who looked half-gypsy anyway.

She felt inclined to tease him a little. "How does one recognise a witch?" she asked.

"It's difficult, I admit." The farmer's eyes twinkled. "But there are some little signs."

"Such as?"

"She'll have eyes like pools of ink. Black hair. Red lips. A pale face, but when she's roused the blood will set it on fire. She'll have a manner which enchants and delights. She'll draw a man like a moth to a candle flame."

"I see." Lalage was intrigued now. "You yourself have dark eyes. Your hair is black."

"True enough." The farmer finished his tea. Folding his arms, he grinned. "Tell me, Mrs Lowell. When you look in a glass, what do *you* see?"

"I – I have a great many things to do today." Feeling her cheeks and temples glow, Lalage stood up. "Mr Morgan, it was most kind of you to visit. I hope you'll call another time?"

"Do you invite me?" John Rhys Morgan looked into her eyes. "You'd like me to come?"

"I would." Lalage nodded. She offered him her hand. "Yes, Mr Morgan. I'd like it very much."

John Rhys Morgan knew perfectly well that he had only to be seen walking with the widow once, and all kinds of gossip would begin. So, when he called one Sunday afternoon and asked if she would like to stroll with him on the Burrows, his fate was sealed.

He meant to marry, certainly. Now he had found his bride. But what a bride! This English woman was old. She was a widow, and childless to boot. The creature was barren as a stony field. She'd admitted it herself.

But, from the first moment he saw her, he had wanted her. Now she was free, he meant to have her. A moth to a candle flame.

Might she yet breed? It didn't seem likely. She was too thin. Even if she did conceive, she would not carry well. If at all. Giving birth would probably kill her. He needed sons and daughters to his name.

They walked on the soft, dry sand. They skirted great, rolling dunes, on which grew sharp, grey-green marram grass. She took his arm. Noticing she was stumbling, he stopped. He asked if she'd hurt herself. "My shoes are full of sand," she replied. She grimaced. "It's hard to walk."

"Stand still. Now, lean on my shoulder here." Kneeling before her, he took off one shoe, emptied it, replaced it on her foot. He did the same for the other. "There," he said, smiling up at her. "Better?"

"Much." Lalage smiled back. "May we go down to the flatter part of the beach?"

"Certainly." Where her hand had rested, his shoulder burned. "We'll walk along the shoreline," he said. "The whole of Llangynnydd can watch us!"

At dusk, he took her home again. "May I call tomorrow?" he asked as Betty, exclaiming at the length of time Lalage had been gone, practically dragged her mistress through the door.

"Do." Lalage offered him her hand. "I'll look forward to it."

He visited every day. Now, it was clear to everyone that he meant to marry the widow. To everyone except the widow herself. For, racked with guilt and misery, Lalage hardly thought of the young Welshman at all.

But then, one fine evening, she went to visit Alex's grave. Walking through the little churchyard, she came across a cluster of identical granite tombstones, each one engraved with a figure of a mermaid. Stopping to read the inscriptions, she found these were memorials to the Morgan family. She thought of her landlord then.

She conceived a desire to see him at home.

Reflecting on the fact that he had now visited her at least a dozen times, she decided it would be perfectly proper – indeed, desirable – to repay his calls. So, she made her way down the lane, walked briskly past her own home and, five minutes later, was within sight of the grey stone cottage where her landlord lived.

She arrived there just as John Rhys Morgan was coming home from work. He and his cowman were strolling towards her, talking rapidly in Welsh. The farmer was frowning – but then, shaking his head, he laughed. He clapped William Parry on the back. Then he saw Lalage.

Turning to his companion, he murmured what must have been good night. Then he smiled. "Good evening, Mrs Lowell." Evidently quite pleased to see her, he held out his hand in welcome. "I'm about to have my supper," he said. "Will you take something, too?"

"I – well, perhaps a cup of tea." Her appetite was almost non-existent these days, and Lalage knew she would be physically sick if confronted with solid farmhouse fare. "Just some tea."

"Come in, then." Pushing open the cottage door, John Rhys Morgan ushered his guest inside.

A bachelor, and an orphan, the farmer was not quite alone in the world. He had a brother. An apothecary's assistant, David Morgan lived in Cardiff.

But John Rhys Morgan had no female relatives. None at all. There were no women of his own blood to make his fireside companionable, or beguile his long evenings of rural solitude. Alone except for a housekeeper, a middle-aged woman who had been his mother's maid, he spent his free time reading.

He read anything. Stock reports, broadsheets, gazettes, political pamphlets, newspapers – all printed publications held something of interest for him. He even bought books, so was probably as well informed as anyone in the area. Better, perhaps. He was able to hold a conversation with the parson, even to argue with that reverend gentleman.

Sometimes he walked into Swansea for the day, and these harmless excursions gave rise to the theory that he must keep a woman there. Two women. Several, even.

But, although he had a rake's reputation, his housekeeper was very surprised to see her master lead the English woman into his own house. What did he mean by it? So, the village gossips insisted he meant to marry her. But they weren't married yet. Mrs Lowell was said to be a fine lady. Not a harlot, who visited men at home.

"Well, John Rhys?" demanded Bethan Davies. "What's she doing here? Did you bring her along? Or did madam chase you up to your own front door?"

"*Meindia di dy fusnes.*" Well aware that Bethan was perfectly capable of taking her broom and sweeping Lalage right out of the cottage, the farmer glowered. He threw his coat on to a chair. "*Dere â dishgled o de. A shapa hi!*"

Bethan glowered back. So she should mind her own business, should she? Bring some tea. Get a move on, too! The housekeeper drew herself up. She folded her arms. "*Oti hi'n aros yn hir?*" she demanded, coldly. "Is she staying long?" she repeated, with emphasis. In case the Saxon woman should imagine she was welcome here.

Lalage blushed.

Bethan scowled.

John Rhys Morgan glared. "Mrs Lowell has come to pay a call," he said. "She'll stay as long as she pleases." Nodding to Lalage to be seated, the farmer went into the kitchen. The servant followed him.

From the doorway, Bethan Davies looked again at Lalage. "So. You bring your fancy woman here, do you?" she demanded.

John Rhys said nothing. He began to wash his hands.

"You bring her into your very own home. Then you expect me – "

"To bid her welcome and offer her some tea. Yes, that's what I expect."

"Is it, indeed?" Bethan bridled. "Well, if your mother were alive today, she'd – "

"She'd offer Mrs Lowell the best chair. Then tell you to fill the kettle. Bethan, you're an impertinent old woman. Stop arguing with your betters, and fetch the tray."

But Bethan stood her ground. She went on grumbling. Soon, her laboured English gave way to voluble, fluid Welsh. Standing at the dresser washing his face and neck, John Rhys Morgan gave as good as he got.

Lalage heard his boots clatter on the flagstones. Then, still in his shirtsleeves, he strode back into the little parlour.

"Well then, Mrs Lowell." He smiled now. "Some tea, yes? Bethan!"

"What?" Appearing in the doorway, the servant glowered. "What do you want?"

"Tea for the lady! *A brysia*!"

"Don't you tell me to hurry up." But Bethan knew when she was beaten. Muttering, she shuffled off.

John Rhys Morgan sat down by the fire, opposite his guest. "It's a pleasant evening for a walk," he said, equably. "When you've had your tea, I'll see you back home. If I may."

"I'd appreciate that. Oh!" As Bethan crashed a trayful of tea things on to a table nearby, Lalage jumped. "But please, Mr Morgan. Do have your supper first."

"I'll have it later." The farmer beamed at his guest. "Mrs Lowell, the kettle's singing. Will you make tea?"

"Certainly." Lalage smiled too.

He met her again one evening, later that same week. She was taking a favourite walk, across the sands at Rhosili.

Falling into step with her, he pushed his hands into his breeches pockets. He began to hum a lilting Welsh air.

"What's that called?" asked Lalage.

"*Fy mabi tlws i*. It's a – what's the word, now? Oh, yes.

A lullaby." The farmer looked at her. "Do you mind if I walk with you?"

"I don't mind at all."

"That's good."

Together, they strolled on. Soon they reached a rocky outcrop. Sitting down on a boulder, the farmer motioned to Lalage to sit beside him. "You're a wicked woman, you know," he said, casually. "Very wicked indeed."

"Am I?" Astonished, Lalage stared. "Why do you say that?"

"Well, why do you think?" Picking up a pebble, he flung it far out to sea. "Your sins are scarlet. If you were caught, they'd hang you. Or even burn you alive."

"Don't be insolent!" Lalage glared at him. "You ignorant lout, how dare you speak to me like this! I've done nothing. Nothing at all!"

"It's all there, you know. Written on your face. I can read it clear as day." Calmly, the farmer shrugged. "You're evil. You're brave, you're passionate – but you're wicked, too. You've lied, you've betrayed." He shrugged again. "You've even killed."

"Nonsense! I – "

"You can't help it." Sighing, John Rhys Morgan shook his head. "Poor soul, you're to be pitied. It wasn't your fault they gave you devil's milk. Your foster mother lay with Satan himself."

"You're mad. Insane." Lalage wanted to weep. The tears gathered, then began to flow. "I'm g-going home now," she sobbed. "No! Don't come with me. Don't even speak to me. Ever again!"

She struggled to her feet. But, as she did so, the farmer caught her arm. "Don't fight your destiny," he whispered, his eyes glittering. "Marry me!"

"What?"

"You heard me, witch. Marry me. Be my wife."

"Your wife?" Lalage sobbed harder. "I'm not treacherous," she wept. "I'm not wicked. I'm not a liar, either. You m-mustn't call me a witch!"

"I'll call you Lali, then." Reaching out to her, the farmer touched her face. "Lali, my darling? Will you marry me?"

Lali? Lalage tried it on her tongue. This was enchantment indeed. Lali. She wanted to hear him say it again. For this wasn't the plain English Lally. It wasn't a debased version of the Greek Lalage. It was a new name. A Welsh name. Her own.

"Well, Lali?" he demanded, breaking into her thoughts. "You don't mind *that* name, I hope?"

"I – I like it very much." Her colour high, Lalage looked away. "But if I've really done all these things of which you accuse me, why do you wish to marry me? If I've committed murder, how do you know you'll be safe?"

"Oh, but you'll love me." John Rhys smiled. "You'll adore *me*, heart and soul – you'll not harm a single hair of my head." He took her hands in his. "Well, *cariad*? May I kiss you?"

Lalage stared at him. "You think I mean to accept you?" she asked.

"I know it," he replied.

"You won't need all your servants," he told her, as they walked on the sands, the wind from the Atlantic tugging at their hair. Today, it had even burned a little red into Lalage's pale cheeks. "So. We'll live in your house. Bethan will come in every day. She'll arrange for a girl from the village to do the rough."

"Very well." Still bemused, Lalage nodded her agreement. "As it happens, Caspar and Sukey came to talk to me last night. They wish to marry."

"Do they, indeed?"

"Yes. I was surprised, too." Lalage sighed. "She's six or seven years older than him. My poor Caspar. He's only a child."

"But old enough to know his own mind?"

"I doubt it." Lalage shook her head. "I expect she seduced him. So now he feels obliged to her."

"Where will they go?"
"To Swansea, they said, to get situations there. That's what Sukey intends."
"What about Betty?"
"She must stay with me."
"Ah." John Rhys Morgan shrugged. "Well, I expect she'll be useful. She can learn to make cheese."

The wedding was in May. By July, Lali Morgan had been transformed.

She put on a little flesh. This suited her. Once again, she had a woman's figure – albeit a slight, insubstantial one. Leaving her hair unpowdered and undressed, she pinned it up in a simple pleat. She folded away her silks and satins, and now wore gowns of plain Lancashire cotton. As befitted a modest matron who was also a respectable farmer's wife, she wore a white cambric handkerchief, which concealed her bosom and kept the sun off the back of her neck.

Betty was disgusted. She loved to see Lalage resplendent in satin and lace, and had spent many happy hours powdering, painting and titivating this most beautiful of living dolls. Now Lalage was no longer a walking skeleton, Betty longed to dress her up again. To coil her lovely hair. To lace her slim but pretty figure into the softest, most diaphanous of silks. To paint her sweet face. Then to show off her handiwork to an admiring world.

But it was not to be. Evidently, John Rhys Morgan didn't approve of other men gawping at his wife. Nor did he wish his wife to attract their attention or their stares. He would never have permitted Lalage to go out in pretty little kidskin shoes which left her ankles unprotected. Or in gowns which exposed her slender shoulders and had bodices cut so low that her breasts were on public display. From now on, stout boots and pintucked cotton shifts, rough woollen mantuas and twill coats would be the rule.

But, as summer became autumn, became winter, as the year turned again and spring bloomed afresh, even Betty could see Lalage was happy. Happier than she'd ever been. Once half-crazed by guilt and sorrow, now she was relaxed. Contented. At peace.

"You may have that." Sorting out her old clothes, Lalage tossed a beautiful blue silk sacque aside. "This, too." A mauve satin morning-gown fell to the floor.

"Oh, madam!" The blue silk was beautiful. Betty had coveted it for years. But when would she wear it now? She could hardly stroll to church in watered taffeta, when her mistress wore black serge or brown homespun. She sighed. She could sell it, perhaps. In Swansea, it would fetch a very good price.

Lalage became a real farmer's wife. She kept hens, and learned to milk the placid Welsh cows. She fed and cosseted the calves, who had been separated from their mothers, but were being reared for stock.

This last was a favourite chore. She loved to stroke the little creatures' soft, velvety heads. To have them butt and nuzzle her. To feel a rough tongue rasping her fingers, as it sucked off the gruel.

Her health was better than it had ever been. She had a spring in her step and her complexion glowed. At last, Lalage had found bliss.

But then, one blue morning in late August, she woke up feeling very ill. There was a dull pain her in her stomach and a catch in her throat. Her head throbbed painfully. Crawling out of bed, she reached the washstand just in time to vomit into the china basin. "John!" she wailed, between bringing up great mouthfuls of bile, "John, wake up. I'm ill!"

"What's the matter?" In the cool morning half-light, John Rhys Morgan blinked his eyes. Waking properly, he sat up. "Lali? What's wrong?"

"I've been poisoned!" Sobbing and choking, retching again but bringing up only watery catarrh now, Lalage cried harder. "Oh, John! I'm going to die!"

He was beside her then, holding her narrow shoulders. "It's all right," he soothed. He stroked her hair, smoothing it back from her brow. Reaching for a cloth, he wiped her mouth. "Any better now?"

"A little." Still distressed, still terrifed, Lalage covered her face with her hands. "Oh, God! I'm not ready to die!"

"It's far too early in the day to talk about dying. So come on. Get back to bed." He smoothed the sheets. He plumped her pillows, then drew up the blankets, tucking them round her shivering form. "Comfortable?" he asked.

"Yes, thank you." Miserably, Lalage sniffed.

"Shall I fetch you something to drink?"

"No. Don't do that. I'd only be sick again." Lalage clung to him. "Don't leave me!" she cried.

He took her in his arms. "Shall I come back to bed?" he asked.

"Better not. You'll be late for milking."

"Oh, Huw and William can manage very well without me." Letting her go, John Rhys took Lalage's hands. He held them between his own. "So, Lali. How long have you been feeling ill?"

"I've had a headache all week." Still sniffing, Lalage shrugged. "Yesterday morning, I felt sick – but I didn't bring anything up. Today, though – "

"Do you still feel sick?"

"Yes!" Lalage began to sob. "I'm dying! My head aches. My ankles are swollen. I've pins and needles everywhere, and my chest is so sore!"

"Dear me." Releasing her hands, John Rhys Morgan stroked her temples. "Cool enough," he observed. "No fever there. When did you last bleed?"

"Bleed? I don't know. I can't remember. Betty always deals with all that."

"From now on, learn to mark the almanac yourself." Reassuringly, the farmer smiled. "Well, Lali. I think I know what this must be."

"What?"

"Can't you guess?"

"The smallpox? The quinsy? My throat's very sore."

"That's from retching." John Rhys shook his head. "Well, then. Shall we have your nightgown off now?"

"Why?"

"Just to confirm my suspicions."

"Suspicions? Oh, God!"

"Hush." He undid her buttons. Slipping the garment from her shoulders, he smiled his satisfaction. "Lovely," he said. "Quite beautiful. Don't you agree?"

"What do you mean?"

"Look at yourself." John Rhys grinned. "You're not ill. Not at all. Look!"

Lalage followed his gaze. Then she grinned too. For the first time in her life, she had a grown woman's figure. She had full, heavy breasts.

John Rhys kissed her. "You're going to have a baby," he cried. "Clever Lali! We're going to have a son."

Chapter 23

For more than a year after the fire, Ellis remained extremely weak. He took cold too easily, suffered from recurrent fits of shivering – and even the slightest exertion left him breathless and exhausted. Frequently, Rebecca feared he would die. That her daughter too would grow up without knowing a father's love.

But, although his health did not improve, Ellis did not die. When Jane Darrow reached her second birthday, it was decided she should have her portrait painted, in the company of her parents. "He flatters *me*," muttered Ellis, sourly. He scrutinised the finished article. "But he hasn't caught a tenth of your beauty. I've a mind to retain half his fee."

"I think he's done a very good job." Rebecca smiled. "Look how well he's painted Jenny. He's captured her expression beautifully. One can almost see her toss her curls. Hear her refuse to go to bed."

"Oh, I'll not deny he has some talent." Ellis shrugged. "But he thinks he's a second Hogarth. I call him a maker of daubs."

The painter had indeed flattered his paymaster. Once a well-made, athletic man, Ellis had grown gaunt and thin. His face was a haggard mask, over which parchment-dry skin was tightly stretched. His hair was turning grey.

Rebecca managed the estate and oversaw the manufactory almost single-handed. Not that she minded this. On the contrary, she enjoyed being in control, having *carte blanche* to do just as she pleased. For Ellis took no interest in anything.

Wandering into the sitting room one morning, he found Rebecca at the window, turning something over in her hands. Weighing it, tapping it, holding it up to the light and squinting at it, she was absorbed in her study and did not hear him come up behind her.

"What's that?" he asked, giving the object in question a cursory glance. "A piece of papier mâché?"

"What?" Startled, Rebecca spun round. "Oh! Ellis. I didn't hear you come in. No, this isn't paper-board. It's metal."

"What's its use?"

"It's for fruit." She passed her trophy across to him. "It's a dessert basket. You know? When one has company to dinner, it sits in the centre of the table, piled high with grapes and apples and nectarines. Everyone admires it, and wants one exactly the same."

"I see." Evidently not impressed, Ellis merely sniffed. "Is it brass? Or copper?"

"Tin. Over iron." Rebecca retrieved her basket. "They plate the iron with tin," she explained. "Then coat it with layers of varnish. They bake each new layer in a hot stove – so, a finish is gradually built up. The painting is done just before the final varnish is laid."

"I see. Did Searle's make this?"

"No." Rebecca shrugged. "There are factories in Birmingham which do turn out this kind of thing. But the workmanship is only fair. I have seen nothing as fine as this basket."

"Where is it from?"

"South Wales. A little town called Pontypool." Rebecca looked up from her hardware. "I was thinking I might go there. To look at the manufactory."

"To spy?"

"No! Of course not." Rebecca frowned. But then, candidly, she smiled. "Well," she admitted, "to look about me. To take note of what goes on. Ellis?"

"Yes?"

"The factory in Birmingham needs a new direction. It

can't remain a little button-works for ever."

"It's hardly that now." Ellis shook his head. "That manufactory is renowned. Famous. Searle's brass and copperwares are known to be the best. Its wrought-iron work is valued far above anything your rivals can produce."

"That's true. But since Lyddy married Matthew Harris, and he took an active interest in our concerns, my eyes have been opened. If a brand new line were introduced, and it found favour with the public, Searle's could do better than ever. Now the problems of mechanisation seem to have been solved, that is." Rebecca grimaced. "That steam engine! It's been far more trouble than it was worth."

"That's the price you must pay for being in the vanguard of change." Ellis shrugged. "You won't lose in the end, will you?"

"Maybe not." Shaking her head, Rebecca sighed. "But if only I'd been more circumspect! If I'd thought it through, and realised what could go wrong – "

"Don't fret about it," said Ellis, kindly. "Mechanisation had to come some day. Now you can say, I saw the way things were going. I was a pioneer."

"I can also say, I listened to an old woman who'd had no youth. Who, since her father died, has behaved like an unbroken colt. Who talked me into innovation for innovation's sake." Rebecca sighed again. Then, firmly, she changed the subject. "Ellis, are you well enough for a jaunt?" she asked.

"Are *you*?" Ellis looked pointedly at Rebecca's belly, hugely distended with her second pregnancy. "When is the baby due?"

"Not for months yet."

"Rebecca!"

"Not for five or six weeks, anyway." Caught out, Rebecca laughed. "My dear Ellis! There must be midwives in Wales."

"Yes, there must. Well, perhaps we could go away for

a few days. If that's what you want." Ellis glanced out of the window. "The weather's a little better now."

"Quite." Taking his hand, Rebecca kissed him. "Today, it's bright. Next week, I predict the sun will shine!"

But the fine weather did not last. Spring that year was so dismal and cold that the trip was postponed once, twice, a third time. By the time the warmer weather did eventually arrive, Rebecca's pregnancy was so far advanced that to travel would have been foolish.

Delivered of a second daughter on the first day of June, by early September Rebecca realised she was pregnant yet again. "A son this time," she promised Ellis, as they lay in bed that warm, summer night. "A boy, to take after you."

"Just the one?" Ellis looked at her. "It's showing already," he observed. "I think you'll be brought to bed of twins. Triplets, even. My dear Becky, if you go on at this rate, we'll have a cricket team by the time you're thirty. Plus reserves."

"Maybe we will." Lying on her back, Rebecca stretched luxuriously. Then, taking her husband's hand, she laid it on her belly. "Ellis?"

Obligingly, Ellis massaged her. "I love you when you're pregnant," he murmured, as he rubbed.

"Only when I'm pregnant?"

"No. I've loved you since the day I met you. You know that." Ellis kissed her. "But when you're with child, I love you even more."

"That's nice." Complacently, Rebecca smiled. She enjoyed being pregnant. Being soft and fat and milky suited her. Now, lying against Ellis in her wide, warm bed, she sighed. "He *is* growing fast," she agreed. "Perhaps I'm further on than I thought. Soon, you'll have an heir."

"I'd quite like another girl, I think." Reassuringly, Ellis patted the child. "Daughters – *your* daughters, anyway – are as welcome in this house as any son could be."

"All the same, this child will be a boy." Rebecca kissed him. "Your colour's healthier these days," she observed.

"You seem to have more energy, too. Dear Ellis – I think you're actually getting better."

"Do you?"

"Yes." Rebecca kissed him again. But now, her arms were around his neck, and her kiss was one of desire.

Gradually, Easton Hall was restored. Slowly, painstakingly, it was becoming a house again. One day, it would be a home.

But it was a long-drawn-out, wearisome process. The Darrows lived in the Dower House for one year, two years. These stretched into a third.

Sometimes, Ellis lost heart. "Is it really worth it?" he asked one winter morning, as he turned over yet another stack of bills. "Sometimes, I think we must be mad."

"Don't be absurd." Fiercely, Rebecca glared at him. "Of course it's worth it," she cried. "Absolutely! Every brass farthing is well spent."

For it was Rebecca who had insisted the Hall be rebuilt. When Ellis was too ill and sick at heart to care if he lived or died, she had hired labour, set her own craftsmen to work and supervised the jobbing builders. Willingly, she had pledged a large percentage of the profits from the manufactory to pay for the work.

Ellis wished he had her faith. Her determination. "But I'm younger than you are," she said, when he remarked on her amazing energy, her boundless optimism, her unbreakable spirit. "I haven't been ill, either."

"It's not just that." Ellis took her hand. He felt for the pulse. "Ah, now here's the secret," he said. "Electric current. How could it be tapped, I wonder? We have steam today. Tomorrow, will electricity power the world?"

"You do talk nonsense." Rebecca pulled her hand away. "Please don't mention steam power to me. Last week, the wretched engine broke down again. Lyddy had three men working on it for five days, and it's still not right. I hate to think what we've lost in production and labour costs."

Ellis shrugged. "We'll get a new engine," he said. "A bigger, better one."

"We can't afford it."

"We'll raise credit." Ellis grinned. "I'll speak to Mr Harris tomorrow. We'll ask his advice."

Rebecca stared. Here was a change indeed.

Over the next few months, Ellis grew more positive still. More physically active, too. Formerly indifferent to just about everything, he enquired into the running of the estate. He visited the manufactory. He argued with his wife. He found fault and grumbled, as well.

Rebecca came down to breakfast one morning to find him tearing open his post with as much dispatch and interest as he ever had in former days. Scanning one particular letter, he scowled. Anger, as opposed to mere irritation, was something she had not seen on his face for months. For years. So now, intrigued, she looked at him. "Well, my dear Ellis?" she began. "What's upset you?"

"That!" He tossed the letter across the table. Taking a bread roll, he reduced it to crumbs. "The insolence of the man! He supposes that because I have been ill, he may take what liberties he pleases. May ask any favour. Nay, may demand – "

Word failed him. He was reduced to grinding his teeth in rage.

Rebecca read the letter through. "Ah," she murmured. "I see."

"Do you?" Ellis glared. "He says I must reduce his rent. Let him off the last few repayments of a loan, which was advanced in good faith, to buy in stock last spring. He says he has lost heavily over the winter. That unless I give him better terms – "

Reaching for his cup, Ellis gulped down a mouthful of scalding coffee. "*I* say we evict him. Today!"

"Do you, indeed?"

"Yes." Ellis jumped to his feet.

"Where are you going?" asked Rebecca.

"To see Robbins." Snatching the letter back, Ellis

crumpled it into a ball and stuffed it into his pocket. Turning on his heel, he stumped out of the room.

Momentarily, Rebecca considered calling him back. Insisting he drink his coffee, eat some breakfast. But then she reflected it might be salutary for Henry Robbins, the Easton land agent, to see his master in a rage today.

For the agent, together with the other servants, had grown slack. In spite of Rebecca's efforts to keep them in line, they had fallen into lazy, slovenly ways. Had learned to cut corners. In one way or another, they all shirked their responsibilities, because they weren't afraid of Ellis any more.

Rebecca poured herself more coffee and buttered herself some toast.

"Simmons!" Ellis's voice echoed down the passage. "Simmons! Damn you, man! Where the hell are you? Where are my God-damned boots?"

Ruefully, Rebecca smiled. She'd never have thought the day would dawn when she would be delighted to hear her husband swear, or take the name of the Lord in vain.

Everyone in the village agreed. An enchantment hung over Llangynnydd. The fine English lady whose haughty expression and insolent manner had made all the villagers hate her, had vanished in a puff of smoke. To fill her place, some genie had created a plain, ordinary dairy farmer's wife.

Lalage loved her dairy. This in turn endeared her to Bethan, who had confidently expected her master's new wife to disdain such lowly tasks as milking and managing the little creamery next door to the beast-house, which Bethan considered her own.

"That's not for the likes of you," she had declared that first morning, as she watched Lalage try, and fail, to skim the cream from a pan of new milk. "Out of the way, now. Let me."

Offended, but curious, Lalage did as she was told. Standing aside she watched closely while Bethan, skilled and deft-handed, demonstrated the mysteries of skimming, churning and straining through butter-muslin. While she took her new mistress step by step through those very tasks which Ellis had watched Lyddy Searle perform, all those years ago.

Soon enough, with sleeves rolled to the elbows and her hair tucked beneath a muslin cap, Lalage was making cheese, churning butter, and expertly separating curds from whey. Contented and fulfilled, she toiled in her dairy from dawn to dusk.

"Don't work too hard, girl." Coming into the dairy one evening to fetch a jug of cream, Bethan was amazed to find her mistress still busy. "Come on, now," she scolded. "Enough is enough. What are you doing? Brining, is it? Let me finish for you, eh?"

"Very well." Pushing a stray lock of hair off her forehead, Lalage stood to one side.

Bethan took the heavy salting-pan from its shelf. "You must remember your little one now," she admonished, as she worked. "If you was to miscarry, think how upset poor John Rhys would be."

"*I* should be miserable, too." Weary now, Lalage sat down on a dairy-maid's stool. "Bethan, when you've finished that, will you make me some tea? I've such a thirst on me today."

"I'll make you all the tea you can drink." Bethan grinned, revealing perfect countrywoman's teeth. "Get off home with you now. Sit by the fire. I'll be along in ten minutes, no more."

As Lalage drank her tea, she gazed into the red heart of the kitchen fire. How comfortable she was. How warm, and happy. "Bethan," she began, "have you seen Betty today?"

"Seen her just half an hour ago. Off up the village, she was. After William Parry."

"William?" Lalage frowned. "What does she want with him?"

"I wouldn't like to say. Not in respectable company like

this." Smirking, Bethan trimmed the crust on her pie. "But I reckon she'll be Mrs Parry pretty soon now. Well before next Whitsuntide, at any rate."

"She'll never leave me." Horrified, Lalage stared. "Bethan, you're a wicked liar! Betty would never even dream of marrying, unless I gave her leave."

"No? Kissing and muttering in the lane last night, they were. Where he had his hands, I don't know. But I'm sure it was somewhere nice and warm." Bethan put her pie into the oven. "Poor Mrs High and Mighty. Your Betty don't take notice of you no more."

But now, seeing Lalage was on the verge of tears, Bethan stopped teasing and went to sit beside her. "Don't mind me," she said, gently. "Don't let an old woman's gossip make you cry."

"But Bethan, if Betty leaves me, it will break my heart! Does she really like William Parry?" Lalage sniffed and gulped. Soon, the tears would flow. "Oh Bethan!" she wailed. "What shall I do?"

"Don't be so silly." Bethan took Lalage's hand. "So Betty marries William. What of it? Why should you care? John Rhys loves you like his own soul. Half the women in Wales would give their eye teeth to be you."

"Would they, Bethan?" Lalage sniffed again. She knuckled her eyes. "You think he really loves me?"

"I'm certain of it. Listen to me, your ladyship. I've nursed him from a baby, so I should know. He adores you. He'd die for you."

"You think so?"

"Jesus and Mary, girl! I know it." Bethan grew solemn then. "Don't cross him, will you?" she whispered. "Don't let him down. He's not a man anyone should choose for their enemy. I'd pity the woman who deceived him, from the bottom of my heart."

Chapter 24

"He does very well, doesn't he? Considering everything, that is." Busy in her dairy, Lalage was wrapping fat, yellow cheeses in muslin. Turning to Bethan, she smiled. "What I mean," she went on, "is that all the other farmers and shepherds round here scrimp, bodge and starve the whole year long. But John Rhys contrives to make a good profit from his land."

"What?" Bethan was admiring the cheeses. "Oh – yes," she agreed, absently. "He doesn't do too bad."

"He's a good manager, that's why."

"If you like to say so." Bethan grinned. She eyed Lalage. "You look like a proper Welshwoman today," she said. "Time you got your tongue around the language, too. Learn to speak like a farmer's wife. After all, you're not a fine lady now. You don't even look like Mrs High and Mighty no more."

"No, I suppose I don't." Clad in a light cotton shift and striped calico gown, today Lalage was also wearing one of Bethan's enormous, white aprons. She laughed. "But as you say, I'm a farmer's wife now. Bethan?"

"Yes?"

"Where *is* John Rhys today? He said he had to go over to Oxwich, but he didn't tell me why. Or for how long."

"Oh, he'll have gone to see old Mr Atkins." Bethan gave the biggest cheese a maternal pat. "You know. Jack Atkins, the Englishman. Him as owns that big house on the headland."

"I know." Nevertheless, Lalage was puzzled. "Why's John Rhys gone to see *him*?"

"They're expecting a ship. So, there's things to be done. Arrangements to be made." Realising her mistress had no idea what she was talking about, Bethan Davies grinned. "You mean to say he hasn't explained about Jack Atkins? You don't know nothing about all that?"

"No." Lalage took down another cheese. "So now you can tell me. What's going on?"

"Ah, now there's a story! If I had an hour or two to spare, I could – "

"Bethan, you're an irritating old woman!" Lalage stamped her foot. "Tell me what Jack Atkins has to do with us."

"Like I say, that would take half the morning."

"Just make a start, then." Lalage fixed Bethan with a gimlet glare. "Well?"

"No peace for the wicked, eh?" Still grinning, Bethan sat down on a three-legged stool. "You say John Rhys does well at farming," she began. "Well, that's true enough. But he doesn't just farm the land. Oh, no. He farms the sea, as well."

"So that's where he goes." Lalage shook her head. Ever since they'd been married, she had noticed that once in a while her husband stole from her bed. While the village slept, he shrugged on his clothes, let himself out of the farmhouse, and walked off down the lane.

She'd been so afraid he had another woman that she'd never dared ask him where he went. Or what he did. Now, relief made her glow. "He's a fisherman!" she cried.

"He is indeed." Bethan laughed. "He nets tea, coffee, brandy, wine. These days, there's excellent French brandy to be had. Casks of fine sherry, as well."

"Sherry wine?" Lalage's relief was very short-lived. Now, she grew pale. Her hands trembled. "You're telling me he's a smuggler?" she whispered.

"He's a trader!" Bethan stood up. Impressively, she frowned. "Now," she rapped, "just you listen to me. John Rhys and Jack Atkins do things properly. Do you understand? They know the right people. They know who to trust.

"So, *they're* not going to commit murder and outrage. They're not going to bring half the redcoats in the country down here, burning, destroying and killing for the fun of it. No, indeed. What John Rhys does is all regular. He and Jack Atkins – "

"Are middlemen. They bribe the Excise. That's an expensive game, I'll be bound." Still shaking, Lalage felt tears well up inside her eyes. "You say they're traders. They're nothing of the kind. They're criminals!"

"Don't dare to talk like that!" Taking Lalage by the shoulders, Bethan held her. "Your man's no criminal!" she cried. "There's no bloodshed. No violence. The excisemen on this coast know their business, it's true. But John Rhys knows his. He knows it well."

"He's still breaking the law!" Her eyes wide, Lalage was actually weeping now. "If he were taken, he'd hang. Oh, Bethan – "

"Hush, hush." Derisively, Bethan sniffed. "Shouldn't have said anything to you," she muttered. "Might have known you would take a fit. Have you finished wrapping those cheeses?"

"Yes, but – "

"Don't pick them up. They're too heavy. Betty can pack them later." With that, Bethan strode out of the dairy, leaving Lalage alone. To think.

"I was chatting with Bethan today," said Lalage, as she and John Rhys walked on the Burrows that evening. "She tells me that in addition to being a farmer, you have other interests too."

"Have I, indeed?" John Rhys grinned. "Well, she's right. I'm a landlord. I own half a dozen cottages, I let some grazing – "

"You're a smuggler! You deal in contraband and prohibited goods!"

"I do, do I?" John Rhys Morgan's grin did not falter. "Bethan told you all about it, eh?"

"Yes, she did!" Lalage's dark eyes flashed. But then, sighing, she shook her head. "You *are* careful, aren't you?" she whispered. "Oh, John! If you were taken – "

"I'd hang. You think I don't know that?" The farmer pushed his hands into his pockets. "My dear Lali, don't fret. There's not a man anywhere on Gower who'd inform on me."

"Isn't there?" Unconvinced, Lalage looked at him. "Don't be so sure. If there were a reward, they might."

"There's no price on *my* head, girl!" John Rhys Morgan laughed. "Oh, my poor Lali, don't worry about me. My men know their master. They also know they'd gain nothing by betraying me, for they'd betray themselves as well.

"Anyway, my darling, we poor Welsh farmers are just small fry. Little mice. We nibble only the tiniest holes in the Englishman's great cheese."

"Do you?"

"Certainly. Mr Atkins makes quite sure of that." John Rhys sniffed. "If he thought I was getting too greedy, it would be the end of me. So, I have to watch my step."

Lalage shuddered. "Why is Mr Atkins so powerful?" she asked.

"He's English. He's rich. He's respectable. He farms acres a hundred times more fertile than any owned by poor Welshmen on North Gower."

"He's the master?"

"Yes. He offers the bribes, and takes three quarters of the profit." John Rhys laughed. "But he couldn't do anything without me! He knows he has to keep me sweet. If I had a mind, I could hang his whole family.

"Then, we poor Welshmen – we dirty barbarians, who were driven out of South Gower to make room for even dirtier Saxons – we could reclaim our own."

"If Mr Atkins were taken, I'm sure you'd be arrested too. He'd make certain of that."

"He could prove nothing against me." John Rhys shrugged. "Come on, Lali. It's getting dark, and I don't want you taking an evening chill. Let's go back."

As he helped his wife across the dunes, John Rhys was muttering to himself. "They tax everything," he growled. "The soap we wash with, the candles we burn, the salt which savours our food, the light which enters our windows! It's a wonder they don't tax the very air we breathe. We must assert our freedom somehow."

"Must you?" A horrible vision of her husband swinging at a rope's end making her shudder afresh, Lalage took his hand and held it tightly. "Be careful," she murmured. "That's all I ask. Take care."

"I've seen my fate." His face barely visible in the growing darkness, John Rhys Morgan's eyes glittered like stars. "I shan't die on the gallows," he said." My end will be bloody enough, but they'll not break my neck."

By the time Ellis and Rebecca finally set off on their trip to South Wales, Rebecca's third pregnancy was well advanced. Leaving their daughters in the care of their nurses, husband and wife began their journey on a fine spring day.

Leaning out of the carriage window, Rebecca waved until she could see her children no longer. Then, sinking back against her cushions, she sighed. "I don't want to go now," she said.

"Shall we turn back?"

"No. But the children – "

"Will be fine." Reassuringly, Ellis smiled. "They have excellent nurses, whom they love and trust. Jane actually told us to go."

"Yes." Rebecca laughed. "So she did."

Now a bossy three-year-old, whose beautiful blue eyes and fair hair were obviously inherited from the Lowells, but whose inflexible will and imperious manner were pure Jeremy Searle, Jane Darrow had watched her parents prepare to leave with great satisfaction. Now, *she* would be in charge. She and Maria would have chocolate every morning, a ride in the phaeton each afternoon, and sugar candy on demand.

The tin plate factory which Rebecca had come so many miles to see turned out to be part of a huge concern, on a site spread over many acres, just outside the little town of Pontypool. The owner, Mr Evan Lloyd, told Rebecca her fame had preceded her. Searle's manufactory was renowned even in South Wales. Far from regarding her as a spy, he was flattered she should take an interest in his factory's wares.

After entertaining Ellis and Rebecca to tea, he suggested they might like to tour the works. Ellis demurred. Making his excuses, he took himself off for a walk about the town.

A puzzled Mr Lloyd watched him go. Did Mr Darrow really trust his wife to understand everything she would be told? He shook his head. Modern manners baffled him. Modern women made him stare in disbelief. Their forwardness, assurance and impertinence embarrassed him. He was not looking forward to the next few hours at all.

But Rebecca astonished him. Walking round the factory and works, she displayed so much plain good sense and business acumen that Mr Lloyd almost forgot she was a woman. He answered her questions in detail and considered her opinions. He spoke to her man to man.

Returning to his office, Rebecca was glad to sit down. Now Mr Lloyd remembered that here was a young woman at least six months pregnant, and he'd spent the past three hours dragging her round an iron works. Poor creature, she must be exhausted. He offered tea and refreshments. She could have whatever she wanted – he would send out specially.

Rebecca accepted the tea, then asked for pen and paper. She made some calculations. Then she offered Mr Lloyd a business deal which the Welshman could hardly refuse.

The next hour was spent haggling over details. Then, when these had been resolved, they discussed the possibility of sending workmen from the Birmingham factory to the Pontypool works, where they could be instructed by masters.

"Well, I think that would be an excellent plan." Accepting Mr Lloyd's offer to train three of her best craftsmen, Rebecca smiled. She offered her hand. "I appreciate your kindness."

"Not at all." Mr Lloyd shook on it. "It's a pleasure to do business with someone like you." Then, meeting Rebecca's cornflower-blue eyes, he saw how very pretty she was. He blushed. He hoped Mr Darrow appreciated his good fortune. Where had he found this wonderful woman? Had she been born like this, or made?

"So, you talked him into giving you *carte blanche* to manufacture his products. In effect, to put him out of business." Picking up his knife, Ellis hacked his food into manageable pieces, then began to eat his dinner. "You smiled. You tossed your pretty blonde curls. He signed his patrimony away."

"It wasn't like that at all." Still elated by her recent amazing success, Rebecca laughed. Then she shook her head. "Searle's could never manufacture tin-ware on the scale Mr Lloyd does," she said. "He has his own rolling mills. His own foundries. He has access to an endless supply of labour, and it's much cheaper than any I could get. Most of his processes are protected by patent, too."

"So what will you do?"

"Buy his excellent tin plate. Then make the goods under license, using processes which Mr Lloyd has developed and perfected."

"Will Searle's still make a profit?"

"Certainly!" Her blue eyes radiating confidence, Rebecca twinkled like a star. "When my workmen are properly trained, we will prepare our own range of goods. Design our own patterns, as well. We shall create an enormous demand, which Mr Lloyd will help us to meet. Both Searle's and Lloyd's will profit hugely in the end. Ellis, this roast lamb is delicious!"

"Yes, it *is* good." Chasing an errant piece of meat across his plate, Ellis nodded agreement. But he knew Rebecca. She was so full of herself just now that she would have found a plateful of cold cabbage delicious, and exclaimed delightedly over dry bread and cheese.

Rebecca's business concluded, she and Ellis spent a few days at leisure in the beautiful county of Monmouthshire. Driving through green valleys overhung by rocky precipices and forbidding dark woods, strolling on the banks of the Wye, exploring the picturesque ruins of Tintern Abbey, their senses were gratified and their bodies exercised. They were thoroughly enjoying their jaunt.

Walking gave Ellis a better colour. Animated by interest and activity, his face seemed slightly fuller, and his features less haggard, less gaunt. Delighted to see him looking so hearty, Rebecca wondered aloud if a little sea air might not be good for them both. "We'll go to Swansea, shall we?" she suggested. "We'll take the coast road. Fresh air, sunshine, light sea breezes. Those are just what you need."

"It's a long way to Swansea." Studying a map, Ellis frowned. "Don't you want to go home? You're missing the children, I'm sure."

"Yes. A little." Reminded of Jane and baby Maria, Rebecca sighed.

Ellis made up his mind. "We'll go to Cardiff," he said. "Look about us, breathe in as much salt and tar as we can stand – then go home by way of Chepstow and the Wye Valley."

"Very well." Rebecca thought that an excellent plan.

To Cardiff they would go.

John Rhys Morgan had business in Cardiff. He could not

put it off any longer. For it concerned his younger brother, David.

When old Mr Morgan died, his will had been short and to the point. The great stone farmhouse, together with all the Morgans' land in and around Llangynnydd, all the labourers' cottages, all the livestock and all the barns, were bequeathed absolutely and unconditionally to the elder son. Except for a tiny legacy from his mother, David Morgan was left unprovided for.

His fate was to serve his brother. To work for wages on his brother's land. To hope, if he were that way inclined, that the heir might die childless.

But, well aware that his brother would hate to work for him and had no desire to be a farmer anyway, John Rhys had taken David for a long walk along the sea cliffs and asked him what he meant to do with his life. Knowing the boy was something of a scholar, he asked if being apprenticed to a physician or surgeon held any appeal.

"Not at all." A small, slim boy of sixteen whose tastes were ascetic and bookish rather than practical, David shuddered. "But I could work for a druggist, perhaps."

"Or an apothecary?"

"If you like." David shrugged. "But I won't be a saw-bones, and that's final."

"I'll write to Mr Gregory," said John Rhys. This was the obliging English apothecary who, as a last resort in cases of desperate illness, was sometimes summoned from Swansea. "We'll see if he knows anyone who needs a junior."

So David Morgan had eventually gone to Cardiff, to train under a Mr Phillips there. Now John Rhys needed to see him again. David had written to say his training was almost completed. Soon, he hoped to open a shop and set up a practice of his own. He needed a few hundred pounds.

John Rhys disliked towns. He found Swansea dirty, noisy and oppressive. The only times he went there were when he wanted to buy a book or bank some money. He loathed Pembroke, which stank of fish, sewers and the English incomers who had settled there. But he hated Cardiff, a mean little rat-hole infested with more Saxon rats than even Pembroke, more than either.

But he had to go. He couldn't trust David to find a property, or to bargain for it if he did. Where financial matters were concerned, the boy was unworldly to the point of foolishness.

Hearing of her husband's obligations, Lalage was wild to go with him. Mad to visit a town. In a town, there would be shops. Milliners, dressmakers, drapers, shoemakers – she *did* need some new clothes, and her boots were all falling to pieces. "I ought to meet your brother," she insisted. "Please, John Rhys? Let me come! I love travelling. A jaunt in a stagecoach would do me so much good."

"Would it?" John Rhys hated travelling post. He considered the malodorous public stagecoaches which plied between Swansea and Cardiff to be nothing more than prison cells on wheels. Dirty straw scratched your ankles, filthy upholstery practically crawled with wildlife, and fellow travellers stank, spat and swore.

He grimaced. "Oh well," he muttered. "I suppose I could take you with me. Then I'd have some pleasant company, at least."

"Splendid!" Delighted, Lalage kissed him. "I'll tell Betty to pack. We'll make it a holiday, shall we?"

Rebecca found Cardiff a dismal little town. The shops were half empty, the people looked poor and dispirited. The castle was a ruin, the docks were dirty and silted up. "Someone should take Cardiff in hand," she thought. "Shake it about. Make it sit up."

Taking a walk round the centre of the town, such as it was, she and Ellis looked at each other, agreed they were bored, and decided to return home. They would start that very afternoon.

"I'll go and buy some tobacco," said Ellis, "then we'll

walk back to the hotel. We'll have our dinner while the girl packs. With luck, we should be away by three."

"Perfect." Rebecca glanced across the empty street. Spotting a dingy little draper's shop, she remembered she ought to buy a present for Jane. "You go and get your tobacco," she said. "I'll step over and see what Mrs Williams has to offer."

As Ellis walked over to the tobacconist's shop, a woman in the garb of a respectable tradesman's wife came out of a narrow alley. She crossed the street. She glanced at Rebecca, who was looking at the draper's window display.

Momentarily, she paused. From a distance of three or four feet, she stared. But then, shrugging, she hurried on.

Hearing footsteps, Rebecca assumed Ellis was coming across the street. She turned from her idle contemplation of an unremarkable bonnet, and smiled – at a woman who was already walking away.

Rebecca stared after her until she disappeared, up an entry. She knew that walk! That arrogant toss of the head, that languid yet haughty air. That was no tradesman's wife. Rebecca frowned. For a moment, she thought she might faint. Her imagination was playing tricks.

Or was it? In her mind's eye, Rebecca could still see her. Shaking, she leaned against an iron railing. She knew she wasn't mistaken. She had seen Lalage.

Protectively, she folded her arms across her pregnancy. Now something else struck her. Something about the way the woman walked. Then she knew. Lalage had been pregnant, too.

"Ellis!" Seeing him at the end of the street, Rebecca ran to him. "Did you see her?" she demanded. "Ellis? Did you?"

"See whom?" Trying to stuff a package into his coat pocket, and damning the flap which was determined to get in his way, Ellis wasn't even looking at his wife. "Well, Becky?"

"Did you see your sister?" Her breathing harsh and her

blue eyes wide, Rebecca shook him. "You *must* have seen her!" she cried. "She passed this way – you couldn't have missed her. Ellis, did you see Lalage?"

"No. Of course I didn't." Fearing she'd been taken ill, Ellis reached for Rebecca's hand. To his relief, it was cool. "You're imagining things," he said. "Daydreaming."

"I'm not!" On the verge of tears, Rebecca stared. "I saw her!" she insisted, butting her head against her husband's chest. "I'm certain of it!"

"Oh." Ellis shrugged. "Well, women in your condition often – "

"Have strange fancies. See things which don't exist. I know all about that. But Ellis, this was no dream. I did see your sister. What's more, she was pregnant. *She* was expecting a baby, too."

"What nonsense." Now quite certain his wife must be ill, Ellis kept her hand in his. "Come along, Becky. Let's go back to the hotel. You must have a rest."

"But, Ellis – "

"Darling, listen. Alex and Lalage live in London. How could they be here?"

"They could be taking a holiday." Rebecca was determined – she would convince him yet. "That's one possibility. Isn't it?"

"I hardly think my sister would choose to come to Cardiff for her holiday," replied Ellis, drily. "Bath or Brighton, now – they are possibilities, I'm sure."

"But why – "

"Lalage likes crowds. Shops. Theatres. The world of fashion. She would not willingly come here."

"How do *you* know?" Rebecca would not give in. "Peoples' tastes change. Their horizons widen. Their incomes contract. Do you know if they still live in London? If they are there now? Of course you don't."

Ellis considered. "I don't know exactly where they are," he admitted. "As it happens, I heard from my banker only the other day. Alex has taken no money from their allowance for almost a twelvemonth now."

"There you are, then!" Triumphantly, Rebecca smiled. "Now agree – "

"I'll agree they may have moved. But I doubt if you – "

"You *will* insist I'm mistaken!" Rebecca was in despair. Why was he so stubborn? Why couldn't he accept what she said? "You will say I'm daydreaming. But I know I'm as wide awake as you are. Ellis, I did see Lalage!"

"You *didn't*!" Growing angry, Ellis glared. "God in heaven," he muttered. "Am I to be hag-ridden for the rest of my days?"

"Ellis! That's hardly fair – "

"Rebecca, you've said enough." Scowling, Ellis walked on. By himself. "She can't be here," he muttered. "Why should she be in Cardiff? She could be anywhere. Anywhere in the world. She might even be dead, for all I know."

"Or care?" Realising Ellis was very upset, Rebecca took his arm. "Ellis, my dear? Do you care?"

"No, I don't."

"There's no room in your heart for forgiveness?"

"None. My heart is closed to her." Ellis looked down at the pavement. "Were she lying in the gutter here, starving, diseased or even dying, I should not lift one finger to help. In fact, I'd watch her die."

"Oh, Ellis! So unforgiving?"

"She meant to kill you." Now, Ellis took Rebecca's hand. He held it firmly in his own. "She wanted you to die. Slowly and painfully, too. So now she's dead to me. Do you understand? She doesn't exist."

"I saw someone I know today," said Lalage. Alone in a public stagecoach, she and John Rhys Morgan were on their way home.

"A friend, Lali?" Relieved and delighted to be leaving that dirty little town, John Rhys smiled. "So who was it, then?"

"A woman. A slut, I should say. From England."

Lalage scowled. "I saw a fat, English slut. She hates me. I ran away. But she may well havc recognised me."

"Oh." John Rhys put his arm about his wife's shoulders. "She can't hurt you now," he said, soothingly. "No one will hurt my Lali."

"No one?"

"Well, *cariad* – they'll have to kill me, first."

Chapter 25

John Rhys Morgan meant what he said. If anyone had even tried to hurt Lalage, he would have cut them to pieces. But now, sitting in an only moderately dirty stagecoach, with his darling wife safe in his arms, he was happy. Comfortably aware that every moment brought him that little bit nearer home, he relaxed. "All right, Lali?" he demanded, giving her a kiss and a hug.

"Yes indeed, John Rhys." Mimicking his accent, which she knew entertained him, Lalage grinned. "Some day soon," she said, "you'll have to start teaching me Welsh."

"Shall I?" Her husband hugged her tight. "Why's that, then?"

"So I can talk to you in your own language, of course. Your child must learn it. Won't his mother be the best person to teach him?"

"God, no. It would hurt my ears beyond endurance, to hear a Saxon mangling the loveliest language in the world."

"Yet you married me." Lalage pouted. "You're always grumbling about the English. Saying you hate us. But you chose to wed a Saxon bride."

"Oh, you're not really a Saxon. You're a fairy's child." Laughing, John Rhys Morgan kissed her again. "Very well, Lali," he conceded. "I'll teach you Welsh. We'll have three days a week when we speak nothing else.

"Listen to Bethan, yes? She may be a servant, but she has a way with words. She's quite poetic on occasions. In Welsh, that is. I know her English is a torment to hear. Lali, my darling?"

"What?"

"You're so beautiful. So soft and lovely! You're like a sweet, ripe apricot."

"Oh?" Appeased, Lalage smiled again. She glanced down at her pregnancy. "I'm a rather fat apricot," she laughed. "At any rate, I am just now."

"Doesn't hurt you to carry a bit more weight. Far too skinny you were before."

They reached the inn where they would stay that night. They went straight upstairs. Taking his wife in his arms, John Rhys held her close. "*Wrach Seisnig*," he whispered, into her hair. "English witch."

In bed, Lalage smiled to herself. She did know *some* Welsh. Quite a bit, in fact. For, in moments of intimacy, John Rhys Morgan's command of the English language deserted him. Welsh took over completely then.

"Another couple of months," said John Rhys. His passion spent, he lay back against his pillows and studied his wife with a farmer's critical eye. The English witch was a piece of livestock now. "Seven, eight weeks," he murmured. "Then you'll have your baby at your breast."

"But won't we get a woman in for that?" asked Lalage. In her experience, only the labouring poor fed their own children. "Can't we – "

"Hire a wet-nurse?" John Rhys shook his head. "Don't be ridiculous. You must nourish him. You'll want to, anyway. You'll see."

"Oh." Lalage wasn't so sure. Out driving in Warwickshire, she had observed many a field woman or tinker's wife squatting in a dry ditch or lurking under a hedge, one sagging breast spilling out of her dirty bodice while her brat took its fill. A perfectly repulsive sight it had always been. "I'll think about it," she said.

"You'll do as you're told. I'm not having some scrofulous creature from Swansea feeding my child." Narrowing his eyes, John Rhys measured her. "You won't grow much bigger," he said now. He pressed her stomach with the flat of his hand. "There's hardly any fluid," he added. "A pint or two at most."

"Is that bad?"

"Silly woman. It's good, of course. Why would you want to carry a gallon of water around? All that weight – it would only make your ankles swell. Fatigue you half to death."

"I'm not at all tired now." Lalage looked at him. "John? Do you love me?"

"What a question." John Rhys took her in his arms. "Of course I love you. I could eat you alive."

"Will you, then?" Lalage's eyes sparkled greedily. "Will you do it now?"

"Well – yes." He laughed at her. "If you like."

"Wonderful." Lalage lay back. She closed her eyes and relaxed. She waited for the rapture to begin.

John Rhys always took his time with her. At first he was teasing and gentle, then fierce and urgent – but today, just as Lalage was almost there, he began to tease again. He even talked to her. "You taste of the sea," he told her. "You smell and taste of the cold, grey sea."

"Do I?" Lalage couldn't imagine it. Contentedly, she sighed. "You tell such lies," she murmured.

"It's true." His clever fingers busy, John Rhys grinned. "I should know, shouldn't I?"

Five, ten minutes went slowly by. Lalage wanted to touch herself. Her hand snaked down her stomach, into the nest of curling black hair, searching for a special place. But her husband knew exactly where it was. He had found it long ago. Now, he would not let her near it. "Wait," he said. "Have some patience. We'll do things my way today."

"Oh, let me!" Fiercely, Lalage pulled his hair. "It's my body," she protested.

"Wait," he repeated. He pushed her hand away, and went on with his work.

He had her now. The lightest touch electrified her.

Aware of his power, he played with her, making her wait a little longer. Longer still.

A gasping sob made him look up. To his surprise, he saw she was in tears. Pitying her, he kissed her again.

The resulting convulsion almost tore her apart.

"So what do you think now?" he asked, as she lay there motionless. Her eyes glazed, her breathing shallow, she was evidently exhausted. "Do I love you, Lali?" he whispered. "Or do I not?"

"You do." Happily, Lalage sighed. Then, sitting up, she looked into his eyes. "Would you do that with anyone else?" she asked.

"What?" He laughed. "Well, there's a question."

"But you're always going off by yourself." Lalage frowned. "Are you ever unfaithful to me?"

"I should think so." Still, he grinned. "Take half the girls in Wales to my bed, I do. Wear myself out pleasuring women."

"Tell me the truth." Lalage shook him. "Do you have mistresses?"

"I have had particular friends. But since I married you, I've been as constant as the turtle dove."

"Truly?"

"Yes, indeed." Solemn now, he kissed her. "You're the moon in the sky," he told her. "You're my love. You're my life. My heart is in your hands."

Back in Llangynnydd, the villagers would have had no time at all for that sort of romantic nonsense. They knew for a fact that the Englishwoman was a child of the devil. The *hen wrach Seisnig* had enchanted poor John Rhys. How else would such an old, dried-up, skinny bit of misery have caught a young, handsome bachelor? Then made him her devoted slave?

She was a spell-binder of the first order. As good, honest Christians, they should take her to the village green, pile up faggots and burn her, without further delay.

Fortunately for Lalage, everyone in Llangynnydd and the area round about was too frightened of John Rhys Morgan even to annoy him, let alone hurt his wife. In any case, he seemed well able to control her. No one could claim she made him neglect his stock or his land. Or his rather less legitimate concerns.

Once one of Lalage's fiercest critics, Bethan thought her mistress was beginning to turn out well after all. She was becoming the handiest of dairy-maids. She was learning to cook. She loved her husband. More than loved him. "Worships him, she does," declared Bethan. "She'd lie down and die for him. Indeed she would."

Betty, now William Parry the cowman's wife, agreed. "She used to be such a madam," she said. "But look at her now. Tame as a pet lamb."

She sighed. "Poor Mr Lowell. He couldn't manage her at all. But as for Mr Morgan! How did he do it? He's brought her to heel and no mistake. I'd love to know how."

"He's tamed creatures wilder than she ever was." Reflectively, William Parry chewed the stem of his pipe. "There's not a man on Gower would cross John Rhys," he observed. He eyed his wife. "No woman, either. You know about the fishing, do you?"

"Bethan told me." Betty shrugged. "John Rhys is a fine fisherman, she says."

"None finer." William Parry stared into the fire. "His catches are always good ones. But he's a hard master. Very hard indeed. He runs a very tight ship."

"Does he?"

"I'll say so." William looked up. "What do you think happens to a man who don't pull his weight? Or – worse than that – tries to cheat his master? Who decides to go fishing on his own account?"

"I don't know. What?"

"It's the marshes for him." William Parry looked grave. "The estuary, Betty. The north shore. A treacherous place indeed. You'll find quicksands there."

"Quicksands?"
"That's right."
"What do you mean?"
"Well, girl. I don't know exactly how it happened, so I don't lay no blame. But a couple of years ago, a farmer by the name of Llewellyn thought he'd try a little fishing. All by himself.
"Did all right until John Rhys heard of it. Then there was trouble. Big trouble. Arguments. Shots fired. Heads broken. Huw Llewellyn was a big man round here. A big farmer, with his own acres and his own flocks. Not a little cottager with one pig and a cabbage patch. No, indeed."
"What happened?" Betty put her sewing aside. "William?"
"One low tide, Huw went missing. At the next, he was found on the marshes. Staked out. Drowned. A warning, if you like."
"John Rhys did that?" Betty was horrified. "Are you telling me he's a murderer?"
William Parry shrugged. "I don't know who took Huw Llewellyn to the marshes," he said. "I've no idea who tied him down."
"But you suspect it was John Rhys. Or some of his men."
"Perhaps." William tapped Betty's wrist. "Listen to me," he said. "Don't go blabbing and gossiping, will you? I'm only telling you this so you know – "
"Oh, don't worry. I can keep *my* mouth shut." Breaking off a piece of thread, Betty sighed. "I have secrets, too. If I had a mind, I could send somebody we know straight to the gallows tree."
"Could you?"
"Certainly." Remembering, Betty shuddered. But now, she smiled. "So, do you think Mr and Mrs Morgan are well-suited?" she enquired.
"They seem very happy together." Glad to get off the subject of murder, William Parry grinned. "She's too old,

mind. Must be at least thirty, and he's not twenty five until gone Midsummer Day. She's a pretty little *dwt*, though."

"I think she's beautiful."

"So she is. Far too skinny – but that don't always signify. Some men swear by lean meat. Insist it's far tastier than fat or rind." William grinned again. "I'd say they were well matched."

"So would I." Betty threaded her needle. "Two of a kind," she murmured. "Two children of the devil. Well matched indeed."

William Parry yawned. Standing up, he stretched. "What you muttering about?" he asked, indulgently. "You're a proper old mumbler. Always talking to yourself."

Betty shook her head. "I was just thinking," she said.

"What about?"

"I'm almost sure I'm going to have a baby." Betty smiled. "In fact, I know I am. Are you pleased?"

William stared. But then he beamed at her. "I'm thrilled, girl!" he cried. "Delighted. Over the moon!"

Even though her pregnancy was well advanced, Lalage still went for the long walks to which she'd become accustomed while Alex lay dying. Often, she was alone. But, now and again, her husband had time to go with her.

One Sunday, John Rhys Morgan announced that since it was such a fine day, they might walk out to the island on Penrhyn Gwyr. "But we'll only go if you feel strong enough," he added, considerate as always.

"How far is it?" asked Lalage.

"About eight English miles. There and back." He grinned. "We'll take a picnic, shall we? Make a day of it?"

"What if I tire?"

"I'll carry you home."

"Very well."

They set out. Hand in hand they walked along the

flat sandy beach, making for the rocky causeway at the southern end of Rhosili Bay. This causeway led to the little island at the tip of Worm's Head, or Penrhyn Gwyr.

The tide was well out, so it was easy to scramble across the great boulders and stones which, at low tide, joined the Head to the mainland. "We shan't be cut off, shall we?" asked Lalage, as she clambered over sharp, jutting rocks. "I don't fancy spending a night on Worm's Head."

"Don't worry." Stopping to help her over a particularly difficult stretch, John Rhys grinned. "Afraid to be left alone with me, is it?" he demanded, his dark eyes glittering, wicked as they come.

"I'm not afraid of *you*." Gathering her skirts and tucking her petticoats up to her knees, Lalage laughed. Taking his hand, she held it tightly. "Why ever should I fear you?"

"Why, indeed?" John Rhys laughed too. "I look at you, Lali – and all I see is that you're beautiful. I forget you're a devil's child. It's I who should be scared."

"What nonsense you talk." Reaching a well-trodden sheep-walk, Lalage let him go. "A babbling, drivelling idiot. That's all you are."

"You know something interesting, Lali? You're the only woman in Wales who's allowed to abuse me like this." For a moment, John Rhys Morgan's eyes were bright. Dangerously bright. But then they softened. "Come along, *cariad*," he said. His voice was controlled. Bland, even. "Let's get on."

So on they went. They clambered over rocky outcrops. They walked on rabbit-bitten, springy turf. They crossed the Devil's Bridge, a fine arch of rock carved by wind and waves. Reaching a grassy knoll, they sat down.

All about them, gulls screeched and wheeled. The wind blew a fine colour into Lalage's cheeks, and the sun dazzled her eyes. "Tired, my darling?" asked John Rhys.

"Not at all." Lying back against a rock, Lalage stretched. Luxuriously, she sighed. "We're Adam and Eve, in the garden," she said.

"You're an Eve, certainly." John Rhys grinned. "I hope I'm not such a fool as old Adam."

"Time will tell." Lalage grinned too. "How can I tempt you?" she asked.

"You can't. Not just now, anyway." Taking a flask from his pocket, John Rhys unscrewed the cap. He offered Lalage the brandy. "Have some of this, eh?"

"What is it?"

"Best Cognac. None finer."

"I don't doubt it." Lalage shook her head. "I don't think I want any," she said.

"Go on. Just a mouthful." John Rhys took some himself. "Warm you up, it will."

"I'm not cold. But I'm very hungry. Did you bring something to eat?"

"My pockets are laden." John Rhys began to empty them. "Here," he said, holding out two pies. "The big one's yours."

Lalage took it. "What's inside?" she asked.

"Rabbit, I should think."

"Splendid."

Watching his wife stuff herself, John Rhys grinned. "You like Bethan's cooking, don't you?" he demanded. "You would say it's the best there is."

"It's excellent." Wiping crumbs from her mouth, Lalage grinned back. "You like it, too."

"I've always enjoyed my food. But as for you! When we were first married, what a sparrow you were. Never saw such a little picker."

Lalage shrugged. "Didn't you?"

"God Almighty, no." Fastidiously, John Rhys took a piece of meat from his pie. "Oh, what's this?" he cried, in a high falsetto. "Oh, John! It's bacon! I can't eat bacon. What's that? Beef? I can't digest beef. I take only breast of chicken. Very lightly fried."

"Oh, be quiet, do." Tearing a piece of bread off the loaf he had brought, Lalage threw it at him. "My appetite soon improved."

"Well, it had to."

"What do you mean?"

"You needed energy. I set you to work, remember? For the first time in your idle life, you had a job to do."

"True." Lalage finished her pie. She looked round for something else to eat. "You make me slave all day," she complained. "You wear me out. You're a tyrant."

"I know." Finishing his meal, John Rhys lay back against a boulder. He closed his eyes. "You can stop all that," he added, as Lalage kissed him, then began to walk her fingers up and down his chest.

"Don't you like it?" Stealthily, Lalage slid her hand under the waistband of his breeches. "You don't have to do anything, you know," she murmured. "Just lie there. Let me ravish you."

"God in heaven." Sitting up again, John Rhys removed Lalage's invading fingers. "Be a good girl, and I'll tell you a story," he said.

"Will you?" Unimpressed, Lalage pouted. "What about?"

"A baby boy." John Rhys glanced at his wife's swollen stomach. "He can listen, too."

"You're sure it's a boy, aren't you?"

"Certain."

"What if it were a girl?"

"She'd be as welcome as the dawn, and I'd love her dearly. But all the same, you're going to have a boy." John Rhys frowned in concentration. "So now. To the story. Once upon a time – "

"Why do all stories begin so?"

"Be quiet and listen. Once upon a time, on North Gower, there was a father who seduced his daughter. In due course, she bore a son. But the child was deformed. Poor creature, he had a badly twisted foot. The people in the village said this was a judgement. They pelted the girl with stones and mud, and drove her away."

"Poor girl."

"Let me go on. Well, the girl took the child to the High King of that country, and asked his advice. The king deliberated and prayed for two whole days. Then, 'wrap the baby warmly,' he said. 'Put him in a wicker cradle – ' "

"Like Moses."

"Stop interrupting, Lali. Yes, like Moses. Put him in a wicker cradle, place the cradle on the river bank, and let the tide take him out to sea. There, God will decide his fate. So this was done.

"Well, the tide carried the cradle out of the estuary, and into the open sea. That night, a great storm blew up. The cradle was smashed to little pieces against the rocks of Penrhyn Gwyr.

"But God was merciful. The baby was unharmed. Then God sent his sea-birds, who pitied the child, and took him up. They laid him in a nest, they warmed him with their feathers, and they shielded him from the rain.

"Soon, the child cried for food. The gulls and cormorants could not feed him, so they asked God what to do. In due course an angel came down from heaven, carrying a great golden bell. At the side of this was a metal breast, and from this the baby took his milk. When the time came for him to be weaned, the angel returned and told him what herbs were safe to eat and which were death. So, the boy grew up.

"He became a very holy man. All the people round about were in awe of him. They said he could work miracles – could heal the sick and make barren women conceive, no matter how old or ill. Then, one day, the angel told him that God wanted him to build a chapel. He must leave Penrhyn Gwyr and walk north across Rhosili sands, towards the Burrows. Crippled though he was, he did so. He built his chapel – "

"All by himself? Or did the angel bring a trowel? Lay bricks alongside?"

"Perhaps he did." John Rhys grinned. "Anyway, the chapel was built. The holy man became very famous. People came from all over Wales to hear him speak, to ask for his prayers, to beg he would lay his hands upon them. Saint Cenydd, that was his name. The remains of his chapel are there still. I'll show you, if you like."

"Saint Cenydd, you say?"

"That's right."

"So his chapel must have been at Llangynnydd. Where *we* live."

"Oh, you're so sharp. Wicked sharp!" John Rhys laughed. "Bright as a new-made pin. Well, at least you've been listening."

But then he stopped laughing. He took her face between his hands. "Lali?"

"Yes?"

"When the time comes for the little one to be born, will you be afraid?"

"Yes. A bit." Lalage shrugged. "I'm so small. I'm almost bound to tear."

"Don't worry." John Rhys took her hands in his. "There'll be no difficulty, I promise. I'll be with you. I shall deliver the child."

"You?" Lalage stared. "What do you know about all that?"

"A great deal more than you." He ran his hands down her sides, then measured her hips in spans. "Yes," he agreed, "you're very small. But you're strong, and you're supple. Your bones will part easily, and let him through. He won't hurt you at all."

"Isn't it time we were getting back?" Lalage looked towards the west. "The sun's going down fast. John?"

"Up you get, then." John Rhys picked up his flask. He threw the remains of the picnic to the gulls. "Want me to carry you?"

"No. I can walk."

They arrived back at the farmhouse to find Bethan in a state. Seeing them approach, she ran down the path to meet them. "A message from Mr Atkins!" she cried. "John Rhys, you're to go at once. You're to take your men. All of them!"

* * *

It was three o'clock in the morning by the time John Rhys finally came home. He walked softly into the bedchamber then, sighing, he sat down on the bed. He drew off his boots, took off his shirt, and groped around for his night attire.

"I'm not asleep." Sitting up in the pitch darkness, Lalage fumbled for flint and tinder. "Just a moment, I'll light the lamp."

"Let me." His eyes more accustomed to darkness than hers were, John Rhys took the tinder box. He lit a candle. He rubbed his eyes, and groaned.

"Well?" Lalage looked at him. "A good catch?"

"So-so." John Rhys covered his face. "We had to kill a couple of excisemen," he said.

"Oh, God." Her heart turning over, Lalage stared. "Why?"

"We had no choice. No bloody choice. Oh, Lali!"

"What happened?"

John Rhys groaned again. "We went down to the beach," he muttered. "The men took the boats into a cave, for unloading. Jack and I stood on the tide-line, discussing fair shares.

"All of a sudden, there they were. Two of them, armed to the teeth. Pistols drawn, shouting their bloody heads off. God knows how they came to be there."

"Someone must have tipped them off."

"I'd worked that out, girl." John Rhys flashed Lalage a look which shut her mouth like a trap. "But who?" he growled. "Who was it? These were men we knew. Fellows Jack Atkins had drunk with, men he'd paid off with gold. When he saw who they were, he went mad. Crazy he was, like a tormented bull."

"Did he kill the men? Or did you?"

"I helped." Remembering how smoothly his knife had slid under one man's ribs, John Rhys shuddered. "They had no chance, anyway. They were armed, it's true. But there were at least two dozen of us.

"From the look on their faces when we all went for

them, I think they were surprised. They'd expected Jack and me to be alone. They'd taken Jack's money, see, so then they were going to take us. Be heroes, like. Have it all ways."

"Oh." Bewildered and frightened, Lalage bit her lip. "What will you do now?"

"Lie low for a while. Hope for the best." Getting into bed, John Rhys took Lalage in his arms. He buried his face in her hair. "Pray," he whispered. "Pray the English soldiers don't come."

"Might they?"

"I don't know. The last time an exciseman met with an accident, a company of redcoats marched down from Swansea. All the people were rounded up. For days together, cows went unmilked, stock unfed. Strict curfew was imposed, you see.

"Oh, Lali! Burning, stealing – that was the least of it. They had great big dogs. Terrible creatures, like wolves. At night they were out, with flambeaux, searching. Anyone they found out of doors – "

"Don't tell me."

"You need to know. They had their fun with the men, but at least they killed them. For the women, it was ten times worse."

"You mean they were – "

"Yes. That, and more. You've seen Dilys Lloyd? Lives with her brother and his wife, in a cottage by the Burrows? Sits in her window all day, staring out."

"You mean the madwoman? Yes, I've seen her."

"They caught her. When her father found her, he lost his reason. Died a month after, of a broken heart. Dilys was his darling. Such a sweet, gentle girl. She was out looking for a stray calf, you see."

"Poor thing."

"Poor thing, indeed." John Rhys grimaced. "English soldiers! They're scourings of the cess pits, the scum of this earth. I'd cut your throat myself before I let one get near you."

"They may not come." Lalage rocked him like a child. "Even if they do, there's nothing to lead them to us. You said so yourself. Mr Atkins – "

"Mr Atkins!" John Rhys glared. "He'd sell his grandmother for ninepence. He'd sell me for a lump of coal. If the redcoats came for him, they'd only have to show him the hot irons. He'd be yelling my name loud enough to be heard in Cardiff! He'd have no – what's the word?"

"Qualms? Compunction?"

"Something like that. Well, he wouldn't care what happened to the Morgans. He'd be certain to give me away."

"But you've always said – "

"He'd definitely betray me. If he were condemned to hang, he'd make quite sure I went with him." John Rhys held Lalage close. "Just hope for the best, eh? That's all we can do now."

Chapter 26

More than anything, Rebecca wanted to be living at Easton Hall again, to be settled in good time for the birth of Ellis's heir. It seemed likely she would realise this ambition. The Hall had been a long time rebuilding, but now it was almost complete.

Walking through its newly decorated rooms, she breathed in the delicious smells of drying plaster, new carpentry and fresh paint. Soon, she thought, soon it will all be done.

One sunny afternoon, she went up to the long gallery. Here, she found plasterers putting the finishing touches to its ornately-sculpted ceiling. Coming down from his ladder, the master craftsman told his journeyman to carry on with the job, while he spoke to Mrs Darrow. "Well, madam?" he ventured, as he wiped his floury hands on a cloth. "What do you think?"

"It's beautiful, Mr Lawley. Absolutely lovely." Looking up, Rebecca gazed in wonder at the swirls and arabesques which turned and twisted in graceful arcs, leading the eye towards the enormous Tudor rose in the centre of the snow-white confection above her head.

She felt tears in her eyes. The son of God himself had been a craftsman. Now, these two perfectly ordinary men had performed their own miracle. "Well done," she said, with feeling. "Very well done indeed."

As if it were in some way connected with the rebirth of his house, Ellis's own health improved tremendously now. That summer, he began riding again. Mounted on a steady grey, the reins clasped firmly but awkwardly in his left hand, at first he had to take things very slowly. But soon enough he was visiting studs and stables for miles around, evidently on the look out for a high-spirited, mettlesome hunter of the kind he'd always ridden before.

He took as active an interest in the estate as ever. He began to talk of draining, of ditching, of enclosing this bit of heathland in the west or that piece of scrub over to the east. He resumed his duties as magistrate, and local felons started to be more careful, anxious as they were not to come up before him at the quarter sessions.

Good health being more or less restored, he took it for granted. "Don't fuss so, Becky," he muttered, when she expressed her concern that a persistent cold might well turn to fever – for he would go out on dull, rainy mornings in a light summer coat, rather than a cloak of thick frieze. "I can hardly let Robbins think I'm afraid to get wet."

Rebecca sighed. Recalling that a mere six months ago, Ellis would have been in bed at this hour of the morning, and would not have cared what his land agent thought of him, she let him go. "Enjoy your day," she said, kissing him. "Dear Ellis, please take care."

"I always do." Ellis picked up his riding crop. "Are you going over to the factory today?"

"Yes, I am."

"Well, order the carriage and be off with you." Ellis grinned. "Go and chivvy your workmen. Order them about. Exhaust yourself, and then perhaps your poor, henpecked husband will get some peace. Simmons! Where *is* the fellow?"

"Sir?" About to slope off for a quiet smoke, the butler came out of the sitting room.

"There'll be three for dinner. Mr Hatchard, Mr Blackwell and myself. Get up some decent claret. Then tell Mrs Webster to make more of an effort today."

"I'm sorry, sir?"

"You heard me!" Derisively, Ellis sniffed. "That beef we had yesterday was as tough as last year's salt mutton. If the woman can't roast a piece of the best sirloin without ruining it completely, maybe we should look out for another cook."

"Sir." Simmons slouched off down the corridor. The days of peace and quiet were well and truly over. In good health and spirits once more, his master was every bit as exacting as he'd ever been before his illness. Only the previous morning, he'd complained that some perfectly acceptable coffee was luke-warm.

Going into the kitchen, the butler sat down at the white deal table. Heavily, he sighed.

"What's the matter, Mr Simmons?" Twirling a strand of hair back from her forehead, Mrs Webster grinned flirtatiously. "What's upset you?"

"Nothing. Everything." Simmons sighed again. "Look here, Edith. Mr Darrow and two of the county magistrates will be here for dinner, and the master wants to impress. You'd better get those geese drawn. Concoct a special pudding. Prepare a rack of lamb."

"But there isn't time to roast geese!" The cook wrung her hands. "As for the lamb, it was only killed yesterday. It needs at least three days to hang."

"Get the geese plucked and in the oven. See that the lamb is pink and tender. Or it'll be the ducking stool for you."

Out in the fresh air, the drizzle fast soaking his clothes but the exercise invigorating and refreshing him, Ellis felt better than he had for years. He was coming out of a nightmare. Out of a black, pain-filled dream which had fogged his vision and stopped him feeling the sunshine.

Seeing his land agent come riding towards him, he kicked Sophie into a canter. His eyes shining, he was as fresh and lively as his mare today. "Good morning, Robbins!" he cried. "Well, I think we'll go over to Handley's Ford this forenoon. See how the Morrisons are getting on these days."

"Handley's Ford? Bit far for your honour, isn't it?" Robbins had been drinking heavily the previous evening, and he'd hoped to spend the afternoon asleep before the fire. He was certainly in no fit state to steeplechase across half of Warwickshire, for his head ached and his eyes wanted the rest of the day off.

Now, he scratched his head. "Pardon my saying this, sir," he began, "but don't you think a long ride might tire you? What with your honour having been so ill – "

"I was ill, certainly. But I'm quite recovered now." The squire looked narrowly at the servant. "Not feeling very well yourself today?" he enquired.

"On the contrary, sir. I was never better."

"Well, then. A good gallop across a nice stretch of open country will suit us both."

Ellis moved off. Morosely, the land agent followed him.

When Ellis returned from Handley's Ford, he found Rebecca standing on the front steps, anxiously looking out for him. "I thought you'd gone to Birmingham," he began. "I – "

"I changed my mind. I shall go later this week." Rebecca was beside herself. "I was speaking to Mr Ferriman just now," she said, her eyes sparkling. "He says that by Wednesday – well, guess!"

"All the workmen will be gone?"

"Yes!" Rebecca beamed. She clapped her hands. "Ellis, your son will be born at Easton Hall!"

"Mama?" Having given her nurse the slip, Jane had appeared from nowhere. Tugging at her mother's skirts, she searched Rebecca's face. "Are we all going to live in the big house?" she asked.

"Of course, my darling." Sweeping the child into her arms, Rebecca sat her astride her pregnancy. With a playful forefinger, she rubbed her daughter's little nose. "You shall be a princess in a castle," she cried. "You and Maria will have a school room, a play room, a music room – and the best bedchamber of all. The one with big windows, above the drawing room downstairs."

"Yes?" Jane was thrilled. She hugged Rebecca round the neck. "I shall love that!"

"Why do you give the girls that room?" asked Ellis, as he and Rebecca walked over to the Hall. "Why not put them in the old nurseries? They look out across the garden."

"The windows of the great chamber overlook the courtyard." Taking Ellis by the hand, Rebecca smiled. "They won't be able to climb out. Ellis, my dear, I remember your old stories only too well. I don't want *my* children scrambling out of their bedrooms windows, crawling off over the tiles. Falling from the roof, and breaking their necks."

"Oh, children must be allowed to take risks. How else do they learn?" Ellis grinned. "You let Jane climb trees. Yesterday, she was in the great oak at the bottom of the drive. Her nurse was frantic. I had to threaten her with a whipping before she'd come down."

"You'd never whip Jane."

"No, of course I wouldn't. But she doesn't know that."

"Does she not?" Rebecca laughed. "Look," she said. "Smoke. They've lit a fire in the drawing room. Let's go and see how it looks."

They quickened their pace.

It was many years since Lalage had climbed a tree, but since the excisemen had been killed she made sure she kept herself fit. If the redcoats came, she might have to run for her life.

The caves with which great stretches of the Gower coast was riddled would provide comparatively safe havens for fugitives. John Rhys had taken her to one of the best hidden, shown her how to make the perilous descent down the cliff to reach it, and arranged for basic provisions and fresh water to be taken there.

But Lalage did not fancy spending time in a damp, spidery cavern. She said so.

"You have no choice," retorted John Rhys. "Or rather,

your choice will be between certain death and possible salvation."

"You exaggerate." Lalage tossed her curls. "You say things like this just to scare me."

"I only wish that were true." John Rhys took her by the shoulders. "If they take me," he said gravely, "promise me you'll hide. They'll make sure I suffer. But at least I'll die peaceful in spirit, if I know you are safe."

"But they wouldn't hurt me. I'm English!" Lalage glared defiance. "I'm pregnant, too."

"You're the wife of a Welsh criminal. As such, you'll be fair game. The fact you're with child will simply add sauce to the meat." John Rhys grimaced, as if in pain. "They'll toss you from one to the other. Use you worse than they'd use a penny whore. Then, when they've done with you in that way, they'll kill you slowly. Just for entertainment."

Lalage shuddered. But then she shook her head. "No, they wouldn't," she said. "Their officers wouldn't let them."

"Jesus in heaven!" John Rhys groaned. "Great God and all the saints, their officers would encourage them! Do you know how the Scots were treated, after the '45? I shan't tell you. But it's past my understanding how a woman can endure such torments, and still live."

"Why are you frightening me like this?"

"For your own safety. I know what I'm talking about, believe you me." John Rhys scowled. "To English soldiers, the Welsh, Scots and Irish are animals. Wild beasts, put here on this earth to provide them with sport. So promise me, darling. If I'm arrested, give me your word of honour you'll come here."

"Oh, very well." Lalage shrugged. "I promise."

But the redcoats did not come, after all. A week went by. Then two. Then three. Betty heard a rumour that the traitor had been discovered. That he had been tried, found guilty, and dealt with.

Soon, it was general village gossip that down on

Llanrhidian marshes a body had been found. That of a local shepherd, its throat was cut through to the bone. Before that final mercy, however, the man had been flayed.

"His face was twisted awful, so they say." Bethan loved a good story, and now she told Betty all about it. "If I'd been him," she said, "I'd have cut my own throat. Long before they came for me." Eloquently, she sniffed. "Like I told Mrs Morgan, girl. John Rhys makes a nasty enemy."

"He's a barbarian." Shuddering, Betty put a newly–ripened cheese to one side. She took down another. "There's justice for you," she muttered, as she mixed brine. "There's law, and there's order. So, he warned the excisemen. He took their gold. But why couldn't John Rhys have had him shot? Why did he have to suffer so?"

"Go to John Rhys and ask him, eh?" Bethan grimaced. "Do you know what they do to Welshmen, in Swansea gaol?"

"No."

"Well, I don't want you to be sick all over these nice clean flagstones, so I shan't tell you now." Bethan sniffed again. "There won't be any more betrayals," she said. "One clear example. That's enough."

"Murderer," thought Betty. Crossing the cobbled yard, she saw her mistress standing at the farmhouse door. Her eyes closed, Lalage had her face towards the sun. "As for her," she reflected, "she's no better than he is. Fits in well she does, among murderers and rogues."

Betty sighed. She loved her husband. Her own unborn baby kicked lustily against her ribs. But she frequently wished herself at home, in the green safety of her native Warwickshire.

Spring was beautiful that year. The villagers began to hope for a good summer. They also began to breathe more easily, for they dared to hope they would not be suspected. The bodies of the two excisemen had been disposed of, and Jack Atkins had presumably squared things with their masters at the Customs House – so the farmers and shepherds assumed they were safe from troops of soldiers over-running their land, searching the fields and woods, assaulting the people and destroying for the fun of it.

For a while, the fishing stopped. Lalage was glad of that.

The baby was ready to be born. Lalage was longing for delivery, but for all her husband's assurances that she would survive childbirth unscathed, she was afraid. Women *did* die in childbed. It happened all the time. That winter, in a village near Llangynnydd, a poor girl had lain in labour for three days and nights. Too large to be delivered, the boy had torn his mother apart, and both had eventually bled to death.

"I'm too small. I know I am." Dolefully, Lalage met her husband's eyes. Not hungry tonight, she pushed her untasted supper aside. "Bethan says I'll suffer the torments of the damned. She says that if she could, she'd have this baby for me."

"Indeed?" John Rhys Morgan shook his head. "I know whose child I'd rather be," he murmured, as Bethan shuffled in on arthritic feet, to remove the supper plates. Her hips were wide enough to brush both sides of the door-frame at once.

"Don't worry, *cariad*," he said, when Bethan had tidied away and gone out again. "You're thin, I agree. But you'll give a little. The baby is small. There's nothing to fear."

"Is there not?" Only a little comforted, Lalage shrugged helplessly. "What shall I get ready?" she asked now. "For when the child arrives?"

"Some old sheets," he replied. "There'll be plenty in my mother's wedding chest, so take what you want. You'll need some linen, cut into strips. Lots of straw, too. Get William Parry to take up a bale of the best."

"Why should I want straw?" Lalage frowned. "I'm not a pig in farrow!"

"No. But you'll bleed a bit, you see. Only a little – but straw under the sheets absorbs the blood." John Rhys took her hand. "Saves the bedding, look. That's all."

"I see." Lalage picked at a corner of the linen tablecloth. "May Betty be with me?" she asked. "Shall Betty help?"

"I shan't need help." Complacently, John Rhys smiled. "Oh – if you want her, you may have her there. She can heat water for washing the child. Tear bandages, cut string, and that."

"She can hold my hand, too. Mop my brow."

"Funny ideas you have." John Rhys laughed. "Mark my words. When this child comes, you'll be too busy to notice whether Mrs Betty's there or not."

In the event, John Rhys was right. Betty was of little real use. Roused from her sleep at three o'clock that same morning, she came running from William Parry's cottage. Clad in a nightgown, shawl and curl papers, she held Lalage's hand while the expectant mother, ably tutored by her husband, pushed and grunted valiantly. Then, riding another contraction, pushed again.

"Nearly there, you are. So not as hard this time." Glaring crossly at poor Betty and willing her not to faint – for she was already a delicate shade of green – John Rhys placed his hand on his wife's stomach. "Just gently now," he insisted. "Once more, Lali. Breathe in. Now, push. Very good."

Perspiration beading her brow, Lalage did as she was bidden. She pushed, she breathed in, she pushed again.

She'd been so terrified of giving birth. But, now she was actually doing it, she was almost enjoying herself. To her great surprise, it wasn't hurting at all. It was hard work, certainly. But, listening for her husband's next instruction, and striving to obey him to the letter, she didn't have time to wonder if she were in pain.

She looked up at Betty. Seeing how pale the girl had

become, she pressed her hand. "Not long now," she said calmly. She smiled. "When your time comes, you must certainly engage the services of this midwife. He's – "

"You can stop that chattering!" As he bit off a length of twine, John Rhys saw the baby's head. "Now, Lali," he said, "take a deep breath. Push, and – well done!"

There was a sound of slipping, of sliding, of slithering out. Lalage wondered what it was. But then, to her astonishment, she heard a baby's cry. "John?" She tried to sit up. "Is it – "

"Clever girl." John Rhys beamed. "He's perfect, Lali. Absolutely beautiful."

"Let me see. Oh, let me see!"

"In a moment." John Rhys was busy with the baby. Reaching for a shawl, he glanced at his wife. He smiled again. "As for you, girl," he remarked, "not a mark anywhere. No broken flesh, no pain, not a single tear. Do you feel well?"

"Well?" Lalage stared. Then, to her great surprise, she realised she did indeed feel well. "Yes, I'm fine," she replied. "John, what are you doing?"

"Just tying the cord. Lie back again, *cariad*. In a few more minutes, the whole business will be over."

Wrapping the baby warmly, he gave him to his mother. He flashed Betty a rather sharp look. "Another pillow under her head now," he rapped. "Come along, girl. You're here to help, not to hinder. Lali, put him to the breast. That's right. It will help to bring on the afterbirth, you see."

Looking at mother and child, the midwife realised he was more or less superfluous now. "Are you happy, Lali?" he asked.

"Perfectly." Watching her son root for nourishment, Lalage smiled a great beaming smile. "I'm the happiest woman in the whole world."

That same evening, Rebecca had gone to bed knowing full well she would not sleep. The child was not due for another week or so, but now she thought he might decide to come early.

He was certainly anxious to be born. For the last few days, he'd kicked and punched her mercilessly, furious to be kept confined when he longed to be in the great world breathing in the fresh air.

About midnight, Rebecca was woken from a light doze. Her son was tired of waiting. He was going to make his appearance without further delay. "Ellis?" Pushing his shoulder, she roused him. "Will you ring for Molly? Tell her to go and wake Mrs Robbins now."

"I'll go and wake her myself." Getting out of bed, Ellis reached for his dressing gown. He slid his feet into slippers. "I'll come if you want me," he said. "Otherwise, I'll be in the old nursery."

"Asleep?"

"Wide awake." Ellis ruffled his wife's hair. "Waiting, and hoping all goes well for you."

The land agent's wife, who was also Rebecca's midwife, was pleased to note that her patient looked well and that her contractions were coming regularly now. Hopeful that this confinement was going to be as free of drama and crisis as the previous two, she sat down in a wide basket chair and was soon nodding off.

Half an hour later, she woke again. Her cushion had slipped and she was resting her head on hard wood. She looked at her watch. Ten past three. She yawned. It would be half an hour yet. An hour, even. If she rang down to the kitchens, where Molly was heating water, the girl could send up some tea. She struggled to her feet.

Rebecca had been dozing for the past thirty minutes or so, but now she too woke up with a start. A terrible, agonising pain gripped her like a vice. "Mrs Robbins?" she cried, panicking. "Charlotte? Where are you going?"

"Just to check everything's prepared." Smiling reassuringly, Charlotte Robbins – who attended only gentry and was accustomed to their imperious ways – came over to the bed. "Don't worry, madam," she said. "Have patience. You're not ready yet."

"I'm ready now." Pushing back blankets and sheets, Rebecca caught her breath. A fresh, even fiercer contraction convulsed her. "Look!" she gasped.

"You'll be another hour yet. At least." But, obligingly, the midwife rolled up her patient's nightgown, in order to check.

"Oh, sweet Jesus!" Throwing back her head, Rebecca cried out. "You see?" she wailed, when she could speak again. "Have patience, indeed! It's the child who's impatient. Not me."

"You're right." The midwife rang the bell. "Well, my dear madam? Shall we get on?"

But Rebecca was now past speech. Contraction followed contraction without a break. The pain was so awful she thought she might die. Tears filled her eyes and poured down her cheeks. Why was it hurting so much? This baby was ripping her apart.

"Not so hard, madam!" cried the midwife, as the child's head appeared. "Madam, for the love of God, stop! The cord – "

"I can't stop now!" Rebecca was held in an iron grip of pain. Tears soaked her pillow and sheets. "I'm sorry, but I – "

Another contraction hit home. She heard herself screaming and knew she would die. She was glad. Then she would be at peace.

The midwife was very experienced. Deftly, she slipped her hand inside the mother. Carefully, so carefully, she eased the cord from round the baby's neck.

Now it slid over the child's shoulders. With the next contraction, he was born. As Lalage Morgan's son drew his first breath, Rebecca Darrow's child sucked in a great, gulping mouthful of clean, fresh air.

"Go and wake my husband." Still somewhat bemused by the speed at which her son had decided to enter the world,

Rebecca was now sitting up in bed. "Please, Charlotte. Leave all that. Go and fetch Mr Darrow."

Mrs Robbins went.

"A boy, Ellis!" Propped against her pillows, Rebecca beamed in both triumph and delight. "Ellis, look! A beautiful, healthy boy."

Ellis looked. He saw his own dark eyes. Deep blue, soon they would turn brown. The baby's features were unmistakeably his. They were his sister's, too.

"He's a true Darrow," he whispered. His heart contracted. But then, taking his wife's hand, he kissed her. "Well done, Becky," he said. "Very well done indeed."

"You're pleased with your son?"

"I'm delighted."

"Good." Rebecca held the baby close. "Ellis?"

"Yes?"

"He's going to look just like you."

"Poor child." Ellis shook his head. "Shall I go and wake the girls?"

"At this hour?"

"Yes. Jane asked me most particularly – "

"So you promised. I see." Ruefully, Rebecca smiled. "That child makes a baby of you."

"She does indeed." Ellis grinned. "She winds me round her proverbial little finger."

He went to fetch his daughter, who was already wide awake, and running along the landing towards her mother's room.

Chapter 27

Ellis did not get his cricket team, far less his reserves – for, after the birth of Rayner, Rebecca's recovery was much less rapid than after her previous confinements. Determined nevertheless to get on with her life, she was up and about on the second day. But then, as her milk came in, she was suddenly taken ill. A slight fever became a tossing, burning ague, which in turn became a raging delirium. This lasted for two dreadful weeks.

"Take comfort, sir," said the famous London physician, called in at great expense and retained indefinitely. "Mrs Darrow is young, and strong. Milk-fever can sometimes be dangerous, but rarely proves fatal."

"Rarely?" Watching at her bedside, trying to comfort and encourage a woman who did not even know who he was, Ellis took a vow. If Rebecca recovered, she would have no more babies. Even if this child were to die, and even if she begged him on her bended knees to give her a second son, she would never be pregnant by him again.

The pet and favourite plaything of two doting elder sisters, the son and heir of a very wealthy landowner, and the light of his mother's life, Rayner George Darrow could hardly help but grow up in peace and prosperity.

It seemed that both fate and fortune had agreed to bless him, for he led a charmed life. Minor childhood ailments were easily shrugged off. The plague, the septic quinsy and the smallpox all passed him by. The alphabet gave Rayner only a few minor headaches, and the rules of elementary arithmetic were so easily grasped that the mild-mannered curate who taught the little boy pronounced him a native genius. So, if Rayner's opinion of himself was high, his friends and family had only themselves to blame.

Against her better judgement, Rebecca spoiled and indulged her only son. Brought up to despise both personal beauty and every other kind of earthly vanity, she nonetheless took the greatest pleasure in dressing her handsome Rayner in the most luxurious velvets and finest broadcloths money could buy. She retained one of the best tailors in Warwick. She had her own lady's maid cut and style Rayner's black, glossy curls.

Ellis did not approve of this at all. "You make an absolute fop of that child," he muttered, one bright Sunday morning, as he eyed his son's new coat of dark blue velvet, the revers of which were edged with silver braid. "Prettify the girls, if you must. But let Rayner at least look like a boy."

"My dear Ellis, he does look like a boy!" Rebecca smiled her satisfaction. It was not every woman who had three such beautiful, well-mannered, intelligent children to show off in church each fine Sabbath day. "Only last week, Lady Westfield herself declared she never saw so stout a lad as your son."

"That's because she has her eye on him, as a possible husband for one of her lumpy daughters." Gratified in spite of himself, Ellis grinned. "Very well," he conceded. "Dress him in silks and velvets. Tie ribbons in his hair. But let him go barefoot now and then. Let him climb trees, dirty his clothes, scratch his face. In short, let him grow up to be a man."

"He's doing his best to avoid growing up at all." Coming into the drawing room twirling a brand new parasol, Jane Darrow went to kiss her father and be kissed in return. "Only last week, while you were at the Assize, he climbed into the great oak by the lodge gates. He fell out of it, too. You should have seen his poor little knees."

She turned to her brother. "Rayner? Have all your grazes scabbed over now?"

"Nell dressed them again this morning. She thinks I shall live." Rayner grimaced. He looked at Rebecca. "Mama, are we walking to church today?" he asked.

"Certainly. Unless, of course, you would prefer to ride?" Rebecca took his hand in hers. "If your legs are still bruised and sore, you and I could order the dog cart."

"We're *all* walking." Ellis took out his watch. He went over to the door. "Maria?" he called. "Where the devil is the girl? Can't she ever be on time, for anything?"

Far away from the tranquillity of rural Warwickshire, Owen Morgan also prospered, was also the sun and moon in his mother's sky. He was fast growing into a courageous, handsome, charming little boy.

But while Rayner Darrow felt all the constraints of manners and education, and was being carefully groomed to take his place in the highest society, Owen Morgan was allowed as much freedom as a gypsy's son. He ran wild.

"Owen? John Owen, where are you?" Coming out of the farmhouse to stand on the steps, Lalage Morgan squinted into the bright morning sun. Then she turned her gaze westwards, towards the sea. There was still no sign of her child. But then, a soft rustle made her start. Looking down, she saw a very dirty little boy grinning up at her.

"John Owen!" Shaking her head, the mother smiled at her prodigal son. "John Owen, you rascal! I've been searching for you everywhere, and so has Bethan. Where on earth have you been?"

"Talking to William, in the new byre." Nonchalantly, the seven-year-old shrugged. "Just talking, Mam. That's all."

"Then why are you so filthy? Where are your shoes and stockings? Whatever happened to your shirt?" Lalage sighed in mock despair. "I'm almost sure that both the sleeves were whole yesterday."

"Oh, Mam!" Glancing at the great tear from elbow to

wrist, which now disfigured the left sleeve of his newest shirt, Owen – as he was invariably called, for his full name of John Rhys Owen was far too much of a mouthful for everyday use – shook his head in disgust. Women! How they fussed! "I don't need no shoes or stockings," he said. "I'm a bit dirty because I helped William and Huw clean out the stalls. I don't know nothing about this tear by here."

"The fairies must have done it. While you slept." Lalage ruffled his hair. She had been seriously worried when she'd found his bed empty so early in the morning. Her husband had gone out in the small hours – and she was afraid he had taken the child with him. In Lalage's opinion, Owen was far too young to go fishing, and would be for several years yet.

Now, however, she had not the heart to reproach him for the anxiety he'd caused. "Come and sit on the step," she invited. "Have something to eat. Bethan's just put a batch of baking to cool. We'll steal a few buns, shall we?"

"Yes!" At the thought of food, the little boy's dark eyes sparkled. He realised just how hungry he was.

Chewing his way through a piece of warm fruit loaf, John Rhys Owen Morgan glanced covertly at his mother's belly. He wondered when the new brother he'd been firmly promised – but didn't particularly want – meant to make his appearance. Not just yet, perhaps. While Lalage was sitting down, there was no sign of it at all. But when she stood up, the bulge beneath her apron was obvious.

He knew she wanted another child. Yearned for one. Last year, she had given birth to a still-born daughter, and been so sad that he had wondered if she would ever smile again. His father had been absolutely heart-broken. John Rhys had actually wept, which was something boys and men just did not do.

But now both parents were their usual cheerful selves again. His mother's merry laughter rang through the farmhouse once more. So Owen supposed the news wasn't completely bad, after all.

Bethan came into the kitchen just in time to apprehend the thief, by now on his second or third sortie. But, instead of clouting him round the ear, the housekeeper smiled her indulgence. John Owen was her lamb, her darling, her best beloved. He could have stolen all the cakes in South Wales and she would have adored him still. "Here," she said, handing him a sample of one of his favourites. "Take one for your Mam, as well. Needs building up, she does."

Lying back against the door jamb, Lalage let the sun kiss her face. "Have you seen your father today?" she asked casually, as she accepted a hot pie.

"No." His mouth full of melting pastry, Owen grinned at her. "He was up long before me. But William thinks he's gone over to Oxwich. Mr Atkins sent a message last night, you see."

"Ah." Lalage grimaced. "He's told you about all that, has he?" she enquired.

"Yes." The boy nodded. "Don't look so upset," he added. "There's no danger. When I'm older – "

"He'll take you with him. That's what I'm afraid of." Lalage stood up. "Well," she said, "it's a beautiful day. We'll have a picnic, shall we? Down on the sands."

Lalage had fallen asleep against a dune. Inside her closed eyelids, the sun had created a warm, red glow, which was the essence of contentment itself.

Suddenly, however, she was aware of childish giggles. Then she heard a growl of grown-up laughter. She opened her eyes, steadied herself on one elbow, and looked up. "John Rhys!" She smiled in welcome – but then reproach dulled the brightness in her eyes. "Oh, darling!" she scolded. "Where have you been, all this time?"

"Over at Oxwich." Yawning, John Rhys rubbed his jaw. "Been there the whole day, I have."

"Doing what?"

"Haggling."

"Oh?"

"Yes." John Rhys Morgan sat down. He took his son on his lap. "Don't know why I bother, though," he muttered. "Don't know for the life of me why I spend whole days and nights shut up in that filthy villain's den. When I could be running on the sands, or snuggled up in my nice warm bed with the two of you."

"What did the filthy villain want to see you about?"

"Oh, my men have been grumbling. Again." John Rhys sighed. "They have cause, mind. Who does all the bloody work? The Welshmen. Who makes all the profit? Those fat English swine."

"What did you say to him?"

"Oh, I just put him in the picture. Told him straight." John Rhys hugged his child. "Who takes the risks, I asked him. Who goes down to the beaches, fair weather or foul, who gets the stuff off the boats? Who's there waiting for the lights in the bay – or the Excise men, to ride up and take us red-handed?"

"What did he say?

"He agreed. Well, in the end he did." Tugging at a piece of marram grass, John Rhys frowned. "A third of all the profit. That's what we'll have from now on. A third of the cash will come directly to me. So, I've done my best. If my men still aren't satisfied, one of *them* can go and argue the toss with the greedy Saxon pig, for I've had my fill of it, I can tell you now."

Parents and child walked home together, their backs to the setting sun. "We Morgans came out of the sea, you know," said John Rhys, conversationally. "We are the sons of mermaids. Did you know?"

"No, I didn't." Lalage laughed. "So that's why Owen swims like a little silver fish."

"Yes, indeed." Now John Rhys took his son in his arms. He hoisted him on to his shoulders. One hand held the child's ankle, while the other circled his wife's thickening waist. He led his little family back to the grey stone farmhouse.

Jack Atkins sat in his study. He glowered down at the papers littering his elegant mahogany desk. "Bloody Welsh," he muttered, as he stirred his evening chocolate with a finely-chased silver spoon. "Greedy barbarians. Filthy, rapacious swine.

"As for that Morgan fellow! He marries some raddled English whore, so he thinks he can treat me as an equal. Very well – he has what passes for an education in these parts. He's cock of the walk on North Gower. But that doesn't give him the right to dictate – "

"You know, we'd get on much better without him." Jack Atkins's son Michael, a large, florid, fair-haired man of thirty or so, with something of the Fleming in his blond good looks, stood up. He walked over to the window. He gazed towards the setting sun. "Father?"

"What?"

"It's high time we gave Mr Morgan up."

"Is it?" Jack Atkins dribbled his spoon through some spilled chocolate. "Well – I don't know about that."

"Think about it." Michael Atkins grimaced. "Do so now."

As the richest, most influential Englishman on Gower, Jack Atkins was a power in the land. A magistrate, and a philanthropist who endowed the local hospice for orphans and the labouring poor, he dined with and visited persons of quality from as far afield as Pembroke, Cardiff and Swansea. He shot and hunted with the local clergyman. He kept company with the other country gentry settled on Gower.

For many years now, he had made a very comfortable living from his rents, his financial investments – and from his other interest. He enjoyed life to the full, and was not disposed to finish his days at a rope's end.

Now, as he thought about John Rhys Morgan, he scowled. "We can't give him up," he muttered. "Not yet, anyway. He knows enough to hang both you and me."

"Does he, though?" Michael Atkins shrugged. "He could tell a fine tale, I don't doubt that at all. But would he be believed?"

"He knows names. Places. Times. He's been involved in this for years. He's – "

"He's a stupid, ignorant oaf." Picking up a pencil, Michael Atkins tapped it against his chin. "He's greedy. He's vicious. But these days, he's presumptuous and arrogant, too. Why, he was almost threatening you this morning. All the stuff about the risks his men take – that was so much nonsense. But the desire for a bigger share in the loot is real. Next, it will be blackmail."

"He wouldn't dare."

"You think not?" Michael Atkins stabbed his pencil through several sheets of paper, scoring the fine veneer of the desk. "Give him up. That's what I say. Hand him and his rabble over, before he puts the Excise on to you."

"There's very little chance of that. I – "

"I know you've squared your friends at the Customs House. I know a dozen or more of them do very nicely out of turning a blind eye. But there are others – "

"Who can't be bribed. You think I don't know that?" Jack Atkins scowled, considering. "Do you really believe Morgan might try to blackmail me?"

"If the idea ever enters his thick Welsh skull, I'm sure he'll get round to it some day."

"So what shall we do? Let the Excise take him?"

"Good God, no. We needn't be as crude as that."

"So what had you in mind?"

"I know a fellow in the Swansea militia. A captain." Michael Atkins grinned. "He's a decent enough chap, but he's immoderately fond of gambling. The poor devil finds it hard to pay his debts of honour. He owes *me* a favour or two."

"I see."

"I could make it worth his while for him and his company to visit Mr Morgan. To take Mr Morgan for a walk. You know what a rough lot soldiers are. Perhaps Mr Morgan will have an accident. Who knows – he might even be dead before they can bring him to trial."

"Ah." The older man was still not sure. John Rhys Morgan had been a loyal lieutenant. Jack Atkins had trusted him absolutely. But, as Michael now pointed out, he was getting above himself. He was a landowner. A Welsh landowner, who made no secret at all of his dislike of the English overlords on Gower. He might turn dangerous indeed.

"This captain of militia," Jack Atkins began. "You think if his men were to arrest our friend, they would do their job properly? Ensure that by the time he reached Swansea, he'd be in no fit state to talk about me?"

"Or even talk at all." Michael Atkins grinned again. "Good. We agree. That takes care of that."

The soldiers came early in the morning. Hammering on the door with rifle butts, they raised the whole household. While his men splintered the solid Welsh oak, the officer in charge stood back. This was going to be a disagreeable business indeed. He wished he was back in barracks, still in his bed.

Just as the lock was about to give, the door opened. Dressed and neatly shaven, John Rhys Morgan stood on the threshold. He was seized at once. Presented to the captain, he was asked to confirm his identity. Then the officer told his sergeant to put the Welshman in chains.

"You must think I'm a very dangerous fellow," observed John Rhys. He held out both his hands. Unresisting, he let the soldiers put the rusty manacles on his wrists. "Tell me. Does it always take a dozen dirty great redcoats to arrest one little Welshman?"

"Shut your insolent mouth." Observing his prisoner's

wife and child – or so he assumed them to be – standing sullen in the doorway, the captain scowled.

John Rhys turned to his wife. "I'll be back," he promised. "Look after Owen. See he comes to no harm."

"What did he say?" asked the captain. For John Rhys had spoken in Welsh.

"Don't know, sir." The sergeant spat. "He was probably telling the woman to alert his friends, down in the village. We had best get moving, I think."

"Very well. Form up."

"Sir."

Well aware that if he had resisted arrest or now tried to escape, Lalage and Owen would suffer, John Rhys co-operated fully. At the command to march, he marched.

Posted to a company spending the summer season in the back of beyond, the redcoats had seen no action for a very long time. Veterans of service in the Scottish Highlands, however, they'd had lots of experience in dealing with recalcitrant Scots. As far as they were aware, the Welshman was much the same sort of pig-headed, ignorant animal as the Caledonian. He could be jollied along in the same sort of fashion.

They led John Rhys away. In no particular hurry to get back to Swansea, they took the scenic paths, wandering down pleasant country lanes and stopping for frequent rests. Calling at various farmhouses and cottages en route, they commandeered refreshment. Thus, they became steadily inebriated. At each place they stopped to drink, they also displayed their prisoner, to silent, surly villagers. The men stared impassively, the women scowled, but the children wept in fear.

Whenever a large enough crowd could be assembled, the soldiers put on a show. While the people watched, they gave John Rhys a series of exemplary cuffs and blows. These, they felt, would serve as a warning to any other dirty Welsh peasant who might feel inclined to defy the King's majesty, and the Excise men.

By evening, John Rhys Morgan had blood on his face, stripes across his back, and murder in his heart. He'd see Jack Atkins hanged! If the Welshman were to suffer for his crimes, he'd make quite sure the Englishman did, too. He made out his case, and planned his defence.

Lalage was beside herself. "What shall we do?" she cried, for the twentieth, the thirtieth time. "Oh, Bethan! Speak to me! What on earth shall we do?"

"Nothing, girl." Since John Rhys's arrest, Bethan had been unusually silent. Now, she sighed. Her eyes were full of unshed tears. "There's nothing we can do for him now."

Chapter 28

His face white and ghostly in the early dawn, William Parry came thumping on the splintered farmhouse door. Staring up at the tightly closed shutters, he willed Lalage to appear. "Mrs Morgan!" he cried, growing desperate now. "Mrs Morgan, please! You must come to my house, straight away."

Wide awake until long after midnight, for the past hour Lalage had been dozing. Now, at the sound of William Parry's voice, she roused herself. She opened the casement, and looked out. "What is it, William?" she demanded, her speech indistinct and slurred by weariness. "Is the beast-house ablaze?"

"No!" William Parry was almost weeping. "Come to my house!" he cried. "Come quickly, on your own – "

"Is it John Rhys?" Hope leaping like a flame in her aching heart, Lalage looked down at him. "William?"

"Come on, Mrs Morgan. Get yourself down here. There's no time to lose." With that, William disappeared into the shadows of the lane.

After checking on Owen – who was, mercifully, still fast asleep – Lalage threw on her clothes. Silently, she left the farmhouse. Two minutes later, she was in William Parry's warm kitchen.

"Round the back," muttered the cowman. "In the old byre there." Taking his mistress by the elbow, he led her out of the cottage, across the yard and into the derelict cattle shed now used for general storage. He ushered her into a clean, straw-lined stall.

Lalage now expected the worst. Crossing the cobbled

yard, she had noticed the thin, dark trail of blood. Her spirits sinking fast, she entered the byre.

But John Rhys was not dead. He was either unconscious or fast asleep. Evidently, he was sleeping. For, as his wife fell to her knees beside him, he groaned.

"Good God." Looking at him, Lalage gagged. Even in the grey half-light, she could see his face was the colour and texture of raw liver. That his forehead was cut, and his chest a horrible mess of gashes, lacerations and grazes, on which half-dried blood stickily congealed. "William?" she hissed. "Why did you bring him in here?"

"Eh?" William did not answer her. He merely shrugged.

"Well?" Glancing up, Lalage met his gaze. Now, she understood. But she saw no need to be kind. "I see," she muttered. "Betty didn't want her nice clean floor messed up."

"It wasn't that, Mrs Morgan!" Embarrassed, the cowman bit his lip. "But if he were found in my house – well, there's Betty to consider. Our little girl, too."

"Yes, I know." Lalage turned back to John Rhys. She saw fresh injuries now, in addition to the marks of irons on his wrists and ankles, the bruising on his face, and the gashes on his chest. He coughed. Now, bright red pulmonary blood began to seep from a wound on his left side.

Aware of someone crouching beside him, the farmer stirred. He opened his eyes. Seeing his wife, he sighed with relief. "Lali?" he whispered. "Tell me. You and Owen – are you well?"

"Perfectly well," Lalage replied. But then she began to cry. "Oh, darling," she wailed, "why didn't you hide? You could have got yourself to Swansea. Or even Cardiff. Why did you come back here?"

"To warn you, of course." John Rhys groped for her hand. "They're coming for you, Lali. For you and the boy."

"But why?" Lalage stared. "What are we supposed to have done?"

"Oh, God! As if you need to have done anything!" John Rhys shook her. "Listen. I'll explain."

"Well?"

"When they took me yesterday, I thought I'd never get a chance to escape. But late last night, they left me outside a tavern. They all went in to get a skinful – "

"They left you unguarded?"

"Yes. Shackled, but on my own. I suppose they thought they had used me so roughly, I wouldn't be able to move." John Rhys scowled. "But the chains were rusty. The manacles were old. I got myself over to a rock, and smashed the leg irons against it. They came apart, easy as anything."

"Oh, darling – "

"It was Jack Atkins!" John Rhys glared. "Do you hear me, girl? Jack Atkins. He betrayed me."

"Did he?" Lalage frowned. "Are you sure?" she asked.

"Certain of it." Coughing up a great mouthful of blood and phlegm, John Rhys attempted to sit up. He failed. When Lalage tried to support him, he pushed her away, and fell back against a bale of straw. "Their officer was talking to the sergeant," he muttered. 'Our friend Jack.' That's what he said. Our friend Jack ought to be well pleased with this day's work."

"I see." Lalage smoothed the hair back from his bruised and bloodied forehead. "That cut on your chest is deep," she said. "How – "

"They heard the manacles being smashed. They all dashed out of the tavern. One of them lunged at me as I ran, and got me there." Coughing again, John Rhys brought up more blood. "But I still ran, Lali! God, I ran. I'd heard them talking, see. They'd forgotten I understood their horrible, brutish language. So I knew their plans."

"Which were?"

"To take me to prison, in Swansea. But a couple of them were to come back here, to Llangynnydd."

"Why?"

"To find all the gold I'm supposed to have hidden. Jack

Atkins told them I was a rich man. So they were going to make you give the money up." The effort of talking exhausting him, John Rhys groaned. 'If she won't talk,' says one, 'we'll persuade her.' 'How do you mean to do that,' asks another. 'Roast the brat,' says the first."

Now John Rhys was gasping for breath. But he was determined to speak. "My God, Lali," he whispered, "what a dance I led them. All night, through woods and valleys. Along beaches, into quicksands. Stupid drunken English swine. They couldn't catch me. But they'll be here soon. I was afraid they'd be here already."

He was obviously dying. As he talked, as he drew each breath and exhaled, more bright scarlet blood bubbled through the encrustation which had already dyed his shirt crimson. The straw on which he lay was spongy with gore.

"Don't talk now." Lalage rubbed her husband's cold hands. "We'll get a doctor," she declared. "I'll send William into Swansea, to fetch the best surgeon there is."

"He wouldn't go. Nor would anyone else. It's far too risky." John Rhys shook his head. "Anyway, a surgeon could do nothing for me."

"Of course he could! If – "

"Lali, my darling, I've had it." John Rhys sighed. "Either way, I'm dead. Here, or at a rope's end. So take Owen and Bethan, and get yourself to England. Go now." Exhausted by the effort of speaking, John Rhys closed his eyes.

Lalage let him rest. Taking a cloth, she dabbed ineffectually at his shoulder, trying to staunch the flow of blood from a wound there.

A minute went by. Two minutes. "John?" Feeling his pulse grow even weaker, Lalage wanted to hear his voice once more. "John Rhys? Speak to me!"

"It's no good, Mrs Morgan." Touching the farmer's other wrist, William Parry shook his head. "You and the boy must get away. You – "

"Fetch Bethan." Lalage stood up. "Go and wake Bethan for me, now."

"But, Mrs Morgan – "

"I want to see Bethan." Lalage scowled at the man. "Do as you're told, and get her!"

Poor Bethan, roused early from her fitful sleep and practically dragged along the country lane, was horrified by the sight in the byre. Seeing Lalage was both hard-faced and dry-eyed, she realised everything the villagers said about her was true. This woman was a witch, a creature from another world, for anyone human would have been weeping. As Bethan wept now.

As her heartless mistress wrapped her cloak around her shoulders, Bethan frowned. "Where are you going?" she demanded. For the task now, surely, was to lay out the dead. "Mrs Morgan? Where are you off to, at this time of the morning?"

"I'm going out. I have a call to pay." White-faced, Lalage glared. "Bethan? Listen to me. You must take Owen away from here."

"Away?" Frowning even harder, Bethan folded her arms. "The soldiers won't touch Owen," she declared. "They won't kill a child. Even the Saxon swine won't hurt a poor little thing just seven years old."

"They would. They're on their way here now, to do just that. Therefore, Bethan – "

Lalage explained what she wanted Bethan to do.

"Darrow." Grimacing as she tried to get her tongue round this peculiar foreign name, Bethan met Lalage's eyes. "Ellis Darrow," she repeated. "Of Easton, in the county of Warwickshire."

"That's right." Lalage willed Bethan to remember. "Take the coach to Birmingham. Then go on to Warwick. When you get there, ask for directions to the village of Easton. I'm not sure where you'll find Mr Darrow. He used to live in a big old house there, but that's long since gone."

"So, this Mr Ellis Darrow. Your employer, was he?"

"He's my brother." Now Lalage felt cold and ill. "He loved me once," she whispered. "He'll not turn Owen away."

"You're sure of it?"

"Certain."

Lalage's self-control was slipping. Owen! She could take Owen now. She could escape. She could get them both back to England, and safety. "Oh, Bethan," she cried, "please go! Look – in the cashbox on the dresser, you'll find sixty English guineas. Take them, get Owen out of bed and get away."

While Bethan wrung her hands and wept, Lalage slipped into the farmhouse, changed out of her bloodstained clothes, then rummaged around until she found what she wanted. She pocketed it.

For a second, she stood alone in the parlour, wondering if she might take just one last look at her child. But then, deciding against it, she left the house. The morning sun was high as, for the first time in her life, Lalage approached the great mansion on the headland, where the Englishman lived.

"I wish to see Mr Atkins." Her inward turmoil masked by a veneer of frosty dignity, Lalage swept right past the neat little housemaid who opened the door. Standing in the entrance hall, she looked about her. "Mr Atkins is at home?"

"Yes, ma'am. Certainly he is. But – "

"Say Mrs Morgan wishes to speak to him. At once."

The housemaid scuttled away.

Left alone in the cool gloom of the hall, Lalage eyed the place. This was a gentleman's home! Fashionable prints adorned the neatly-papered walls, an expensive Turkey carpet lay on highly-polished boards, and thick, velvet drapes festooned the large windows. Smelling sweetly of beeswax and fresh flowers, this was no smugglers' lair. Lalage wondered if she'd come to the right place.

She had never met the man she was here to see. As she hurried along the lanes towards Oxwich, she'd wondered what he was like. She had imagined a big, rough buccaneer, a great English lout who ruled his smuggler rabble like a pirate king. But now, she hardly knew what to expect.

"Mrs Morgan? Will you be so good as to come this way?" The little housemaid smiled at her. "Just along the passage here. Mr Atkins will see you in his study." Reaching a panelled oak door, the housemaid tapped once. She opened it, and ushered Lalage inside.

Jack Atkins was small and slim. He was old, too. At least sixty. A neat, trim, grey-haired gentleman, he was clad in a suit of good broadcloth. His linen was fresh, his cheeks were newly shaven and his hair was lightly powdered. He looked every inch the plain country gentleman. A pillar of the community. An honest English squire.

"Come in, Mrs Morgan." Politely, Jack Atkins nodded a welcome. "Do sit down. A dish of tea? Polly, my dear? Will you see to it?"

Only when Lalage was seated did Jack Atkins sit down himself. "Now, dear lady," he said, kindly. "What may I do for you?"

Lalage stared at him. Although she'd had no idea at all how she would be received, she certainly hadn't anticipated this softness. This courtliness. This bland *politesse*. She'd meant to confront Jack Atkins with his treachery, curse him to hell, then –

She was completely nonplussed. "My husband has been arrested," she said.

"Arrested?" Jack Atkins frowned. "When was this?"

"Yesterday. The soldiers came at first light." Lalage began to weep. "They took John Rhys away," she sobbed. "I don't know why. Mr Atkins, my husband is an honest farmer. He's done nothing wrong!"

"Hasn't he?"

"No!" Lalage wept harder. "Sir, you're a magistrate. Can't you do anything to help?"

"Well, now. Let me see." Jack Atkins reached for a pen. He found some paper. Reassuringly, he smiled.

Looking at his visitor, he saw she was pretty. Beautiful, in fact. He had been led to believe that John Rhys Morgan's bride was a scrawny old hag with dewlaps and a cast in one eye, who had somehow tricked the young bachelor into marriage. How wrong he had been.

For, this woman was absolutely lovely. She was a few years older than her husband, certainly – but she was still quite young. Slender, soft and comely, she had the bloom of a peach and the dusky radiance of a summer rose. She even had the air of a lady. Her carriage was graceful, and her manners perfect.

She was pregnant, too. Now Jack Atkins smiled again. If that greedy Welsh lout survived long enough to be brought to trial, the brat might even see its father face to face. Albeit in the market place in Swansea, swinging from a rope's end.

"Humour the creature," he thought, as he wrote the deposition. Fob her off. She was English herself. Hopefully, therefore, she would prove rather less excitable than the average Welsh peasant. Sweet words and false assurances would keep her quiet for a few days. Possibly even a week.

Glancing at her again, Jack Atkins remembered he was a widower. Once this poor but exquisite creature was widowed, she was sure to be courted again. Who would be more eligible than her dead husband's colleague and faithful friend? The very idea put new life into his dry old bones.

"I'll do everything I can," he promised. "I'll speak to the authorities in Swansea. I'll use all my influence there." Still wearing his Judas smile, he rose to his feet. "Mrs Morgan, rest assured I'll do everything in my power. If there's been a mistake, if he is in fact innocent of any crime, we'll soon get your husband released." He walked towards the door.

He had his back to her. Now, thought Lalage. It had to

be now. She felt for the handle of the knife. She grasped it firmly.

She ran up behind him. Clumsily – for she'd never done anything remotely like this before – she grabbed Jack Atkins by the collar. She yanked his head backwards and stabbed him, between his skinny shoulder blades.

The knife took so long to penetrate! Razor-sharp though it was, the mass of cloth, skin and gristle obstructed its progress. As her victim squirmed, Lalage felt her hand slip. The handle of the knife was now pushed back against her own chest.

Desperation made her strong. With a sudden jerk, she pulled the weapon away. She stabbed again. She drove the blade upwards, towards Jack Atkins's cold, perfidious heart.

His screams were heard all over the house. Almost immediately footsteps clattered on boards and flagstones, and within a minute the room was full of relatives, servants and hangers-on, all talking, all exclaiming, all shouting at once.

Lalage stood silent. Blood streaking her gown and splashed all over her shoes, she was clearly guilty. Now she stood like a statue, as servants and relatives hung over Jack Atkins's prostrate form.

For moment or two, everyone was more concerned with him than with her. This gave her the chance to slide the weapon under her cloak. To hide it behind her back.

Tenderly, Jack Atkins was helped to his knees, then laid face down on a sofa. His coat was eased off and cloths applied to staunch the blood. An old woman, an upper servant it appeared, for she wore a good black stuff gown and a spotless linen cap, now examined him. She said the wounds were not deep. His life was in no immediate danger.

Michael Atkins turned to the would-be assassin. "Hold her," he said. "You, Robin. Henry, too. Hold the bitch fast."

Lalage did not struggle. Calmly, she met Michael Atkins's pale blue gaze.

"You'll suffer for this," he told her. "You'll die by inches. Days, it will be. Weeks, even."

Lalage winced. Looking up at Michael Atkins's hard, Flemish face, into his almost colourless eyes fringed with sparse, pale lashes, she understood that here was a ruthless killer who meant exactly what he said. She would suffer the torments of the damned. Recalling how cruelly her own husband had dealt with traitors, she felt sick with dread.

Now she remembered the baby inside her. Poor child, would they tear it from her womb, and laugh as they watched it die? She thought of Owen. She'd had such high hopes of John Owen! Such a clever boy, such a handsome child, he was a son to make any mother proud. Lalage sighed. So this was it. This was the end.

The knife was still warm, its handle still damply sticky in her hand. She would have to do it now. Soon, they would search her – indeed, it amazed her they had not done so before. So now, she twisted away from the men who held her. Immediately, there was a rush to bar the windows, to block the door. But Lalage stood where she was. Falling forwards, she stabbed again.

This time, the blade slid in easily. Sweetly, smoothly, John Rhys Morgan's knife pierced his widow's willing flesh, and found its home in Lalage's heart. With no more than a surprised whimper of astonishment that it should be so simple, Lalage drove the blade home, right up to the hilt.

As Michael Atkins leapt to restrain her, to cheat her of a clean and easy death, Lalage slumped against him, lifeless.

"He'll survive." Summoned from Swansea, the surgeon finished bandaging his patient. He smiled encouragingly at Jack Atkins's anxious son. "He'll be weak for a month or so. But provided mortification does not set in – and I see no reason why it should – he'll certainly live."

"Good." Michael Atkins sucked his teeth. "What about her?"

The doctor glanced at the woman laid out on the table. "She's past my help," he said. "Poor lady. Young, and so pretty – pregnant, too. What happened?"

"She had a grievance against my father. She tried to kill him. Fortunately, we prevented her from causing him serious injury. Then she turned the knife on herself."

"Were there witnesses?"

"A dozen, at least. Maybe more." Michael Atkins shrugged. "Apparently, she was well-known in Llangynnydd. Was disturbed in her mind, so they say. My people will be making statements this afternoon."

When the doctor had gone and Jack Atkins was safely put to bed, Michael Atkins called Robin and Henry to the study. "That's the dog and vixen accounted for," he muttered. "Now to deal with the cub."

But, before his mother's limbs were even stiffening or her eyes glazing over, little Owen Morgan was running. Taken from his bed and hurriedly stuffed into a suit of clothes, he was soon scrambling along beside his nurse. They were making for the high road from Port Eynon on which, if they were lucky, he and Bethan would meet the Swansea coach.

"Oh, Bethan! Where are we going?" His face still creased from sleep, the child tugged pathetically at his nurse's hand. "Bethan, I'm frightened! Where's my Mam? Where are we –

"We're going to England, my lamb." Breathless now, Bethan held her aching side. "We must get on a coach – "

"A coach? But Bethan, what about Mam?" Almost in tears now, for bewilderment and fear had made him quite unlike his usual jaunty self, Owen began to wail. "Bethan, what about – "

"Tell you later." Grasping Owen's hand more tightly, Bethan stifled a sob of her own. "All you need to know

now is that we're going to England. To your uncle. To safety. Come along, *cariad*," she gasped. "I can hear the coach coming now. Run a bit faster for me."

Two hours later, Bethan and Owen were in Swansea, swallowed up amidst the market-day crowds.

"There's a person to see you, madam." Finding Rebecca in her little sitting room, where she was playing a game of chess with Rayner before he went to bed, Simmons pursed his lips in distaste. "It's a rather peculiar old woman," he went on. "She has a child with her."

"What does she want?" Seeing her queen in mortal peril, Rebecca moved it – only to find that, with a crow of triumph, Rayner now took her one remaining bishop. At seven, he was far more of a strategist than she would ever be. "Well, Simmons?" she asked, standing up. "What's her story?"

"She doesn't have one, madam. She asked to see Mr Darrow first. When I told her he was away from home, she said she would speak to your ladyship, instead."

"Oh. Well, I expect she needs food. Or some other sort of relief." Smiling, Rebecca conceded defeat to her son. She told him he took after his father, and was sure to be a great man some day. She turned to Simmons. "Is this woman from the village?" she asked.

"No, madam. She's a stranger. Welsh, I believe." Sniffing, Simmons turned to go. "If your ladyship is busy, I could tell one of the maids to give her some scraps from the kitchen. Then send her on her way."

"No, don't do that. I'll see her now." Always mindful of her obligations to the poor and needy, the squire's lady followed her butler out of the room.

As Rebecca walked into the service passage, she saw a very stout, plain, middle-aged woman in voluminous red petticoats and a striped flannel gown. An outlandish-looking person, she had a great willow basket on her arm and a black, high-crowned bonnet on her head. Hearing footsteps, she turned to look at the mistress of the house.

Rebecca opened her mouth to speak. But then she saw the child at the woman's side. Cold and dirty, his clothes travel-stained and his face smudged with fatigue and recent tears, Rayner Darrow was standing there.

But Rayner was in his mother's sitting room, putting away the chess set. Rebecca blinked. She looked again.

Black-haired, dark-eyed, this child was unmistakeably a Darrow. There was no doubt of it. Generation after generation of faces exactly like his had stared solemnly from dozens of those family portraits which had graced the long gallery, in the days before the fire. Now, looking at Owen Morgan, Rebecca knew straight away whose son he must be.

The sound of a door slamming shut behind her made Rebecca start. Now, her husband's familiar tread sounded on flagstones. He had presumably gone into the gun room. Leaving the woman and child standing there, Rebecca ran back down the passage. She found Ellis talking to Simmons, who was helping him take off his outdoor clothes.

"Ellis!" She fell into his startled embrace. "Oh, Ellis! She's sent him to us. She's given us her son!"

"Do you think the woman was telling the truth?" Having got over her initial shock, Rebecca was calmer now. "Ellis? Do you think Mrs Davies's story can possibly be true?"

"I've no reason to doubt her word." As astonished as Rebecca had been by the sudden, dramatic appearance of Owen Morgan, Ellis shrugged. "It's a rather gruesome tale, but I don't see why it shouldn't be as she says."

"What do you think has become of Lalage?"

"God knows. But I shall have enquiries made, and I shall certainly find out." Ellis stood up. He walked over to the window and gazed out at the darkening summer evening. "It would appear," he continued, "that Mr Morgan was an extremely unpleasant piece of work. He seems to have met with a singularly appropriate fate. As for that Atkins fellow – *he* will be thoroughly investigated. There'll be an official enquiry, I expect. Down there in the back of beyond, he doubtless thinks he's safe from the laws of this land. But he'll find he isn't."

Ellis turned to his wife. "Well, Becky? What have you done with the boy?"

"I had Molly make up two beds in the old nursery. He and his nurse, or whatever she is, have taken themselves up there. Poor creatures, they're both exhausted."

By late evening, Bethan Davies was down in the kitchen again, drinking dish after dish of strong tea and relating her adventures to the housemaids and the cook. Her little charge, however, still slept. Rebecca and Ellis went upstairs.

"He's the image of you." Rebecca looked down at the sleeping child. "He has your face. Your features. He could be Rayner's twin. It's astonishing."

"It's rather unsettling." Turning away, Ellis frowned.

But Rebecca gazed on. Searching the child's face for malevolence, she saw nothing but childish innocence. Well aware that any son of Lalage must have at best a mixed inheritance, she refused to consider it. Owen was a Darrow. He was her own dear Ellis, born again.

"You'd love him for my sake?" asked Ellis, doubtfully. "If we kept him here, would you accept him as readily as a son of our own?

"Yes." Looking up from her contemplation of Owen, Rebecca took her husband's hand. "He needs us," she said simply. "Poor helpless child, who will love him, if we do not?"

for that sort of fellow. He'll be the [illegible] expected. There'll be an official enquiry, I expect. Even those in the back of beyond, he somehow thinks he's exempt from the laws of the land. But he'll meet his match.'

[illegible] turned to his wife. 'Well, [illegible]? What have you done with the boy?'

And Marie came up [illegible] and [illegible]

[illegible]

In the evening, [illegible] in the kitchen [illegible] den of [illegible] the [illegible] and the cook [illegible] Rebecca and Ellis were [illegible]

[illegible] looked down at the [illegible]

[illegible] he refused to [illegible]

[illegible]